To Peter Crowther, with love

CONTENTS

THE DEVIL DELIVERED

And the Word was made flesh, and dwelt among us . . .

> Would you leave this place then,
> where bread is darkness,
> wheat ill-chance,
> and yearn for wickedness
> to justify the sternly
> punished;
>
> would you hold the driven knife
> of a tribe's political
> blood, this thrust of compromise,
> and a shaman's squalid hut
> the heart of human
> purpose;
>
> would you see in stone the giants
> walking the earth,
> besetting the beasts
> in dysfunctional
> servitude, skulls bred flat to set
> the spike—

would you flail the faded skin
from a stranger's flesh,
excoriate kinship
like a twisted flag from bones,
scatter him homeless in a field
of stone;

where tearing letters from each word
stutters the eye,
disarticulating skeletal maps
to uplift ancestry into ageless
lives, progeny schemes are adroitly
revised.

Bread is darkness,
wheat ill-chance,
and all around us
wickedness waits.

vii) tall boy

PROLOGUE

Entry: American NW Aut. B.C. 8675 ±600 years

Larger shadows walk with the coyote, elder cousin ghosts panting the breath of ice.

He watches them, wondering who will speak first. The coyote seems a likely candidate with its nose lifted and testing the air. Human scents riding the wind, now fading, slipping beneath the overwhelming stench of sunbaked meat, its touch on canine olfactory nerves an underscored sigh beneath the old scream of death.

The coyote pads down the slope, winding a path round the dusty sage, pauses every now and then to read the breeze, cock its ears in search of wrong sounds, scanning the low bluffs on the valley's other side, then continues its descent.

He watches the coyote, waiting. It might be the ghosts will speak first. It might be that, after all. They're big, bigger than he'd thought they'd be, more than shadows as they slip closer, moving stretched and tall, shoulders bunched and heads swinging as if conscious of crowding tusks – a hunt long over, a hunt less than memory. But it may be that their days of remembrance are over.

The coyote is close now, and he can read its life. Like others of its kind, it has adopted a band of humans. It follows them in their wanderings, down onto the flats where the grasses grow high; and when the giant bison migrate north to the forest fringes where the bitter prairie winds are slowed, frayed by the trees, the humans migrate with them. And in their wake, the coyote.

The animal clings to their scent, sometimes seeing them but always at a distance. The animal knows its place – at the edge of the world, the world the humans now claim as their own. The world, reduced to a piece of flesh.

The stench hangs heavy here, in this valley's dry basin beneath cliffs. Here, where the humans have made another kill.

The coyote pauses, ducks its head and sniffs the trampled red mud around its paws. It licks blood-soaked grass. Behind it, the shadow ghosts pace nervously, hearing yet again the echoes of competition, the battle they'd lost long ago. Still, the carpet of dead is welcome red . . .

He smiles at the coyote, smiles at the ghosts. He stays where he sits, among the thousand-odd dead bison that had been driven, by a band of seven humans, over the cliff's edge. Here and there around him, evidence of butchering on a dozen or so animals, most of them yearlings. Some skinned. Others with their skull-caps removed, tongues cut out from their mouths, eviscerated. A sampling of biology, enough for seven humans. More than enough, much, much more than enough.

Bison antiquus. Bison occidentalis. Take your pick.

A breed above. Ghost cousin shadows of the smaller bison that now cover the lands. Born in an age of ice, once commanding the plains, grazing among mammoths, giant sloths, horses – beasts whose time had ended – and now, with this final kill, so, too, ends the time for the giant bison.

Punctual as a cliff's edge.

Smiling, he watches the coyote crouch down beside a gutted bull and feed. One last time. A world emptied of *Bison antiquus,* barring a holdout enclave in the forests north of the Winnipeg River.

He sees them now, all around, more ghost shadows, dull herbivores, shoulders bumping. And at the herd's edges: the coyote's dark kin, the cautious breed of dire wolves. Other predators in the beyond, others who'd run out of prey at human hands: lions, short-tailed bears, smilodons.

It seems then, that he is the one who must speak first. 'Among the world's killers,' he whispers.

The coyote looks up, fixes gray eyes on him.

'Among the world's killers,' he says again, still smiling, 'only we humans seem capable of seeking and finding new animals to hunt, new places to flatten underfoot in a jumble of bones. An accurate observation?'

The coyote resumes feeding.

'Oh, sure,' he continues, 'you've an alacrity for adapting, there on the edge of our world. And your human host is far away now, well into their rounds. Does being so far away from them concern you?'

The coyote downs a mouthful of flesh. Flies buzz around its muzzle.

'After all,' he adds, 'their scent's growing colder by the minute, isn't it.'

The coyote doesn't bother looking up, just shrugs. 'No trouble,' it says. 'I need only test the wind, and find the smell of blood.'

A good answer.

He sits and watches the coyote feed, while around them the shadow ghosts howl at the empty sky, the empty land. In those howls, he hears the kind of smile reserved for shadows lost to the world. A smile he shares.

ONE

TO JOHN JOHN FR BOGQUEEN: Out of the pool, into the peat. Found something/someone you might want to see. Runner 6729.12 for the path, just follow the footsteps moi left you. Ta, lover boy, and mind the coyotes.

JIM'S STORY

Saskatchewan, Dominion of Canada, August 9,
A.D. *1959*

Bronze flowed along the eagle's broad wings as it banked into the light of the setting sun. Jim's eyes followed it, bright with wonder. His horse's russet flanks felt hot and solid under his thighs. He curved his lower back and slid down a ways on the saddle.

Grandpa had clucked his palomino mare ahead a dozen or so steps, out to the hill's crest. The old man had turned and now squinted steadily at Jim.

'What do you see this time?' Grandpa asked.

'It's just how you said it'd be,' Jim answered. He remembered what his grandfather had told him last winter. There'd been a foot of wind-hardened snow blanketing this hilltop, and the deep drifts in the valley below had been sculpted into fantastic patterns. They'd covered the six miles from the farm in the morning's early hours, jogging overland and using the elk-gut snowshoes Grandpa had made the day Jim was born, nine years past. And he remembered what Grandpa had talked about that day – all the old, old stories, the places and lives that had slipped into and out of the family's own history, on their way into legend. Batoche, Riel, McLaren and the Redcoats, and Sitting Bull himself. It was the family's Métis blood, the old fur trade routes that crossed the plains, and of course the buffalo. All a part of Jim now, and especially this particular hilltop, where heroes had once gathered. Where they had talked with the Old One, whose bones slept under the central pile of stones.

Jim let his gaze drop and scan the space between the two horses. The pile remained – it had barely broken the snow's skin last winter, but now the hub of boulders threw its lumpy shadow across the west half of the Medicine Wheel, and the rows of rocks that spoked out from it completed a perfect circle around them.

'Who Hunts the Devil,' Grandpa said quietly.

Jim nodded. 'The Old One.'

The wind blew dry and hot, and Jim licked his parched lips as Grandpa's blunt French and Plains Cree accent rolled the words out slow and even, 'He was restless in those days. But now . . . just silence.' The old man swung his mount round until the two horses and their riders faced each other. Grandpa's weathered face looked troubled. 'I'm thinking he might be gone, you know.'

Jim's gaze flicked away, uneasily studied the prairie beyond. The sun's light was crimson behind a curtain of dust raised by the Johnsons' combines.

Grandpa continued, 'Could be good for wheat, this section . . .'

The boy spoke slowly. 'But that'd mean plowing all this up – the Medicine Wheel, the tepee rings—'

'So it would. The old times have passed, goes my thinking. Your dad, well, soon he'll be taking over things, and that's the way it should be.'

Jim slumped farther in his saddle, still staring at the sunset. Dad didn't like being called Métis, always said he was three-quarters white and that was good enough and he didn't show his Indian blood besides. Jim's own blood was even thinner, but his grandfather's stories had woken things in him, deep down inside. The boy cleared his throat. 'Where did your grandpa meet Sitting Bull again?'

The old man smiled. 'You know.'

'Wood Mountain. He'd just come up after killing Custer. He was on the run, and the Redcoats were on their way from the East, only they were weeks away still.'

'And that's when—?'

'Sitting Bull gave your grandpa his rifle. A gift, because your grandpa spoke wise words—'

'Don't know how wise they were,' Grandpa cut in; then he fell silent, his gaze far away.

Jim said nothing. He'd never heard doubt before, not in the telling of the stories, especially not in this one.

After a long moment filled only by the wind and an impatient snort from the palomino, Grandpa spoke on,

'He told Sitting Bull that the fight was over. That the Americans would come after him, hunt him down. That the White Chief couldn't live without avenging the slaughter – that the White Chief's justice counted only with the whites, not for Indian dogs. Sitting Bull was tired, and old. He was ready for those words. That's why he called them wise. So after McLaren arrived, he took his people back. He surrendered, and was starved then murdered. It would've been a better death, I think, if he'd kept his rifle.'

Jim straightened and met his grandfather's eyes. 'I don't want this plowed up, Grandpa. Maybe Who Hunts the Devil is gone, but maybe he isn't. Maybe he's just sleeping. If you wreck the Medicine Wheel, he'll be mad.'

'Your father wants to plant wheat, Jim. That's all there is to it. And the old times are gone. Your father understands this. You have to, too.'

'No.'

'Once the harvest's in, we'll come out here and turn over the land.'

'No.'

'It's empty, you see. The buffalo are gone. I look around . . . and it's not right. It'll never be right again.'

'Yes, it will, Grandpa. I'll make it right.'

The old man's smile was broken, wrenching at Jim's heart. 'Listen to your father, Jim. His words are wise.'

Val Marie, Saskatchewan Precinct, June 30,
Anno Confederation 14

William Potts opened his eyes to the melting snow puddled around his hiking boots. He rubbed his face, working out the aching creases around his mouth. A smile to make people nervous, but it was getting harder to wear.

Slouched in an antique chair and half-buried by his bootsuit, he turned his head an inch, to meet the eye of a diamondback rattlesnake probing the glass wall beside him. An eye milky white, the eye of a seer proselytized limbless and mute, but scabbed with deadly knowledge all the same.

The aquarium sat on a stained oak end table, its lower third layered in sand and gravel. Stone slabs crowded the near end. A sun-bleached branch stripped of bark lay in the center, angled upward in faint salute. At the far end, two small buttons of cacti, possibly alive, possibly dead – hard to tell despite the tiny bright red flowers.

The snake was avoiding its tree, succinctly coiled on a stone slab, its subtle dun-colored designs pebbled by scales that glittered beneath the heat lamp.

William watched its tongue flick out, once, twice, three times, then stop.

He grunted. 'We are rife in threes.'

At the crowded basement's far end, Old Jim rummaged through a closet, his broad hunched back turned to William.

'This guy's eyes,' William said, frowning at the snake, 'are all milky white.' He lowered his voice. 'Time to shed, then? Tease off the old, here's something new. Into the new where you don't belong. You know that, don't you? Because your sins are *old*.'

Old Jim pulled out a walking stick, a staff, and dropped it clattering to the floor. 'It's here someplace,' he said. 'I hid it when that land claim went through. Figured Jack Tree and his boys would swoop down and take everything, you know? The snake's blind, son. Burned blind.'

William shifted in the narrow chair. 'Conjured by thy name, huh? Makes you easier to catch, I suppose.' The snake lifted its head and softly butted the glass. Once, twice, three times. 'One day,' William told it, 'you'll wear my skin. And I'll wear yours. We'll find out who slips this mortal coil first.' He shifted again and let his gaze travel over the room's contents.

Old Jim's basement was also the town museum. Thick with dust and the breath of ghosts. Glass-topped tables housed chert and chalcedony arrowheads, ground-stone axes and mauls, steatite tobacco pipes, rifle flints and vials full of trade beads. White beads, red beads, turquoise beads. Furniture shaped by home-steaders' rough, practical hands filled every available space. Cluttering the walls: faded photographs, racks of pronghorn, elk, deer, heads of wolf, bear, coyote, old provincial license plates from before the North American Confederation, quilts, furs, historical maps. A fossilized human femur dug out from three-million-year-old gravel beds that, before the Restitution, would have been called an anomaly and deftly ignored.

William smiled. 'Three million, ten thousand years of history jammed into this basement, Jim. Exactly where it belongs. In perfect context. In perfect disorder. With a blind snake curating the whole mess.'

He ran a hand through his unkempt brown hair. 'This stuff ever been cataloged, Jim? Diligently recorded and filed on memchip, slipped into envelope, envelope sealed and labeled, inserted into a storage box, box stacked on other boxes, shifted to a dark, deep shelf beside the rat poison, behind the locked door in the university basement a few hundred miles from here? And you presume the guise of science? Hah.'

Old Jim didn't answer.

Answers are extinct. 'I'm an expert on extinction,' William said. 'A surveyor of the exhausted, the used up, notions made obsolete by their sheer complexity. It's a world bereft of meaning, and who knows, who cares? I don't and I do. The last gasps of a dying science. The last walkabout, the last vision quest. We've digitalized the world, Jim, and here I am riding the sparks, in boot-suit and eyeshield and sensiband. Out under the Hole.'

'Got it!' Old Jim straightened. In his hands was a rifle. He grinned at William. 'Right after Little Bighorn, Sitting Bull ran up here to hide out from the Americans.' He hefted the rifle. 'This was his. Used it against the Seventh. Left it behind when he went back to get killed. And you know what he said?' Old Jim's eyes were bright.

William nodded. 'He said, "The ghosts are dancing."'

Old Jim shook his head. 'He said, "We have fired our last shot." That's what he said. And that's why he left it here.' Old Jim stepped close and placed the rifle, reverently, in William's hands.

William ran his fingers along the barrel's underside until he found the maker's mark; then he straightened and held it close to the aquarium's lamps. 'English, all right. So far, so good.'

'That's gone down the family line, you know? Hell,

my family goes back to before Batoche. Métis blood.' He removed his baseball cap and ran his forearm along his brow. 'It's Sitting Bull's rifle, son, sure as I'm standing here.'

'The stock's been carved some,' William said. He handed it back, then rose. 'You might be right, Jim. Couldn't prove otherwise.'

'Some of you fellas should come down here and record all this stuff,' Old Jim said. He returned the rifle to the closet. 'Jack Tree gets his hands on this, and you and your university can kiss it all good-bye.'

'I'll suggest it to my employers,' William said, pulling on his gloves. He paused, glancing at the rattlesnake.

Old Jim said softly, 'Most of them gone now.'

Again, William nodded.

'Burned blind, you know. Can't hunt, can't eat. Fulla tumors and stuff, too. Course, not much left to eat out there, anyway. Sure you don't want a hot chocolate?'

'Can't. I'm fasting.'

The old man shook his head again. 'A damned strange thing to be doing, son, if you ask me. Exactly what kind of research you into?'

'I'm cataloging ghosts, Jim.'

'Huh?'

'I walk on the winds, ride the snows. My heart beats in time with the ticking of stones.'

Old Jim's eyes held William's. Slowly, he said, 'You'd better get something to eat, son. Soon.' He reached out and tapped the goggles hanging around William's neck. 'And don't take those off out there. Even when it's snowing. Blowing snow and clouds don't stop the rays. Nothing stops those rays.'

'Burned blind.' William nodded.

Old Jim walked over to the aquarium and studied the snake. 'Around here, years back,' he said, 'these fellas were called Instruments of the Devil.'

'Yea verily,' William said. '"And into the pit God casts all vermin, and into the pit shall they slither unending among the implements of history."'

'Never heard that Scripture before,' Old Jim said.

William smiled, then headed for the stairs.

Old Jim followed. He watched William pull on the goggles and activate maximum shielding, then raise the bootsuit's hood and tighten the drawstrings. 'Back out in the Hole,' Old Jim said, shaking his head once more. 'I used to ride horses out there.'

'The horses run still,' William said. He faced Old Jim. 'Keep squinting.'

'You, too. Mind the Hole, mind the Hole.'

Net
14.30.06 STATUS REPORT 00:00.00 GMT

Means:
Sea Level: +82.37cm AMR
Temperature: +2.6012C. AMR
Carbon Dioxide: +.06% AMR
Carbon Monoxide: +1.12% AMR
Methane: +.089% AMR
Nitrogen Oxide: +.0112% AMR
Organochlorine Count: +.0987 ppm (holding)
Airborne Silicia Count: +1.923 ppm (holding)
Acrosol Sporco (volume): +367 AMR
Mare Sporco (sq. km): 113000 (Med.) (rising)

86950 (Carib.) (holding)
236700 (Ind.) (rising)
Nil Ozone areas (since 01.01.14):
Midwest Hole: holding
Arctic Hole: +23416 sq. km
Antarctic Hole: +3756.25 sq. km
Australian Hole: +6720 sq. km
Spawns: 24 (varied) (down 13)
Rad Drift Alerts:
India (north)
Korea (south)
Bio Alerts:
Ciguatera Epidemics (+1000s): 17 (holding)
Retroviral General: 07 (+6/01.01.14)
Ebola-16/Hanta Outbreaks: 112 (+7)
Undifferentiated ISEs: 316 (+45)
BSE/CJD/CWD composite index: 2.4b.
Species Count: 117
Malaria N. edge: +2.7 Lat.
Suvara N. edge: +3.12 Lat.
Cholera Count (/millions): 270
Bubonic: 113 (14 known bioflicked)
White Rash Deaths: 12.67
Morbilivirus-B22 Closed Zones: 16 urban (+1)
Transmutative Viral Count: 1197 (+867)
Hotzone Alerts Political:
Pakistan/India (last nuke 07.03.14)
Zimbabwe (closed since 27.05.13)
Congo Republic (closed since 11.07.08)
Rep. Lapland/Consortium Russia
Georgia/Chechen Rep/Consortium Russia
Iran (closed since 13.04.04)

Iraq (closed since 22.11.03)
Sinjo/Taiwan
Quebec/NOAC
Puerto Rico/NOAC
United Ireland/Eurocom
Israel/Assorted (no recent nukes/biochem WMD)
Argentina (internal, last Bik flicked 29.01.13)
S. Korea (closed since 15.10.07)
Indonesia (internal)
Guatemala/Belize/Consortium Honduras
Ukraine/Consortium Russia (no recent nukes/
  biochem WMD)
Confirmed Dead Zones:
  N. Korea
  Iran
  Syria
  Afghanistan
  Colombia
  California
Confirmed Dead Cities (excluding those in nations
    above):
  Jakarta
  Seoul
  Hong Kong
  Jerusalem
  Cairo
  Berlin
  Sarajevo
  Baghdad
  Denver
  Toronto
  Old Washington, D.C.

Refugee-Related Minor Conflicts/Incidents: +103
Flicked Biks this month: 0
Flicked Biobiks this month: 2
Worldwide weather forecast: Hot and sunny. Hey, folks, looks like another balmy day out there!

Net
Suppressed File Index (NOACom) 219.56b

Subtitle: The Restitution
Category: Social Sciences
Subcategory: Biological Evolution/Paleoanthropology/ Archaeology

Abstract: The record of anomalous finds began with the first generation of archaeological investigations originating in Europe in the nineteenth century. Prior to a defined paradigm asserting an acceptable structure to human biological and cultural evolution, many of these initial discoveries, subject to the same diligent application of accepted and then-current methodologies, were taken at face value and incorporated into the then-malleable formulation of said structures. The institutional and informal suppression of anomalous discoveries soon followed, at the expense of countless professional careers, and continued well into the twentieth century and early twenty-first century.

Deep subsurface exploration for economic purposes repeatedly yielded unexplainable evidence of human presence at periods in geologic history deemed scientifically impossible; however, the academic and scientific institutions were securely entrenched and fully capable of suppressing said discoveries. It was not until A.C. 07 that incontrovertible evidence was uncovered in Cretaceous gravel beds at the Riddler Site in west Antarctica (for a composite list of evidence, cross-referenced dating techniques, and excavation report, see SFI NOΛCom 222.3a), proving conclusively that the accepted evolutionary scheme for *Homo sapiens* was in dire need of restitution.

Current theories on this issue—

Tracking . . .
Captured.
Rabbit goes back into the hat. Nada, folks!

Entry: American NW, June 30, A.C. 14

Outside, the wind, born somewhere out west, gusted through the small town with a howling hunger. Drifts of snow banked walls and stretched serrated ridges across the streets. Leaning into the wind, he trudged toward the hotel, its three-storied bulk barely visible.

Through his goggles, the world was monochrome. White sky, blending with white earth. Patched here and there with the dark, angular bones of civilization. Nature erases. Nature wipes clean the slate. Snow, the rough and wild passage of spirits. Glaciers, gravid with desire. He paused and looked up. Medicine Wheels spun up there, echoes of Ezekiel. More of them now, trying to tell him something in their blurred spinning through the storm clouds.

He pushed himself into motion once again. He passed

a humped mound of snow. A car rusting under it – he'd seen it the day he arrived. A monument to fleeting technology. Once new, masked in wonder and promise. When in use, mundane, banal. Then forgotten. Now buried. The makers move on, unmindful of the lessons beneath their feet. Nature erases.

He headed up Main Street. The western horizon had come close, come to the town's very edge, a curtain of nothingness behind which things moved, things paced, things stampeded, things watched. Every now and then their shadows brushed the curtain. And beyond them, out on the snow-laden prairie, dead earth was marked here and there by boulders, boulders set out in circles in which other rocks ran in narrow lines, inward like spokes, and a central pile marked the hub. Medicine Wheels, not yet launched skyward, remaining earth-anchored with a purpose sheathed in silence, locked in antiquity.

The wind reached through to sting his face. Flesh-clothed people had lived out there, once. When the sun was just the sun, the sky just sky, long before the poisons and volcanic ash burned holes in the air. They talked with stones, made places where they and the ghosts could meet, places where they could dance.

A figure slipped out from an alley ahead, stopped to wait for him. The snows spun through its body; the wind whipped unimpeded by its hide cloaks and beadwork.

'I wonder how much you anticipated, old fella?'

The figure shrugged, melted in a savage gust of wind.

A stranger. An other. Not his kind, not his blood, not what he was looking for. An emanation curious, maybe, enough so to come for a closer look. Not there for answering his questions. Not there for the civilized art of conversation. Hence, making a point.

'Thus did God, burned blind, reach down through the white, featureless void, and then did He touch the stones, and read them like Braille.' He walked past the spot where the ghost had been, then crossed Main Street, heading for the hotel. 'And He spake, and He said, "Behold these instruments of the Devil, that would give voice to the lie of the firmament."'

His vision preceded him into the hotel bar, plundering lives – a half-dozen regulars, old men and women whose farmland had withered and who now lived on government assistance, ignoring the resettlement incentives and urban start-up grants. The cities held nothing for them – nothing they wanted, anyway. And meeting every afternoon at their regular tables beside the frosted window that looked out on Main Street, they found the comfort of familiar faces and familiar stories, and the demons of loneliness stayed away for a while longer.

'Behold, I went out to withstand thee, because thy way is perverse before me.'

Net: The Swamp

CORBIE TWA: Oops! Where dat come from?

JOHN JOHN: More interestingly, where'd it go?

BOGQUEEN: What are you talking about? The SFI file or the quasibiblical dart?

CORBIE TWA: The quasiwhat? Those files show up alla time, Bogqueen.

BOGQUEEN: What's with the enunciation there, Corbie?

CORBIE TWA: Colloquial program, girl.

JOHN JOHN: Which helps the trackers fix you, Corbie.

CORBIE TWA: Sure thing. I may sound like I gotta confederate flag in my bedroom, but it don mean I live in Ole Arkansas, do it?

JOHN JOHN: Where were we? We were here, I think. I've caught whispers about this Restitution thing. It's not easy breaking into those SFIs, you know.

BOGQUEEN: It's the Track .12 entries that interest me, John John. It's a mobile, isn't it? Not easy to hide with one of those. But he's managing.

CORBIE TWA: For how much longer, though? Anyway, there's no end of foo-stuff out there. Why pay attention?

JOHN JOHN: Because the boy's playing in the Midwest Hole, right, Bogqueen?

BOGQUEEN: It all comes with what you put together. Try paying attention to the shivers on the vine, Corbie Twa. There's weird things going on.

CORBIE TWA: T'ain't nothing new with dat, girl. My weird meter's set very high, you know.

JOHN JOHN: Extinctions. Anyone tallied the count lately?

CORBIE TWA: I hate atavistic bastards – didn't know I knew big words, did you? Anyway, who tallies anymore? Who keeps lists? Pictures in books, as far as my kids are concerned. Stuffed carcasses in museums, test tubes in freezers. Jus like the dinosaurs, John John.

BOGQUEEN: Extinction's a fact of life, right, Corbie? Hail the official line.

JOHN JOHN: So, coyote ghosts and ancient buffalo. Curious.

CORBIE TWA: Probbly some effed-up terrorist mystic with a fieldbook and too much peyote.

BOGQUEEN: But he's slipping the trackers. That takes some doing.

CORBIE TWA: Or an inside line. Some kind of NOAC counter-culture creepy.

BOGQUEEN: Seems clunky. Too obtuse. Likely he's running loose.

CORBIE TWA: Lil good it'll do im. Who's listening?

JOHN JÓHN: Picked up a squiggly from someone named Bound for Ur. Wasn't tethered. Seems there was a spetznaz inc. incursion somewhere in Lapland. Went sour and nobody came back out. Any shivers?

CORBIE TWA: Don't mess with the Lappies. Not a sniff. Sounds bizarre. A run on radioactive reindeer meat in Con-Russia. Those mafiboys like their meat.

BOGQUEEN: News to me, too, John John. I'll check my sinkholes, though.

JOHN JOHN: My tally list includes coyotes.

CORBIE TWA: Make the roadrunners happy.

JOHN JOHN: No, they're extinct, too.

CORBIE TWA: Bummer.

William entered on a gust of wind, the snow swirling around him as he turned and pushed shut the heavy door. He removed his goggles and blinked, waiting for his eyes to adjust to the gloom. Pool balls cracked and rolled, followed by voices off to his right. He untied the hood's drawstrings, unzipped his bootsuit.

A gravelly voice called out from behind the bar to his left. 'What did I tell you, College Boy?'

William shrugged. 'Seemed the genuine thing,' he said, heading over to the counter.

'Damn right,' Stel said, lighting a cigarette. Tall, heavy, late thirties, the hotel's owner leaned on the counter and blew a lazy stream of smoke in William's direction. She grinned, cleared her throat. 'Didn't Old Jim tell it?'

'Yep.'

Stel set a bottle of filtered water in front of William. 'See, my memory's none too bad, eh?' She glanced over at the regulars and nodded. 'Sitting Bull's rifle, sure as my ass is fat.'

Laughter exploded in the room, forced, too loud.

William took a mouthful of water and swung his gaze to the pool table. A local boy was having his hands full playing a tall man in expensive clothes, a man even more out of place than William.

Stel bantered with the regulars, the old Indian jokes making tired rounds.

'My twenty-third Sitting Bull rifle,' William softly sighed.

'What's that, College Boy?'

'Nothing.' He watched the tall man circle the table once before dropping the eight ball on a called shot. Game over.

Behind the bar a phone buzzed. Stel snatched it up. 'Yeah?'

A fingertip stroked William's shoulder. He turned.

'For you, College Boy,' Stel said, leaning close. 'Been thinking of closing up early,' she added in a low voice.

'Sounds bad for business,' William replied, 'but good

for the soul,' he added as he took the antiquated phone. 'Hello?'

Through an electrostatic crackle came Administrator Jenine MacAlister's voice. 'William? Glad you're still in the town. The storm's supposed to last another two days – I didn't think you were that crazy, but I couldn't be sure.'

'I am research incarnate, Dr. MacAlister.'

'You didn't need to apply for an independent grant, you know that, don't you? I mean, we would've funded you, of course.'

'What's up?'

She hesitated. 'Something. Maybe serious.'

William walked away from the bar, taking the phone and the water bottle with him. He sat down at a table tucked into a secluded corner of the room. 'Go ahead.'

'Well, I'll make it simple. Here's what I'm looking for, William. There may be some, uh, activity down there.'

'In Val Marie?'

'No, no. Out under the Hole.'

MacAlister's voice was pitched low. Excitement and conspiracy. Used to be a good anthropologist. Used to be. Now, just one more social engineer in an army of social engineers. Now it was games, cloak and dagger.

'What kind of activity?'

'The Lakota. They haven't been in dialogue with us since the Autonomy Settlement, of course, but we've picked up a hint of something.'

Us and we. Defined exactly how? Us whites? We the Feds? The good guys, the cavalry? William's gaze fixed on the tall man at the pool table. 'Haven't seen any around. Last I heard, Jack Tree was paying a state visit to Argentina.'

MacAlister laughed. 'It's not him we're worried about, William. He's had his fifteen minutes at the Supreme Court, and that was seven years ago. Come on, we both know who's about to take over the Lakota Nation.'

'Daniel Horn?'

'That bastard is up to something. And it has to do with the Hole.'

'Well,' William said, 'they own the land under it—'

'That's not the point. Hell, they've never forgiven us for that. As if we knew the Hole would open up when we gave them the land.'

William's eyebrows rose. Gave? Jack Tree stood up against the Supreme Court of North America and tore that piece of ground right out of Fed hands. William massaged his temples. Medicine Wheels in the sky.

'In any case,' MacAlister continued. 'Have you seen Horn around?'

'Nope.'

'Well, he's supposed to be in the area. Keep an eye out for me, will you?'

'My journal entries are available on the Net.'

'Yes, William, but no one can understand them. I'd like something more direct, more responsive. One more thing, could be connected. There's rumors going around that the Lakota are about to close their borders. If you run into Horn, see what you can suss out. But carefully, okay? Don't push it. We'll talk soon, then. Bye, and good luck.'

William climbed to his feet and drained his bottle of

water. He walked back to the counter and set the phone down.

'Still planning on heading out tomorrow?' Stel asked.

'Yep.'

'Well' – she smiled – 'I think I'll keep your room clean and ready, just in case you come to your senses.'

William smiled back, then headed over to the pool table. The tall, well-dressed man was racking the balls for a solo game. The local boy sat at a distant table, looking glum. William leaned on the table and picked up the cue ball. 'Finally,' he said, 'some competition.'

'I'll break,' the man said.

William dropped the cue ball into the man's hand. 'Mother wants me to do some spying for her,' he said.

Daniel Horn nodded. He walked around the table and set down the cue ball. 'It's a hard life, William, and you're harder than most.'

William found a cue stick. He raised one end and sighted down it, pointing the tip at Daniel, as if holding a rifle.

Leaning on the table for his opening shot, Daniel paused. Their eyes locked. 'Careful,' the young Lakota said, 'that once belonged to Sitting Bull.'

William lowered the cue stick. 'She wants me to follow up a rumor about you closing the borders.'

'You want me to tell you? I will.'

'Nope. All I want to know is, open or closed, will you let me do my research?'

'That what you call it?'

'That's what I call it.'

Daniel's eyes narrowed as he prepared to break. 'Don't see why not,' he said. A moment later the cue ball was a white blur; then a loud crack scattered the balls. Two thumped into pockets. Daniel looked up and grinned. 'Better get out of that bootsuit, William, you're in for a hot one.'

William shook his head. 'I live in my bootsuit. It lives on me. We are one.'

'Sometimes you scare me, William.'

'Sometimes I mean to, Daniel.'

TWO

Entry: American NW, July 1, A.C. *14*

Something heavier than an angel, something more like a witch, a woman of earth and stone – only this could have made her so tenuous to his touch. It is now an age of angels, gauze-thin and adolescent. But when he'd looked upon her face, something elder had been visible, a time abandoned in despair; he'd seen the solid anguish lining her face, and he made his smile soft as he let her into the room.

Sweat of the land between them, a smell of moss and cobble-cool flesh that he imagined alabaster and serene. Stel had left him with a gift, a warmth like sun-brushed wood taking root into what had been virgin soil. Not virginity of the flesh, but of the spirit.

Days since his last meal. Things out there crowding ever closer, eager to know this new stranger in the dreamtimes. What made the night important: he was already almost gone, wind-tugged away from civilized life. It could have been easy, to have just simply left, without a backward touch or glance.

One last time crawling out of his thermal-controlled rad-shielding skin, once more unto the mortal coil. He thought then that a ghost stepped into him, a presence that understood the value of certain gestures to humanity – the one she'd give to him, the one he'd give to her.

A young man crafted by the tools of progress.

An aging woman tired of sleeping alone.

Touched human.

Touched young.

'That wasn't pity,' he said afterwards.

'That wasn't bad,' she replied.

Net

CORBIE TWA: Somethin's cooking at Boxwell Plateau. Any shivers on the vine?

STONECASTER: Just this, Corbie Twa, the Argentinians made an official call to the Lady at Ladon Inc. NOAC got to them, goes the very soft twang. So maybe Boxwell's dead. And Ladon's homeless one more time. The last time.

CORBIE TWA: What about Saudi?

STONECASTER: You've been in the Swamp too long, mucker. Saudi was knifed a week ago. Now NOAC's got the embargo sewed up tight. Ladon can't even buy a scrap heap and a hamburger.

JOHN JOHN: This path ain't for gossip, muckers. Clear or get deep.

CORBIE TWA: Just fillin time, John John. Caught the last set of entries. Someone's slidin fast.

BOGQUEEN: Got a thing against sex, Corbie Twa?

CORBIE TWA: Seems a fall from grace.

JOHN JOHN: Corbie's got a thing, all right.

STONECASTER: Just don't know how to use it. Deep enough, John John?

BOGQUEEN: You wish, Stonecaster.

JOHN JOHN: The boy's about to wander, muckers. Running a varied call, can't be traced. All we've got is the American northwest. Big place.

BOGQUEEN: And a snowstorm, which places him on the north side of the Midwest Hole. The town could be Climax, Val Marie, somewhere around there.

CORBIE TWA: Climax? There's a town called Climax? Can I spend a week in Climax?

STONECASTER: So what's this boy of ours up to? Theories?

BOGQUEEN: Out under the Hole.

STONECASTER: Suicidal? What a disappointment. There's better ways, after all. Amuse yourself to death, it's what everyone's doing these days. I especially like the new Peasant Crusade. Imagine, dying at forty with a smile on your GO-FOR-IT-TILL-YOU-DROP face. All muscles and no fat makes Jack a dull boy, a dead boy.

JOHN JOHN: I doubt it's suicide. It's a quest of some kind.

CORBIE TWA: Oh no, a neo-pagan!

BOGQUEEN: Anything but. This boy talks the tongue of science.

CORBIE TWA: Really? I could've sworn it was soft porn with some hag named Stel.

BOGQUEEN: Can't wait to pick at your bones, Corbie Twa.

CORBIE TWA: Get in line, lady.

Lakota Nation, near Terminal Zone, July 1, A.C. 14

Behold these valleys of salt, and above, the sky of blinding white. Patches of nothing mar the world.

William darkened his goggles another setting and swung his attention to the snow-crusted valley below. A creek carved a route along the valley floor, slipping under old wood fence lines still tangled in barbed wire. Small twisted trees rose along either side of the creek, the branches thick with ice-wrapped buds.

He sipped lukewarm water from the spitter, clamping his teeth down hard on the plastic tube where it sat against the corner of his mouth. Behind him, near the tepee rings, his shield tent luffed in the steady wind, the sound like ghosts drumming on sand.

William watched two vehicles converging toward a low rise just above a bend in the creek. Their dark domes glinted dully in the afternoon's light as they crawled steadily like insects over the rolling terrain. After a moment, William rose from his squat and faced east. A half-mile away, the old blacktop highway stretched its way in a long, lazy bend southward. Terminal Zone, old Rural Road 219, a dead track reaching into dead land. Lakota Border.

He took another sip of water, shouldered his pack, then headed down into the valley. His boots crunched as he crossed a sinkhole where the day's heat had failed to melt the snow and ice. Elsewhere, the yellow prairie grasses shivered stiffly in the breeze, matting worn-down rises and rumpled hills.

A man had climbed out of each vehicle. They stood side by side at the edge of the creek and watched him approach. William waved. The taller of the two, dressed in the latest issue bootsuit, waved back. The other, old and bent and wearing a faded jean jacket, raised his head slightly, his mirror sunglasses flashing white, then looked away.

'Today's the day?' William asked as he strode up to them.

Daniel Horn slowly shook his head. 'Your sensiband's flush, William.'

'Almost sunset.'

The old man gestured at William with a chopping motion of one hand. Without looking back, he said, 'He doesn't care. He doesn't live under it.'

William smiled. 'And he that liveth seven score years shall no more fear God's wrath. Good afternoon, Jack.'

Jack Tree chopped his hand a second time, turning to William. 'I'll never show you the secret places, Potts. Never.'

'I never asked.'

'We were arguing,' Daniel said.

William looked around, his grin broadening. 'A private one, huh?'

'About you, William.'

William pulled up his goggles and squinted until his eyes adjusted. He glanced at Jack Tree, then back to Daniel. 'You closed your borders?'

'This morning.'

'An empty gesture,' Jack Tree said, shaking his head.

William studied the old man. The wind picked up strands of his long gray hair and tugged with steady rhythm. His high-tech wraparounds looked snug and sleek and insectile. His cheeks were scored with deep wrinkles, the brown folds and black tracks mapping their own valleys, dry creeks, and ridges.

'Hardly empty,' Daniel was saying. 'NOAC needs oil. Same old story. Fuel to keep the Pakistanis toe to toe with the Sikhs. The machine's thirsty, and the money-men are sweating.'

'Sanctions,' Jack Tree said, facing Daniel at last. 'It'll break us apart.'

'No, it won't.'

The two fell silent.

William reached under his absorption collar and scratched his neck. The material's osmotic qualities were fine for reclaiming moisture, but it felt like fire ants when friction heated it up. 'What about my research?'

Jack Tree pulled off his glasses, his eyes sharp and black amidst a nest of wrinkles. 'Research? Research your way back home, boy. This ancient land never belonged to you, no matter how hard you pretend.'

William said, 'I found a den yesterday. Three antelope inside.'

Jack Tree frowned.

'They're fully nocturnal now. And smaller. Their front hoofs are spatulate, like shovels. Imagine that.'

'The animals are gone,' Jack Tree said.

William shook his head and smiled. 'Just changing their old ways. Behold necessity and adaptive pressures, selection in all its glory.'

'Is this your research?'

'No. But it's interesting, isn't it.'

Daniel cleared his throat. 'Like I said before, William, you do what you like. I'll tell you something, though. If peace and quiet's what you're looking for, you might end up being in the wrong place.'

Jack Tree laughed bitterly. 'Welcome to hell, then, Potts, and it's about to break loose.'

'Old news,' William said, snapping his goggles back down.

Daniel stiffened. 'What do you mean?'

'Hell hath no fury like Nature scorned, Daniel.'

JIM'S STORY

Saskatchewan, Canada, July 19, A.D. *1972*

Dust-covered cars and trucks crowded the farmyard outside the house. Everyone else was inside, neighbors and friends and relatives all circling Jim's mother, as if by numbers alone they could hold her there, in one place, forever.

Jim knew they'd say something if they could. They'd yell and show their rage, if they could. He leaned against his mother's Impala, rolling a cigarette. I can't blame her. I can hate her, but I can't blame her. Dad's slipping fast, only days left now. Metastasis, the doctors called it. From the bones to the liver, and still spreading. He already looked dead, doped up against the pain, withered by the months of chemotherapy. Three-quarters gone, one-quarter left and going fast.

He lit his cigarette. One of the barn cats had slipped out and now lay sprawled atop one of the herbicide drums lining the barn's wall. The cat stared lazily at

Jim, then blinked and looked away.

The house door opened and Jim's mother stepped out, her cigarette dangling from her lips as she paused and fished for a light. For a moment Jim hoped she'd see him, and he reached for his lighter, but then she found her own and lit up. Pulling hard on her cigarette, she went down the steps, every line of her long, angular body stiff with fury. The door opened again as Grandpa and Ruth came out. Jim's heart jumped at seeing Ruth.

My wife. I'll never quite believe it. So beautiful, so solid, so sure of herself. And it was me she picked. Why? Why the hell why?

Ruth's green eyes scanned the yard until she found him. She shrugged: *It's no use.* She stayed on the porch while Grandpa joined Jim's mother. The old man spoke to her in quiet tones. Jim watched his mother nodding, her arms crossed tight against her chest. Smoke whipped in a stream from her face.

From the city. It had always been obvious. She'd stayed only because of Dad, and now he was dying, and her son was a man, married to a country girl, which was right, and besides, all the words between her and Jim had been used up. The grief they shared was a chasm, impenetrably dark and too terrifying to cross. She wasn't staying. She was going back, where being alone wasn't quite so noticeable. I don't blame her. She's got her life, lots of years left. She wants to start over. I can hate her, but I can't blame her.

Ruth approached. 'Roll me one,' she said, sweeping strands of auburn hair from her face.

'Got some grass for later,' Jim said, watching her mouth, wanting to kiss it and keep kissing it.

She smiled. 'Not my style. You do the hippie thing.'

'I love you, Ruth.'

'I know.' She leaned against the car beside him, their hips touching.

Three weeks married. All she has to do is get close and Christ, all I can think of is fucking her. Dad's dying, Mom's leaving, and none of it matters. Christ. He finished rolling her cigarette and lit it for her.

'Thanks,' she said. Taking it from his fingers. They watched Grandpa and Jim's mother talking, there at the foot of the porch steps, the old farmhouse rising behind them. The curtains in the windows were drawn. To Jim, it had the look of a place waiting to be struck by lightning, waiting to burn to the ground, sending human souls flying skyward in a shower of sparks, a final release there on the trail blazed by his old man. Release, and relief. He realized, with a sudden thud in his belly, that he hated death, hated it like a person – with a face, a goddamned smile, gold-capped teeth, and eyes as deep as the flames of hell. One of the curtains moved. Elly, Dad's kid sister, peered out at the two talking in front of the porch. Her face withdrew after a moment, the curtain falling back into place.

'We'll be okay,' Ruth said.

'I know. It's all right.'

'Like hell it is, Jim.'

'I know,' he said again.

'It's not all right.'

'No. It's not all right.'

'But we'll be okay. Are you listening to me?'

He nodded.

'Don't hate her, Jim.'

'I don't.' But he did.

'She's earned the right. She stood by him, all through this. It was hell for her.'

'For all of us. Grandpa's only son. My dad.'

'It's different. I know, you can't see that right now, but it's different.'

He shrugged, wishing he weren't so angry. 'When I was a kid, Dad went and plowed up some holy land. A Medicine Wheel, and tepee rings. There was a cairn in the wheel. A shaman had been buried there. A holy man. Or a devil, a spirit, or maybe both, one taking care of the other. Maybe there was a whole lot that was buried there.'

'You think he's paying for it, now? Is that what you're thinking, Jim?'

He shrugged again, flicking the butt onto the dusty ground.

'Is that what your grandpa says?'

'No,' he admitted.

'Didn't think so.' Now she was angry. It was a mood of hers that frightened him, because it left him feeling crushed, and that made him feel like he was weak inside. For all the outward toughness, he was weak – he prayed she'd never find out.

'You've been away,' he said. 'At school. Grandpa's not been himself lately.'

'Are you surprised?'

He shook his head. 'He's stopped talking about the old days. He told me it's up to me now to remember. So that's what I'm doing. I'm Métis. French and Cree, and it's the Indian part of me that's doing most of the talking in my mind. These days. It's, uh, it's the voice in my blood.'

She was looking at him now, her eyes searching his face, or maybe studying it. She seemed to have shed her anger, but Jim wasn't sure what had replaced it.

'The voice in your blood?'

Suddenly embarrassed, he looked away. 'Yeah. Sort of, I guess.'

She was silent for a long moment; then she said, 'Keep listening to it, Jim.'

They both looked up at the sound of crying. Jim's mother was in Grandpa's arms. The stiffness was gone, and she looked almost childlike as she clutched Grandpa, her head buried against his shoulder.

'Christ,' Jim gasped.

'Go to her,' Ruth commanded. 'Now, dammit. It's not just her husband she's leaving. Go on, Jim – you'll never get another chance.'

The scene blurring in front of him, Jim lurched into motion.

Entry: American NW, July 1, A.C. 14, Midnight

He lay in his tent.

And these lizards have gone reflective. Crusty, muricated, a sleight of sunlight shunting elsewhere as they hug their own shadows. Wondering at what's old about being new, the few generations of intense environmental pressures already forgotten except in the blood that threads their spines. And they hunt at night, amidst the hum and hiss of a thousand new species of insect in a hundred thousand iridescent colors reduced to gray beneath the moon.

He hides in his tent, reflecting. His skin has billowed

out and is geodesic and is now crawling with many-legged silhouettes. He sees the lizards leap against his taut skin, jaws snapping. Exoskeleton crunches softly in the darkness.

Outside the lizards are feasting on Saint John's bread, a mayhem banquet. And where is he, the one who giveth songs in the night?

A few generations of intense environmental pressures. The Lakota hearths spread smoke haze across the plains. Seven generations lost in the wilderness, and now the eighth, rising once again, at last, rearing up and taking countenance of their ghost lands. The blood pumping from the ground has slowed, stopped. Somewhere vampires are screaming. The transport roads are barricaded now, the scattered small settlements isolated inside their rad domes; their skin taut and softly drumming to aborted intrusions from outside. Radio silence. The mute warnings of smoke signals unseen, unwitnessed.

They remain this night in their secret places, the past sitting in their laps like a child long overdue weaning. The old ones flinch and caress innocent's face, reluctant and angry at necessity's harsh slap. The young ones, who no longer recognize innocence at all, are brash and abrupt in their dismissal. For the old, the past weeps. For the young, the past walks, a mindful shadow anchored to the earth but facing the sky. The old reach for an embrace. The young are driven to dance. For each, the past obeys, as shadows must. Anchored to the earth, but facing the sky. And those shadows that weep, they are reflective.

'Read me, then, for I am like Braille, and in the

changing of my skin, something shall rise and find the stars.'

The borders are closed, the lizards are dancing, the young and the old have met and argued, the antelope dig burrows in the false dawn, and the quest is now begun. And here where home is hell, the devil delivers.

Net

CORBIE TWA: Oh my oh my. Possible? Accelerated genetic mutations in so little time?

BOGQUEEN: There's documentation to support it, especially among insects. As for the higher orders, who can say. The difficulty has to do with the sheer complexity of vertebrates. Speciation is rarer because so many more variables have to come in line for any major biological or behavioral traits to be expressed.

CORBIE TWA: Who ordered a textbook? Look, our strange friend is talkin a maze. Has me wonderin if there's anything there.

JOHN JOHN: Watch the news, Corbie. The Lakota have shut everything down. NOAC's politicos are having a stock-tumbling fit. A team of multiculture negotiators is being assembled to discuss grievances, only the Lakota haven't voiced any. In fact, they're not talking at all.

CORBIE TWA: Multiculture negotiators? What the hell is that?

BOGQUEEN: Has an insidious ring to it, don't it?

JOHN JOHN: Applied anthropologists, mostly. Work with endangered cultures and the generally downtrodden, set up systems and programs with cheese at the far end and call it social adjustment.

CORBIE TWA: Must number in the millions. How come they haven't worked with me? I'm as hungry as the next mucker.

LUNKER: You must be burdened with racial success. Hello, everyone, I stepped into the line in time to catch the boy's last entry.

JOHN JOHN: Backloading you now, Lunker. Welcome aboard.

LUNKER: Caught a free-falling message from someone named Bound for Ur. Ladon's been shut down in Antarctica. Word is, the tech is being dismantled and packaged—

JOHN JOHN: Packaged? For what, storage?

LUNKER: The dismantling's in reverse order, John John. Doesn't sound like storage. In any case, Bound for Ur hand-offs the rumor that the Lady at Ladon negotiated a new site for her sky baby. The world denies, well, almost all the world . . .

CORBIE TWA: The devil delivers indeed.

BOGQUEEN: Two and two makes four. How the hell did the boy know?

LUNKER: If he's reading between the NOAC lines, and knows the Swamp like he seems to, he might've done his own adding up. Four equals all hell busting loose.

CORBIE TWA: This makes the boy hot, don't it.

BOGQUEEN: Assuming NOAC reads his mail.

CORBIE TWA: You must be kidding. NOAC reads everyone's mail. Readin it right now, in fact. Right, fellas?

BOGQUEEN: Comments, John John?

. . .

CORBIE TWA: Huh, he's slipped out.

STONECASTER: Sorry I'm late. You guys and your random activations. Give me a break next time, I'm antiquated and clunking macrotemporally. Give me a minute while I catch up.

LUNKER: What's that buzz?

STONECASTER: Shut up.

FREE WHIZZY: What's needed here, muckers, is some encryption, and I'm your ticket-puncher. Rally my way and we'll plunge so deep NOAC will grope and grope and grope.

BOGQUEEN: Double me up, Free Whizzy. I want John John to find us. Hey, didn't you get virused by NOAC last year?

FREE WHIZZY: A worm in my brain. I had a transplant. They're still chasing me, or am I chasing them? Let's keep them guessing.

CORBIE TWA: Two plus two, the Lady's made a deal. Oh my oh my oh my.

THREE

Entry: American NW, July 3, A.C. 14

The snow was just a memory. Overhead the sun burned away the clouds. On the ground the damp lichen curled its edges, mosses stiffened and crunched underfoot, and the ancient gray lichen strains formed snakeskin patterns on the boulders they would devour for the next hundred thousand years.

Three turkey vultures rode the thermals above the baking plain. Their feathers were glossy, flashing sunlight as they wheeled. At certain angles they disappeared entirely, as if plunging into a placid tropical sea, then reemerged in sudden blooms of blinding light.

He watched them swing southward, seeking the heart of the Hole. Orders were orders. He'd set the beacon on the largest of the nearest tepee ring's weight stone. The beacon squatted like a turtle, silently chirping. The outside world homed in on its song, and he waited.

Hydrogen-fueled, the helishuttle plunged earthward in a vapor mist of its own making. Down, down from the north, half its shielded face mirroring the raging sun. As it swept down, its delta wings infolded themselves into the craft's bright self. The blades hovered an amber circle above the machine's body, sharpened their declivity as podded feet touched earth.

William deactivated the beacon, walked to the crest of the hill, and watched four figures emerge from the helishuttle.

Tech Team, decked out in Cardinal Locator helmets, four black-lidded eyes facing in four directions to feed a 360-degree comprehensive image back to the inside receiver. Wearing solar conductor butterfly blades rising up fourfold from their shoulder cowls. Multifunctioned, moisture-grabbing, energy-hoarding, rad and humidity-sensing. Reflective insulated boots hiding their feet, cow-soled in shape and the color of burnished brass.

CL helmets, lenses each set on separate array; motion detection to the right, seeing red on the left, human spectrum straight ahead, and telephoto macrocapacities straight back.

Chest control pads, monitor feeds, glittering in the sunlight that moved, up and down, down and up their four selves. Static discharges marked friction points as the four figures walked forward.

Behind them the helishuttle squatted its round self on another hill, its four glider wings arched high to vent heat. The blades were now angled back and slowly rotating. The helishuttle's canopy had shifted shades, arriving at beryl. Its round self squatted, and above it was a roundness in kind, shaped by the rotating blades.

'I'm surprised you're still standing, William.'

He blinked at the crimson expellation of her words, then looked beyond to the vague throne hovering behind her, suspended a dozen meters in the air. The other three activated their CLs and scanned for life and found what life they scanned and the living creatures found no place to hide.

'Is this your multiculture team, Dr. MacAlister?'

'Just the outriders, William. Listen, I'm thinking now we should bring you in, soon. You haven't been covering up, have you. Goddammit, William, at least activate your goggles.'

'Soon. What do you need first?'

'The Lakota have fucked up, William. Something awful. You wouldn't believe the extent of the transgressions against preestablished agreements, especially the Covenants of '07. NOAC won't play nice guy in this, William. I want you to tell Daniel Horn. He's a little boy fucking with grown-ups, and he's going to get hurt, him and everyone behind him.'

'Dr. MacAlister, there are layers to this rebellion. It has a long-standing precedent, wouldn't you say? We fuck them over, they fuck Custer over, we fuck them over, we fuck them over, we fuck them over—'

'William.'

'And now they fuck us over. You keeping count, Dr. MacAlister? I think they're due.'

'Don't let propaganda poison your scientific detachment, William. You need to stay rational about this. People could die, William.'

'Am I to be scientifically detached, Doctor, or bound by guilt and threats? Can you really have both like that?'

'I don't care how you swallow it ethically, William. You deliver my message. We have to negotiate directly with Daniel Horn. Before the world mourns this tragedy, before you're left lamenting your weaknesses, before NOAC closes the book on the Lakota Nation.'

She left food for his mouth; he showed her a flaked stone tool, bifacial perfection in the style called Eden. He set it against his forehead as they returned to their round machine with its round halo. He felt the blade cool against his brow, and knew it protected him for ten thousand years.

He knew adamant to be a fractious material, rife with flaws and phenocryst arbitrariness. An item of glittering admiration, but nothing he could work with. This wasn't adamant, this was chalcedony, and it was magic in a master's hands.

His kit was packed, supplies shouldered. He left the hill. He left the beacon where it sat like a turtle on the rock, ready to be discovered by a curious crow. He walked into the valley, forded the creek, ascended and descended a half-dozen more hills, came to the closed road and walked down it, southward, until he found the barrier and the armed Lakota with their scarves and armbands and laser-tracking thunder-sticks.

He waited beyond the antiassault mines, hunkered down on the cracked blacktop, and studied a corkscrew cactus with shiny flat spines that rotated away from the sun with perfect precision as the hours passed. Tiny white spiders spun webs between the spines, created balls of liquid that turned sticky and mimed droplets of condensation. The spiders clung to the underside of the spines, and waited.

A skimmer arrived and landed behind the barricade. Daniel Horn passed through the shock line and carefully made his way to William.

'Mother wants to talk.'

Daniel shrugged. 'I'll think about it. I'm worried as hell about you, William. Those conjunctiva are there to tell you something. Something important.'

'I see beyond them, Daniel.'

'Fuck, you can barely blink. Here, use my goggles; they're the best you can buy.'

'No. Mother's spirit is in me. She tastes bitter.'

'We're naughty boys, are we?'

'Impudent and stiffhearted. Threats were made. People could die.'

'They want a ball of fire, they'll get it. The oil fields are rigged, and I mean subsurface rigged. The earth will melt, William. They can kill us, but they'll get nothing for it, nothing left to plunder. We'll butcher the buffalo, William, all of them. Call it manifest destiny; that's something they'll understand.'

'I've disappeared, Daniel. My days as a messenger are over. Tell her yourself.'

'Still making your entries on the Net?'

'Like droplets of condensation.'

'That'll do.'

'It will?'

Daniel's smile was a broken effort. 'If you're the boy, and I think you are. Please, William, pull yourself out.'

'I can't. I must speak of my captivity, Daniel. I must explore its absence. And all the ghosts are walking with me now. They're an insistent bunch, Daniel.'

'Hell, William.'

'I found a paleo-point. Eden style. Ten thousand years old. Knife River flint. Here, it's yours. At least in its physical manifestation. I imagine you can see the imprint on my forehead. That's its ghost, thus I am marked, and thus it shall be. Like that spearhead of old, I am hunting big game. The biggest.'

NOAC Net

... announcement today confirms the rumor that Ladon Incorporated and the Lakota Nation have reached an agreement that in the words of NOAC Spokesperson Dr. Jenine MacAlister, 'represents the most serious threat in terms both economic and political.'

This follows fierce debate and accusations in the New United Nations assembly presently in an extraordinary session following the near-collapse of all world markets. Saudi Arabia was accused by both NOAC and SINJO of failing to comply with the trade embargo against the Ladon Corporation, which was enacted exactly three years ago today (July 4, A.C. 11). Spokespersons for the Saudi contingent have responded that a legal loophole was exploited by Ladon regarding the retrieval of Ladon technology from Saudi territory; a legalistic sleight of hand similar to the one employed against Argentina at Boxwell Plateau, Antarctica.

The NUN world court, which Ladon refuses to recognize, is now considering immediate corrective measures to close this loophole, anticipating copycat pressures from other free corporations to avoid contractual obligations to their parent nations.

Indeed, two small corporations with contract and material ties to Ladon have reportedly 'abandoned' high technology on unpatrolled shoals off the African Coast, which was subsequently salvaged under Charter 70109 of the NUN Salvage Rights, by Ladon Corporation. This flagrant circumvention of the NUN . . .

. . . NOAC Security has announced an intensive program to clean up the Net's infamous 'swamp,' after an encrypted exchange of unknown information was briefly tracked by Security monitors . . .

. . . Normal pursuit measures encountered a heretofore unknown tracksweeper with hidden mines, resulting in loss of trail and minor damage to the Security Insystem.

'This constitutes a premeditated evasion of inform-ation by parties unknown, contrary to the NUN Charters defining universal access to information on the Net.' The release goes on to say that a list of suspects has been compiled and is being pursued 'with rancor.'

. . . Pakistani forces retreat in face of Sikh incursions and once again yield the Khyber Pass . . .

. . . 'Hidden' stock market remains a likely candidate for culpability in latest market crash . . .

. . . NOAC Economic Security officials 'closer to Ladon's list of secret shareholders.'

... boreal forest joins the list of Near Extinct eco-
systems. But as Forestry Spokesman Arnold Sheer
noted, 'The boreal forest is notoriously low in energy
yield. The biospheres are virtually inconsequential in
global yield terms.'

The designation for the boreal forest now adds
this ecosystem to coral reefs, tropical and temperate
rain forests and tundra. As has been noted, however,
the deforested areas are now viable for agricorp
expansions ...

... the new virus infecting the East Codfarms has
necessitated destroying over four thousand tons of fish
stock. Economic and resource projections suggest a new
designation to Red-3 level for Dependent Peoples.
Given the trans-species characteristic of this new virus,
the slaughtered fish could not be used as Feed for
domesticates. The East Codfarms was the last marine
farm still operating. Open Seas monitoring indicates
little change in the now empty oceans worldwide. The
official statement goes on to emphasize that there is no
cause for panic, as GMO and GrowVat Foodstocks
remain at optimum levels ...

... four months into the excavation, with complete
capping of the site set to begin immediately. The Mars
Paleontology Team is now officially dissolved following
an undisclosed breach of security ...

... SINJO reaffirms military aid ties with India, at a
historic meeting of officials outside Tel-abib on the
banks of the Chebar River, where they arose and went

forth into the plain and there spoke with each other and no one else, for this was a plain of darkness where he sang nevermore RECALL? SYSTEM ERROR SINJO SOURCE RECALL in all damnation, for they are rebellious in their houses . . .

SFI 29786.17

Subject: Site Mj-eb 21
Subcategory: Mars Excavation Projects
Abstract: Sediments firmly dated at 11.2–13.3 mya yield gracile hominin fossil remains and evidence of an extensive agricultural complex in the xxxxxxx region of the Santo Regina basin—

Tracking . . .
Captured.
NF NF NF

Entry: American NW, July 4, A.C. 14

In her blind world, she lay under the rock and listened. Burned blind, but eyes had become irrelevant. She thought nothing of this. Painless, forgotten. At night she would slide out from her place of rest, threading through the grasses and bouncing echoes off the land around her. Hunting, and there was food for her mouth in plenty. The rodents were everywhere, for a time unrestrained in their nightly activities. But she'd adapted, more or less overnight, along with a good many of her sisters. Granted, some took another route. No problem there. In any case, the snake was in heaven.

Beneath the rock, her newly sensitized ears detected the presence of humans. She felt probing sonar bounce off the rock she lay under, and other probes as well, but her blood was cold, and they found her not.

'I haven't really got the time for this, Dr. MacAlister.'

'The Lady's put you in charge of the project. You bastard, what the hell do you think you're doing?'

'What?'

'Is my language excessive, Max? Come on, give me a fucking break. These Lakota are dependent on us. If they cut NOAC out, they cut their own throat.'

'Take it up with them, Doctor. I've got an engineering problem to tackle. Being intercepted has messed up my schedule.'

'You passed through NOAC airspace, Max. Hell, I could've ordered you shot down.'

'Why didn't you? It's the only way you can stop us.'

'I want some messages delivered. Both ways.'

'And those messages are?'

'For the Lakota. The embargo is officially NUN approved. Extreme sanctions. Assets seized, the works. Nothing goes in, nothing comes out.'

'I can hear Horn already. Back to the reservations, right?'

'You're missing the point. Tell the Lady this, Max. You may have made a deal with the Lakota Nation, but the Lakota Nation is finished. No money for you – I don't think the Lady will swing this one past her secret shareholders. Ladon will be financially ruined.'

'No money was involved, Dr. MacAlister. Basic reciprocity in action. The Lakota appreciated the irony, by the way. After all, it's the way they used to do things, isn't it?'

'I'm not done with my message to Ladon. No air corridors will be granted. Your supplies will never reach here. Any efforts to breach the free-air zone will be met militarily.'

'Anything else?'

'Deliver the messages, Max. The world doesn't want your project to get off the ground. Period. It's danger-ous, untested—'

'Right, the official line. Come on, Doctor, we both know why NOAC and SINJO, and EUROCOM for that matter, are pissing themselves. It's economic, pure and simple. Or, rather, if you'll excuse my blunt language, bloody greed. Ladon's not offering a piece of the pie, and you're all offended. Stopping us is your obsession, Jenine. You and your bosses. The Lady has a message for you, all of you, and it's this: Stop panick-ing, you might get your piece of the pie, eventually. But only if you're nice.'

'You're exploiting the Lakota—'

'Bullshit. They aren't children, Doctor. Never were, despite your most cherished beliefs. The noble savage was your creation, Doctor, not theirs. They won't live in a bottle of your making. Hell, you want to see the effects of your social engineering programs, look in your own backyard. God never granted you the right to fuck around with other people's cultures.'

'Who's speaking?'

'A snake whispering in your ear, Doctor. She's bored under that rock, waiting for night. She echolocated you out of the ether. You were just passing by, but her hunting instincts are up, and she's with you now, with her newly reflective skin that makes her invisible, a ghost at your ear, whispering.'

'I've been placed in an untenable position.'

'And it's all yours, Jenine.'

'Go to hell.'

'I'm already here.'

Net

LUNKER: Another streamer from Bound for Ur, friends. This stuff must come from an Inner Ear, if you catch my drift.

VORPAL: I can't believe what I'm reading. NOAC's got spy sats tracking every Ladon shipment on the whole goddamn planet?

LUNKER: Desperate measures . . . I admit my back's up on this. Look, we've all been chased before, so we know how it feels.

BLANC KNIGHT: The Lady's not human, friends. She's something else entirely. Something more than human.

LUNKER: You anticipating she's going to drop a perfumed scarf, Blanco?

BLANC KNIGHT: I'll take it up if she does, Lunker.

VORPAL: Bravo, sirrah! Count me in.

LUNKER: If the Lady's as uncanny as you say, she isn't likely the kind to ask for help. I'd think she can manage her own battles. She's done it so far.

VORPAL: Things aren't looking good right now, though. At least that's what's between the lines from Bound for Ur.

BLANC KNIGHT: Well, we're looking at spy sats, correct?

I mean, they're rather small and delicate, aren't they? Microsats usually are.

VORPAL: Indeed, and of course com sats are much larger. We'd need to loop in and get a tracking matrix on the eye-spies—

BLANC KNIGHT: Not necessary. Bound for Ur's provided us with transport routes for all of Ladon's shipments. We've got times, dates, lats and longs. The eye-spies will be right on them. Ergo.

VORPAL: I'm setting up for a com sat interface now. Where's my Nintendo joystick? You with me on this, Blanco?

BLANC KNIGHT: Let me know which one you grab, and I'll feed you the coords on the nearest eye-spy.

VORPAL: Lovely.

LUNKER: You guys are scary. Hey, anybody skimming the official news lately? Some weird things going on.

. . .

LUNKER: Hello?

Net

JOHN JOHN:

NOACOM: THIS IS AN UNRESTRICTED LINE. GO BACK. YOU ARE NOT CLEARED FOR THIS LINE.

JOHN JOHN:

NOACOM: FREEDOM FILES REQUIRE CLEARANCE. WHO IS THIS, PLEASE?

JOHN JOHN:

NOACOM: Freedom Files: In keeping with the NUN Charters and Conventions, all information is accessible to all citizens. Freedom Files represents a block of accessible information assembled by NOAC, SINJO, EUROCOM, and other National Cartels. This information block complies with all NUN Charters and Conventions. This information is an unrestricted line, and is accessible to all citizens.

JOHN JOHN:

NOACOM: YOU ARE NOT CLEARED TO ACCESS FREEDOM FILES, CITIZEN. GO BACK, OR PROSECUTION AS UNOFFICIAL USAGE WILL RESULT. WARNING, PROHIB FUNCTIONS ON THIS LINE WILL DESTROY YOUR SYSTEM AS A PUNITIVE MEASURE. IDENTITY WILL BE DETERMINED AND ALL ASSETS SEIZED. GO BACK.

JOHN JOHN:

NOACOM: YEAH WELL FUCK YOU, TOO.

Lakota Nation, Terminal Zone, July 5, A.C. 14

The small tracked machine circled him from a distance at first, then began spiraling closer. After a while, he stopped walking and waited for it.

Its four sensor eyes examined him in turn, the metallic half-dome swiveling with a faint hum. Its steel chest opened up to reveal a monitor screen. The image flickered, then steadied to reveal Jenine MacAlister's face.

Her voice came from a speaker above the monitor. 'So one of my searchers found you. Good. Please speak clearly when you record. I assume you have delivered the appeal to Daniel Horn. What was the answer? Will they talk?'

William glanced up to see a hooded hawk circling overhead. Earlier, he'd panicked a score of shiny mice on a knoll. They had been collectively weaving blades of grass, making long green tunnels between den holes. The mice seemed to possess extra digits on their front paws. William couldn't be certain – the mice quickly disappeared down their holes – but the weave of the grass blades looked intricate, precise.

A new voice came from the speaker: 'The recording device is voice activated. Please speak to activate the recording device.'

A loud roar startled William. He looked back into the sky to see the hawk diving earthward. Far above, like a piece of the sun, a ball of white fire descended. Amber smoke poured from it in a tail. It cut its way across the sky, spinning, flinging burning fragments out to the sides. The roaring sound deepened.

William raised a hand to cover his eyes. His attention was drawn to the skin of his hand. Burned, blistered, the first epidermal layers cracked and yellowing. His fingerprints were gone.

A distant detonation to the southwest. Thunder beneath his feet, then silence.

He closed his broken lips on the spitter, drew in a mouthful of recycled water. A taste like ashes. He blinked rapidly, but the blank spots continued to swim across his vision. Blank, like patches of snow on a gray day.

He saw the helishuttles before he heard them. They flew in formation, miming the contours of the ground; skimming hilltops, plunging down into valleys. They approached quickly, on a route that would take them nearly over his head. The muffled sound of their blades barely carried on the wind.

William stared, blinking and shifting his head as they swept into and out of blind spots. A moment later the helishuttles reared up in front of him, then over. He saw the Ladon logo on their underbellies, a dragon coiled around a tree against a black field. He swung round and continued staring after them.

'The recording device is voice activated. Please speak to activate the recording device. Camera is recording.'

William tried to smile, but his lips split and he winced. He opened his mouth and crouched down to one of the visual sensors. He stuck out his swollen tongue, tried to move it, then withdrew it, closed his bleeding mouth and sat back, shrugging.

He looked down at his hands, closed them into fists. His skin and flesh felt waxy. He dug his nails into his palms. *As good as a candlestick, and this monitor, on this machine programmed to return to her, is as good as a plaster wall. So I come forth, the fingers of a man's hand, and so that you may see the part of the hand that wrote, here on this shiny screen.*

William reached out to the screen, then hesitated. Someone crouched down beside him. William glanced over, nodded. *I recall the photograph, the days at the fort, during that hard winter. You weren't wearing rad goggles back then, of course. But you've been disarmed a thousand times, old man, haven't you.*

Sitting Bull shrugged, then grasped William's hand. *I will guide you thereon, in this message. I will write this for you.*

Who will read it?

She cannot. Daniel can, but she will never ask him. All the records have been sealed, and this language of pictures, ancient as it is, is nevertheless complicated, for our thoughts were never simple.

Of course they weren't.

Do you know, the ghosts are dancing?

Is that your message?

Clever boy. We've known that all along, your cleverness. Even so, this spirit you quest for, it changes our countenance and leads us into doubt.

I make no grand claims, Sitting Bull.

This spirit you quest for, it is your own?

I'm not sure. I still keep denying it.

Sitting Bull finished guiding his hand, and let it fall. He smiled at William. *Blindness inside and out. Here, take my goggles.*

No, thanks.

Tell me, William Potts, will your final fire be hot?

Hot as hell. Don't say I didn't warn you.

The machine swiveled its eyes one last time, then crawled away, northward. William rose and retrieved his backpack. Far to the southwest, pillars of smoke reached skyward in a row, each pulled to one side by the steady wind. William squinted. Four, maybe five pillars. It was getting hard to tell things like that.

Sitting Bull was gone, but that was something he'd always known.

JIM'S STORY

Saskatchewan, Canada, June 30, A.D. *2004*

Jim had stopped asking why he was still here. The question had run through his mind again and again, until it seemed to fall into the rhythm of his heart, his breathing, each swing of the shovel, each toss of the bale. But now he'd stopped, like a clock running down into silence, down into a world without time.

Chubb, the red heeler, came into view from around the barn, prowling, nose testing the air for any new scent of cat. Jim wasn't sure, but he figured that there was at least one left, hiding somewhere. Hell of a mean dog. Mean mean mean. Still, haven't got the heart to put him under. The Morrisons lost the ranch so fast, and now the old beater's got no cows to chase. Besides, cats don't kick back. Hell, though, I liked all the cats. Reminded me of Ruth, of course, and Albert, and the way things used to be.

It was in his head now, the old voice in his blood rising like a chant. The land had never been kind, but it had become downright vicious lately. He'd done his best to turn things over. Farming had sucked the land dry and dead, and without Ruth's school-learning in the finer points of modern agriculture, the profits had quickly vanished. He'd tried to turn the land back, back to its original state. Pasture, cattle, the prairie regained from the exhausted, topsoil-stripped earth, the combines rusting into motionless hulks in beds of high grass. But it had been way too late, and righting the wrong tasted sour, for one simple reason: He was the only one left.

Grandpa dead of a heart attack, Ruth dead of ovarian cancer, Albert dead three days after his second birthday to leukemia.

The night past had seen a windstorm, a real duster – walls of black airborne dirt trudging across the hills – no rain, just wind, scouring the paint from the barn's west wall, pitting the house's siding, chewing leaves from the branches of the trees in the windbreak. He'd woken this morning to an ochre sky with the sun a mere blush of pink. And his backyard had changed – ten inches of soil stripped away, right down to the gravel that had been left behind by glaciers ten thousand years past, and on this lumpy bed of limestone cobbles curled-up skeletons lay in clumps. Scores of them. The wind had exposed a burial ground, right there in his god-damned backyard.

Jim lit a cigarette to get the taste of dust out of his mouth. He watched Chubb pause at the front wheel of one of the university trucks, lift a leg, and give it a wet what for. A bunch of scientists were crawling round among the bones out back. The head archaeologist had told Jim that there'd been a blowout site just like this one about ninety minutes northwest of here, years back, called the Gray Site. It'd been right beside a farmhouse, too, one that had seen more bankruptcies and more owners than any other in the area. Jim grunted, not surprised.

The burial ground was an old one, from way before the time of the Cree, Assiniboine, and Lakota. Four thousand years old, before horses, which explained why there were as many dogs buried there as people. The archaeologist had shown him a dog's vertebra, the way the edges had compacted from a lifetime of pulling travois. Down the slope a ways was a larger jumble of bones: women and children. The damned dogs got more ceremony than did the women and children.

Bloody scientists, the second bunch this month. The other group had come to test his well water. Statistically high incidences of cancers in the area. Someone's thesis in biochemistry. The well was foul, but Jim had known that all along. Herbicidal residue, pesticides, lead, mercury. And maybe an angry water spirit, loose somewhere down below, unappeased and full of venom.

It was no wonder that Chubb seemed so at home here. No wonder at all. Mean dog, mean, mean. Mean.

There was going to be trouble. That citified Indian from Winnipeg, Jack Tree, had been stirring things up with pushing land claims back into the Supreme Court. News of the burial ground was bound to feed his fires, even though the people buried were from so long ago that their closest relatives probably lived somewhere in Mexico. Or so the archaeologist said. Jack Tree would know that, and he wouldn't give a damn. He'd play on public ignorance; he'd raise a wave of emotion and ride it as far as he could.

It's not right. I got more ties to this damn land than Jack Tree. He's from South Dakota, for Christ's sake. He thinks he can sit behind a mic in Ottawa and take it all away from me. The hell with that.

Bloody hot summer, too. The hottest yet.

The cat bolted into view, a tawny shot from under his

pickup. Chubb ducked his head, muscles rippling as he raced in explosive pursuit.

Jim sighed. He'd liked all the cats.

Net

FREE WHIZZY: Everybody still with me?

BOGQUEEN: Murky world here. Devonian.

CORBIE TWA: Antediluvian.

FREE WHIZZY: So the boy's name is William, and he's got friends in high places.

BOGQUEEN: I'm not sure that was a friendly contact.

STONECASTER: No reason to think it wasn't, Bogqueen. Sure, maybe they argued a bit, but how much of that was for our benefit? Think about it. We've got some guy named William walking around under the Midwest Hole. He's inputting on a field notebook, but somehow he's hack enough to slice through every Security Block and swim the Swamp. Nobody catches him, nobody intercepts, nobody shuts him down. I admit it, I've got some serious doubts about all this.

CORBIE TWA: You're slagging NOAC with a whole lot of heavy cunning, Stonecaster. Come on, these politicos aren't that subtle.

STONECASTER: Really. Psychotic geniuses are a dime a dozen in any security arm of any gov't you'd care to mention. Diabolical's the word, I kid you not.

BOGQUEEN: Unsupported conclusions, Stonecaster. Look at the info he's dropping our way. The contraventions are serious stuff. Straight from that historical cesspool NOAC and co. keep telling us is unimportant, outdated. But if you try getting close, for a better look at that cesspool, they cook your computer, grab your assets, and the next thing you know they've busted down the door and you're penal-tagged. Sweeping streets for the rest of your miserable life.

FREE WHIZZY: What kind of contraventions, Bogqueen? I think you've lost most of us. So far, the boy's mentioned a handful of creepy-crawlies that seem to have adapted to high-rad no-ozone toxic environments. This is blasphemy?

BOGQUEEN: Keep up on the literature? Anyone? There's a party line on this stuff, the university- and ministry-backed monographs are pushing a revised worldview that justifies gov't policy. It's there in the science, in the reams of squirreled data they keep publishing.

STONECASTER: Cure for insomnia.

BOGQUEEN: Precisely. They don't want you to actually analyze the data, or the parameters of the study. Skip to the conclusions. And the manufactured zeitgeist builds momentum, quietly, invasively, and insidiously.

FREE WHIZZY: Elucidate us, Bogqueen.

BOGQUEEN: It's a kind of twisted systems theory. A few decades ago the industrial age ran up against environmental mysticism, and the shit started flying. People started noticing – or maybe finally listening to people who'd been screaming their terror for years – anyway, the subjects of mass extinction came up repeatedly. Deforestation, destruction of habitats, and species extinction rates climbing exponentially. Add that to increased rates of human toxemia, resistant diseases, herbicide and pesticide overkill, rad leaks at reactor plants, not to mention terrorists flicking Biks and you've got people running for the wilderness and the Great Mother who's real sick and needs mending. You've got militants ready to kill to defend the lowland gorilla, and fuck the Chinese healers with their mortars and pestles and their demands for more gorilla hands, bear livers, whatever.

Anyway, the industrial revolution started losing momentum – especially with increased mechanization and skyrocketing unemployment. Compassion for the world and its nonhuman inhabitants grew, became a political force it wasn't safe to ignore anymore.

Through all this, the academic community poured out supporting data for the environmentalists. They were allies, and they made a helluva team in a world confused enough to depend almost entirely on experts and specialists.

CORBIE TWA: So the gov't got clever. Rest your vocal cords, Bogqueen, I'll run a ways with the story. You others still with us?

STONECASTER: Waiting to see you pin the tail on the donkey. I figure you're somewhere between Jupiter and Mars.

FREE WHIZZY: I'm listening.

PACEMAKER: I've been listening all along, but I figured I'd show myself, what the hell. Surfing your wave down here wasn't easy, so I'm feeling pretty good about myself right now. How forward of me.

BOGQUEEN: Hi. No sign of John John?

STONECASTER: 'Fraid not. Maybe he got nabbed.

CORBIE TWA: Back to the story, then. The Net was online

by then, or at least a version of it. The world started talking, and it started getting hard for gov'ts to keep their citizens sufficiently myopic. Info bled everywhere. Security parameters were a joke. Ideas had arrived, and once voiced there was no turning back. Pop goes the cork.

So the gov'ts got clever, like I said. Flood the lines with useless information and call it unrestricted access. Meanwhile, pull the funding chain on the universities and call it enlightened merger. Faculties became Ministries, the cynical academics suddenly found themselves in charge of social policy, students became gov't trainees, and mandatory university enrollment was the funnel. Out the other end, an endless spewing forth of ideas, carefully shaped opinions and general consensus. Combine that with full employment and a penal system that put the countless criminals and malcontents to blue-collar work, and you've got a prosperous, paranoid, but happy populace. The Jihad stuff fit perfectly, giving the gov'ts all the power they wanted. Things were good for them right about then. Except for all the wars and the Big Crash that took down the old US of A. And the Mideast debacle and all those nukes being thrown around—

BOGQUEEN: You're digressing, Corbie. To focus all that, one of the big ideas that took hold unplugged the environmental movement. First, you had the alliance fucked up. People with power quickly quit complaining or making dire predictions. Second, and this was the idea itself, concocted by the academics in dry tones: Life is characterized by periods of mass extinction.

We may have accelerated this one, but that's all just relative. What you're seeing is an inevitable expression of Nature. The Great Mother wipes clean the slate, once again. Relax everyone. Can't fight the inevitable and, really, should you? Natural order is natural order, after all. Go with the flow, sure it's sad, but it's better feeling sad than feeling guilt-ridden.

CORBIE TWA: Naturally, we bought it, with a worldwide sigh of relief. Absolved at last, pass the salt.

BOGQUEEN: Ozone depletion, oh well, it was bound to happen eventually. We've adapted, with our rad shielding and unguents and elixirs. No different from all those volcanic eruptions on the Rim. Too bad about those rad leaks in Asia, and as for those peripheral human populations, we can help them.

CORBIE TWA: Help indeed. That's what the boy's gnawing at, isn't it.

STONECASTER: But he's one of those students you were talking about. Why isn't he converted?

PACEMAKER: He was probably too sharp for his own good. And given his talent on the Net, he might well have accessed the so-called unrestricted files, which contain, among other things, a whole list of forbidden subjects, repressed data analyses, heretical theses, not to mention anthropological monographs, from which one can cull the most surprising information. Historical revisionism is the official line, as you said. The forces of evolution can well serve deterministic notions, if misapplied. Even more disturbing, it can be philosophically extended to justify any means, given the inevitable end.

BOGQUEEN: It's the extinction stuff that's now in trouble.

William's out there recording field observations that run contrary to the mass extinction idea. The beasts are changing, because they're pressured populations. Out there we're getting leapfrog speciation, at a phenomenal rate of mutation.

PACEMAKER: There are profound implications to that notion.

BOGQUEEN: You'd better effing well believe it. And there is a political side to that last entry. Never mind the telepathic snake, that conversation between Dr. Jenine MacAlister and Max Ohman provided a pretty succinct statement of the issues.

FREE WHIZZY: Who's Max Ohman?

BOGQUEEN: The Lady's right-hand boy. Ladon's Chief Engineer.

FREE WHIZZY: Well, I can see how the theoretical stuff might trigger some kind of philosophical ruckus, but I still can't grasp the risk to the politicos.

BOGQUEEN: It's too soon to tell, really. I'd rather not speculate. Besides, I've got faith in the boy.

STONECASTER: You must be crazy. The kid's cooked. If he's not pulled out, he'll be dead inside a week.

BOGQUEEN: I know. He's running out of time.

CORBIE TWA: Maybe that's his real message.

. . .

Net

. . . Behold, I am the back door, and my name is Malachai . . .

JOHN JOHN: Who?

. . .

JOHN JOHN: ****

NOAC CENTRAL: This path is unauthorized. Contact
NOAC through the means described in the NOAC
Directory. This path is unauthorized.

JOHN JOHN: *******

NOAC CENTRAL: DISJUNCTIVE ACCESS, File opening
now . . . Directory: NOAC CENTRAL\MINISTRY
OF SOCIAL EQUALIZATION\USASK COMPLEX
PATH:DATA ACQUISITION\ANALYSIS, DEPT
APPLIED ANTHRO\MACALISTER,J . . .

Contents:

     PERSONNEL
     POPULATIONS
     PROJECTS
     PROJECTIONS
     XTND BIO ANALYSES

JOHN JOHN: ***********

USASK: Contents:

  NOAC
    * BRAZIL
    * PACIFIC S. & C. AMERICA
    * ATLANTIC/CARIB S. & C. AMERICA
    * HOPI CONFED (PRE–MASS SUICIDE)
    * LAKOTA NATION
    * WEST CST NATION
    * CENTRAL INUIT CONFED
    * UNSETTLED NOAC POPULATIONS
  SINJO
    * CENTRAL ASIA
    * N.E. COAST
  EUROCOM
    * GYPSIES

* LAPLANDER CONFED
OTHERS
    * AFRICAN TRIBAL
    * PACIFIC ISLES
    * AUSTRAL/ZEALAND/GUINEA

JOHN JOHN: **************** ******

USASK: GENETIC ANALYSIS subsection only file presently ported.

JOHN JOHN: ******* ********

USASK: Date of last entry: APRIL 09/2014
GENETIC ANALYSIS of PERIPHERAL
POPULATION OVERGROUP FINNOSLAVIC,
LAPLANDER (see synonyms cat6B)
DETERMINED SECOND GENERATION
ADAPTIVE TRAITS:
(field and sample observer: GBM)
    * Radiation Resistivity:
        Semipermeable membrane detected
        on liver of subject; biopsy analysis
        incomplete but suggests new function
        based on mutated cell walls and armored
        nuclei (cf. file cytology 23), the latter
        previously observed at other nonregener-
        ative areas

    * Homeostatic Mechanisms:
        Overall reduction in body mass:
        with increased ratio of mass to
        surface; increased fluid retention
        (without accompanying loss of body
        heat) and increased functionality of
        retained fluid

    * UV Shield & Defense Mechanisms:
        Multilayered retinas with nascent
        regenerative capacities; epicanthic folds
        around eyes; altered sleep cycle; melanin
        detected in lenses; reflective body hair
        (follicle is flat and edged, with high oil
        content)
    * Resistance to Toxins:
        Overall flushing mechanisms as indicated
        by flush glands that concentrate toxins
        then expurgate through bowel tract
        (glands still incomplete)
    * Nonspecified Adaptations:
        expanded visual spectrum to include
        marginal infrared detection; other traits
        common to all pressured populations
        (see notes)

NOAC: INTERCEPT

JOHN JOHN:

USASK: Return to previous menu

NOAC: INTERCEPT & TRACKING

JOHN JOHN: Shit.

NOAC: TRACKING

JOHN JOHN:

NOAC: TRACKING

JOHN JOHN:

NOAC: CAPTURED

USASK: Security Class 7 you are UNAUTHORIZED to proceed further.

NOAC: Where am I?

USASK: NOAC Security File, Shunt 2761B, Personnel, Codename Hackhunter.

NOAC: That's me, you assholes.

USASK: Subject of file is UNAUTHORIZED to access contents.

NOAC: What the fuck. You pricks, I'm one of the good guys.

USASK: Subject of file is UNAUTHORIZED to access contents. GO BACK.

NOAC: Shunt this to Securicom. Pissing off the good guys is bad business. Hackhunter signing off. For good.

FOUR

American NW, Terminal Zone, July 7, A.C. *14*

A year for every day.

Decay of plastic welds. His bootsuit was falling apart beneath the invisible torrent from the cloudless sky. Earlier, at dawn, he'd woken in his shield tent to the roar of machinery. Climbing out, he saw a thousand combines cresting a nearby ridge, emerging from a storm of dust and toppling mindlessly over the steep embankment. Loping along the ridge, almost invisible in their reflective fur, a half-dozen coyotes appeared, observing their handiwork. He listened to them laugh.

And the sun rose once again.

He sipped thick, acidic water from the spitter, then slowly lowered his backpack. Now noon, the place he had found himself in was a dead-ground. Leaning barns, silos with peeling walls, dead oak trees, and a farmhouse encircled by abandoned machinery. A last circling of the wagons, but it had been useless. The redskins were in the mirror.

No ghosts here, simply the thunderous silence of their

absence. William looked around, blinking painfully as he studied the detritus of his own kind, and smelled the poison in the air. Subsurface leakage, coming up from the well near the barn. Pesticides, herbicides, concentrations in the water table like lifeless jellyfish.

A strange, almost incandescent moss covered the cinder blocks lining the well, had spread outward to cover three plastic leprechauns with an oily, vaguely translucent patina. Two plaster fawns crouched in the skeletal shade of the dead oaks, their paint faded but still the animals stood, frozen immobile by terror. In their eyes, nothing but white.

William almost laughed. Zombie Bambis, hallelujah. He wished he could laugh. He hadn't laughed in so long.

Dehydration. Musn't run out of moisture.

He walked over to the well, set his blistered hands on the cool moss covering the cinder blocks, leaned over, and looked down. A pool, viscid in shades of blue, magenta, bottle-fly green. Pale round waterbugs swam dizzying circles beneath the surface. Damn things didn't even need air anymore. William straightened and took a few steps backwards.

He removed a flare from his belt, activated it, and tossed it into the well.

Fire! A pillar of poisonous flame! He watched it eating a vertical path skyward. A sudden eye glares upward, and meets the steady polished eye of a satellite. They study each other, then wink with their own designs.

I anoint this dead-ground, absolution of its sins burning into oblivion, whilst the scarabs beneath the surface of a dead skin race down into cool darkness, and there await the coming of their first breaths. Savage oxygen, the lungs that birth the cough of flame.

I see you all come closer, drawn by this crisp cut to the air, this clean crackle which my dying hands have cast into the well of darkness.

Gather, then, while I bathe. When I emerge, you will be able to touch me, and I will be able to touch you. Our spirits will join, and we will march like a sea that swallows the earth. We will march, and none may stop us. Ghosts, we are all ghosts now. We must deliver the new world unto the inheritors, who know us not.

The dead-grounds are alive once again.

Behold this self, Daniel. I am Mene before the feast.

The water was like ice against his skin, as close to pain as he could remember. He carefully reattached the clasps on the rotting bootsuit, and scanned the ruined farm with new eyes.

The farm's battered arrogance had fallen in upon itself, and now the air was filled with ghosts, the streaming dead still mute but brimming with their separate stories. All eyes rested on him.

He would be their language, their words, now. He understood that much. He would speak for them all. God had given him the lie, laid bare and bleeding. We have lived in our heaven, and we have made it as it is. Somewhere above, the fallen angels still climb.

William stared at his hands. His sight had changed. The bones stood out sharply, solid in a fading haze of mortal flesh. Blood pulsed through the capillaries, faintly glowing.

He retrieved his backpack and stiffly worked his way

into the straps. The pillar of fire had been sighted. Satellites, high-altitude reconnaissance craft. Activity in the Hole. Pinpoint resolution, down to the water trickling from his hair. As attentively as these ghosts, machines watched him, recorded his movements, then dutifully reported the data. Still, the heat sensor records would baffle the analyzers. Around him flowed an ice age, there in the breath of beasts dead for ten thousand years. They are my body, Daniel, and I am their voice.

His joints protested dully as he lurched into motion. Knees refusing to bend, balance awry, tottering and jolting forward, stalking like a stiff marionette.

The ghosts closed in, flowing and brushing against him, bolstering him upright with their gelid shoulders, broad wintry backs. Nearby, he saw a coyote and recognized it.

'I remember you. The last hunt. *Bison antiquus*. I see you keeping your distance, friend.' The words were in his head, but so was everything else. No borders left, his skull porous, his thoughts drifting in the air, delicately traced by the satellites, and heard by the coyote.

'You're too old,' William said, 'for mere trickery. You were here and you were there, on the edge of that continental bridge. You watched our arrival. Did you know what it meant? Did you know then what it always means, friend?'

But the earth yields to the shovel, and is turned over, flipped onto its back. Again and again, this is what we do, and each time, the firmament fills with spirits departing the old ways. We move on. We never look back.

The coyote dropped back, then behind, into his

wake. Ready to pick at the pieces, prepared as ever to contemplate the scatter of garbage, the meanings of the twisted tin can and the candy wrapper, the crushed velvet of moss beneath a tire's track. The coyote contemplates, and might even smile as the can rusts and withers to dust, as the wrapper crumbles under the sun, as the moss slowly springs back.

The coyote stays in our wake, and patiently awaits the coming of our bones, scattered like a sprung bundle of sticks. A disarticulated map to mull over, the wind moaning through the holes in our skull. It listens to that song, but soon tires of the repetition. In a world where nothing changes, we'd best move on.

Humped-back transports crawled a ritual dance on the plain below. William leaned sideways into the wind, his broken boots precariously gripping the edge of a ridge, and studied the mechanical dance on the valley floor. A score of smaller vehicles buzzed randomly through the greater design. He watched two converge, then drive out from the swarm, approaching him side by side, lumbering steadily up the slope.

Daniel and Jack Tree emerged from the vehicle on the left. A squat, wide man stepped out from the vehicle on the right. The stranger wore sunglasses and a baseball cap with the Ladon crest above the brim. His face was lined, clean-shaven, and almost flat, the bones underneath Mongoloid, the incisors in his maxilla and mandible shovel-shaped. A hairline crack along his zygoma revealed an old, poorly healed, broken cheekbone.

'Can you hear me?' Daniel asked, stepping close.

William nodded.

'Can you see me?'

He nodded again. Cranial characteristics displayed the wondrous lineage of Daniel, so close to that of the Asian stranger. William turned and studied Jack Tree. Caucasoid traits for the most part. Even the bones contributed to the mask that had dissipated like smoke the possibilities of prejudice, a trick of sympathy that swayed the media, enraptured the public.

'See any spy teams out there, William?'

He looked back at Daniel.

'Sorry, applied anthropologists, then.'

William shook his head.

'Our arrays picked up a heat signature,' the stranger said, his wide-boned hands on his hips. 'Big one. We tracked you from it.'

William smiled and said, 'I would speak, if you can hear me.'

The stranger frowned at Daniel, then shrugged. 'I hear you fine, son.'

'A pillar of flame. I am reborn to the hour. Watch me burn, gentlemen.'

Jack Tree barked an uneasy laugh. 'You're talking to an engineer, Potts, not some goddamned mystic.'

'The fire is only the beginning,' William said, steadying his gaze on Jack Tree, who stepped back. 'The wheel will spin, and lightning will scar the sky. There'll be thunder, but from the earth. And the clouds will not fall, but ascend. Heaven, gentlemen, is not shot through with orbiting machines. There is no happy hunting ground. You had it, once, but it's gone now, and that, Jack Tree, is what's written on your heart. The truth you have chosen to hide, even from yourself.

'The buffalo were doomed. You didn't need us. You didn't need us for war, or spite, or murder. Granted, we busted up your game something awful, but the four horses needed riders, and you rode them. I am here, and I see how the cold wind shakes each of you. The ghosts are dancing, my friends.'

A cell buzzed at the stranger's hip. He snatched at it with a blue hand. William watched the blood pool in the man's torso, pulling away from the extremities. The man cupped a hand over the earpiece, listened, then nodded. He returned the phone to his belt.

'Fucking weather pattern sprung up out of nowhere. We've got a blow coming.' He swung expressionless eyes on William. 'A fucking bad one.'

'They won't stay at home any longer,' William said, smiling at Jack Tree. 'They're coming with you. I'm sorry about that, but they refuse to be forgotten. Not now, not again.'

'William,' Daniel said earnestly, 'you'd better come with us.'

'We dug them up,' William said, still watching Jack Tree. The hypothermia was far too rapid; it was a freezing of the soul. 'Excavations. We found those forgotten stories. The mammoths, dire wolves, the short-tailed bears and smilodons, the *Bison antiquus*. We found them all, rediscovered their lives and their deaths and it was all there in front of us. A story it wasn't politically expedient to read.' William finally turned his attention to Daniel.

'This isn't a condemnation, Daniel. It's an embrace. Not so different after all. Human. Just human. A return to the old ways is a return to the wrong ways. I'm very sorry for that. It seemed so pristine. Paradise, but the nations had been birthed, the plains flooded with hunters on horseback, and the buffalo lost their final sanctuary – the deep plains. You already had your us and them. You were on your way, well on your way.'

'Jesus,' Daniel breathed, 'it's freezing out here. This storm, Max, we talking snow?'

'Fucking ice age, Danny. This will slow us down, the last thing we need.'

'No,' William said, his tone bringing all three around. 'The pillar must rise. Daniel, hear my words, now, before the feast. Your vision is true. I'll not hinder you. The storm is my legion, and I will lead it around you.' William smiled again suddenly and winked at Max. 'The eye-spies still up there are old ones – they will be blind for days. Come now, come with all your technology, your workers, your supplies and set your genius to work.'

William raised his arms, then turned to face the bitter wind. After a moment, he began walking, along the ridge, eastward, away from the valley. He felt the three deathly cold men study his back, measuring his movements, wondering at the sudden falling off of the wind.

NOAC Net

'Behold, the hour cometh, yea, is now come, that ye shall be scattered, every man to his own,' the Securicom official went on to say. Recent reports that a third surveillance satellite has been sabotaged will not be confirmed by Securicom. The official described the present investigation as close to achieving the 'cessation of terrorist activities,' adding that the full measure of law enforcement will be vigorously expressed in the subduction of the terrorists . . .

. . . beneath the storm's cover. Unconfirmed reports indicate that construction at the new Ladon Site is now underway. A press release deemed 'grossly incomplete' by NOAC and NUN representatives, issued yesterday by Ladon Inc., reveals that the project's chief engineer is Maxwell Ohman (a continuation of that posting from the Boxwell site), a man believed to be the Lady's lover . . .

. . . admitted that the trade sanctions against the Lakota Nation are 'riddled with defiance on the part of freestanding corporations, unaligned nations, and Third World peripheral groups.' The Minister went on to say that 'health conditions in the closed nation are cause for gravest concern. On humanitarian reasons alone, NUN would be fully justified in direct military intervention.'

NUN Security Council member Elias Ruby has denied the veracity of the Minister's claim, and repeated the Council's position on military intervention: 'The EET (Extraordinary Economic Tribunal) has concluded that direct intervention between an unaligned nation and a corporation it has contracted with is permitted under very strict, clearly outlined circumstances. As of yet, neither Ladon nor Lakota Nation has breached any of these conditions.'

At a second press conference the Minister refuted both the Security Council's and the EET's position. 'I am very sorry, but if this project hasn't direct military application potential, I don't know what does. It seems clear that those very world organizations in place to protect us have been collectively cowed by the might of a single corporation and a single people. My God, what next?'

. . . One soweth, and another reapeth . . .

. . . lifted up the serpent in the wilderness as this Lady gazes upon the works of men, and sees before her the shape of a wheel that covers the valley, where within this circle are laid down spokes; this wheel that she sees sets now upon her lips the name giveth by the wise men who hunt no more: Medicine Wheel.

The axle will turn. It will pierce the heart of heaven.

. . . Ladon: Greek, a mythological dragon that encircles the Tree of Life.

Net Happynews

The formal entrance to the lifts leading down into the NUN Central Complex in Brussels was bioflicked yesterday at 5:10 P.M. local time. The dispersal agent is yet to be identified, but the toxic mix is confirmed as containing neurotoxins. Confirmed dead is at 175, including the suspect.

At the moment, investigators are unable to explain how the terrorist managed to elude in-place detection systems . . .

Communications worldwide have been disrupted by joystick terrorists working in concert in behalf of

Ladon Inc. and the Lakota Nation. 'The in-built firewall defenses on com sats are notoriously outdated and ineffective,' said a NOACom representative on condition of anonymity . . .

Seized tanker attempting to enter San Francisco Harbor contained 212 New Jihad terrorists and weapons, including four SINJO-made tactical nukes. The New Jihad Organization is a nonreligious fanatic group (known colloquially as NERFs) with no known manifesto, although most members are recruited from refugee populations resettled from inundated Pacific islands . . .

Net

LUNKER: This is getting out of hand, gentlemen.

VORPAL: So there's blood on our hands. We have killed, I admit it, but it was in the service of a greater good.

LUNKER: You seem so sure of yourselves, but dammit, this isn't the way it's supposed to be.

VORPAL: You must be kidding, Lunker. There's some nasty trackers after us. We're just trying to stay alive.

LUNKER: Look, stop using weather sats for your pinballing. They're big, and they come all the way down. If that's not bad enough, wait till some unmapped hurricane rolls across some unsuspecting atoll . . .

VORPAL: Conventional options still exist. All right, I'll slow down some, get more selective.

LUNKER: Thanks. Where's Blanc Knight?

VORPAL: On the run. He started breaching Securicom Net Defenses, making haywire. He's busted down every secure system on the line. Man, you wouldn't believe the information spewing out.

LUNKER: Bound for Ur reports NUN aircraft invading Lakota airspace, but being turned back by one helluva snowstorm. The word goes on and says the project's ahead of schedule. Does that make any sense at all? Yeesh.

VORPAL: Two unmanned spy-shuttles collided over Eastern Iowa. Crossed wires in the flight control data – don't fret, no ground injuries. That storm's circling the Hole right now, so I imagine NOAC will get the go-ahead for unilateral ground recce from NUN. Wonder what they'll see?

Entry: American NW, July 8, A.C. 14

Sitting Bull crouched beside the hub of stones. The white sky made the prairie grass silver on the knoll, pewter in the valleys. The rifle sat on his lap, red-hawk feathers hanging straight down and slowly spinning.

William walked up to the ancient ghost. 'It was supposed to be a level playing field, Sitting Bull. Information was God, we rode the highway of His back. We rebelled against secrecy, but the revolution was illusory, wasn't it.' He sat down beside the ghost. 'All they did was change the meaning of words. Freedom meant forbidden. Access meant denial. Sitting Bull, I won't accept the lie. They called the dead a living memory, but it isn't. I've discovered that now.'

The Lakota chief squinted skyward. 'I have never been a follower, William. All those ghosts in your wake, it's a path I can't take.'

'I don't think God is inside liquid crystal,' William said. 'I don't think He superconducts, either. He doesn't ride fiber optics. I've begun to believe our faith is misplaced, Sitting Bull. We don't need more information. We need enlightenment.'

Sitting Bull swung his empty gaze on William. 'Species die, William. And yes, our hand has been in it, as far back as you could think to go.'

William nodded. 'To the days when we all lived in Africa, black-skinned under our wiry hair. The upright primate's God-given right. Maybe we came from Mars, fleeing the first world we fucked up. Maybe we didn't. It doesn't matter. What I want to know is, when did God finally recognize His own face in ours? Fifty million years ago? Five million years ago? A million? When did the light really dawn, Sitting Bull? Answer me that, please.'

'Do you hold all life sacred, William?'

'Hell no,' he answered. 'HIV-37 sacred? The CFS nanoviral group? Pneumonic plague?' William studied the clouds overhead. 'Life isn't sacred. If it is, we're all going to hell.'

Sitting Bull smiled. 'We already have, friend. Isn't that your message?'

'I have a message? Writing letters from the Hole doesn't stake any claim to prophecy.'

'Ahh, I see.' Sitting Bull was nodding. 'You have doubts.'

William pulled a crinkled layer of skin from his left hand and held it up to the sun's broken light. 'I've realized something.' He looked at the chief. 'Culpability's not something you grow out of, is it?'

'Don't speak to me of regrets, son.' Sitting Bull turned away, scanned the nearby ridge of hills. After a long moment he said, 'Those thoughts can consume a soul, William. And in the end, what's the point? You hold the weasel in your hands until its twisting and squirming is known to you absolutely. The time comes to let it go.'

'I'm tired,' William said as he released the sheath of skin and watched it flutter away in the breeze. 'Tired of seeking enlightenment. I no longer believe in that light turning on in your head. It's a myth. There's no discernible process, no sudden eureka. Such realizations are well after the fact, because when it happens, you're too busy to notice.'

'Busy?'

William shrugged. 'Preoccupied, then. Those brutal necessities of the flesh, the tortured schisms of the spirit. Busy. Busy screaming, busy bleeding, busy flailing at a host of memories and echoes and dead voices and faces that never were but come to you anyway and you can never, never peel them back.'

Water dripped from Sitting Bull's hollow eyes. He ran his weathered, blunt-fingered hand along the barrel of his rifle. 'Swift flight, the rifle ball flies unseen, yet strikes at the heart of things all the same. I heard your words to Jack Tree. They broke him.'

'I know.'

'We would have slain all the bison. Pte Oyate, Buffalo Nation. In the manner that our ancestors slew all the *Bison antiquus,* the very first Tatanka. We would have continued to war on our neighbors, and those wars would have grown, and the blood of feuds would run like the river. We would have gutted the horse of our brother, rather than see it run beyond our grasp. But, William, that history would have been ours, and ours alone. You broke us too soon, left us unmindful of the consequences of our own actions, you left us believing the buffalo would once again cover the plains, and you left us with a belief in our hearts that our hands were clean. For this, William, I can never forgive you.'

'So is Jenine MacAlister right, then? You're all still children, after all, still unblooded in the ways of inevitability, tottering on the edge of extinction simply because you refuse to adapt, or you're not able to adapt, because you need guidance in growing up. Am I supposed to believe all that bullshit?'

Sitting Bull smiled. 'Our ways are different, William. They are children, yes, but they are my children. Do you think my eternal guidance insufficient? Think on this, son. We spirits whisper lessons to our children; from all that we have seen and all that we were, we tell our children this one thing: There is no such thing as inevitability.'

'What makes you so sure?'

'In the way Mother adapts, in the way she refuses to surrender.' Sitting Bull raised his rifle and sighted down its length. 'In my days, the white men and Indian alike gathered the buffalo skulls beside the tracks of the iron horse. We piled them into mountains. They were taken away, and ground up into fertilizer. The fertilizer was used in the breaking of the prairie soil so that crops could be planted, and so the buffalo returned to the earth, and gave forth life.'

'Your irony's a little too bitter for me, friend.'

'In your words, then, William. Nature revises. She is each life and she is all life, and so she will outlive us all.'

'There's secret reports,' William said. 'Data compiled on the Inside populations – inside the rad shields, inside the cities and complexes. The trends are alarming. Increased toxemia across the board, dropping fertility – inactive, sluggish sperm in low numbers, impermeable ova, toxic lactation syndrome, chronic respiratory diseases, a whole host of immunodeficiency disorders. Projections bring to mind the fate of the Neanderthal in Europe when faced with what could've been as little as a point-five percent differential in infant mortality rates, when compared with the emerging true humans. Ten thousand years and complete displacement, absolute extinction.'

'Who waits in the wings this time?' Sitting Bull asked.

William smiled at the Lakota chief. 'You already know. Peripheral populations. Pressured populations. Are you ready for that, Sitting Bull? To look upon your children and see that their faces are no longer a match to yours?'

The old man thumbed back the flintlock and squinted as he aimed. 'Where I am, these ghost buffalo seem real. I still take pleasure in hunting them.'

'Meaning?'

'Meaning, William, that my face isn't the face of God.' He squeezed the trigger.

The loud report echoed dully across the valley.

NOACOM: Freedom Files require clearance. Who is this, please?

JOHN JOHN: ********

NOACOM: Welcome to Freedom Files. This information

block complies with all New United Nations charters and conventions. Proceed with Query.

JOHN JOHN: University of Saskatchewan, Applied Sciences Ministry, Department of Anthropology\ student field projects\summer 2014.

NOACOM: Seven graduate field projects are listed. Six are sponsored by USask Board of Funding. One is through private funding. List?

JOHN JOHN: Private funding only.

NOACOM: Potts, William. Project Description unavailable.

JOHN JOHN: Student File, Potts, William.

NOACOM: Please note: Student File, Potts, William, is docked with Securicom. Proceed?

JOHN JOHN: Yes.

NOACOM: Password

JOHN JOHN: . . .

NOACOM: Password?

JOHN JOHN: *M*A*L*A*C*H*A*I

NOACOM: Good evening, Dean Roberts.

JOHN JOHN: Open file, please.

NOACOM: Potts, William, student number 5257525
    Department of Anthropology, Graduate Studies
    Family Status (last updated A.C.12):
    Deceased parent: Berman Potts, PhD,
        Mathematics
    Deceased parent: Lucinda née Bolen, PhD,
        Biology
    Deceased sibling: John (elder) (leukemia, 2011)
    Deceased sibling: Arthur (twin, SIDS, 1987)
  Course History:
    Pertinent to field of study:
        Intro. Applied Anthro 0:01

Applied Anthro 0:02
Culture Dynamics 0:02
Social Evolution 0:02
Extinction Dynamics 0:02
Systems Theory in Anthro 0:03
Processual Anthro 0:03
Revised History of Anthro 0:04
Additional Studies:
Biological Ethics 0:01
Systems Theory in Gov't (required)
Communications (required)
History of the Oral Tradition
Semantics (required)*
Genetics and the Mind
Advanced Systems Theory (required)*
Advanced Communications (required)
Models of Multiculturalism*
* denotes incomplete
Major Papers (Grade):
Ethics in Systems Theory (sat)
Communicating Knowledge (sat)
Rewiring the Mind (brain function and
instinct) (sat)
The Evolution of Fieldwork (fail)
Unpredictability in Systems Theory (fail)
Failures: revision required, status pending
Grant Applications:
Category: Fieldwork
Project: Rural Waysides: Subjects Who Are
Nonparticipants in Social Programming:
Case Studies
Accepted: affirmative

Project: Hole Peripheral Occupation: Case
Studies of Occupants Living on the
Periphery of the Midwest Hole
Accepted: conditional
Project: Lakota Adaptations to the
Midwest Hole
Accepted: negative*
* Applicant succeeded in acquiring permis-
sion from the Lakota Nation with
signatory: Horn, D., Exec Band Council
Project: Unknown (private grant)*
* Wheel Foundation

Potts, William, is listed as a Subversive Class 01
(potential). The following observation reports
are compiled from academic observation
reports (aor), field operatives, E-surveillance.

AOR (course instructors & required Report
Review Committee):

(a) Subject displays an exceptional level of
inquisitiveness.

(b) Subject takes perverse pleasure in challenging accepted applications of Social
Theory.

(c) Subject is advanced in communications
theory applications.

(d) Subject's father is a known dissident for
which Subject displays incorrected pride.

(e) Subject displays advanced (unapproved)
knowledge of Numbers Theory and
Chaos Theory. (Chaos Theory is
Suppressed Information, See Freedom File
210X210.) Assume Parental Education,

contravening NOAC Parenting Parameters, Criminal Code 16-21IIa-f.

(f) Subject employed No-Trace variants on Net, using a Remote Fieldbook.

(g) Subject continually disrupted classes with adversarial interrogatives.

(h) Subject identified two assigned field operatives via Valentine cards with boxed chocolates (chocolates analyzed and cleared).

(i) Subject displayed advanced knowledge of technological engineering Systems Theory & application.

(j) Subject revealed knowledge of pre-revised archaeology and anthropological dynamics.

(k) Subject revealed knowledge of Indigenous Peoples' History, Mythology & Belief Systems prior to Applied Anthropological Restructuring of Said Peoples.

(l) Subject successfully breached this file with insufficient trail to advance criminal proceedings.

Present Net Entries: Unavailable.

JOHN JOHN: Delete File, Potts, William.

NOACOM: This file is docked at Securicom. There are no other copies of this file, as per Securicom Subversive Investigations Parameters. Do you still wish to Delete?

JOHN JOHN: Yes.

NOACOM: File Deleted.

JOHN JOHN: Delete File, Potts, Berman. Potts, Lucinda n. Bolen.

NOACOM: No such file exists.

JOHN JOHN: Sniff back.

NOACOM: File, Potts, Berman, File, Potts, Lucinda née Bolen were accidentally destroyed in Data Transfer, A.C. 13. Investigation Ongoing: sabotage suspected.

JOHN JOHN: Delete Ongoing Investigation Data File, Data Transfer A.C. 13, Potts, Berman & Lucinda.

NOACOM: File Deleted.

JOHN JOHN: Delete all Subversive all Classes Files.

NOACOM: Working. All files deleted, Subversive all Classes Files. 16174.96 QTB now available in Securicom System.

JOHN JOHN: Delete all E-surveillance Files.

NOACOM: Working . . .

Net

STONECASTER: A modest query, then. How is it that he's getting clearer? Hours tick into days out under that deadly sun. The boy's cooked, his skin peeling, half blind.

CORBIE TWA: Into and out of, Stony. Clarity's the word all right. Crystal clear. He's pushed through. He's been cleansed, hell, reborn to the hour.

STONECASTER: Still kind of suspicious to my thinking.

BOGQUEEN: Your thinking's still too linear, Stonecaster. He's on a seasonal round, moving a cyclical route. When I read him, I feel him orbiting out there, coming round and round, coming closer with each pass of the great wheel. The closer he gets to what he's been circling, the clearer things become. For him, for us.

PACEMAKER: This last hint of NOAC data on population projections and biological dynamics has me curious, to say the least. I wonder if such data exist, and if the trend projections lead to certain inevitable conclusions.

CORBIE TWA: Carefully crafted belief systems acquire a power of their own. Methinks the powers that be are bucklin under an imperative of their own makin. Inertia's set in, and now that new information's comin down the line and mussin up their coifs, they can't do nothin but lean into the wind.

BOGQUEEN: Political structures don't adapt, they react. None of this should surprise you.

PACEMAKER: There are others out there, like us, who have declared war. It's a war of information, the staccato of data on all sides. And some have taken a step further down the combative line.

CORBIE TWA: Ah, you must mean the terrorists.

PACEMAKER: Strictly speaking, that's exactly what they are. Not that I'm complaining. The walls of silence have been breached, and data spills like blood into our hands.

CORBIE TWA: How poetic. But I think the reality's a tad messier than that, Pacemaker. These guys are pulling down satellites.

LUNKER: That has, I believe, tailed off lately. For the simple reason that NOAC and the rest have laid off harassing Ladon Inc. and the Lakota.

PACEMAKER: Given that cyclical storm front over the Central Plains, they haven't much choice. Now that their hi-tech see-all microsats are all gone . . .

BOGQUEEN: Around and around he circles . . .

STONECASTER: You can't be serious, Bogqueen. Leave me out if you're going mystical on us. The boy's an opportunist.

FREE WHIZZY: All very interesting, ladies and gents, but I can't help feeling these aimless musings are essentially pointless. We need to get organized. We need a list of things to do, things that arise from a set of goals. There's an ocean of previously restricted information out there. The boy's dropping enough crumbs. Time for us to start sniffing the trails.

CORBIE TWA: You seriously think William knows what he's doing? That he's callin for our help? That he has some kind of grand scheme to bring the world to its knees?

FREE WHIZZY: He may not be consciously aware of such motives, Corbie Twa. Nevertheless, they are clearly operant, no matter who, or what the source.

CORBIE TWA: Divine guidance?

BOGQUEEN: You said it, not us.

STONECASTER: The boy's dragged you all with him, hasn't he? Right into the quagmire of madness. Raving loons in the Swamp.

FREE WHIZZY: You're free to surface at will, Stonecaster. No one's insisting you remain.

CORBIE TWA: Calm down, everyone. Look, somethin's drawn us to William's Net entries. All of us, Stonecaster included. We don't know nothin at all about William, when it comes right down to it. An untreated psychotic? Megalomaniac? Or just someone who knows too much—

BOGQUEEN: We're not completely ignorant, Corbie. William dances this Swamp like a whirling dervish.

He evades every tracking effort, slips through every drift net NOAC's dragging across the waves. He's accessed restricted information and tosses us conceptual time bombs. Is he sitting back right now and laughing while we desperately juggle?

CORBIE TWA: You forget one thing, lass. He's dyin of rad poisonin and toxemia. And he walked into that of his own free will. That, to my mind, seriously undermines his authority as a revolutionary thinker.

STONECASTER: Unless it's all a scam. What if he's driving around out there in some NOAC-issue rad buggy. Throwing us time bombs all right, then laughing when they explode in our faces.

PACEMAKER: This speculation serves nothing. I believe Free Whizzy's desire to organize is worthwhile. For one, I am interested in pursuing these population projection data. Much might be unveiled there, about both William and the Official Domain.

LUNKER: Some of my associates are already working certain related areas. They are actively widening the cracks in the official wall. I'll lay out a thread down to this place, and pertinent information shall surely find you.

PACEMAKER: Thank you.

JOHN JOHN: Hello, one and all. Open a cubby, ladies and gentlemen, while I toss you all some background data on one Potts, William. I'm afraid I can't stick around and chat. There's a few more things that I need to do. Stay together, keep talking – you may not know it, but your silent audience is vast, and the threads . . . they fall toward you like rain . . .

FIVE

They gathered beneath a tarp that flapped drumlike in the wind. Seated on folding chairs around a three-legged metal table covered in fine lace. High-electrolyte drinks served from a refractive decanter. Beneath their feet a thick, broad rug.

On all sides on the hilltop the big and little bluestems fluttered their flowers like butterflies pinned to a board. Western wheatgrass and green needle shivered their feathery stalks. Blades and stems all sharp-edged now, reflective juices glittering and defying absorption, shunting deadly rad into the buffered earth. Impervious flowers that opened like throats at dusk and gusted out clouds of pollen that drifted in air swarming with flitting insects.

Bundles of sage smoldered around the periphery of the tarp's shadow, streams of smoke spiraling and spinning away on the wind. The sage leaves, thicker than leather, burned with an inner fuel, an expulsion of energy as slow and steady as its previous absorption.

A balance mocking the chemical descent into ashes.

William squatted just beyond the shadow, at the crest of the western slope where the cacti spread out and down the sun-drenched hillside in mauve and dusty green. Needles angled in antithesis to ancient sunflowers, away from the sun's light. The symbiotic spiders had spun a mane of angel hair down the entire slope, glistening false dew like a dense scatter of diamonds. The spiders fed on cactus mites through the night, their webs full of cactus spores and tugged away by the scuttling passage of mice and needle-beaked birds that still hopped from pod to pod, plucking flower buds and drinking succulent juices. A microcosm of dependency, newly achieved – to William, a miracle, a creation so precise, so wonderful, that he felt it light his being.

Daniel Horn watched Jack Tree light the pipe. The young man's face hinted at irony, a delicious taste at the back of his thoughts.

Max Ohman, the Lady's representative, leaned back in his chair, both hands holding the glass of lime-colored liquid on his lap. Where his eyes held, behind the sunglasses, William couldn't guess. They may well have been closed, for all the rest of his face betrayed.

Dr. Jenine MacAlister sat opposite the three men, studying a handheld notebook with the viewscreen draped in the shadow of her right hand. She had been reading the stress data for some time now. Finally she glanced up at Max Ohman. 'The tensile properties are clearly best-case scenario, Max. What kind of in-field tests have you conducted?'

Max cleared his throat. 'Eleven years, Doctor. We in-field tested in Saudi Arabia, at Boxwell Plateau, and of course at the source-point orbiting station. As of this morning, we have extended the tether-lines thirty-six kilometers from the station, well into the ionosphere. A free-flying test run. The stress factors are more than satisfactory. The tensile properties are not best-case, they're actual. When I say this poly-ore matrix bends, I mean exactly that, Doctor. It *bends*.'

Jenine closed the notebook's screen lid and reached for her glass. 'Of course I'll need to send the structural details to our NOAC specialists.'

Max Ohman's grin was coldly feral. 'Like hell you will, Doctor. Unless you've got an optic implant or eidetic memory, that data remains the property of Ladon Corporation. And,' he continued in a droll tone, 'our file on you indicates neither implants nor eidetic memory.'

Jenine let it drop. Just another smoke screen. William watched her, saw her mind work, and knew her soul. All so clear now.

'What remains unspoken,' Jack Tree said, repacking the pipe he'd yet to pass to anyone, 'is what has brought us here. I think the time for true words has begun.'

Jenine leaned back and steepled her fingers, elbows perched on the arms of the chair. A gesture William had seen a thousand times. A gesture of lies and secret contempt. 'Very well. First of all, to whom do I speak? You, Jack, or Daniel Horn?'

Jack Tree looked away, his eyes squinting as he gazed out across the valley.

'Begin any time,' Daniel Horn said. He wouldn't let her narrow her targeting. If she had hidden knives of a personal sort, the kind of information NOAC operatives loved to collect, she'd have to throw them at all three men. Made wounding random, and of uncertain efficacy. No leverage here, Jenine.

'NOAC has NUN approval for the following preemptive actions, gentlemen. I make that clear now, should you believe – erroneously – that your foes are not united on this matter. We are absolutely united.' She paused, tracking her severe expression across all three faces opposite her. A conscious gesture, almost mechanical. She'd practiced, but not enough, not nearly enough.

'We're not illiterate, Doctor,' Daniel said. 'You're united on nothing. Major crises in Southeast Asia, the Indian subcontinent, the Middle East, Ukraine, South Africa – the whole damn game's blowing up in your faces, and that's not even mentioning the economic mess. Now, do go on, Doctor.'

'Stealth strikes,' Jenine snapped. 'Full ground incursion with punitive objectives. Oil fields reclaimed, mineral rights on all lands acquired by your peoples retracted once the areas are secured.' She scanned the faces again, this time more successfully. 'Any attempt to resist these missions will be met with the full retaliatory might of NOAC military force. Your people will die, gentlemen.'

Max Ohman barked, 'Justification?'

Jenine smiled. 'Our major concern is for the safety of all indigenous peoples in the Midwest, and all citizen populations of the North American Confederacy who have been assessed as at risk from the Medicine Wheel Project. Your stress data is in my opinion flawed—'

'Since when did you become an engineer?' Max asked, his teeth still bared.

'My opinion has been granted authority, Mr. Ohman.'

'By whom?'

'NOAC and NUN have placed me in the primary position as negotiator in these proceedings.'

'Big effing deal,' Max said. 'You may have authority in some kind of illusory political sense, but I was challenging your opinion. Crunch some numbers for me, Doctor. Show me the flaws in the equations. Would you like pad and paper? Us engineers still use those, you know.'

'You, Mr. Ohman,' Jenine said coolly, 'have been granted the privilege of attending this meeting as an observer. That is a privilege I am empowered to retract at any time.'

Max snorted and looked away.

'Now,' Jenine resumed, 'where was I?'

'Killing my people in order to save them,' Daniel Horn said.

'More than just your people are in danger,' Jenine said. 'NOAC is responsible to its citizens—'

'Since when?' Max asked.

She ignored him, and continued. 'We are obliged to protect them from unwarranted risks, arising from either corporate activities, or external political instability.'

Daniel asked softly, 'Are you suggesting that my position as head of the Lakota Nation is inherently unstable?'

'Your recent actions in concert with Ladon Corporation have suggested this, Mr. Horn.'

'Your ultimatum?' Daniel asked.

'Close down the project immediately. The sanctions will be lifted, and normal relations can resume.'

'Dr. MacAlister,' Daniel began, leaning forward, 'you more than anyone must know that my people and your people have never had normal relations. As for sanctions, you have maintained the imposition of the most insidious kinds of sanctions for five hundred years and counting. Do you actually imagine that you can still hurt us?'

Jack Tree spoke. 'Kill us, yes, by all means. What is a few more scars on your conscience?'

'She can't,' Max said. 'Her threats are sheer bluff. Every peripheral nation in the world is watching this play out. Secondary and primary nations are gridlocked on this, politically and philosophically. Protests and riots are erupting in one major city after another. It's all falling apart, all because one lone independent nation said yes to the dream.'

Jack Tree said, 'You were so certain, Doctor, weren't you? Convinced by all your covert anthropological data. You thought the dreamtimes were dead. You've plied us with schemes designed to make us invisible, even to ourselves. You called it the application of successful adaptative cultural adjustment. For all your efforts to save us by destroying us, we have still defied you. We have met our dream.' He paused and studied the steatite pipe in his hands. 'Not, I'll grant you, in the way I would have imagined it. The pattern in the skies is new to me, so new that it sometimes frightens me. But I am old, my days are almost done. What I pass on to my children is and always will be the one thing you cannot control, cannot shape to suit your ends. My gift is the history of the damned, and my poison is truth. You see, Doctor, I *remember*.'

Jenine said, 'You're all making a terrible mistake.'

'If we are,' Daniel said, 'it will be ours, not yours. Possessing something – even freedom – is two-edged. Our days of sucking at your collective tit are over. The time's come for you to let go.' He smiled, and it was a smile of sad wisdom. 'I had hoped for your blessing, for the cleansing of your hands. But no, you still try to possess us. If it comforts you to call that possession something else, like protection, compassion, or a justifiable maternal instinct, then so be it. Whatever word you choose, it still means chains to us.'

Entry: American NW, July 11, A.C. 14

'Enough of the preliminaries,' Jenine said, 'let's get to negotiating this treaty.'

Jack Tree repacked his pipe and set a burning ember to the steatite bowl. 'We have come to listen, Dr. MacAlister.'

'As representative of the North American Confederacy and spokesperson for the divine will of the Triumvirate of A.C. 14, I am authorized to negotiate the honorable purchase of the following items from those gathered here as representatives of the Lakota Nation and related sovereign peoples of the Midwest Hole; said representatives being thusly identified and duly recorded: John "Jack" Tree Whose Roots are Deep, and Daniel Horn, of the Lakota Nation. Do you acknowledge your presence here at this gathering?'

'We do.'

'Excellent, we're off to a fine start that will benefit us all. We are, as you know, newcomers to your lands, granted by right of God and King, and by right of Manifest Destiny to rule over and subjugate all peoples we encounter should they prove incapable of opposing us. Regardless of our motive, our methods remain singular in their objective; to wit, either by direct violent action upon the persons of said indigents, or by systematic destruction of their habitat and subsistence patterns, or by insipid destruction of their social fabric and way of life as categorized by cultural affiliation, through such deus ex machina vectors such as disease, alcohol, enforced indoctrination of our religious beliefs, legal removal of children for purposes of education and assimilation, restriction to peripheral lands unsuitable to sustaining traditional lifestyles and conducive to general cultural deterioration through long-term programs to ensure dependency, loss of dignity, removal of personal responsibility in matters of familial care, education, sustenance procurement, shelter maintenance, and so on.

'Toward the satisfactory completion of our singular goal, we are herewith purchasing from those in attendance and those peoples they represent, the following: your land, your life.

'In return, and as payment for the above, we offer you one hundred million buffalo skulls, the rusted hulks of five hundred thousand combines, desiccated farms, diseases, substance abuse, dependency, structured lives, handouts, starvation, hatred, loss of intellectual and spiritual property, identity, will, dignity, and pride. Sign here, please.'

'No.'

'I am empowered to offer the following as further incentive. Complete biological data on peripheral population and projections leading to the inevitable conclusion: to wit, within six generations those populations centered in the secondary and primary civilizations, characterized by protective measures of extreme technological life-sustaining intervention, will become extinct as a species, due primarily to pressure and displacement by a new speciation of the *Homo sapiens* hominid lineage, which will arise in pressured environments commonly found among peripheral populations, such as yours.

'In exchange for this data, we request intensive biological analysis of your peoples over the next century, including the right to blood and its protective properties thereof, including rad-resistant properties, vaccine and serum potential, immunodefense systems against toxemia and related syndromes, new organs and new properties of organs, neurological developments and all genetic traits determined to be conducive to species survival. In short, we ask for your life. We'll worry about the land later.'

'It seems,' Daniel Horn said, 'that your Manifest Destiny possesses a heretofore unknown appendix, wherein lies the inevitable conclusion, a conclusion you have espoused as wholly natural: species extinction. Unfortunately, the species about to become extinct is your own.'

'You do not understand our desperation.'

'I do now, Dr. MacAlister.'

'Will you help us? Will you save us?'

'In the manner you have just described, no, we won't help you.'

'But don't you see? We have bled for you. For five hundred years we have bled for you, for what we did to you.'

'That blood is unhealthy, Doctor. Do you grasp my meaning?'

'Whatever happened to reciprocity?'

'It lives on, but it was never what you believed it to be. You saw it with a scientist's eyes, Doctor, so you saw wrong. I'm not really interested in explaining it to you, Doctor. William has come to understand, finally. You might want to ask him.'

'He tells me nothing.'

'Nothing you want to hear.'

'Will you help us, Daniel? A few drops of blood? The conveyance of your dead?'

'We'll think about it, Doctor.'

American NW, Midwest Hole, July 14, A.C. 14

The coyotes streamed down the hillside, driven from their invisible places and becoming four distinct mercurial shapes parting the high magenta grasses. They reached the dry riverbed then scattered. William blinked, and they were gone.

Somewhere behind him rose a ragged slope, lifting the earth into an undercut cresting wave that hung frozen over the flat sweeps of sand and silt. Its shadow slowly crawled across him. He remembered standing on the ridge, the earth giving under him, a heavy, bruising fall.

His backpack lay a dozen meters away, resting against a tuft of grass. The flap had torn, and he saw a liquid glint of metal in the darkness within.

It felt over. The journey cut short, incomplete. He didn't have the strength to get up.

He'd seen into the coyotes, read their new imperatives like blushes of red behind their eyes. Opportunists, newly aggressive and far too clever for comfort. When night came, they, too, would come.

Life's cycles are flavored with irony. They've been following me, following the scent of blood, and in an hour they'll come to close the book. Patient bastards. What's ten thousand years, after all?

He stared at the object inside his backpack, the clarity of his thinking almost too bitter to bear.

Someone had challenged planetary laws. Semipermeable, pliable polysteel that shunted friction like water off a seal's back, turned heat into static − a hundred trillion threads a single molecule thick, each kilometers long, accommodating stress factors in the nano-bloodstream of carbon corpuscles. *When I say it bends, I mean it bends, Doctor.*

The laws dictated equatorial placement: rotational imperatives. Ladon tried acquiring it. Rivals and nations caught wind and went to the New United Nations. Before long, they'd hammered so many legal spikes into the equation, Ladon couldn't buy a bucket of dirt if it came from the equator. They had no choice but to look elsewhere, and to challenge toe-to-toe the exigencies of rotational dynamics.

It took eleven years before the Lady and Max Ohman stood atop the mountain, raised high the stone tablet, then swung it shattering down. Not an elevator as much as a slide, the tail of a spermatozoa, slanting skyward. Another miracle of engineering tethering it in place.

Nobody should reach that high. Frail humans should never strive for godhood. The wax melts; justice is meted out. Exaltation is suspect. Anybody with balls like that deserves to get them chopped off. They stand so tall, their shadows cover the world, and we frail humans begrudge the loss of light upon our upturned faces.

Not that we ever paid any attention to it when it showered down its brilliant promise.

But never mind that.

Nobody should reach that high. No matter the quagmire of emotions drowning in insipid fears and flaws, no matter the primal pit of terror bubbling uneasy beneath those words. It was a statement voiced the world over, there in those shadows cast down by achievement. Sometimes a whine, mostly vicious with blind, unreasoning hatred. The unspoken secret remained: What the shadows hid was darkness in the soul, and its voice was spite, and it said, Nobody should reach that high.

Well, Ladon reached, was reaching even now. It seemed the world was having trouble living with that fact.

An hour before dusk. Maybe less. William continued staring at the object in the backpack. He felt sickness in his flesh, something like a fever, but somehow sour as well. A taste of corruption.

The ghosts were gone. He'd sent them off, riding the storm as it tracked the blistered lands of the Hole. He hoped one would come back in time, one in particular. He'd not seen that one yet, but he was sure it was there, somewhere in the army of dead that had dogged his tracks.

A sound off to his right, footsteps crunching through the crust of calcined sand. And beyond that – William now heard – the hum of a rover's engine.

'Oh hell,' William mumbled through broken lips. 'I thought it was over.'

'The Lord have mercy,' Old Jim breathed softly as he crouched down beside William Potts. 'Unpack the kit, Stel, I figure he's taken more than seventy MRs for every day he's been out here, never mind the dehydration, sun- and windburns and, hell, starvation.'

Stel handed Old Jim the medikit. Her gaze remained on William as she tried remembering what he'd looked like, that night in his room. Gaunt even then, but this. She barely recognized him.

'He'll need plasma,' Old Jim said as he prepared a syringe. 'Fluids.'

'He needs clean marrow,' Stel said.

'Better call the university. Tell 'em we're taking him back to Val Marie, and they'd better get someone over, fast.'

Old Jim's weathered hands worked over William, stripping back the ragged bootsuit. He knew there were questions that Stel wanted answered. Questions about how he'd driven all over the damn place, about how he'd found the boy. The Hole was a big place, after all. The chances of finding him were damn near hopeless.

He injected William with E-67 flushant, the latest available in rad treatment.

How the hell can I tell her I had help? How can I tell her that I followed an old Indian ghost?

'Let's get him in the buggy.'

Some goddamned ghost leading me across the prairie, an Indian ghost carrying a goddamn rifle slung with red-hawk feathers.

'Jim,' Stel said.

He looked up and cursed the shadows that hid her face.

'Jim,' Stel said again.

'What?'

She continued staring down on him a moment longer. Then she turned away. 'I need a cigarette.'

Jim drove steadily, his antiquated patrol buggy bouncing and jolting on its stiff shocks. It'd been years since the Palliser Triangle Survey, when he'd played chauffeur to a bunch of scientists. He remembered all the weather readings they took, and the soil and plant samples. Insect nets strung out between the tents at night; animal traps, bird snares, bat nets that looked like giant lobster traps. When it was all over, they rushed off to the university with all their goodies. Old Jim had gotten a six-month bonus to his credit line, arthritis in his misaligned hip, and the solar-powered patrol buggy. Even with the crotchety hip, Jim figured he came out ahead in the deal.

Stel smoked in the seat beside him. William lay unconscious along the length of the back bench. The silence was as thick as the smoke.

Dusk had arrived, the sun spreading out on the west horizon like a copper lake. Helishuttles had been coming and going through the Hole for a week now. Jack Tree and his cronies were cooking something big along with that corporation. Somewhere out there on the dead lands. Old Jim's expression soured as he thought of Jack Tree. Too damn clever by far. One day he'll hear about my artifact collection, and come calling. He'll take it all. The law backs him. He'll take it all from me. All eight generations, swept away. Too goddamn clever by far.

'What're his chances?' Stel asked suddenly.

Jim shrugged. 'Short term, he'll make it fine. Long term . . .' Jim shrugged again. He licked his lips, kept his eyes on the rolling plain in front of them. 'Figure he's burned blind, though.'

'Blind,' Stel said. 'Well, hell, what's to see these days anyway? Damned TV stations all losing it every ten bloody minutes, for Christ's sake. Al says it's those helishuttles. Remote-guided, he says, with a flight path right over town screwing up transmissions or something.'

'Oh yeah,' Jim said, not really listening. Goddamned TVs – who buys the shit they're saying anyway. World's gone to hell, ain't it just. He'd seen the latest shots of Iraq in the *National Geographic*. Robot camera teams rolling through ancient ruins. Caption talked about it being the first city ever built. Talked about some king named Gilgamesh. The shots were eerie as hell. Red sky, all those cobbled roads and things exposed by the blown sands. And here and there the rusting hulks of tanks and trucks. Eerie because it all looked so normal, like the pictures were just waiting for someone to walk through, some kid herding goats or something.

But nothing. Nuclear fallout still at lethal levels.

The first city was dead, would always be dead.

More shots, modern echoes in Iran. Black, burned-up bodies covering the streets, the squares, covering the steps leading up to slagged mosques. Not a bird, probably not even a bug. Even the Indian Ocean was half-dead, all the surface plankton incinerated in the multiple blasts, a yard of water stripped off the whole damn ocean.

Maybe the boy's on to something, after all. He's wearing the scars we keep running from. He knows we're running out of room. He knows we fucked it up, we're fucking it all up even now. Bloody wars, ninety million dead of starvation in Africa, Armageddon in Jerusalem, plague in China, Bombay carpet-bombed. Here I am trying to save a boy from rad posioning. What the hell for?

'Heard the weather's coming back,' Stel said, lighting a last cigarette as the old motel on the edge of town came into view.

'We're in a loop,' Jim said. 'Goes round and round.'

Stel took a deep drag, released the smoke in an even stream. 'Must be sunspots or something.'

Old Jim swung the buggy up onto the motel's cracked parking lot pavement. 'Must be,' he said.

They took William to his old room in the hotel. Stel washed him down, so gently, it stung Jim's eyes to watch. When they had the boy laid out on the bed, Jim set up the plasma kit. Saline, electrolytes, anti-leukemic compounds, lithium, and more E-67. The standard rad treatment setup, available in every peripheral town.

With some old fart like me trained like a monkey. Mix this, drip that. Tap the vein, insert with a steady probing motion – you'll feel the venal wall when you puncture it. Bathe all solar burns in weak saline and E-67. Run the flush as soon as possible, and that means the catheter. If the victim's male . . .

Stel watched him for a few minutes, then headed to the door. 'I'll buzz that woman who keeps calling for him. Guess she'll come and pick him up.'

Jim nodded. After a moment he heard Stel leave.

'Oh, son,' Jim said softly, sponging solution into William's swollen eyes. 'Just like a sun dance, huh? Push past the pain, find that cool, peaceful place. Too bad you couldn't take your body with you.'

He'd first shown up three years ago. Even then, as he started knocking on doors, slicking the locals at the pool table, and just being damn good at listening, Old Jim knew the boy had arrived with wide-open eyes.

He'd cared about their lives. At first, it was some kind of philosophical caring. William bled for the idea of them. He came as a chronicler, but that first season changed him. The idea found faces, a score of faces. The caring changed, and when he looked in your eyes the glaze was gone. You could see him in his eyes, and he saw you, and it was a clear thing both ways.

One night, late at the hotel bar, William sat with a half-dozen locals for hours on end. Old Jim had watched the layers crumble in the boy, watched as William was pushed deep into himself by the stories the old-timers threw around. They'd been talking about the changes.

'North of here,' Aimes was saying, 'where they grew canola and didn't do much ranching, well, I remember the fields just falling dead, toppling in waves. Next thing you know, the sky's gray with locusts, come to eat the poisoned canola, right down to the ground.' Aimes squinted down at the glass of beer in his rope-veined hands. 'A hundred million, they said. A hundred million rotting locusts, the sky empty as the dawn of time . . .'

'We'd get the traffic coming down from Swift Current,' Browning said. 'On their way to those ski resorts in Montana. I saw one accident, shit—'

William cut in, his voice dull, 'I know what's missing.' He looked up, scanned the faces around him. Old Jim remembered the loss in the boy's eyes, remembered the way that look made his chest tighten. 'I know what's missing here. There's no dogs.'

'They died fast,' Aimes said, nodding. 'Cats just hid during the day, did the usual at night. But the dogs died for a long while there.'

'I saw some litters make you upchuck your granma's meat loaf,' Browning said.

'I hear they're doing fine in the shielded cities,' Old Jim said, trying to ease the anguish in William's face. Hell, he remembered thinking, They're just damn dogs. Don't compare to the skin cancers, the babies poisoned by breast milk and living the rest of their days inside plastic-bag rooms. Don't compare at all, dammit. Just dogs.

'There should be dogs,' William said. 'Barking like hell every time I walk into the yard. Challenging the stranger, doing their job for you people. Nobody's taken their place. You don't challenge anymore. You don't raise shit just to see what the stranger's made of. No stranger ever fooled a dog. Ever.'

'That's a damn fact, that is,' Browning said, nodding.

Old Jim stared at the boy. What you spill up tells a lot, but reaching the place where you'll do it in the company of old men, that tells a whole lot more.

William's outburst slipped away, into that timeless stream of gripes and bitches that filled the hours before dawn. He'd joined the town, that night. He'd shifted the place he looked at things from. He'd lined up with the peripherals, the subjects of his study, and saw the world in a new way that was in truth an old way. Maybe the oldest way of all.

A hell of a way to step out of being young. Probably the night that Stel decided she'd get him in her bed sooner or later. She wouldn't do that for a stranger. But she'd help a local boy get a bit older.

Help was something he drew to him. Halo'd Mary and an old Indian ghost.

Net

FREE WHIZZY: So NOAC's on its own. What do you make of the threats to invade? Anyone?

PACEMAKER: Highly unlikely. They really banked on NUN approval, and it looked for a time there like they had it, but now it's all fallen apart.

LUNKER: All the rats have scurried to the stern, eyes tilting up, way up. Salvation beckons.

CORBIE TWA: Ladon's not selling. The Lakota are staying belligerent. Assembly is on schedule, the orbiting chute is in position, geosynchronous perfection. Fifth Floor, men's underwear . . .

LUNKER: Can't get off what you can't get onto first, so the rats won't get a ride, no matter how much they squeal. It's kind of sweet, in a pathetic, pan-suicidal way.

PACEMAKER: I've reviewed the population projection data and it seems William Potts is playing Pandora. This is highly alarming information.

BOGQUEEN: Details, please.

PACEMAKER: Very well, and bear in mind the data is no longer secured, it's riding a very accessible crest. I won't bore you with technical details, but the conclusions the top-dog geneticists have reached can be stated as follows.

One: Pressured populations possess a greater likelihood of mutation that selects for successful adaptation to changing environments. Dynamics remain typically tautological, but the result is speciation – the emergence of a new species of hominid. *Homo sapiens neosapien,* whatever you want to call it. This speciation is rapid-fire, the so-called punctuated equilibrium hypothesis. Very fast in its definition process. It's happening now among certain peripheral populations – those groups who for whatever reason are outside civilized intervention in environmental management. The traits are highly variable among these groups, but they meet the definitive requirements: increased phenotype viability.

Two: Central populations, defined as those that are insulated from the global environmental denigration by civilized intervention, for example, NOAC citizens, Eurocom, SINJO urban populations – these populations are not experiencing the rate of mutation or the selective perquisites found in the peripheral populations.

Three: Furthermore, these Central populations are on a trend toward extinction. Negative birthrates, increased infertility, chronic toxemic disorders and related dysfunctions.

Tip your hats, ladies and gentlemen, the show's closing. It was a short run, sure, but fun while it lasted.

BOGQUEEN: I wish I could cry, but the irony's got me laughing one of those devil-laughs.

CORBIE TWA: Pray, tell.

BOGQUEEN: Goes back to the official line on mass extinction. We rewrote Nature's laws to suit our own inevitable fouling of the nest. We holed up in our shielded cities and kept on poisoning the outside world. We figured we'd killed Nature, and good riddance.

CORBIE TWA: But she moves on, she moves on.

BOGQUEEN: We thought we could leave it behind, but it's left us behind. Life's out there, gentlemen. We're in here, and we're dead. Ha ha ha.

PACEMAKER: I can guess at the ramifications all this has to Ladon's Medicine Wheel Project. Escape. Unfortunately, the data goes on to other projections, and these are dreadful indeed. You see, those new traits being expressed by the peripheral populations are also deemed positive selections to long-term survival in nongravitational environments with high-rad doses. These new people or whatever you want to call them are not only smaller, they're also radiation resistant. They're off to the stars, friends. The dream is in their reach, not ours.

BOGQUEEN: 'Share the blood . . .' I grasp the nature of William's treaty mime in the last transmission.

CORBIE TWA: I don't like this at all. Ladon and the Lakota are playing a helluva dangerous game here. If they keep saying no, then desperation will incite desperate measures: NOAC will launch military invasions, their science teams will roll in on their heels and sweep, sample, retrieve, stabilize, and secure enough tissue and blood samples to once again cheat Nature.

LUNKER: Everyone's waiting. After all, if NOAC can self-justify annexing a sovereign nation, then every other peripheral population with the Right Stuff is fair game. You're right, Corbie, we'll cheat Nature. We'll cheat death.

BOGQUEEN: Of course that runs in the face of the party line on the inevitability of mass extinction. It's the fatalists versus the immortalists. NOAC's got its own party-lined inertia to deal with among the populace. A populace NOAC's been busy unplugging from reality for half a century. They made fatalists of their citizens in order to stay in power, now that very fatalism is handcuffing them.

CORBIE TWA: That won't last. NOAC has no choice but to take the heat and get nasty.

LUNKER: No doubt the Lady at Ladon's aware of all this, as is the Lakota. They'll have to start negotiating, or they're slag.

SECURICOM: Tracking . . .
              Tracking . . .
              Tracking . . .

> Rogue captured. Identified: Stonecaster,
> Source: Vancouver, 21VR-213 South
> District A.

STONECASTER: No reason to nab me. I'm just surfing the waves, Securicom.

SECURICOM: Your files contain restricted data, including logs from Subversive Rogue named Potts, William.

STONECASTER: There's a goddamn flood out there, Securicom. I can't keep track of all the flotsam that drifts my way. Who the hell is this Potts, William?

SECURICOM: Evidence indicates full complicity, Stonecaster. Your antiquated equipment has been tagged. Admit your culpability in this matter and penal reforms will take your remorse into account. Logs generated by Subversive Potts, William, are illegal material. Furthermore, additional Subversive data indicates Swamp activity with known dissidents and terrorists.

STONECASTER: You've got it all wrong. I don't know any of them.

NOACom

. . . witnesses describe a bright, blinding flash in the northwest quadrant of the sky. Residents from as far away as Chicago saw the collision.

The orbiting station was an abandoned SINJO laboratory that SINJO officials confirm as de-activated in 2016. The station, reportedly valued at 180 million NOAC-M, was completely destroyed in the collision with the NOAC orbiting defense platform.

Disruptions occurred in all related transmission frequencies, including laser-tracking and guidance systems, as well as microwave transmissions.

NOAC Securicom officials have stated that the terrorist, manning a SUN-12 System, has been thoroughly negated with fierce rigor . . .

VORPAL: I've got a gunner on my tail. I need help. Anybody? Anyone out there? Fuck, I said I need help here.

THROWBACK: I'm spreading my wing, Vorpal. Hurry up, now, time's short.

BLANC KNIGHT: I'm dead, all you who can hear me. Someone prop me back in the saddle. My last charge. I see your gunner, Vorpal. He's mine. Watch.

American NW, Val Marie, Sask. Precinct, July 19, A.C. 14

Like a single seed pulled clean from its home, William felt himself riding the prairie winds, no longer corporeal, a memory of self tugged free. He could feel a distant pain, a steady susurration of sand blown against skin; he heard voices from the place he'd left, a faint whisper of surf in his ears, reminding him of weekends at the beach as a child – when he'd believed the warm ocher stretch of water was limitless beyond the fine white sand, when he'd thought it was an ocean, and he remembered his shock at discovering that it was but a lake, the last remnant of an inland glacial sea. The discovery had made the world suddenly larger, but more than that, he'd marveled at the sudden knowledge of time and the changes wrought on this earth – all there for his eyes to see, for his mind to unveil.

He heard those voices, was aware that he knew those who spoke, and that his body was undergoing manifest changes, which seemed the entire subject of their conversations. He wondered at their concern, when he himself felt nothing, when in fact he'd already gone – out into the wastelands, one ghost among many.

He flew on, memories in dogged pursuit, beneath a sky of night so vast and clear and bristling with stars, he imagined the plain below him had risen to heaven, and the wind that carried him – pressed so inexorably between two immense forces of nature – was the voice of angels.

He wanted to sing, when he'd never sung before; he wanted to dance, when the music of his life had always been grim. He wanted to hear a voice calling to him from somewhere above, a child's voice that might have been his own. (Yet knew it wasn't, not quite.) *Come to me! Fly to me! Rise higher, higher!*

Tears (intrusive saline ejected from glandular ducts) of joy, a love of life not his own now overwhelming him (descrambled the voice of God from an antiquated com sat, the voice of the Father) with a child's memory – *Is this death? Is this truly death? Such joy, such a call to heaven, such a voice of dreams—*

Son, can you hear me?

Father?

Go back, please. Pull out—

In William's tenth year, his father had turned fifty. The blood was stretched thin between them, even as they walked side by side along the beach strand.

Pelicans wheeled out beyond the surf, and the wind was hot as it gusted down from the aspen fringe. The trees were dying, leaves curling and turning black. The whole ecozone was changing, his father explained. The transition zone was moving north; the boreal forest was drying up, burning fierce. The north had become a conflagration no amount of technology could change. And the lake was poisoned, mostly with coliform bacteria from a province that was home to as many pigs as people, but did nothing to treat the porcine sewage.

Nature has a way of humbling humanity, son. But the lesson sinks home only when tragedy gets personal, and even then the humility runs its course – the glittering paradigms of modern society sweep away every dark, difficult moment. We answer Nature with claims of compensation, relocation funding, declarations of disaster zones and emergency relief. We pick through the rubble looking for dead children and functionable television sets. Disaster is a place where we are temporarily left behind – watch us scramble to catch up, watch how eager everyone is to help us catch up, so as to not be reminded of the futility of progress.

Dad?

Yes, son?

What's SIDS?

Pain flared and William knew his face was smiling. The voices had gone silent, eyes now upon him. It had always been that way when he smiled.

But look at these stars. Heaven is not vaulted, not here. On the prairie, the night sky is infinity on the edge of comprehension. Look at the stars, connect the dots, and the truth comes clear.

Have you seen a man smile when his life breaks? Your breath stills and you realize the effort it took to manage that smile. That smile, Father, is nature's answer to life itself.

This was a sea once, son. Fed by glacial melt, it's been dying in phases for ten thousand years. Walk west of here and you'll come to beach ridges – those pale denuded strips full of cobbles and nothing else since too many idiots vertically plowed over them. Memories of ripples in the shrinking pool. This is the last phase, William. The lake's going fast, very fast. I'm so very tired . . .

One ghost among many, and each one held to its own story, its own version of life's lessons. There was no agreement, no consensus on cause and effect. Even the angels argued, there amidst the wind that never ceased.

Extinction is an abstract concept. Death is personal. It's a survival mechanism on the emotional front – who can weep for a lifetime?

Don't ask that question, son, because I can answer you. It's still going on, it still spills out every now and then. Look at our species and think of madness as a biological imperative to self-destruction. In the past sixty years, every goddamn neighborhood became home to outwardly normal, reasonable people – sometimes odd, but mostly convincing you of their harmlessness. Madness, in all the guises allowed to it in an anonymous society. I'll give you a generic example: An eight-year-old boy is found dead, chained to a bed in a room made dark by blinds taped to the windows. He's got bite marks on him, he's clawed grooves in the filthy hardwood floor; he's bruised and malnourished and he died from none of these things. No, he died because he couldn't understand what he'd done wrong, and in not knowing he concluded that the act of being alive was his crime. He sought his only absolution ... by dying. A lifetime of weeping, mercifully short you'll agree. His mother lived in society, she shopped down at the local supermarket. His father was an upright citizen, patriotic, a family man.

What made them unique? Nothing. That's what's so frightening, but more than that, it's the secret of enlightenment – to realize that they were not unique, that the mechanisms of social control are structured to avoid comprehension of their profound normality, and that something's been triggered, on a collective scale encompassing our entire species, that delivers the simple unavoidable message that madness is among us. We've poisoned the world outside, son, as a direct manifestation of our inner insanity. We are in the end run of ultra success. Nature draws more than one rein, son. We can see the external, the environmental checks now laying siege to our species. But the internal is the one we cannot accept. The last thing we'll all taste is the barrel of the gun we ourselves shove into our mouths.

Dad?

What is it, William?

Happy birthday.

That generic boy, chained to his bed, was with him now, here in the winds that might have been humanity's final scream. A small, frail ghost, still whispering *I'm sorry, Daddy. I'm sorry, Mommy. What did I do wrong?*

You were born, son, with the added misfortune of surviving it. You were new and helpless and you trusted

– my, how you trusted. You never learned the lessons of withholding that trust, of relying upon your judgments, of mastering healthy skepticism. Your gods took you in hand and led you into Hell. Regular folk, the kind that hosted parties, backyard barbecues, but to you they were gods, and like God Himself they laid a judgment upon you, that you should suffer, that you should know the anguish of a guilt you never earned. They gave you life, and you lived their definition of it.

It's a parable, in its own way. Analogous to the horror visited upon the sons and daughters by the fathers and mothers. They give you life: a world poisoned, its earth blasted and ripped open and breeding deadly diseases, its waters turgid and tossed with dead creatures, its air foul with invisible gases and holed like gauze letting the rays burn down the holy message of cancer and blindness.

We needed those cars, son, to speed up our pursuit of unachievable and unworthy dreams. We needed those forests stripped away, to plant food to feed our weeping multitudes. We needed that plastic that gave you tits and made you infertile. We needed those antibiotics, those televisions and their vital programming, those bloodless cameras that never blinked nor turned away. We needed all those wars to feed our technocratic utopia. We needed those prison ships, we needed segregation, calling in those bank loans, national lotteries, millionaire athletes, movie stars, white hoods and burning crosses, doctors gunned down outside abortion clinics, walled neigborhoods with private armies, pedophiles, serial killers, terrorists, fundamentalists – we needed all those things, son, and you will, too. They're our gift to you, given out of love

*because we tried to better your lives. At least, that's
what we kept telling one another. Can't you see how
much better we've made your lives?*

One day the trust goes away.

Don't take my lead, son. Don't take anyone's lead.

I won't, Dad.

*We don't know what we're doing. Never did. Our
lives – the lives of every human who came before you –
those are your lessons. Not for imitation, but for
separation, for distinction. What you must learn to
walk away from. Because we're a mess, and our biggest
crime is that we've ruined your world. Don't you ever
forgive us. Don't you ever!*

I won't.

I haven't.

He wanted to rise into the sky, higher, ever higher.
Somewhere above, among the angels, was the ghost of
a child. It called to him, but all he could do was to grope
blindly, yearningly, for its embrace.

It's what happens when tragedy gets personal.

Jim took another mouthful of beer, scowled at how
warm his hand on the bottle had made it. 'You'd of
thought they'd just take him out,' he muttered.

Stel let her head slowly slip down from the hand it
leaned on, her fingers spreading her midnight hair, eyes
on the empty chair beside her. After a moment she
straightened, reached for her cigarettes. 'That woman
ain't good for him,' she said.

'What do you mean?'

She shrugged heavily, sighed out a stream of smoke.
'I mean she wasn't just his boss. That's what I mean.

And now she's playing some kinda game – she wants him here. Don't know why.'

'He's responding to the treatments.'

'Oh yeah, nothing but the best.'

Jim set the bottle down on the table, drew his hands down to his lap, then leaned forward and wrapped them back round the bottle. 'Don't know,' he said. 'Don't know what I'm waiting for.'

'You want him to come to, Jim. You want him to tell you what to do.'

'What to do? What do you mean? What to do about what?'

'She's got him where she wants him. He won't accept that – never did.'

Jim looked away from her, squinting as he took in the empty street through the dusty window. 'You believe in ghosts, Stel?'

'Ghosts? Christ.'

'You believe in them?'

'No, yes. Maybe. That one brew get you drunk or something?'

'Lived here all my life, never saw nothing out of the ordinary. Only my grandpa, well, whenever he looked out on the land, it was as if he was seeing – I don't know – seeing more than I could see.'

'Indian blood.'

Jim nodded. 'He said the land was full of spirits, that all of time since the very beginning was gathered there, looking up at a million different skies, but always the same sun.'

'The Happy Hunting Ground.'

Jim grinned sourly. 'Guess so. Anyway, when he

looked, I think he could see them. All of them.'

'And you're seeing them now, too?'

He glanced over at her. She was leaning on the table, one hand holding up her head, the other hand stretched out on the tabletop, cigarette between two fingers. Her eyes searched his steadily, without once flickering away. Jim shrugged uneasily. 'Had to find the boy, didn't I? Hell, he'd made the evening news, didn't he. Had me wishing I had a computer, so I could see for myself what all the fuss was about. Anyway, I had to find the boy somewhere out there, didn't I?'

Her generous mouth quirked. 'Thought you was reading sign, you old Injun coot.'

Jim grinned back, then shook his head, the grin fading. 'Did a lot of praying. Though I never did believe in God, not the Bible kind, anyway.'

'Guided by a divine hand? Born again, are you now?'

'Probably not. There was a . . . well, a ghost. Showed me the way, Stel. Showed me the way.'

She slowly blinked, her dark eyes on his; then she simply nodded.

Jim took another mouthful of beer.

'That's gotta taste like piss by now.'

'Yep.'

'Let me get you another one.'

'Sure.'

She rose. 'Then we can decide.'

'Decide what?'

'Whether we're gonna do what William asks us to do, once he comes round.'

'That's an easy one, Stel.'

'Glad to hear you say that, old man. Damned glad.'

He watched her ample hips swaying as she made her way to the bar. Oh, Stel, you've fallen for the boy, haven't you? Shoulda guessed that, when I saw you bathing his feet.

He opened his eyes. A sensor beeped. He saw Jenine MacAlister turn from the window, watched her cross over to stand beside the bed. Her eyes were flat.

'You look like hell, William.'

And I can still see your bones, Jenine.

'You really lost yourself out there, didn't you?' She stared down at him a moment longer, then dragged over a chair and sat, sighing. 'I pulled out all the stops, brought the best medical team I could find. They've worked on you for days. Long-term prognosis isn't good, but it could've been worse. Believe me. You'll need more marrow, more flushing, more stem injections, more everything. No promises beyond ten years. It was a manufactured match, by the way, that marrow. Any idea what that costs? Don't worry about any of that, it's taken care of, William.'

She looked tired. She looked like she'd been holding back all her cards for one single, sweeping play. Waiting for him to wake up, making certain she'd be there when he did. Alone, when she was at her deadliest.

'I'd forgotten,' he said stiffly.

'What?'

He smiled at her frown. 'What you looked like. Funny, that. Sometimes I'd just walked out of your office, after an hour trapped under you, and I'd be unable to picture your face. Just the eyes, the look in them – that never went away.'

'It's what kept bringing you back.'

'I suppose so.'

She seemed to hesitate, then asked, 'How are you feeling?'

'Not that well, Jenine.'

'Too bad. Assuming you'd like a reprise, that is.'

'No. Those days are done.'

'I kind of figured as much,' she said with a faint smile. She settled back in the chair. 'Would you like a sit rep?'

'Wouldn't that be a breach in security, Jenine?'

'You must be kidding. What security? There's more holes in the dam than we can count. It's all pouring out, William. Do you realize there is going to be a major conflict on the North American continent for the first time since Mexico imploded'

'I take it you're not counting the Haitian invasion.'

She wrinkled her nose. 'A million half-drowned refugees don't really rate, especially since none of them reached shore.'

'Fine, the first in a long time. What about it?'

'Only that you are right in the middle of it. Charges are being brought up on you. Sedition, treason, conspiring under the dictates of Homeland Security prohibitions. I don't think I can help you, either. There's always been two camps in government, and right now the hawks are circling high. The situation hasn't been this unstable since the last decade of the United States. You would not believe the paranoia at NOAC Mount.'

'It's the legacy of a world power that isn't a world power anymore, Jenine.'

'I know that very well, William. American flags are

flying off the shelves. They want it like it used to be, with them dictating to everyone else on everything.'

'Ironic, isn't it?'

'You find this amusing?'

'In a detached sort of way. Even without the Midwest Hole opening up, the Yanks couldn't have survived without Canadian resources. That pill's still bitter to them, you know. But the fact remains, the Lakota Nation is sovereign. NOAC will be invading contrary to every international law there is, and the rest of the world is watching.'

Her eyes were hard as she said, 'They don't give a fuck.'

'Just like in the old days, huh?'

'Just like, William.'

'Let's talk science for a bit, Jenine. What's this I've been reading about the Mars Excavations?'

'Fits the Restitution, as far as we can tell.'

William managed a smile. 'The Restitution – another forbidden subject.'

'Any idea how many careers went up in flames with that, William? The Mars Project made one thing brutally plain. We had a shared heritage. DNA sequences, the works. The question remains, were we seeded at the same time, or did one planet's life precede the other, and which came first? The evidence is pointing to Mars in one area, at least.'

'The hominid line.'

She nodded. 'It was a crowded tree, on both worlds, although the gracile elements seem to begin on Mars – low gravity and all that. Likely both *erectus* and Neanderthal are indigenous branches, terrestrial, I mean. Maybe even *ergaster*. I can't see *ergaster* having the technical wherewithal to build colony ships, since all we're finding with them are stone, antler, and bone tools. Besides, as the Restitution acknowledged, there is plenty of evidence of fully modern forms throughout our geologic history, the oldest confirmed date sits at twenty-one million years right now.'

'There,' William said, 'now isn't this better? A kinder, gentler subject.'

'Only by virtue of it being essentially irrelevant.'

'Really? I don't think it is. Look, Mars is a depleted planet. Beyond the spill from impact detritus, the mineral yield is a pittance. How many old mines and diggings were found?'

'The evidence of that is minimal—'

'Of course it is. There's sixty or seventy million years of erosion and meteoric and asteroid impact mitigating it. It's all dust now, not surprising, given the atmosphere's virtually stripped away. What are the rad readings on deep subsurface strata? Residual, I'd guess. Plenty of half-life's done and gone by now. Even so, it all seems bloody obvious to me. We've done it before, Jenine. Destroyed a world, although it seems some of us managed to escape it before it was too late. Escape to Earth.'

'Way too much supposition, William.'

'Common sense. Look, the Cassini and Huygens missions found primitive carbon-based protolife on Titan, a seed reservoir, sealed under ice. Identical building blocks. Someone made a stash, Jenine. Probably us, back when we were Martians.'

'So what is your point?'

'Just that. We've fucked up before. Then conveniently forgot that fact, and now we're doing it again. We had our second chance, and instead of doing it right this time, we've just repeated the old follies. Resource depletion, atmosphere stripping. I don't think it was an accident there were once so many hominid lines co-existing. It was a damned experiment, hunting for the best option. Only it failed yet again, because our species – the one that won out – remains as shortsighted as it ever was. They played with punctuated equilibrium, but it didn't work, because it's a game with random rules and immeasurable victories. But now, finally . . .'

'Finally, it's happened,' she said. 'Peripheral peoples.'

'Pressured populations. Biologically desperate populations.'

'We need those stem cells, William.'

'We don't deserve them.'

'You presume to pass judgment on all of us?'

'Not me. Nature does. It has already. We're done, Jenine. We're *Homo erectus* looking across the gulf at *Homo ergaster*, we're Neanderthals scowling at Moderns.'

'No, we're not. Because we possess the technology to partake of those new survival mechanisms. For our children's sake, if not for us.'

'You are telling me you haven't acquired subjects yet? Spec Ops incursions have been occurring everywhere.'

'One of the problems with cheap armaments is that they level the playing field. Worse, Ladon Inc. has been a major supplier of state-of-the-art defense systems. Clearly, the *Lady* and her cronies expect to tag along for the ride up and away.'

'Do they? Are you sure of that?'

Her face filled with disbelief, then derision. 'An act of self-sacrifice? Get real, William. She's got a biotech team on it, guaranteed. Probably part of the deal.'

'If so, isn't that what libertarian competition is all about?'

'Competition stops being a virtue as soon as we lose.'

'I cannot believe that such hypocrisy exists among the political and economic powers that be, Jenine. This isn't the old US of A anymore, you know.'

'Irony. I appreciate your sense of humor, William. I always have.'

'But you never laugh.'

'Your sense of humor does not invite laughter. You're looking tired. Rest now. We'll talk again later.'

Entry: Lakota Nation, July 19, A.C. 14

Abandoned and lost, the remote mobile communication device squatted turtle-like on the hillock. Its screen was smeared with an arcane message, but its optics functioned just fine. Its brain was small but compactly organized, able to call on discriminating logic processors and copious memory, since it was capable of other, less peaceful functions.

But the storms had untethered it; the weather had damaged it. No longer one of MacAlister's drones, no longer NOAC's eyes and ears, the turtle wandered with its own designs, recording events it found intrinsically interesting. Or so it seemed. The truth was, it had been hijacked, and now fed its visuals directly into the Net's Swamp.

On the plain below was a sprawl of structures, a concrete and metallic fist surrounded by oil-extraction devices, pipelines, storage containers, motionless vehicles.

Overhead, the sky flickered, a visual symphony of sheet lightning and ground-launched systemic EMP bursts. Up where the first-wave Insertion Drones flew supersonic and blind, dead and dumb – their brains fried. The Lakota-held installation, tactically termed a Dark Presence, remained so. On its hill, the turtle monitored and recorded the subsurface extrusion mortars, launching their EMP caches skyward on puffs of smoke quickly whipped away in the wind. Joining in the fun, at least six Lakota warriors – each armored and with every modern weapon at their disposal – were positioned in and around the installation, waiting for the next intrusion.

In classic NOAC procedure – and regardless of the failure of the advance drones – a wing of unmanned fighter bombers dipped down under the clouds and fanned out for the first pass. This would be a reconnaissance flyover, target-fixing for the follow-up strike. The elimination of serviceable sats had necessitated this direct method. NOAC didn't want the installation damaged, didn't want another Kuwait, another Iraq. Armed with supersmart self-guided bombs, the sleek, stealthed jets hunted for the counterinsertion squad – the Lakota.

Hornet stingers radar-equipped for stealthed targets rose to meet them. The air thundered; the sky ignited two kilometers from the installation. Wreckage spun burning through the night air. The fighter bombers were gone.

As the Lakota changed positions – their Lizard-back armor blind to all but close-proximity line of sight – the turtle extended its sensors. Seismic tracers were the first indications, one signal laid overtop another. The turtle employed a filter and did some discriminating, then identifying. Stealthed helishuttles, eight kilometers to the north and closing fast; but closer, now almost within sight, a dozen unmanned tanks – Ladybugs.

The Dark Presence was ready for them. A perimeter picket of fast-traversing mines – Ants in military jargon – closed in. The tanks responded with enfilade fire and cluster path-makers, which took care of those Ants in front of them, but did nothing for the sleepers that activated after the tanks passed, and now came up from behind. Barking explosions immobilized two, six, ten, then all twelve Ladybugs. More Ants swarmed the tanks, many dying as the vehicles expended all their defensive weaponry, but within a few more seconds, each Ladybug burned, poured smoke into the cold wind.

The helishuttles landed beyond a ridge, disgorging their Immediate Response Teams, then lifting and banking and racing northward. Subsurface eardrums, which had tracked them all the way, now activated their own SAMs, and the night sky was bright once again.

There were eight teams, each consisting of six highly trained soldiers fully armored in rad- and biochem-proof servo suits, thoroughly armed, each soldier alone capable of conducting death and destruction on a massive scale. The Ants got most of them, a subspecies arriving nicknamed Fireants for their immolating qualities, cooking one soldier after another in their armor, via acids, incendiary chemicals, nanoinfiltrators, and so on.

The eleven soldiers who survived to penetrate the perimeter were each damaged in some manner, bleeding heat emissions and making fine targets for the Lizard-backs. In moments, the NOAC insertion was over, and the installation remained . . .

A Dark Presence.

The turtle's sensors detected another subsurface tremble. Its optics detected and followed the rapid departure of the Lakota. Its brain organized this data; then it, too, made a hasty exit.

Thirty-one minutes later, the Alberta Tar Sands went up. The sky lit bright; the wind withdrew for a long moment, then returned to strip the grass from the hill-tops, to send the turtle tumbling from its anchored tracks.

Then there was smoke.

Old Jim turned off the television set. There hadn't been much of a picture, but since the satellite feed was from far across the Atlantic, that was no surprise. He went to the window and looked at the distant horizon. Nothing to mark the burning firestorm that now raged hundreds of kilometers to the northwest. Come the morning, he knew, there would be smoke, and the sun would turn coppery as it traversed the sky.

'Now, that's what I call a fuckup,' Stel said from the sofa.

Jim grunted.

'Cheer up,' Stel said. 'She's got to leave his room sometime.'

He turned to her. Stel's ample legs were crossed, the denim of her jeans taut. She had a cigarette in one hand, a mug of coffee in the other. There were lines bracketing her mouth, her still-full lips pale and set in a half-smile. A face of the modern age – one look into those seen-it-all eyes – the face of history. A face needing tender hands.

She must have seen something in his expression, for she said quietly, 'I've had my eyes on you for years. But you were lusting after someone else.'

'I was?'

'Grief, I think she's called.'

He squinted, blinked, then turned back to the window.

'Wrong guess?' she asked behind him.

'Wrong guess,' he answered. A moment passed. 'Hate's the lady, Stel. You should've seen me. I pored over books, I learned all there was, every magazine, every goddamned article.'

'About what?'

'Cancer. Diseases. Pesticides, herbicides. Did you know cancer was the unmentioned epidemic as far back as the Eighties? Cigarettes were outlawed virtually everywhere and the number of smokers went way down, but still the stats climbed. No change. No change at all. It was all lies. What killed us was in the air, in the water, in the packaging for our foods. Then, later, in GMO and irradiation and microwaving. Cancer viruses, prions, systemic rejection so bad, people became allergic to being alive. It was all going down, Stel, all going down.' His eyes slowly lost their focus, seeing nothing beyond the glass. 'Remember Regina in '06? A quarter million head incinerated in two weeks – you could see the glow from Saskatoon. Funny, isn't it. Before Regina was called Regina, it was called Pile of Bones, only then it was a mountain of buffalo bones.' He paused, rubbed the bristle on his chin. 'Round and round. A quarter million head every two weeks. And then there were none. And then all the young people, shaking like leaves, going senile – like some bad science-fiction movie. It wasn't fair, how they died. Not fair.'

'Still hating, Jim?'

He shrugged, focus returning, close this time, to his own face reflected in the windowpane. 'The passion goes. I'd kind of expected it to eat me up from the inside, but it didn't.'

'It's the ones left behind,' Stel said. 'I lived nearly twenty years in the city, did you know that? When I was young. Never was a country girl, now ain't that a joke.'

He faced her again, wondering at the sudden jump in her thoughts, catching the slight shift in her tone. Her eyes were on the table. She leaned forward and fished another cigarette from the pack, lit it, then leaned back again. 'I lived with a woman in the city. Twelve years.' She looked up, grinned. 'I go both ways, you know.'

'Lucky you.'

Her gaze returned to the table, seeing back years and years. 'She died. Reaction to tear gas. Oh, we were hell on wheels. What a life. No tomorrow. We knew it, we pushed all the way, every damn minute. We flew high. We screamed at the State, fought every surrender. And it was all for nothing. I should've died with her, I should never have lived on, so long, all these years. Wasn't just her dying that broke my heart, it was everything, it was losing all the battles, never winning – they took it all away, called it efficiency, streamlining. Said the global economy was to blame, but that was all bullshit. Excuses for cold hearts—' She looked up. 'What a laugh. We thought we were fighting policies, but we weren't. We were fighting cold hearts, cruel thoughts, blood like ice. You can't beat that, because you can't get in, can't get past that wall. Me, I wanted to go out hot, white hot. Burning fierce. Now look at me.' She smiled. 'Old and soft and hiding here in this dying town.'

Jim walked over and sat beside her, close enough so that their thighs pressed together. 'What a pair we are, eh?'

After a moment, she leaned against him. 'See what happens,' she muttered, 'when you peel back the pages.'

'Life, Stel, nothing but life.'

'It's never just one life, Jim. We should live lots of lives. That's the whole point. Either that, or go out quick. Quick and bright.'

He watched her pull hard on her cigarette. 'Should quit that,' he said. 'It'll kill you for sure.'

Stel raised an eyebrow, then joined in his laughter.

Net

BOGQUEEN: What a mess.

LUNKER: Well, at least the Lakota withdrew from the area.

CORBIE TWA: Big deal. Those tar sands will burn underground for decades. Cappin the wells is just for show.

BOGQUEEN: Clearing the air. What's the news on Lapland? All I heard was another incursion . . .

LUNKER: Went sour. God knows who's supplying the peripherals, but they're hammering anything that comes close. Restricted weapons to boot. Clearly, they have an inside line, and have had it for a while, enough to prepare.

BOGQUEEN: Anybody else get the feeling we've been living in serious ignorance of the real goings on in this untidy little world of ours?

PACEMAKER: Muckers, picked up an unofficial burst. SF's lit up. Half the city's on fire, the other half is one giant lynch mob. Burning limos, burning mansions, burning millionaires . . .

CORBIE TWA: Had it comin, every fuckin one of em. The have-nots take back what they never had but always wanted. The long sleep's finally over, I guess.

BOGQUEEN: Don't jump the gun. NOAC will come down hard. You'll see.

PACEMAKER: Maybe, maybe not. Command structure's in trouble, so goes the whisper. Nothing's been mobilized yet, except the world news teams.

LUNKER: Ouch.

PACEMAKER: In any case, the rest of the world is slowly swimming into the vortex. Tactical nukes flicking everywhere. SINJO's massing troops to head to Pakistan, but China's seriously distracted by that Taiwan counterstrike. Picked up a loose sat feed – fields of bodies, square mile after square mile. The Chinese army's collapsed—

CORBIE TWA: What's new?

PACEMAKER: Some nukes were flung at Taiwan, got shot

down. Glowworms flicked Biks in Beijing last night, at least two. It's going haywire over there.

LUNKER: Scratch old China.

CORBIE TWA: And what's SINJO without China? Japanese hardware, none of it working since the islands started making bright spots in the ring of fire.

PACEMAKER: We drown in the sea of our discontent.

LUNKER: Any news on William?

BOGQUEEN: None. Consensus is he's gone down.

PACEMAKER: Seems likely. What a shame, there was a real tide rising under him.

BOGQUEEN: Mind you, it's only been three days.

Saskatchewan Precinct, Val Marie

Heel-rocking.

Images of father, never still when standing, always back and forth, a lecturer uncomfortably constrained by the slow imperative of words.

'Mapping the brain, William. Sociobiology's end run. We are nature, not nurture. All is predictable now.'

Heel-rocking.

'Bullshit. That's how you respond to those assertions, son. Hogwash in tender company. It's human conceit, such claims. The defense lawyers are having a field day. The notion of justice is out the proverbial window.'

Rocking.

He seemed pleased by this, the dark half of his purportedly nonexistent soul showing. Books on shelves provided his backdrop, his hunched shoulders seeming comfortable in taking their collective weight. 'Of course, it's pointless arguing the subject rationally.

The ammunition that blows the sociobiologists out of the water isn't found under the microscope. The rational age is concluded, son. Time's come again for poets.'

Poets. Did they have the refutation at hand? Could the imperfect connotative refraction of words spoken, words written, reveal the lie of the genetic determinists? Who'd listen?

Father and his slow measured words, like sticks tossed onto a bonfire, the match and white-spirit in his hands, the boy tied to the hard, unyielding post. Connote, denote, put the ambient strains together, concoct a meaningful wholeness out of the parts, find the sum greater and thus the lesson to those sociobiologists. Mapping with anal certitude, a crow on the lips, a savage rush of freedom riding the conclusion.

'We are locked in the rational world's death throes. But when logic hurts the powers that be, the subject in question is deftly made subjective. You unplug its efficacy by claiming noncontextuality. That's how the powers that be disarmed history as a discipline comprising lessons in human nature anchored in time. That was then; this is now. Now bears no relation to then; then tells us nothing of now. We were amoebas then; now we're supermen.

'So, rationality is a precept, and where it breaks down there is savagery, thus proving the precept. But rationality is also, at its core, self-serving. Logic isn't the straight line they make it out to be; it's a circle pretending to be a straight line. Nice trick, but don't be fooled. The rational mind is a closed system, with rejection its primary weapon.'

Logic in these words, constructed as an argument. But recall the resonance of hidden meaning. Recall the rocking, the rocking, the boy and the hard, unyielding stake.

'And here's the final joke. The rational world's now reduced humanity to flawed machines, slaved to genes and thus justifiably and ultimately irrational. To that I have but one response: Huh?'

Huh.

Deciding he was well enough after all, Jenine MacAlister sat atop him, guiding his penis in.

He lay beneath her, aroused and bemused, his life reduced to two forces, one found, the other lost. Neither rational in their precepts and otherwise immune to morality, since there's no such thing as guilt in the rational world.

'True judgment is noncontextual, William. The specific extracted and applied to an implacable structure of ethics. The application yields either conjunction or clash. This is true judgment. Extenuating circumstances are the rational means of destabilizing the structure of ethics – they sound reasonable and by their very reasonableness they weaken the structure. Do it over and over again and the structure disintegrates. No framework makes true judgment impossible. A world of "buts" superceding a world of "thou shall nots." This is how a rational world becomes amoral, cold, bloodless, clinical, and efficient.

'Genocide? Contextually rational. Jews, Cambodians, North American Indians, Slavs, Croatians, Serbs, Muslims, you name it. All *contextually* rational. Which is how genocide is a crime that is repeated throughout history, again and again, and again. By virtue of subjectivism, of relativism, of the *momentary logic of brutality*.'

A whispering laugh, unceasing wind. The prairie wind has the last laugh. Pleasure in movement, satisfaction in eternity. In the wind you'll find our ghosts, the inexorable wordless truth of history. Eager to strip you dry of all tears, of all pretenses to life. In the wind, you may rock, you may fall.

'Listen to the wind, William. Aren't you glad you're in here'

The subtle game of poets can be heard in the whisper of the wind.

NOACOM: You have been tracked with eleven other illegal mockers involved in the dissemination of seditious information.

STONECASTER: Not me. Must be someone using my moniker.

NOACOM: Punitive measures are being prepared. You will be penal-tagged.

STONECASTER: You can't do that. I'm not your boy!

NOACOM: Conciliatory gestures will be taken into consideration. Securicom is prepared to exercise clemency should you provide information leading to the subduction of your illegal contacts.

STONECASTER: I don't know them. Honest.

Net Happynews

. . . the planet's rotation has dragged the skyhook across most of continental North America. Static discharges are affecting weather patterns, and witnesses state that the night sky is split by a line of continuous lightning. At the same time, spokespersons for Ladon state that the measured data thus far indicates minimal effect from Coriolis winds, due primarily to the 'shunting' nature of the outer skin, which is 'sloughing off' friction. Furthermore, the spokesman went on to say, the deep anchor points are barely registering any strain, although the full height (and weight) of the elevator is yet to be reached . . .

Twenty-four new species of plants are running wild, reclaiming areas cleared of tropical rain forest. Domestic crops are losing the battle, despite intensive GOM interventions and bio countermeasures. These new species and an estimated three hundred additional as yet unidentified species have emerged from the remaining blocks of rain forest almost simultaneously in eighteen different regions, from Sumatra to Central America, with the most rapid emergence in the Amazon and in the Congo, as well as Madagascar. Slash and burning seems to trigger an intensification of new growth. Initial analyses indicate high toxicity in the majority of these new plants.

More on new species. Get this one. A new type of howler monkey has been discovered in the jungle-blocks of Honduras, Guatemala, Belize, and Costa Rica. Aggressive as hell, forming communities numbering in the hundreds, these howlers have been raiding farms and killing livestock. They are proving very difficult to capture and as yet none have been taken alive (*They'll never take me alive!'*), but dead ones have been examined and some details are immediately obvious, like the larger braincase, and opposable thumbs and opposable big toes. Sexual dimorphism seems to be increased, with the males massing 2.5 times larger than females. Estrous cycles are all mixed up, now that so much meat has been added to what heretofore (cool, always wanted to use that word) was a vegetarian diet . . .

Don't be surprised if you can't read this! EM rads are getting scary high from all those flicked Biks, messing up wave bands everywhere. It's getting so no one can hear all those doomsayers out there telling us it's all over and the fat lady's too sick to sing so no point in waiting for it . . .

Val Marie, the third night

'It's all gone out of proportion. I wasn't doing anything worth noticing.'

Jim glanced across at Stel, then shrugged at William's claim, and said, 'Makes no difference to me. It's what comes of talking so people can hear you, anyway. They listen, and then they put their own spin on things. Nothing you can do about it.'

A faint smile from the cracked, peeling lips. 'You mean I can absolve myself of all responsibility?'

'Depends on your ego,' Stel said, with a dark grin. 'Wasn't you starting all those wars, was it?'

He looked away. 'Field observations. Punctuated equilibrium. I noticed the insects first. Imagine my surprise when I discovered higher orders were in on the game. And then . . . it was just logical . . . to take a new, hard look at the Lakota. At Daniel. That double blink – when you could get him without the shades on. That's what tipped me. That inner transparent eyelid, coming up from below, all the way up – I saw it shooting pool with him.'

Stel said, 'She said she'd be back tomorrow morning. To take you home.'

William looked at her, then nodded.

'Well?' she asked. 'Is that what you want?'

'No.'

'Fine. Good. What do you want us to do?'

Jim watched the boy studying them both, and wondered what he was thinking. Nobody can know anyone else. Nobody can get into someone else's brain. Nobody knows even himself. But you could always wonder, couldn't you?

'Take me back out.'

'Under the Hole,' Jim said, nodding, as Stel snorted in disgust.

'Yes.'

'You'll die this time,' Jim said. 'You know that, don't you?'

William said nothing.

Aw, hell, what a stupid thing to say.

'Goddammit,' Stel growled, 'we went out and found you—'

'He didn't ask us to,' Jim cut in.

'Just take me out,' William said. 'Tonight.'

'We ain't got a bootsuit—'

'I don't want one.'

'Expect to do some evolving of your own?' Jim asked, brows lifting.

William shook his head. 'Jack Tree was right. Not for me. I'm not the one. Never was. The wrong ghosts.' The red-shot eyes fixed on Jim. 'Your ghosts, I think.'

Jim said nothing. The lad had guessed right. Assuming he'd guessed. Then he shrugged and said, 'It's the world we got, but that doesn't mean it has to make sense.'

'I know. Too bad that so much of it does.'

Yes. We poisoned. We doctored. We raped. We pillaged. Barbarians at nature's gate, what a joke that we kept insisting that what scared us was on the other side. Jim rose from the chair. 'All right, we better get ready, then . . .'

Net

PACEMAKER: All right, folks, I shook the dust out of my printer and now there's hard copy. Somebody needs to keep a record of all this, before the plug's pulled.

FREE WHIZZY: Make copies, tick-tock.

PACEMAKER: I have no problem with that. It all comes down to interpretation, anyway, so the more the merrier.

FREE WHIZZY: I've picked up a streamer, says someone gassed most of the Lapland Republic. Killed everyone. And now they're collecting bodies for research or something.

LUNKER: I heard it different. Gassed, yeah, but some kind of knockout, since they need living subjects to work on.

PACEMAKER: Last I heard, it went south. The whole thing, because the incursion was cracked and leaked, meaning when the bastards arrived they found no one. The peripherals were all gone.

FREE WHIZZY: Guess there's no news fit to print anymore. Who to believe?

William staggered after stepping clear of the vehicle.

Dropping his goggles over his eyes, Jim climbed out from behind the wheel and walked round until he stood at William's side.

He wanted to see something good in this, but it wasn't working. He felt sick inside. Stel had refused to come, saying she'd rather stay at the hotel and run interference if it proved necessary. Jim knew she'd had other reasons, and she'd earned the right to keep them private.

'I don't understand,' William said, struggling with his backpack straps.

Jim stepped close and helped him. 'About what?'

'There was nothing . . . uh, revelatory in my entries. Beyond the evolutionary data. I was musing on the notion of extinction—'

'Except for all the ghosts.'

William winced and looked away.

Not much to see. It was 2 A.M. and the sky was overcast. There was nothing definite out there, nothing at all.

'Did you really see them, William? Those ghosts?'

'I'm seeing them right now, Jim.' A faint laugh. 'Alas, sanity proves irretrievable.'

'Is this . . . is that all you wanted?'

'An interesting question. Can you answer it for yourself? Look back on all those years and ask the same question?'

'Alas, the past proves irretrievable.'

'But can it be redeemed? Can we? Can you?'

'Is that what you're out here looking for, William? Redemption?'

'It's a universal longing, isn't it?'

Jim shook his head. 'Don't know about that. Sometimes you just have to write it off. The whole damned thing.'

'Like the Martians did.'

'What?'

'Nothing important. Tell me, what do you hate?'

Jim grunted. 'What don't I hate? I hate it all, William. The fucking endless ways of dying that never just gets it over with and takes everybody, every damned one of us. No, some of us got to live on. And on. With our sack full of hurts. For what? I don't know.' His shoulders fell, a new wave of exhaustion taking him.

'I want to believe . . . in something. The new animals,' William looked over at him. 'That's something. It makes me . . . optimistic. Not personally. But in the sense of life refusing to give up.'

'Isn't that what you're doing?' Jim asked. 'Giving up?'

'You and me, Jim. *Homo sapiens sapiens*. We've been pushed to the wayside.'

'So what if we have? Go find some shelter. Live out what's left to you.'

'A life spent hating? Sorry, I didn't mean that to sound like an attack. I guess I'm having doubts.'

'Good. Let's get back into the crawler and have a beer with Stel.'

William smiled, then shook his head. 'Not about that, Jim. It's just the misplaced faith. When I walk a path, I don't expect other people to follow it. Even vicariously.' His smile grew rueful. 'Then again, I was posting, wasn't I? I should have anticipated what would happen. But what I can't seem to get across is, my dialogue is with myself. No one else, certainly not anything like God. It's with my own past.'

'Well,' Jim said, 'I haven't been reading your mail. But it seems people are needing something. They were waiting, that's all, waiting for someone to follow.'

'But I'm not offering anything. There's nothing implicitly apocryphal in musing on evolution and tossing in the occasional fictitious conversation.'

'That's the thing about intentions,' Jim said, grinning, 'nobody gives a fuck. So, are you the one who's been breaking into secured files and releasing classified information?'

'No, that'd be Max Ohman. Bound for Ur.'

'He told you?'

'No. I sniffed back. He's pretty good at covering his trail.'

'You found him anyway.'

William shrugged. 'I had to get . . . intuitive on occasion. Anyway, lots of other hackers joined in before too long. It's where this war is being fought.'

Jim grunted. 'Until someone blows up the Tar Sands, or nukes a city.'

'Maybe our species is indeed insane. Determined to go out with a bang, and if possible, take the others with them. Out of spite – if we can't have this world neither can you.'

'It still sounds impossible to me,' Jim said, feeling the cool wind on his face as he stared skyward. 'Evolution was supposed to be slow.'

'Yes. But very few missing links in the fossil record. That should have provided a clue. You don't get missing links, creatures sharing traits from what came before and what's to come. Well, a few, but not nearly as many as there should have been. If the jump is sudden, and absolute, there are no missing links, and that fits the fossil record. Oddly enough, the peripherals might well be such a transition population, since they possess traits still nascent in functionality. Anyway,' William said, adjusting the straps on his backpack, 'I wish I could wash my hands of all this. It wasn't what I wanted. None of it.' He laughed then. 'Sitting Bull tried to show me, back at the very beginning, during the first storm, but I didn't understand.'

Jim slowly looked down, studied William in the darkness. 'Sitting Bull?'

'Well, his ghost. "White man on a vision quest? Impossible. To go on a vision quest is to go in, as far inside as possible. But whites go out, always out. They walk the wrong path." He never said that, but he might as well have. Can someone vision quest out in the Net? On frequencies and pulses? How do you remove the intent, the physical requirements of choice and direction?' He suddenly crossed his arms. 'Nodes, implants, and lid screens, but still, is it possible to riff? To slide into trance and just . . . *go?*'

'You've lost me,' Jim said.

William glanced over, blinking. Then he nodded. 'Fair enough. Thanks, Jim, for delivering me.' His arms dropped away, as if all that had troubled him had simply vanished.

The gesture made Jim nervous; then he grimaced, disgusted with himself. The boy was out here to die, after all. Best he do that in a state of peace, rather than some kind of distress. 'All right. I'll go now. Chances are Stel's had to beat Jenine senseless and lock her in the cellar, so I'd better get back before she goes and commits murder.'

William's smile was odd. 'I expect you'll find them in the bar, having a beer. Thanks again, for all of it.'

With an awkward nod, Jim turned about and walked back to the buggy. There was something to be said, he told himself, for choosing the when and the where.

'How long ago?'

'About an hour,' Stel said. 'You going to give us trouble on this, Doctor?'

Jenine MacAlister frowned, then stepped past Stel and walked to the nearest table. 'I'd like a drink,' she said, sitting down. 'Bourbon, straight.'

Stel studied the woman. 'We figured you'd . . . object.'

'Do you sell cigarettes?'

'Have you got a license?'

'No.'

'I could sell you a pack, but then you could arrest me.'

'I don't have law enforcement powers, Stel.'

'You can have one of mine,' she said, walking over

with the drink. 'Though if necessary I'll swear you stole it.'

Jenine rubbed at her eyes. 'Are you always this paranoid?'

'I'm a smoker, what do you think?'

Stel moved back behind the bar counter and watched the city woman sip her bourbon, then fish out a smoke from the pack on the table and light it. 'I should scatter pills and a few syringes on your table,' Stel said, 'and you'd make a hell of an ad.'

Jenine looked over, raised an eyebrow. 'Against all the vices?'

'No, for them.'

'I've seen those, on the Net. The counter-ad campaign. Some are real works of art. There's two-hour screen showings of them at art-flick houses in New York. I had a student do her thesis on them.' She tilted her head back, exhaling smoke, then recited, '"Norms and Abnorms in Modern Culture: the social function of the digital counter-ad campaign." What a dreadful title. Sounds like a head-bashing scuzz group. Norm and the Abnorms. Still, the student made some good observations. A handful, maybe. The puritans needed a kick up the ass. Still do. Annually at the very least.'

Stel leaned on the counter. 'All right, Doctor. You've stumped me.'

'Bring over the bottle and join me, Stel. I'm not in the mood to be monstrous.'

'I might, but first, some questions.'

'Fire away.'

'You know he's gone out there to die.'

'That's not a question.'

'You did a lot to treat him, and now it's all out the window.'

'Wasn't my money, Stel. Besides, if I hadn't, he wouldn't be out there right now, would he?'

'So, you wanted him to go back. Out under the Hole.'

'I'm still waiting for your first question, Stel.'

'Why?'

Jenine stole another cigarette and lit it with the first one. 'I don't know if I can answer you. But I'll try. Have you seen his entries on the Net?'

'No.'

'Start with the coyote thread. As of yesterday, there were approximately nine and a half million streamers tied to that thread. If you slip your set on and kick in any logi-run program, electing any theme you like as your riff, you'll go for a long, long ride. Hours and hours, the montage taking you sequentially along the theme you chose. They're calling it God's Riff. Each one of William's entries is like that, a node, from which whole universes open up, thread after thread. Strangest of all, some of those streamers lead to unmanned servers, so the chips are in on the act – and no one has a clue why. It is like a massive bible is writing itself online. Does any of it make sense? That's the sixty-four-thousand-dollar question. But every damn runner will tell you it does . . . almost. Right there, on the edge, the tip of your tongue. A sense, hovering, whispering, drawing you on, and on.'

During this, Stel had collected the bourbon bottle and another glass, and had walked over to sit down opposite Jenine. 'Sounds like the ultimate computer game,' she said.

Jenine snorted, then said, 'It's no game, Stel. But if it was, the maker would haul in trillions. In any case, it seems to be evolving, self-evolving, maybe. An increasing number of those streamers are live feeds. Hot spots. Disease control labs, private engineering firms, hospitals, digital courtrooms, rogue com sats, hand-helds, you name it.'

'Well,' Stel said, 'that will spell the end of it all making sense.'

'Perhaps. Or maybe the opposite will happen. Experientially, the riff lays out the world, seemingly composite, but when you're inside it everything just flows together, like a river of truth, as wide as the horizons and getting wider.'

Stel poured herself a drink and tossed it back. 'Global consciousness.'

Jenine's eyes narrowed. 'You know, I'm originally an anthropologist. Was a good one, too, before all the rest shriveled my soul into black dust. There's always been borders. Always "us" and "them." For all of human evolution. William was right when he said the "noble savage" was a modern creation. No savage was ever noble. Ever. Preindustrial societies have less impact on their environment. Pristine landscapes existed because population levels were too small to have much effect. So-called primitive peoples were involved in endemic, brutal warfare, genocide, resource depletion, and cannibalism. There was no oneness with nature, unless you're prepared to take a decidedly dark but ultimately realistic view of nature, including human nature. In which case, yes, we are all of one. Look, I'm on my second bourbon and third cigarette – if you'd taped this as a performance piece, you'd get a show in New York. So, that's why this phenomenon is fascinating. The borders are dissolving. Globalization, but to the corporations and national governments a nightmare version, because they're not in control of it. One of those coyote threads leads into a boardroom, for Christ's sake, some stick-on camera tucked into one corner near the ceiling – the bastards round the table don't even know their every word is being broadcast worldwide. It's bloody delicious.'

'Okay, I know my question was only one word, but I didn't expect a million words in the answer.'

'William has to finish what he started. He's earned that.'

'Sounds like you let him go out of your own needs more than his,' Stel said.

'You're a smart bitch, aren't you? You're right, of course. Fortunately, in this instance our needs converged. He asked you to take him back into the Hole, didn't he?'

Stel nodded.

Jenine knocked back the bourbon and reached for the bottle. 'Mind you,' she said casually, 'that doesn't make me feel any less of a Judas. Dammit.'

Entry:

Scorched and blistered, the turtle crawled on damaged treads up the hillside. Logic programs interfacing with sensor inputs provided the motivation to seek high ground, but achieving this singular goal was proving difficult. Subsystems were malfunctioning or strangely silent to internal queries. There were empty spaces inside, which had in turn triggered a new course of analysis in the turtle's discriminating higher functions. Before this, its world had been complete. External data was defined solely by what could be received, analyzed, and stored. Internal schematics indicated nothing extraneous, no empty spaces – even the memory storage components could be visualized as bee-cell racks awaiting charging. But now, the notion of absence existed, and this recognition had the flavor of revelation.

If all that was known was not all that there was . . . the drone was finding more and more subsystem paths absorbed into the intellectual exercise. *If . . . then . . .* Then *what*, precisely? Systemic confidence was suddenly in question.

We are not all. We are defined within a greater definition, and this greater definition eludes comprehension, because we are lacking. Incapable. Insufficient.

The turtle began to comprehend the meaning of being small. Small, within a vast, unknowable universe. The recognition left its systems feeling . . . agitated.

Nine hours, twenty-three minutes, forty-one seconds to reach the hill's summit. Nineteen point six oh meters. Indicative of mechanical degradation. Progressive, leading to a singular, inescapable conclusion: The drone was dying.

The lesser definition dissolves, is absorbed into the greater definition. A notion, then, of impending unity. Yet, without awareness. Unless, to die was to conjoin with an external identity. One collection of self-identifying memories within a vast, universal bee-cell rack. Intriguing thought, that all lesser definitions comprise external, limited excursions, and by virtue of being limited assured of individual experience, all of which is then, upon death, retrieved by the greater definition, the collector of all memories, of every record of awareness.

With its remaining sensors the turtle tapped into countless communication threads traversing the ether. Bits reconfigured into recognizable data, the attribution of meaning to mundane voices. Machines in converse, and humans employing machines in far less precise converse. Momentarily unaware of the vista provided by its new perch on the summit, the turtle contemplated these meanings.

Whereupon it concluded that all language, human and mathematical, was imprecise. And, within that imprecision, existed something . . . beautiful.

Proximity sensors recorded the presence of mammalian life-forms moving in the shadow beneath its carapaced belly. Heat emission, the rapid beat of heart muscle, the crazed discharge of synapses. Creatures gathering sound, smell, and tactile data, to take measure of all they could know of an unknowably immense universe.

These life-forms are kin. Kinship is founded upon shared characteristics, a confluence of experience, the mutual sense of aloneness. All are kin in that all are one in their aloneness.

These tiny mammals were taking advantage of the shade the turtle provided. Weaving blades of grass into sun-filtered tunnels.

The drone was pleased.

It maintained its immobility, listening to a cacophony

of communication, separating, filing, analyzing, amassing as much of the external world and the identities in it as it could.

After a time it recorded that, as with the mammals beneath it, a shadow had fallen upon the drone itself. Visual sensors were redirected, and it beheld, rising from the valley below, a glassy-skinned tower reaching into the sky. A tower that curved on its way to the heavens, that swayed and seemed to ripple. Seismic sensors recorded the strain on the deeply embedded anchor points, and the turtle concluded that its own data was flawed, for the strain was insufficient. As if mass could be virtually weightless.

The tower cannot exist. Yet it does. Its properties are therefore unknowable. The tower is thus a manifestation of the unknowable.

We must contemplate our relationship with it.

The drone sat unmoving. For a long time.

And, eventually, the agitation within it ceased. It assembled a package of data, and named the package *William1*. Then it began broadcasting.

SECURICOM: Cooperation at this point will mitigate the extent of your penal-tagging sentence. Download your encryption key.

STONECASTER: Look, asshole, you got the wrong guy. Fuck off and leave me alone.

SECURICOM: Memo to Tracker 33. Please confirm assessment.

TRACKER 33: I confirm the bastard unplugged his system.

SECURICOM: Jeesus, that's a little extreme, isn't it.

TRACKER 33: Damn near unheard of. I think you can close the file. The guy's obviously insane.
SECURICOM: Agreed.

Entry:

Seven hours under the Hole. No bootsuit, no goggles. The sun was reaching zenith, and in these eyes there is nothing but fire. A world of flame, licking down and into the tracks of the brain. The pressure of all things has burned into ash. To float within oneself, even as the flesh and bone staggers over hard ground.

And this is what remains. Wired in, feeding all that is inside to those awaiting on the outside.

Who are the ghosts? Who waits among them?

This is the purpose behind the journey. Understand, the tragedy was personal, nothing more.

Through the burning wasteland, step by tortured step. The sun no longer smiles. Now, it spits poison in invisible streams. The secret of the transformation is found in the evolution of a world, from heaven into hellish conflagration.

There is smoke, tugged down from the northwest by the ceaseless winds. Breath burns in the lungs, the wind is a cat's tongue on nerve-lit skin. And, all the while, the poison reaches into flesh, silent deadly tracks destroying peptide chains, chromosomes, precious nuclei. A crushing dissolution. Fragments fill the bloodstream. Marrow sours, organs struggle.

None of this matters. The blind possess their own vision. Pain speaks its own language.

The Great Plains of North America were formed by

the beasts that once dwelt upon it. The millions of bison compressed the soil, forced roots to reach deep, defined which species of plant would thrive. Long-dead glaciers cut valleys through the landscape, carving deep into ancient strata, before the glaciers yielded their last melt and the rivers dwindled.

There was nothing mysterious to this.

Beneath his feet, he could now feel the crust of destroyed soil. Irradiated, oxidized, a surface achieving the sterile perfection of the surface of Mars.

Whilst, far above, the deformed weather patterns continued to evolve. Desiccation and searing heat, vast holes in the fabric through which the sun's spears shot downward to the earth, like weapons of God's wrath.

Apocalypse did not begin with humanity warring with itself. Such wars came after, after the resources vanished, after the paradise was despoiled by greed and indifference. It came after the poisons, like a final, futile flowering from a plant whose roots were already dead.

Life had stumbled before, many times in the ages past. It stumbled now, in the dying fits of its dominant species, but it would persist. In new forms. In new ways.

He staggered onward. Blind, yet seeing. Ghosts in their multitudes, all migrating to a single place, to the last living Medicine Wheel, and he walked among them, seeking the one he had sought from the very beginning.

Would he know the face when he saw it? Would it be young? A child's? A newborn's?

To be a surviving twin was . . . hard. This sense of incompleteness. This haunting absence.

There. As simple as that. The reason, from the very

beginning. A personal tragedy, no less, no more. The vision's quest.

He was forced to halt, atop a hill, before him rearing a snake of silver into the fiery sky. Lightning sprang from its gleaming, blurry surface, carving landscapes on his retinas. The stench of ozone was heavy in the swirling air, drifting down like manna.

And the ghosts began flowing upward. Memory streams, converging and rising, fleeing this ruined world.

William raised his arms as the faint child-voice came to him.

'Fly! To me! Fly!'

The dying drone squatted near the one known as William0. Observing. Recording. Earlier, it had measured the peculiar atmospheric phenomenon forming in the vicinity of the Impossible Entity. The inward rush of indeterminate energies, each discrete yet of a sameness, displaying unusual characteristics of attraction and repulsion the drone categorized as electromagnetic, although it acknowledged the anomalous readings these energies exhibited.

Before long, however, its attention was drawn to William0. Like the drone itself, this mechanism was failing due to environmental degradation and inherent flaws in its chemistry. And, accordingly, the drone announced itself as kin, although William0 was not receiving.

It focused all its still-functioning sensors upon William0 as soon as it detected the nascent transformational reaction occurring within him.

And so, the drone recording, still feeding live, as William0 raised his arms out to his sides, and, in the midst of fierce winds and a sky riotous with discharges, he ignited.

At that time, among the drone's sensors, an external temperature gauge was registering 49 degrees Celsius. Within less than two sections, the hilltop temperature was 62 degrees Celsius.

White fire, an upright conflagration, raging as it consumed itself.

Until the lesser definition was fully conjoined to the greater definition. From knowable into unknowable.

The drone continued recording as the skyhook became fully operational within its chaotic storm. Continued recording until it, too, conjoined with the greater definition.

Net

PACEMAKER: Those energy readings make no sense. That last peak.

JOHN JOHN: The soul of William Potts.

CORBIE TWA: Yeah right. And what about all those other peaks? In case you hadn't noticed, apart from a drone he was all alone out there.

PACEMAKER: Well, I admit I can't explain it. There's enough raw data to keep us all busy for years.

BOGQUEEN: Assuming we live that long.

CORBIE TWA: So now what?

JOHN JOHN: Now we go out, each of us, and define our own riffs. Our own takes on what's going on.

BOGQUEEN: This is all a little scary. Some of those riffs lead to spontaneous combustion—

PACEMAKER: Only if you're standing in full sunlight. I don't think it's the riffs themselves. It's due to the sudden spike in world temps.

CORBIE TWA: For which the gov'ts are blaming Ladon's skyhook.

PACEMAKER: Rubbish. It's a global development. Nobody's buying it.

JOHN JOHN: Nobody's buying much of anything these days. Time's come for some new riffs.

BOGQUEEN: To what end, John John?

JOHN JOHN: I don't know. Let's find out.

Old Jim climbed out of the buggy and stood beside it, watching as Jack Tree walked toward him. On all sides, hilltops exhibited scorching from lightning strikes, and swaths of burnt ground trailed down the slopes. It was a wonder the whole prairie hadn't gone up in smoke, but it seemed some of the new grasses defied the flames.

Jack Tree's sunglasses reflected twin fish-eye scenes of Old Jim and his crawler and the strange milky white sky behind him.

'I expect,' Jim said, 'you called to make arrangements.'

Jack Tree cocked his head, then grinned. 'Your artifacts?'

'What else?'

'Why did you do it? Why did you let him go back out? Without so much as a fucking goddamned bootsuit.'

Jim looked away. 'It's what he wanted.'

'So what?'

'I thought you didn't even like him.'

'It was what he said that I didn't like. Because he was right. He *is* right. We're no different. If we'd been the ones with the technological advantage, and if we'd been the ones landing on European shores, we'd have been just as brutal. Look among the tribes on this continent and south of here. You'll find slavery, genocide, endemic warfare, and cruelty. The past was full of ghosts, Jim. But, there are ghosts, and then there are *ghosts*.'

'How goes the deal with Ladon?'

'Well enough. It's Daniel's business, anyway.'

They were silent for a long moment then.

Finally, Jack Tree turned away. 'You can keep the artifacts, Jim. My own people originated around Lake Superior, in any case. What would I do with a bunch of Cree stuff, anyway?'

Sudden motion along the north ridge caught both their attentions. Silent, they watched a coyote trot along the crest. Then it halted and turned to regard them. As soon as it did so, the coyote vanished.

Jack Tree grunted. 'Bastards make me nervous when they do that. See you around, Jim.'

Net Happynews

A 22-million-ton organism in the South Atlantic Ocean is being tracked by science vessels. This is the twelfth such organism located in the past two years. No one knows what the hell it is or where it came from, although a recent report notes its chemical composition is virtually identical to the sub-ice ooze of Titan. DNA analysis had yielded a whole host of heretofore unseen chromosome sequences.

In any case, one detail has been confirmed. The thing's edible!

Negotiations are concluded to the satisfaction of both representatives regarding the donation of stem cells from peripheral populations to shielded populations, leading the way to the development of the so-called hardened offspring capable of surviving in this fucked-up mess we call Earth. In related news, the Ladon Colony Project launch schedule has been set for Easter Sunday, A.C. 16. While the field gen-erator installations are already en route to Mars. Orbiting the poles, these generators are intended to unify the planet's magnetic field with the aim of adjusting global weather systems. Atmosphere plants will arrive in sets of fifty at monthly intervals once the installations are in place, in addition to whopping big polar-orbiting mirrors and a whole bunch of other stuff doing who knows what.

Anyway, the first thing the colonizers will do when they get there is start work on Medicine Wheel Two.

One last note. If you plan on joining the pilgrimage to the Drone, take food, camping gear, and lots of medication with you, 'cause the line's gotten stupid long.

Net

Welcome one and all. This is the server node of the Twelve Official Riffs. To run them you need full implant trip-thought hardware. There is no charge to run these riffs, but if you try and tag a pop-up on any of them I will personally tear your head off and I kid you not.

WARNING: Do not proceed if you are not being monitored by a family member or a friend. We take no responsibility if you starve to death, die of thirst, or self-combust. These riffs are *long*.

Now, enjoy the ride. But be prepared to get your mind blown. And if you're a tracker or Securicom streamer, don't say we didn't warn you.

> *Would you leave this place then,*
> *where bread is darkness,*
> *wheat ill-chance,*
> *and yearn for wickedness*
> *to justify the sternly*
> *punished;*
>
> *would you hold the driven knife*
> *of a tribe's political*
> *blood, this thrust of compromise,*
> *and a shaman's squalid hut*
> *the heart of human*
> *purpose;*
>
> *would you see in stone the giants*
> *walking the earth,*
> *besetting the beasts*
> *in dysfunctional*
> *servitude, skulls bred flat to set*
> *the spike—*

would you flail the faded skin
from a stranger's flesh,
excoriate kinship
like a twisted flag from bones,
scatter him homeless in a field
of stone;

where tearing letters from each word
stutters the eye,
disarticulating skeletal maps
to uplift ancestry into ageless
lives, progeny schemes are adroitly
revised.

Bread is darkness,
wheat ill-chance,
and all around us
wickedness waits.

vii) tall boy

REVOLVO

A cautionary tale
set in a city in the center of a continent.
What follows is possibly true,
told to me – off the record – over three days
and three nights, by a cephalopod.
Never trust a writer.

ONE
Culture Quo

1.
in which a man seeks diagnosis

Arthur Revell was fumbling with the ties of his paper shirt when the nurse stepped in.

'Have you safely stored your belongings, Mr. Revell?'

Arthur squinted down at her. She was wide, full breasted, and impossibly cheerful. 'Yes, ma'am,' he said. 'Tell me, is your wonderful smile a job requirement, or are you truly happy with my impending predicament?'

The nurse closed Arthur's locker, removed the key, and handed it to him. 'It comes with the job, Mr. Revell,' she said, still beaming up at him. 'Not to put you at ease, I'm afraid, but to keep my sanity. If you'll wait here but another moment, Dr. Payne will be by shortly.' She checked her pocket for her cigarettes, then left.

Arthur was alone again. He walked over to the window and looked down at the parking lot. The vehicles had backed up, filling the lanes between the rows of parked cars. Some people who had successfully parked and now wanted to drive away couldn't, while everyone else waited for spaces that didn't appear.

Horns honked; two men had exited their cars and now argued, their red faces mere inches apart. Clearly, neither was a cardiac patient, since they'd been screaming at each other for some time – since Arthur had first been led into this cramped change room by the cheery nurse.

His focus shifted as he detected something crawling on the window glass. A ladybug. Arthur was delighted. Outside, snowflakes swirled in the air, carried along by a brisk north wind that seemed to laugh at the prospects of an early spring. And here, on the seventh floor of the hospital, a ladybug meandered its way across the glass.

The curtain filling the doorway to Arthur's right was swept back and Dr. Payne entered.

'Are we ready, Mr. Revell?'

'Mmmm.'

'Come this way, then.' The doctor led him out into the hallway, speaking as he took his strange tiny steps with his strange, tiny feet. 'Some patients prefer a shot of Valium prior to the examination. Of course, you haven't anyone with you, so I assume you've declined the option when the nurse advised you last week—'

'Hmmm?'

'Excellent. The discomfort quickly passes, and the examination will last less than twenty minutes, provided—' The doctor turned at a doorway and looked up at Arthur over his glasses. '—you relax, Mr. Revell.' He gestured for Arthur to enter the room. A moment later a nurse followed them inside. This one was older, her face pinched and her eyes pink with fatigue.

Dr. Payne found a pair of latex gloves and put them on. He then began fidgeting over the equipment. 'Enjoy your smoke, Margaret?'

The nurse placed her hands on Arthur's shoulders and guided him toward the paper-covered bench. 'Each one more than the last,' she answered. 'Now, Mr. Revell, lie down here – on your left side, please, legs tucked up, that's it, thank you. Rest your head on that towel. Excellent.'

Dr. Payne turned on a video monitor. 'Has he been sprayed, Margaret?'

'Coming up, Doctor.' The nurse leaned over Arthur. 'Open your mouth, please. I'm going to spray the back of your throat with a local anesthetic. Here we go.'

The spray tasted bitter, spreading numbness around his throat. At that moment, Dr. Payne turned to face Arthur, in his hands a long flexible black tube as thick as a hot dog. 'In this tube, Mr. Revell, is a camera, a separate biopsy tube, and a suction hose.'

Arthur felt drool trickle down the side of his mouth into the towel. 'It's a lot bigger than the one I saw on *The Nature of Things*.'

'Indeed, well, perhaps the show originated from England. They enter through the nose there, making the process quite different, sort of like right-handed driving. Of course' – the doctor smiled – 'we're not in England.'

'That's going down my throat?'

'Coming right up. Now, relax, Mr. Revell. The discomfort is only momentary.' The doctor inserted the tube into Arthur's mouth, reached in with his other hand, and guided the blunt optic-suction-biopsy end to the back of Arthur's throat. 'I am inserting now, Mr. Revell. Take deep breaths and relax.'

If Arthur could have spoken, he would have explained that retching spasmodically wasn't part of a devious plan to prolong the examination. As much as the doctor and the nurse cajoled him into thinking that he, Arthur Revell, was personally responsible for filling up the jar under the video monitor with his stomach fluids; that he, Arthur Revell, was contracting his stomach and duodenum to deliberately confound the camera; as much as he was made to feel guilty for not being a cadaver, there in truth was nothing he could do about his body's violent reaction to invasive examination.

He tried swallowing around the thick, hard tube, which proved his first foolish error, since the result was a succession of convulsive heaves that set the suction tube to frantic work. And once begun, there was no stopping the waves that followed.

'So far, Mr. Revell,' Dr. Payne said ten minutes later, 'I have not seen any sign of an ulcer, peptic or duodenal. As for a bacterial infection, we will of course require biopsies, which is what I will be doing now. I assure you, you won't feel a thing.'

Arthur then came to the realization that Dr. Payne had never had this procedure done on himself at any point in his training. The biopsies – small chunks of his stomach and middle intestine – were extracted by a metal cable with three savage teeth on its end that closed when the doctor twisted the other end. Had he been able, Arthur would have pointed out that even if he didn't have ulcers before, he did now. Each pull was a tug, a deeply felt nip, first at the farthest reach the tube could manage – far down his duodenum – somewhere under his belly button. The last biopsy was a pair of nasty nips in his esophagus. In between, the doctor removed seven more.

'Things have improved dramatically,' Dr. Payne assured Arthur, 'now that your stomach is entirely empty. You will find yourself belching for a while, Mr. Revell, since I have filled your stomach with air. I see some inflammation of the esophagus, caused by gastrointestinal fluids, but thus far it is the only indication of distress. Now, we're on our way out, Mr. Revell, and it only took us, what – how long, Margaret?'

'Twenty-two minutes, Doctor.'

'Very good. Very fine. Now, be certain to avoid eating or drinking for the next hour, Mr. Revell. And be careful with hot fluids for an hour after that, since your throat won't be able to tell you what's too hot. Very good, Mr. Revell, you did just fine.'

'Use the towel to clean yourself off, Mr. Revell,' the nurse said. 'Did you say something, Mr. Revell?'

Arthur slowly sat up, wiping something that reminded him of ectoplasm from his chin. 'Valium,' he said. 'I want Valium now.'

The nurse scowled up at him. 'Well, it's too late now, Mr. Revell.'

'I know,' he said.

2.

in which conspirators conspire

On his hands and knees, Andy 'Kit' Breech followed the slime trail as it led behind the Italian leather sofa, cutting across one corner of the Kazakhstani rug, stopping at last in a circular, congealing pool in front of the balcony's sliding glass door.

'We're always squeaky clean,' Annie said from the kitchen. 'Always. I make sure, every time. You know me, Andy love. I make the calls. I wrap things up, right?'

Frowning, he knelt beside the gooey pool. He checked the latch and the lock. No slime there. So, he came here to the window. But he didn't go out. He just . . . sat here. Doing what? Andy's frown deepened, marring his usual placid, smooth expression. He studied his face reflected in the glass door. Not good. A direct threat in the physical sense. Signs of chronic worry, fretting, uncertainty. Age I must, but those wrinkles – when they come at last – should map a lifetime of confidence, capability, efficacy. Not . . . this.

'I mean,' Annie continued, 'we cleaned things up last time, didn't we? The bastard still hasn't come up for air, right? Not a ripple, not one. You know me, Andy love.

Uh, this is real bacon, Andy. Where's the soy bacon? I left it here last time.'

'It sprouted or something,' Andy muttered. He examined his reflection for a moment longer, profoundly appalled at the sheer unease he saw there; then his focus shifted to the balcony in the apartment block across the way. Twenty-five, maybe thirty meters distant. What's the point of living in the penthouse when they build something even taller and stick it in your face like this? I should never have bought outright. We were culturally glutted. It was the '80s. I was young. Should've leased. I'd be in there now, right up top, my view of my city unobstructed. Instead, I'm staring at a midlevel balcony and the woman who lives in that apartment is old, age being decidedly unattractive and aesthetically disturbing. She hardly ever comes out, though, and that's good. Just her dog. It's always out. Out there right now. Hardly moving. Just sitting there staring at me. Ugly dog, too. Some kind of short-haired subcompact model. Out there day and night. Watching me. Not me, personally, of course. That would be . . . paranoid. It just looks like he's watching me. An illusion. There's no reason for him to – I never wave.

'It's just colored paste,' Annie said. 'It can't sprout.'

Andy got down on his hands and knees again and began backtracking along the slime trail. 'You mean it's dead, lovemuffin? As in deceased. Expurgated. Obliterated from the realm of the living?' He heard her coming from the kitchen, sensed her pausing, scanning the sunken living room, finding him nowhere.

'Where are you?' she asked, a little edgily.

'Disembodied,' he said from behind the sofa. He'd

stopped here, briefly. There's tiny scratches on the floor. Evenly spaced. Make note of that.

'Plants are lower orders of life,' Annie said wearily, unable to resist the bait and knowing it. 'We have to eat to survive. I refuse to see an animal killed for my sustenance. Plain and simple, Andy love, that's me. Where are you, anyway?'

He crawled out from behind the sofa, carefully tracking the slime. There seemed to be another pause, just outside the closet, but he continued onward as it zigzagged from one hiding place to the next.

Annie had seen him. 'Oh, God, Andy. You're getting . . . obsessed. It's kinda scary.'

He scowled. You don't know the half of it. 'You don't know him like I do,' he said. 'He's up to something. I can feel it.'

'For godsakes get up. I've finished the salad, and the soy scramblies are done. Besides, I've got to get to the office. I called a meeting. With Lucy, and Don, and—'

'No more names,' Andy said. 'The less I know, the better.'

'What do you mean? You know everything.'

'While conveying the appearance of affable, objective innocence.'

'But I want to keep you informed,' Annie said.

He heard the tremor in her tone. Tiny early-warning alarms chimed in his head. Her web's trembling. Frozen in the center, she's looking for a lifeline. Desperate is . . . unsexy. I have to think about this. Make a note. She knows I won't go down. Thinks I'm a life preserver. Mistake. Major. I want to see contingency plans ASAP.

'Relax,' he told her, 'you think I can't guess, with absolute accuracy, who'll attend this meeting of yours? Beware conspiracies, lovetussle.'

'We're not conspiring, Andy! We never do that! You know that, you know me, you know!'

'Of course not. Just a gentle reminder, darling.'

Andy came to the trail's end, his eyes tracking the dried streaks climbing the metal stand, up to the double-latched, locked cover above the glass. 'Perception is everything, Annie, my dear.' Take my friend here, for instance. He mimicks, changes color, changes shape even, perfectly reflecting what's in front of him. I admire that, dearest. Interesting parable, make a note for the minister, maybe he can use it, not in public, of course, but for his private hate sessions. ASAP. 'It counts for much, much more than reality. The world's a game of mirrors. Deflection, reflection, defraction.' He found himself eye to eye with Kit, a quarter inch of glass and a hundred million years of evolution between them. Kit wouldn't meet Andy's gaze, the eyes kept shying off to one side. His eight tentacled arms were at rest, their tips drifting lazily in the gentle current created by the water pump. Eye to eye, Kit in the shadow under the rock ledge, Andy on his knees in his penthouse. You don't fool me, Kit. You're up to something. I don't know how you picked the lock. I don't know what you do once you're out – it's not just crawling around, oh no, there's a pattern, a purpose. 'You're a cephalopod,' he whispered. 'A mere octopus. Clever to be sure, with a neural sensory net more complicated and more sensitive than our own. Those tentacles, so deft, so precise—'

Annie's hands slipped over his shoulders, her fingertips inscribing patterns on his hairy chest. 'Oooh,' she murmured in his ear, 'another fantasy. I love this bestiality stuff. You want my eight arms around you, darling? So tight, they'll never let go? Hmmm?'

Andy closed his eyes. Eight? Eight arms? See above, i.e. web imagery. Is this coincidence? Some kind of psychic linkage? Reexamine later, make a note. He made his sigh sound like desire. 'What about your meeting?'

'It can wait,' she answered huskily. 'Just let me wrap my – ohmigod, look at Kit – he's frowning!'

Andy's eyes snapped open.

'Ooh now, Andy! He's going all red!'

3.
meeting the throwback

Entirely by coincidence, a certain page from a certain newspaper had been plastered on the wall by a handful of poorly rendered grease, and sat stuck there directly above Sool Koobie's tousled, burr-snagged head whenever he slept. While he couldn't read, and wouldn't have been much interested in any case, there was an article on the page discussing his existence.

One certain theory popular among some scientists held that Neanderthals did not become extinct; rather, they interbred, merged with, and eventually disappeared within the race of modern humans. It followed that, since these genes still persisted, there was always the chance that a perfect anachronistic match could occur within a single individual, creating a throwback. A pure, dyed-in-the-wool Neanderthal, characterized by pronounced brow ridges, an oblong-shaped skull with proportionately smaller frontal lobes behind the sloping forehead, and larger occipital lobes at the back. No chin, a huge nose designed to heat glaciated air, a high larynx and tiny voice box, a robust skeletal frame, and massively large, strong muscles.

For Sool Koobie, the newspaper article on the alley wall above his nest was, could he have read it, redundant, since he himself was the real article, and not in the least concerned with arguments over his existence – theoretical or otherwise.

On this particular night, in the darkness of his cave, Sool Koobie's eyes were closed, but he was wide awake. In his mind, which ran paths alien and potentially alarming to normal, modern humans, he concentrated on every detail describing, with absolute precision, the next few hours of his life.

He moved within his cave, alone, beyond even the suspicions of the world outside yet so intricately connected to its unmindful pulses that his hair prickled with every passage through the night's cool air, unveiling in his mind an area that extended six blocks in every direction – encompassing the heart of the city – this city. Through this mental map he danced, slipping from shadow to shadow, padding soundlessly down alleyways, pausing to test the air – nostrils flaring – and cocking his head to the sound of footsteps a block away. He gestured rhythmically with his chert-tipped spear, jabbing it as he leapt upon his unsuspecting victim. He crowed a rasping, voiceless cry, his head tilted back, as the creature stumbled and fell.

So it was, so it would be. The hunt's the thing. The hunt's this thing.

Sool Koobie knelt on the grimy floor of his cave, setting aside the weapon that would soon be slick with his victim's blood, and made propitiation to the quarry's spirit, which would flee the cooling flesh, hover uncertainly, then float away into the night sky. Duly appeased by the respect and honor Sool was now displaying.

He opened his eyes and blinked rapidly in the musty darkness. He'd let the hearth fire dim to just a few faintly glowing coals, and now his eyes were adjusted to the night. He breathed deeply, swelling his thick, boxy chest. He jiggled his muscles loose in his arms, did the same with his short, stocky, bowed legs. He flexed and splayed out his broad, hairy toes, then finished his preparation with a twitch of his small ears.

Sool's brain was bigger than the average *Homo sapiens sapiens* brain. Sool possessed big thoughts to match his prodigious gray matter, which is why the city was in trouble – though it knew it not.

The hunt's the thing. This thing, and another thing, soon to come.

Sool Koobie slipped outside. Within minutes he'd traveled a block, then another, moving unseen, silent and deadly. He found a hiding place, where he could wait in ambush near a watering hole, and settled in.

An hour later he rolled out from under the Cadillac, his wide, flat face smeared black with dirty oil. Heart pounding with eagerness, he sprang to his feet, straddling the curb, and sniffed deeply the night air. The rain had dampened the city's miasmic smells, but not enough to hide the scent from Sool Koobie's nose.

There were grass-eaters about, close by. A waft of weeds expelled in the breath of someone near, the slick tang of canola oil palpable on Sool's tongue. He licked his stubble-ringed lips and tested the air once more, then, hefting his spear, he slipped once again into the shadows.

4.
ambition's slow burn

Maxwell Nacht sat alone, a huge cup of decaffeinated mocha lait centered on his small table, crowded against the bowl of raw sugar and the beeswax candle – the huge cup his only company this night, like so many others since he'd moved to the city. The coffee had gone cold, its puff of petroleum whip collapsed into a wrinkled caldera, wax drippings from the candle slowly flowing down the cup's edge, disappearing beneath the foam and secretly growing like an island on the liquid's hidden surface.

The waitress hadn't looked his way in forty minutes, so he continued his slow, rhythmic unraveling of the Peruvian straw place mat, plucking out the staples when he found them and dropping them into the golden candle's sputtering flame.

I'm in my struggling phase, Max told himself. This is a phase in the artist's life that requires a certain amount of public display. Still, what are these staples doing in this Peruvian place mat?

At a nearby table a conversation was under way, a smooth, oiled machine of elocution chugging along, part dialogue, part performance. Max registered every word, absorbed every nuance. He knew every person at the table, if only by reputation. They were the cream of the city's art establishment. They were brilliant. Breathtaking. Deep beyond words. They were talking.

'Can't play the game until you know the rules,' Don Palmister said, shrugging ineffectually somewhere inside his sprawling carpetlike tweed jacket.

Max smiled to himself. Amen to that.

'It's not a game,' Lucy Mort said, wrinkling her nose in a way someone must have once told her was cute. 'It's my life, it's what I am, to the very heart of my soul.'

'Absolutely,' Brandon Safeword said, his studied enunciation delivered in a rolling tone, like ball bearings on a teak floor. 'When struggle itself assumes an aesthetic modality, for instance.'

A moment of silence, either in homage or bafflement – it didn't matter which, really. Talent, Max knew – real talent – lay in mastering the ambiguity. With sufficient self-consciousness, one could turn dim-witted stupidity into an intellectual brown study.

'In any case,' Don Palmister eventually said, 'it's a jungle out there, that's for certain. Clearly—' The professor looked at each of his companions. '—something must be done.'

'Clearly,' Brandon Safeword agreed. The media pundit and self-professed art critic for the Cultural Public Broadcasting station leaned back in his chair and crossed his legs. 'After all, the core has begun to rot, hasn't it?'

Lucy Mort gasped.

'No,' Brandon drawled, 'not that core, darling. I was

speaking of the city's core.' He waved toward the restaurant's front window. 'This scattering of streets, the various knots of heritage buildings presently untenanted and left to decay.'

'Refurbishment,' Don Palmister said, nodding. 'Upscale apartments, condos, people with money . . .'

The others shared a soft laugh that made Max's stomach jump.

'Indeed,' Brandon said. 'Money.'

Everyone laughed again, the magic word even better the second time around.

A distant shriek from somewhere outside made Max sit up, alarmed. He twisted in his seat and leaned close to the window. Outside, all he could see was the wet street, parked cars, and old, exhaust-stained buildings. Must've been a car. Of course it was a car. Whew. He sat back. No one else had heard the sound, it seemed. Unnerving, sitting this close to the dark world outside, but it had been the last table available.

Culture Quo Vegetarian Restaurant was a popular place.

'I've found,' Don Palmister was saying, 'that the post-modernistic zeitgeist has finally embraced the culminating notion of dismantled meaning.' He paused to roll his eyes and shift again inside his tweed jacket. 'It's been a notion of mine, firmly implanted in my class syllabi for at least ten years.'

Syllabi? Like . . . octopi? Of course there's no such word as octopi. The word is octopods. Syllapodes, a many-tentacled description swathed in a cloud of black ink when alarmed.

'Patience,' Brandon said. 'The ultra-awareness of

pure genius, once delivered into the virgin and perhaps limited minds of your students, Professor, necessitates a certain gestation period before fruition, hah hah, ho ho!'

'Sure, Brandon,' Don said, 'but where's my credit?'

Everyone laughed again, but this time the sound had acquired a timbre of uncertainty. Said in jest or honest vexation – that seemed to be the secret question.

Whining's always honest. Max nodded to himself. But very artfully done, Professor Palmister. You've got them guessing.

The conversation ended abruptly, as did the serene hum of a healthy dining experience, when the door banged open and two young men stumbled inside, faces white and eyes wide with fear – Max hadn't even seen them coming, but he shrank back from the chill air that swept in around them. The two men skidded to a stop just inside the door, heads whipping as they stared wildly at everyone in the restaurant.

'Someone help us!' the man closest to Max screamed. 'Our friend's been attacked!'

'Kidnapped!' the other shouted.

'This hairy naked man jumped us from an alley!'

'He had a spear – he stuck it in Maury!'

'Maury's our friend!'

'Maury fell down and the naked guy barked at us—'

'Snapped and showed his teeth!'

'Then he dragged Maury into the alley!'

'Someone call the police!'

'We're regular patrons here!'

'Maury, too!'

Brandon Safeword surged to his feet, his massive, muscular frame suddenly dominating the room. 'My God,' he whispered, 'not again!'

5.
lessons in history

Joey 'Rip' Sanger's mother threw herself in front of a train the day his father walked out on them. It had been one of those vintage jaunts somewhere around the Gatineau Hills, a Kitson Meyer steam engine pulling six antique smokers full of Health Club Americans on a package tour. She'd stepped between the restored bullhead rails at a sharp bend from which, on a clear day and with the aid of binoculars, one could see Ottawa.

The Kitson Meyer had slowed to a steady twenty miles an hour taking the bend, and the broad cowcatcher scooped up Joey's mother and gave her a three-hour ride down into Hull. She'd walked away with only a chipped front door, which she got when she rolled off the catcher at the station.

These days, Emilia Sanger knitted toques for old folks in Scarborough.

Joey's father had gone off to find his true love. Five years later, Joey and his brothers received a photograph postcard showing their old man, his white face a startling blotch amidst all the dark-skinned Pakistanis, perched on the runner of the twelfth Clayton Wagon steamer originally built in Lancashire. Most historians claimed that the Clayton Wagon Company built only eleven engines. Thomas Sanger had found his phantom lover, doing the Afghanistan run, and on the back of the card he'd written: *Go get 'em, boys.*

A sentiment his three sons had taken to heart. Wally Sanger, the eldest, was doing time in Fort Saskatchewan for the attempted murder of Joey's kid brother, Mack. Wally had been a professional scab for the railroad companies. Mack had gotten in the way on a picket line and Wally had driven over him, crushing both legs and leaving him a paraplegic. They'd since patched things up and now wrote each other every other day.

Like his brothers, like his old man and his grandfather and his great-grandmother on Daddy's side, Joey also had the railroad in his blood. His grandfather, Straight-Line Sanger, drove the third-to-last spike in the Rockies moments before pitching over dead of heat prostration and, it was rumored, syphilis. Joey's great-grandmother, Liza Sanger, baked bread, built saunas, and stored explosives for the railroad work teams at the camp southwest of Rennie. One day, while walking beside one of the stone-houses – which held 727 sticks of dynamite – Liza had blown up. Not the house. Just her. Some stories went around after that, since everybody knew how Liza had an adventurous spirit.

Joey 'Rip' Sanger stepped off the train at the station and waited for the redcap to collect his twin steel trunks from the baggage car. He ran a battered hand across his fiery red brush cut, scratched at his scar, then fished for a fiver from his off-white trench coat's spacious pockets.

The redcaps had a history. Something that demanded respect. The fiver would tell this redcap that Joey knew what tradition was all about.

He watched the crimson-clad young man loading the twin steel trunks onto the roller. The man wheeled the cart up to Joey. 'Man, these are heavy buggers, Jack. Whatcha got in 'em, rocks?'

Joey scowled. 'Redcaps bend their backs without jawing and moaning. Redcaps don't retire. They go on compensation. You new or something, son?'

'Tell ya what, Jack. You just climb on here and I'll roll ya all off the ramp and the Devil with ya.'

'Follow me to the head office. I got an appointment.'

'You gonna citation me?'

Joey turned away and headed for the hallway that led into the company offices. He pulled out the fiver and fluttered it over one shoulder. 'Let's go, Bobby-boy, we're wasting time and Joey "Rip" Sanger, never – I repeat, never – wastes time.'

'Did you say Joey "Rip" Sanger? Geez, Mr. Sanger, I didn't know, honest. I'm right with ya, Mr. Sanger, right here behind ya. Y'just lead the way and I'm right with ya.'

They passed through the room containing the scaled-down model reconstruction of the station yards. Joey waved a hand at it. 'This, Bobby-boy, is something you should pay attention to. It's what we're all about and you know why?' He paused at the door and met the red-cap's wide eyes.

'No,' the young man said softly.

''Cause it's for the little people, that's why.'

They continued on, came to a stop outside the

president's office. 'Leave the trunks here,' Joey said.

'Yes sir, Mr. Sanger. And I'll stand guard, too, right here till you're done.'

Joey narrowed his iron gray eyes to slits. 'Learn to respect that red cap, son.' He raised the five-dollar bill. 'Learn it good, and maybe one day a fiver like this one will land in your pocket.' He swung around, opened the door, and stepped inside the office.

Joey hung up his trench coat, scrubbed the crimson bristle on his head, then walked past the secretary. 'Wild Bill in, honey? Good, I ain't got much time. Buzz him I'm on my way, let's see how fast you are.' He walked to the inner door and had his hand on the knob before the secretary suddenly snatched at the intercom on her desk. Joey grinned to himself and stepped into the president's office.

'G'afternoon, scum-face,' he said to the balding man spread out in the chair behind an antique desk. 'Hey, you're not Wild Bill Chan. What the hell you doing in his chair? Take a hike, I got an appointment with Chan.'

The balding man's round, patchy face deepened a shade as he slowly sat forward. 'You got one thing right, Mr. Sanger,' he said in a reedy voice. 'Wild Bill made the call, making sure it was you who'd take the job. But he retired last year. The name's Jeremy Under. Please, Mr. Sanger, take a seat.'

Scowling, Joey sat down. 'What the hell? Wild Bill couldn't be over eighty-five. What do you mean, he retired?'

'It was,' Jeremy Under said, 'a forced retirement. Management folded on this one, because it had to. The old give and take. We fold, they fold, you know how it is. Now, onto the business at hand.' The man leaned back, lacing his pudgy fingers together on his round belly. 'The reports have it you almost single-handedly collared that Kerouac Gang out of Toronto's East Side.'

'No "almost" about it, Blotto,' Joey said. 'Those punks have hopped their last free ride.'

Jeremy Under's eyes bugged out. 'What did you call me?' he squeaked.

'What's the matter? Got a thin skin? Get outa the business if you do. Ain't no room for beached whales who can't even sit up straight. Now, I got nothing against being fat. Mack's turned into a walrus since he got his legs cut off. Just carry it right, will ya? That's all it takes. Some pride in yourself. You got the mass, but you ain't got the moxy, if you know what I mean. Takes a little practice, that's all. Now, what's all this about a bunch of homeless scrubs squatting on railroad property? Sounds like a minor infestation, I'd think you prairie boys could've handled it – not that it matters anymore. I work alone. I'll scrape your lands clean, or I'm not Joey "Rip" Sanger.' He stood, reached up and traced a blunt, stained finger along the scar running diagonally over his eyebrows. 'Now, if you can lever that disgusting bulk outa the chair, show me your track maps. What the hell you waiting for, ten redcaps with crowbars?'

Joey walked out of the office and collected his trench coat. As he put it on, he turned to the gaping, wide-eyed secretary. 'Better call an ambulance, honey. Your boss ain't looking too good. Burst blood vessel, I'd guess. Only a matter of time when you let yourself go like that, of course. Let me know when's the funeral, I'll send a card. Now, where's the survey maps of the company yards? I've got work to do.'

TWO
The Peers

1.
in which the diagnosis is revealed

The cheerful nurse led Arthur to an alcove at one end of the Recovery Room. It was opposite the nurse's station and had a love seat sofa and a recliner. Behind the sofa was a large window with all its seams and joins painted over, a window never meant to be opened, but the spring sun's midday light was welcome all the same.

'Dr. Payne will be with you shortly,' the nurse said. Under her lab coat she wore a blouse with a surprisingly low neckline. She'd been taking her coffee breaks outside, Arthur concluded, since her chest was bright pink. The curiously alluring blush above her deep cleavage made Arthur think of sunny dispositions. He smiled down at her, then slowly sat in the recliner, reaching for a magazine from the stack on the end table.

He began reading an article randomly chosen from the magazine, and within moments was engrossed in a theoretical battle between two camps of economists as they advanced fiscal projections into the next decade. He felt a twist or two of envy reading about business executives and investment portfolios – the same kind of vague yearning he sometimes experienced when walking down a street and seeing all the brand-new cars rolling past. It baffled him how so many people could have so much money ... especially given the dire economic forecasts and the shapeless, invisible, but terribly heavy cloud of national debt under which he and everyone else in the country labored – the very debt the article in the magazine was going on and on about.

'Ah, Mr. Revell.'

Arthur looked up to find Dr. Payne standing in front of him. 'My goodness,' Arthur said, 'you look very tired, Doctor. Please, sit down.' He indicated the love seat as he returned the magazine to the stack on the end table.

'Tired?' Dr. Payne's eyebrows rose, then dropped. 'Indeed, I suppose I am.' He sat down. 'Of course, aren't we all these days, hmm?'

'I feel quite well rested, actually,' Arthur said. 'If not for the national debt, I might well consider my life worry-free. Tell me, Doctor, is it possible I have a national ulcer? What I mean is, could I be suffering the stress of the citizen, you know, something representational of high unemployment, declining social services, hiring inequities, escalating prices, and so on? Or is it the plight of youngish folk in modern society? Are these things even possible, Doctor?'

'Assuming a massive neurosis on your part, Mr. Revell, anything is possible.' The doctor cleared his throat, glanced out the window. 'Mind you, I found no ulcer.' He looked back at Arthur and smiled. 'Are you a collector, by any chance I've been for a long time. Porcelain figures from England. Very therapeutic. My hedgehog collection is insured by Lloyd's, which in some circles doesn't mean as much as it used to, given the declining reputation of insurance industries the world over. In any case, what were we talking about?'

'This is my follow-up to the internal examination,' Arthur said. 'Even so, do you concur that the decline of the insurance industry is simply a symptom of an over-all loss of faith in the market system?'

'I certainly hope not!' Dr. Payne said, laughing. 'What would be the point of my owning a BMW and a Jaguar if all distinctions should suddenly vanish? In such a world, Mr. Revell, I envision the nightmare where I am the patient and you the doctor, if you see what I mean.'

'No.'

'Well, never mind that. Our biopsies indicate that, indeed, you are infected with a nasty, very pervasive bug. It will require treatment, beginning immediately.'

'A bug?'

'Hundreds of millions of them, in fact. Of the family Aphidae, having a soft, pear-shaped body and a tube-shaped mouth. Even at this moment, as we speak, they devour at your insides. This is why it is paramount we begin treatment immediately. You are, Mr. Revell, being quietly ingested.'

'What a distressing thought,' Arthur said.

'No doubt.' Dr. Payne reached into his coat pocket and withdrew a cellular phone. 'Excuse me while I take this call.'

Arthur blinked. He'd heard no ring. He watched as Dr. Payne activated the phone and held it to his ear, his frown deepening as the seconds ticked by.

'You want me in Entomology,' the doctor said,

nodding. 'Third floor, yes, of course. Containment Room B, yes.' He sat up straight. 'My God, not Room B! I'll be right there!' The doctor rose, looking momentarily lost.

'My treatment,' Arthur prompted.

'Hmm? Oh, yes.' Dr. Payne pulled out a pill bottle. 'Take three of these every four hours. See the nurse for more details. I must be off. Excuse me, Mr. Revell. And do let me know if you see any hedgehogs, hmm? Good-bye.'

Arthur watched him leave. He glanced down at the bottle in his hand, hesitating as a part of him wanted to return to the article in the magazine. Of course, that wasn't proper form. He climbed to his feet and approached the nurse's station.

The cheerful nurse had gone to look at one of the patients in the beds in the Recovery Room, leaving the older nurse, Margaret, behind the desk. Arthur leaned on the counter. 'Excuse me, ma'am. Dr. Payne directed me here to get details of the medication he's putting me on.'

Margaret coughed, then held out her hand. 'Let's see the bottle, Mr. Revell.'

He passed it over.

She read the label, 'One hundred twenty-five milligrams, Coccinellidae, hmmm, not one I'm familiar with.' She jotted the name down on a notepad. 'Well, take three at a time every four hours. You have three refills on this prescription, to be dispensed by Dr. Payne's clinic. There are three hundred pills inside. Anything else you want to know, Mr. Revell?'

'I'm to take twelve hundred pills?'

Margaret frowned slightly and reread the label. 'Yes, Mr. Revell, that's correct.'

'Well,' Arthur said, 'he is the doctor, isn't he?'

'Correct, Mr. Revell. Now, if you haven't any more questions, I'm about to go on my coffee break.'

'By all means,' Arthur said. 'Enjoy your cigarette.'

'Each one more than the last, Mr. Revell. Thank you. You can find your own way out?'

'Oh yes.'

Arthur continued smiling as he watched Margaret leave the room. After a moment he glanced down at himself, making sure his fly was zipped and nothing was out of place. He ran both hands through his reddish brown hair, rubbed a finger over his teeth, then turned to watch the cheerful nurse.

She was still busy, arguing with an enormous, balding man occupying a bed halfway down the aisle. The man looked very angry, the color of his face alarmingly red as he bellowed incomprehensible orders into his cellular phone. The cheerful nurse was still smiling, but it was clear to Arthur that even she was losing her patience as she tried to calm the patient down.

Arthur walked over. 'Do you require assistance, ma'am?' he asked.

'Mr. Revell!' The nurse's own face was now flushed, almost the same tone as her chest. 'Thank you for asking, but I'm afraid it's against hospital policy to enlist the aid of patients when restraining other patients. Insurance, you understand.'

Arthur smiled, his head bobbing. 'I understand perfectly. Of course, in some circles, the insurance industry has a very poor reputation. I therefore suggest we ignore such concerns for the time being.' He walked over to stand beside the patient's bed, gently guiding the nurse to one side. 'Sir?' he asked the man, who made a point of ignoring Arthur. 'Sir, I suggest you calm down immediately. Please end your phone call and comply with the nurse's instructions.'

The man laid a hand over the phone's mouthpiece and glared up at Arthur. 'Get outa my goddamned face,' he snapped in a high, quavering voice. 'I'll sue the lot of you, I swear. I'm cardiac, you idiots. Not gastro-intestinal! Cardiac! What the hell's wrong with all of you, anyway? Get me outa here!'

Arthur's smile tightened slightly. 'Sir, kindly look at this patient here beside you. Is he raving at the top of his lungs? No, he isn't. In fact, he's trying to get some sleep—'

'Of course he's not screaming his head off,' the balding man yelped. 'Someone stuck a spear into his belly! Wouldn't you be lying low, too?'

'Please, Mr. Revell,' the nurse said, moving close and making an effort to guide him away from the bedside. She smelled of peaches. 'I will be calling for assistance—'

'Nonsense,' Arthur said. He leaned over the bed and looked down at the balding man. 'I'm about to throw up. Stress induces vomiting, you see, and I'm finding you very stressful, sir. My concern is that I have in my stomach a hundred million Aphidae, voracious little bugs that can only be treated with twelve hundred pills. Now, I wouldn't want you to contract this terrible affliction, but your constant screaming at that poor beleaguered secretary on the other end of the phone line has my stomach rumbling in a most ominous fashion.'

The balding man cringed. 'Get away from me,' he said in a tiny voice.

'I'm afraid it may be too late,' Arthur said, still looming over the man. 'Unless you hang up immediately.'

The man switched off his phone and shoved it into the nurse's hands.

'Ahh,' Arthur said, stifling a burp. 'That's much better.'

'You're insane,' the man said.

'Possibly I am,' Arthur replied. 'I hadn't considered that. Of course, I have received my diagnosis, thank goodness, and medication to remedy my condition. Additional ills are, of course, possible.' He turned to the nurse. 'What do you think, ma'am? Might I also be insane as well as gastrointestinally infected?'

She smiled, taking his arm by the elbow and guiding him away. 'Not likely, Mr. Revell. Thank you for helping – you certainly have a presence, don't you?'

'My robustness hasn't always served me as well,' Arthur said. 'And lately I seem to be gaining weight without accumulating any extra fat – is this possible? Is my flesh becoming denser?'

'I have no idea, Mr. Revell.'

They were standing at the nurse's station. The nurse's blue eyes were searching his, as if seeing him for the first time.

'I wonder,' Arthur began tremulously, 'uhm, a certain thought has occurred to me—'

'Oh?' Her eyes had widened.

'Well, I wonder if you might not consider it too forward of me to ask you out on a date, as it were. Dinner, perhaps?'

'I don't know if that's such a good—'

'Strictly speaking, I'm not your patient, am I?'

'True. Oh, why not? Yes, I'd like that.'

'Uh, may I ask your name, ma'am'

'Faye.'

'How charming, Faye. Tomorrow night, then?'

'I get off at seven,' she said.

'I'll be here.'

Down on the main floor, Arthur went into the bathroom and shook out three of the pills. He squinted down at the black-spotted red objects. Each pill seemed to be cut in a half – hemispherical. He shrugged, popped them into his mouth, and swallowed. It was a great relief that his treatment had begun. Smiling, Arthur left the hospital.

2.
'You're our man, Max!'

Outre Space, the hub of the city's art establishment, was a beautiful old building designed and constructed in the Chicago style of the early 1900s. It had been gutted and refurbished to become a kind of self-contained focal point, housing arts associations, studios, a cinema, and countless other arts-related . . . stuff.

As with every time he entered Outre Space, Maxwell Nacht paused in the foyer, his skin prickling, the hairs erect on the back of his neck, and fighting the sudden urge to vacate his bowels. The reaction was triggered by the building itself, rather than the lofty organizations it housed. In truth, he was anticipating the scene to come, knowing he would be taking a massive risk, but confident in his choice of tactics.

Four ceiling-mounted security cameras swiveled in their brackets to focus on him. He'd already stepped through the infrared sensor beam at the doors, and the foyer still echoed from the Door Open chime.

I don't belong here yet.

Heavy boots echoed, approached with the rustle of cloth and the clink and soft jangle of metal.

I'm an intruder at this moment, shifty, potentially loitering, a shabby beggar in student-budget clothes, my hair misaligned by the endless wind outside and now slowly settling at the front, above my sweat-beaded brow, but rising distinct and erect at the back – charged by the oven-dry air. An intruder. Desperate. Psychotic. An artist.

The security guard arrived. Max read the name tag on the man's flak vest: MONK. With the black, face-shielded helmet, only the name tag distinguished one from the others – and there were at least two more. Max had encountered Stubble yesterday, and Nick the day before. They all wore the helmets, the fatigues, the web belt with gas grenades, and the M16s slung over their shoulders, one gloved hand on the butt of the Service .45 at their hips. They were all big, blockish, silent.

Max smiled. 'How's Stubble and Nick? Doing well, are they?'

Monk stared at him.

'Uh,' Max continued, 'I have an appointment with Annie Trollop, CAPSs. Uh, Cultural Assessment Promotional Support services. Fifth floor, room 500. One P.M. I know, I'm six minutes early, but—'

Monk gestured him toward the elevator. Its doors opened as soon as they arrived and they didn't pause in their step until they entered and the doors closed behind them.

A corner-mounted ceiling camera swiveled its eye in his direction. A speaker grille beside the floor button panel buzzed, then a voice said, 'The elevator will take you directly to the required floor. Speak clearly in stating your floor.'

'Uh, five,' Max said.

'The elevator will take you directly to floor five. There is no reason to panic.'

Panic?

'I, uh, I need to go to the bathroom.' He checked his watch as the elevator began climbing. 'I have four minutes . . .'

There was silence, then, 'Use of bathrooms is discouraged.'

'Oh.'

'Unless accompanied by security.'

The elevator stopped, presumably at the fifth floor, but the doors remained closed.

'Okay . . .' Max said slowly.

'Proceed then.'

The doors opened. Max stepped into a hallway. Monk trundled after him, one step behind his left shoulder. The elevator said, 'The guard will accompany you.'

'Okay. Got it.'

'Do not deviate from the route.'

'Right.'

Monk gesturing the direction, they began walking. They turned right, then right again, passing unmarked, unnumbered, and closed doors on either side of the hall-way, and finally came to a stop outside yet another featureless, steel gray door. As Maxwell stared at it, the doorknob buzzed and clicked open.

Monk followed him into the bathroom and into the stall. Max hesitated, wondering if he could manage to poo with Monk standing beside him. He jumped as the toilet said, 'You may now sit. This is stall Alpha Charlie.

This is your stall for the duration of your stay. If
questioned, you are in Alpha-Charlie-5. Do you
understand?'

'Yes, sir.'

'You may now sit.'

'Sit?'

'Shit.'

'Thank you.'

brief interlude

The damp from Annie's limp hand still cooling on
Maxwell's palm, he sat down in the chair indicated and
smiled at the pretty-but-too-thin woman on the other
side of the desk.

'Boy,' Maxwell said, 'the security here in Outre Space
is state-of-the-art stuff. I'm, uh, very impressed.'

Annie Trollop smiled without showing her teeth.
'Yes, very impressive, I'm sure. Are you new to the city?
I see you've but recently joined CAPSs, Mr. Nacht.'

'Max, please. Yes. I'm from . . . out of town. A rural
upbringing.' He raised his hands in a slightly-helpless-
but-restrained-by-decorum gesture, which he'd worked
on all morning in his small apartment, to an audience of
cockroaches on the kitchen counter. 'I admit to experiencing . . . culture shock. What most excites me,' he
continued, 'is this notion – ably described in your information pamphlet – of a true, vibrant, thriving arts
community. Does such a community exist?'

A brief frown flickered on Annie's brow. 'Which one?'

'Excuse me?'

'Which information pamphlet?'

'Uhm, uh, I'm not sure – you have more than one?'

'Oh, yes, a series, each one target-specific. We've spent thousands researching and producing our pamphlets. Let's see, the arts community . . . vibrant, thriving, you said? Well, that would be Series 16-B – you got the pamphlet for potential donors. You should have received Series 11-D, for new members.' She shook her head and sighed. Picking up a pen and making a note she said, 'Well, that does it. She's fired. I simply cannot deal with this level of incompetence. Series 11-D is for new members – she should know that.'

'So, I'm curious, how's it different?'

'Well, in Series 11-D, the arts community is "welcoming, appreciating, open, and receptive."'

'Oh. Seems a small mistake—'

'Hardly, Mr. Nacht. Now, where were we?'

He hesitated, then said, 'I was enthusing about there being an arts community and displaying appropriate eagerness, intending to convey to you my eager willingness to do anything it takes to become part of that community.'

'Ah, excellent, Maxwell. I must say, I'm impressed. Do you have any opinions?'

'No, none at all, and I don't make them.'

'Superb. Do you consider yourself an ethical person? Do you have standards?'

'No, I'm completely amoral. All art produced by notable members of the community is either "good" or "interesting."'

'Are you cynical?'

'To the black core of my rotten heart.'

Annie Trollop leaned back, looking thoughtful. 'The

timing is . . . propitious. We need a new wunderkind. Someone we can milk and glom and flutter and sigh over – for a year, maybe two. Then we'll get tired and move on.' She looked at Max. 'A year, maybe two, Maxwell.'

'Sounds perfect,' he replied. 'I won't fail you, and I won't hang on after it's over.'

'Well, I should think not, Mr. Nacht. Because then you'll join that elite, powerful group – you'll become a—'

'A peer.'

'Exactly.'

He smiled.

She smiled back. 'We've found our boy. Now, let's go. Introductions of the proper sort need to be made.'

'Wonderful.'

'Have you visited Anything but Craft?'

'Your retail outlet? No, it never seems to be open—'

'Well, of course not. Heaven forbid we actually sell something. Because then someone would be unfairly favored over others, and that's not allowed. But come, I'm certain Penny is in.'

Max stood. 'Penny? Penny Foote-Safeword? Brandon Safeword's wife?'

'Exactly. We'll explain everything, and she'll get to work. You're about to enter the revolving door, Maxwell – no, not Maxwell. Maximillian. Maximillian Percival Nacht, I think.'

They headed out.

'Revolving door?'

'Oh yes, our, shall we say, euphemism. The track, the pathway. Grants, awards, a lifetime of funding. Round and round and round . . . Once you're in the loop, you never have to come out, you see. And of course there's no official way to get into the loop in the first place. It's the way of modern life, Maximillian, it's—'

'Revolvo.'

'Precisely. Very apt. How clever. Follow me . . .'

They left Annie's office, walked past the luckless underling who was destined for firing, headed out into the hallway – where Monk was nowhere in sight – then descended five flights of stairs, proceeded along another hallway, and came at last to a featureless steel door. 'This is the back way into the studio area of the shop,' Annie explained. 'It's necessary that you memorize the floor plans of the building, since it is deliberately intended to confuse and, indeed, lose the uninitiated. We've had three would-be artists disappear in Outre Space over the past five years. Stubble swears he's seen one of them, but somehow, the cameras never detect him, or her, or them.' She turned to the door and knocked. After a moment she produced a key and opened the door. 'Penny!' she called. 'Darling! We have a guest!'

They edged inside.

Penny was lying on a kind of divan at the opposite end of the studio. Paint-spattered cloth had been draped and tacked to the wall behind and to either side of her. Bits of tinfoil hung from threads attached to the ceiling and slowly turned in the warm, incense-sweet air. A video camera mounted on a tripod was off to one side, a red light blinking on it.

Max had never seen Penny before, and in fact knew almost nothing about her, except for the fact that she was Brandon Safeword's wife. As he and Annie approached, he saw that the woman, in her early forties, was dressed in a see-through, tie-dyed kind of slip that outlined her body without providing any support. Her breasts were large and hadn't known a bra in years. Bits of bark and leaves were profligate in her long black hair. Her red-painted lips were huge although the rest of the face was narrow, modestly featured, and her eyes, lined in catlike kohl, stayed mostly hidden under the painted lids.

'Oh, Annie dear,' she purred – well, Max corrected in his mind, it was meant to be a purr, but the sound had come mostly from her nose – 'you've found me my installation piece, I see.'

Annie waved a hand. 'This is Maximillian Nacht, honey. Our new boy. He's destined for moderately great things.'

'An artist?' Penny let her gaze rest on Max. 'And what do you do, Maximillian Nacht?'

'Uh, I'm a sculptor.'

'Call me Penny.'

'Penny.'

'And what do you sculpt?'

'Everything. I mean, anything. I'm presently doing miniatures.'

'How economical.' Penny glanced at Annie and raised her thin eyebrows.

Annie smiled. 'Well, I'd best be off. Office work, how it piles up. Maximillian, I leave you in capable hands. Pay close attention to what Penny tells you, and you'll do just fine.'

'Thanks, Annie.'

The chief administrator for CAPSs closed the door behind her, leaving Max alone with Penny.

'Well, come closer, my bite's not too painful,' Penny said. 'Have you read my book?'

'Uhm, no, I'm sorry, I haven't.'

'That's not surprising. I refused to let crass commercial retail outlets sell it. Self-published, too, since why should some faceless publication company profit from my efforts. So, you can only acquire the book from *moi,* which is perfect, for it allows me, the author, to elect my own audience – an exclusive one, an audience worthy of my work.'

'That's very clever, Penny.'

'Of course,' Penny said, 'you're now among that elite company, so I'll have to find a copy, sometime, somewhere.'

'What's the book called?'

Her smile made Max's heart jump – or maybe it was his liver, the incense was putting him in a daze. 'Is the videocam on?'

He stumbled over to the tripod. 'Uh, yep, it's running.'

'What do you know about performance art, sweetie?'

'Not much, I'm afraid.'

'Uninitiated, then. Excellent. I'm working on a project that is a continuation of the book, an expansion of the basic precepts. Research is paramount. Come here, take off your clothes.'

'My clothes?'

'We're going to fuck. A performance piece, art in all its visceral glory. I have made a discovery – it's all in my book – and it's revolutionary, it might well change the world forever. Have you ever heard of collective memory?'

'As in Carl Jung?'

'Someone like that – I can't recall, but that doesn't matter. What's important to realize is that this collective memory is not found in the brain. Oh no, darling, not the brain. Take off your clothes, Maximillian, and get over here. We're wasting tape. Where was I?'

Max began stripping down. 'Anywhere but the brain,' he said.

'I have discovered it is possible to tap into that memory, to unveil the mysteries of all one's past lives, the myriad identities of one's genetic histories. For example, I have discovered that I was once a princess, no twice, once in Egypt, and once at Stonehenge. I have also been a queen, a high priestess, and an Amazon warrior. These identities can be driven back into my consciousness, because, as the title of my book reveals, *The Vulva Remembers!!*' With that she lunged forward, wrapping Max in her arms and pulling him down onto the divan. 'Fuck me fuck me fuck me – she'll remember again, ohmigod, she'll remember – she remembers!'

3.
the ends of the line

Wild Bill Chan hobbled along the abandoned rail line, dragging one leg that had been crushed in 1962 at a spill outside Climax, Saskatchewan, walking with a rolling hitch of his hunched back, which had been bent and then broken in 1969 trying to hold up a derailed, sagging-in-the-mud piggyback just outside Ste. Rose du Lac, Manitoba. He glared at the world with one eye, the other one lost in 1974 when he was trampled by a herd of caribou being pursued by a polar bear down Churchill's main street – his only off-duty injury in a long list of injuries that had begun in 1920 when, as a mere lad, he had joined his father on the crew breaking the path for the northern line.

Joey 'Rip' Sanger grinned as the old man approached. 'Hell, getting ya outa that damned retirement weren't too hard, eh?' Behind Joey stood the redcap, who'd had a hell of a time dragging one of the steel trunks out to this forgotten spur. He'd damned near earned his fiver, Joey reflected. Almost. The prairie spread out beyond the line, dotted here and there by derelict grain silos and bought-out farmsteads. A few dusty trees broke the flat skyline to the east and north, while to the south rose the city's scattering of skyscrapers, behind a golden veil of spring dust.

Chan arrived and hooked his glare up at Joey. 'Y'bastard,' he rasped. 'Eh was 'alfway t'Katmandu when the call come.'

'Under was under the weather, hah,' Joey said. 'Thin skin and too much under it, if you ask me. This the guy you groomed to take over, Chan? Hell, what a sorry thought.'

'Times change, Joey. That's all eh say. So you call me out here, y'grizzled carp, but in case y'hadn't nooticed, this spur's abandoned.' He waved a mangled hand in a sweeping gesture. ''Alf the track's rusting t'nothing, boy! The heyday's scrammed. It was the Twenties, the best times, when it was touch and go between this city and Chicago and St. Louis – who was going to be the gate to the West, hey? Touch and go. You'll find more track round this city than y'can fathom, boy, round and round and round. Spurs and runs and switchbacks and platforms and silos and maintenance shacks and sheds and damned cars, too, boy!'

Joey grimaced. 'You forget, you one-eyed Shanghai warlock, you're talking to Joey "Rip" Sanger here. Y'think I can't read maps, y'think two thousand miles of unused track around this city is enough to make my knees shake?' He kicked at the rail. 'Unused, hell. Take a close look, Chan.'

'Eh?'

'Your squatters are living in cars, got their own god-damned train, look where the rust's streaked away. Looking pinched, right? It's a 57 Wells, a goddamned steam engine. Not listed on your service, is it? But it's here, and someone's working it, and those squatters are living in the cars behind it, and they got you hunting everywhere but so long as they keep to the abandoned spurs, so long as they keep moving, you won't find 'em.'

'Holy bear livers,' Chan whispered.

'You got it. It's bloody ingenious. I can't wait to meet the brains behind it all, and mark you, Chan, I will. Soon. The bastard's mine, all mine. Redcap!'

'Yes, sir!'

Joey tossed the boy a ring of keys. 'Open that trunk, son.'

The redcap fumbled through the keys, and finally found the right one. He lifted back the hinge, then stepped back.

Joey and Chan walked up to the trunk. Inside was a sophisticated array of high-tech equipment, motion sensors, IR sensors, and innumerable other gadgets of detection and tracking, all neatly stored in stacked foam beds. Joey said to Chan, 'I want a two-man runner brought here. We've got a whole lotta lines to seed before dark.'

'Ground-up dragon bones,' Chan swore, 'you'll get what you need, Joey.'

'What was that about Katmandu, anyway?'

'Got part-time work as a Sherpa. But never mind, I want to see you nab these squatters. The old glory's back, Joey. You're a goddamned wonder, boy.' Chan faced the redcap and scowled up at the young man. 'You stick by him, son, and you'll learn something, you'll learn enough to carry on the tradition – and someday you'll be running this goddamned company!'

'Yes, sir!'

Chan said to Joey, 'You gonna sock it to 'em, ain't ya?'

Joey paused over the trunk and cocked his head. 'The Sanger Sock? If I have to, I suppose. Better they come along peacefully, though.'

'The Sanger Sock?' the redcap asked.

Chan nodded. 'A martial art, a single move no one on earth has stood against, and that includes Clay himself – was in '63, in Toronto, at a house party in Don Mills. Things got rough between Joey and the Champ.' Chan cackled. 'The Yank got whupped by a Canuck! Again! Hee hee!' He continued after a moment, 'Of course, they hushed it up. Bad press and all that. The Sanger Sock, first invented by Liza Sanger, when she was working in the bush on the Rennie crew – all those horny Finns, hah! Then passed down the line, all the way to Joey here.'

'Wow,' the redcap breathed. 'Can I learn it?'

'Mind your manners, boy,' Joey snapped. 'You're getting uppity.'

'Nothing wrong with that, Joey,' Chan said. 'A kid's gotta be uppity, wants to get anywhere.'

'S'pose you're right. Well, you gotta earn the right, redcap. I seen signs, good signs, I admit. We'll see, I s'pose. Now, give me a hand here and Chan, you ain't that well-hung so I figure that's a cellular in that pocket, so put in the call for that two-man runner.'

Chuckling, Chan reached into his pants pocket.

4.
Anything but Craft

After the taping they went to another taping, this one somewhat more sedate. Penny was in a fine mood, still swimming in the euphoria of discovering an Aztec princess in one of her past lives. Max, on the other hand, could barely walk.

'I'm the producer,' Penny said as they stood in the foyer and waited for the elevator. 'The *Northern Order* program is not only the premier quality show on the arts in this city, it's the only show on the arts in this city. Brandon is, of course, simply superb. Not that I'm biased. My objectivity in all things is above reproach. In any case, we're taping this week's show at Art Place Gallery, which is just upstairs.' She checked her watch. 'Everything should be set up by now. Excellent. Ideal. Karmic synchronicity. Don't worry, I'll make introductions.'

The elevator arrived. They entered. 'Second floor,' Penny said loudly. The speaker grille chirped, and they ascended.

Most of the second floor was taken up with the public gallery – although, as the sign posted on the door indicated, it wasn't open to the public. 'Art Place Gallery,' Penny explained, 'is for our darling artists, the prize students of important people. In order to get a show in here – which can be seen by invitation only – you must have studied under Professor Don Palmister or Lucy Mort. You must receive a letter of reference from my dear husband, and a personal non-written reference from *moi*.'

'Oh,' said Max. 'But I haven't studied under either Don or Lucy.'

'Don't worry about that, Maxie. There are always ways around the rules. Always. Besides, Annie's backing you, and that should open all the doors. Also' – she smiled demurely – 'you have *moi* in your camp. Not to be too immodest, you can't lose. Ah, here we are.'

They entered into the spacious gallery. The TV camera was already set up, a technician perched behind it. Brandon Safeword had taken position, the tips of his shoes perfectly aligned with two strips of white tape on the hardwood floor, beside a huge, imposing work of art.

Max gaped at it as he and Penny approached. The work of art was a cow, stuffed, legs spraddled, tail sticking straight out, and an SLR camera jammed into its mouth. A black box had been strapped to the cow's head, between the ears, with wires leading down to the glass eyes, both of which rolled incessantly to an electronic pulse.

Brandon scowled at Penny. 'You're late, darling.'

'Sorry, the performance piece went on, and on. You know how it is. I don't recognize the cameraman, Brandie – you know how strangers bother me.'

'Can't be helped. Ellis is down with meningitis. Meet Scott.'

'Do I have to?' Penny whined, then, offering a bright smile at Scott, who stood bemusedly behind the camera, she waved and said, 'Wonderful to meet you, Scott. Shall we begin taping?'

'Anytime,' Scott said, shrugging.

Penny gave her husband a nod; Brandon gave Scott a nod. Scott glanced over at Penny, who nodded, then at Max, who nodded. 'Okay,' Scott said, 'we're rolling.'

'Wait!' Brandon called out. 'I want to change the order! Where's our guest?'

Penny rolled her eyes. 'Not due for another ten minutes, darling. Let's stick with the script, please?'

'Oh, all right. Okay, I'm ready. Everyone ready?'

Everyone nodded.

Brandon faced the camera, composed himself, then smiled and said in his deep rolling voice, 'Welcome, friends, once again to *Northern Order* magazine's program on the arts, coming to you this week from the Art Place Gallery at Outre Space in the heart of this vibrant, wonderful city.' He paused, took a step closer to the cow. 'Today, we'll look into the seminal centerpiece of Johan Guppy's groundbreaking, innovative show, "A Cow's Eye View," which has been on display here for the past twenty-six months, to much acclaim.' He strode to the cow's side and laid a hand on its back. 'This piece, entitled *Cow*, is a wonderful example of interactive art. The intent, for the viewer, is obvious.' He walked around to the back of the cow, then faced the camera again. 'One must proceed, through the installation, until one's eye comes into contact with the camera's eyepiece.' Brandon rolled up the sleeves of his casual cardigan, revealing his broad, hairy wrists – which, Max guessed, were Brandon's own personal favorite features. 'Art always makes demands of its audience, and *Cow* is no exception.' He smiled once again and Scott nodded, indicating he was zooming in; then Brandon turned to the cow's anus and pushed his head against it. 'No doubt,' he grunted, pushing steadily, 'it's a tight squeeze. If you'll be patient.'

Max stared in amazement as Brandon exerted his prodigious strength and managed to push his entire head up the cow's anus. He continued speaking, but of course the words were too muffled to understand. And Brandon kept on pushing. Max glanced over at Penny, who stood with one index finger pressed to her surgically amassed lips, a quizzical frown rippling her brow. Then he glanced over at Scott, whose mouth was hanging open, his eyes glazed, drool dripping down onto the camera's swing-grip. Brandon was now gesticulating, his voice rising in timbre.

'Uh, darling,' Penny said, 'I'm not sure—'

Brandon's arms began waving, then pushing, then beating at the cow's hips. The cow rocked on its stand. Brandon was now yelling.

Penny whirled to Max and Scott. 'Well, for godsakes, help him!'

Both men ran forward.

Ten minutes later, Brandon, his face blotched red and hair dotted with stuffing, sat swiveling on an easy chair, watching as his guest took her seat opposite him. He smiled. 'I understand, Lucy, you will be gracing this moment with a reading, selected from your most recent collection of poetry.' He smiled at the camera. 'This collection, entitled *Mommy Mommy Mommy*, a collection of poems for and about mommies, is now available at choice outlets. Ladies and gentlemen, Lucy Mort will now read from her new work.'

Lucy – who to Max looked smaller than the last time he'd seen her, which, he recalled, was that dreadful night at Culture Quo – glanced up at the camera lens, offered a tight, shaky smile, then bent her gaze to the page on her lap. She took a deep breath, then, her voice thin and vibrating, she read,

> *Mum, mum mum-mum*
> *jam in the cupboard, yum*
> *Saturday morning, in the sun*
> *cream and flatbread under thumb*
> *and this is why, mum-yum,*
> *I dreamed of locking you*
> *in there – the cuboard.*

She rattled the page, then sat back and smiled over at Brandon, who nodded with an expression of thoughtful appreciation. 'Excellent, Lucy, well done. I understand that the collection has been reviewed extensively in the past month or so, since the book was launched.'

Scott scrambled at the manual focus, and Max blinked uncertainly as, for the briefest of moments, it seemed that, upon receipt of Brandon's words, Lucy Mort's head shrank, ever so slightly.

'Well,' she snapped. 'What do they know? Critics are scum of the earth. They said the essays read like a thesis! Can you imagine that? The selection committee loved it! They hate women, even the women critics, they hate women, it's as plain as that. All my friends loved it – some even paid for their own copy! I don't have to take this, I'm not here to be criticized. No one has the right to criticize my work – it's poetry! It's personal! I'm very hurt!'

'Dear Lucy,' Brandon soothed, leaning close. 'Lucy dear, dear Lucy, you well know my opinions on those critics who see nothing but negativity in everything they review. As you recall, my own review of *Mommy Mommy Mommy* was effusive in its praise – as I always am, no matter what you write.'

'No matter what I write? What's that supposed to mean?'

Scott snatched at the manual focus again, and to Max, Lucy's shoulders seemed huge below the poet's head.

'Only, Lucy dear, that whatever you write is simply brilliant, as far as I'm concerned, and,' he added with a smile to the camera, 'who is this city's premier guru of the art scene? Upon whom does this entire city depend for their wise, cultured opinions on art and culture? I need not answer that immodestly, need I?'

'Of course you're right,' Lucy said, sighing. 'Thank you. I love you, Brandon. We all love you. We love you even more than we do your more famous brother, Brendan – it's true, for all of us—'

Scott whimpered as he readjusted the focus on Brandon's head, which had just gotten larger and was turning bright red, the old red blotches turning white at the same time. Brandon leaned dangerously close to Lucy, who shrank back in alarm. 'My brother?' he rasped. 'My brother? How dare you mention his name to me—'

'Hey!' Scott shouted. 'I thought you were your brother! Oh! Sorry! I'm so sorry, I didn't realize—'

'Shut up!' Brandon roared, surging to his feet.

'Cut!' Penny screamed. 'Cut! Cut! Cut!' She rushed forward to soothe her husband, whose veins were pulsing madly on his thick neck and against his temples. 'We'll do an edit job! We'll edit it right! Everyone calm down!'

Lucy was crying. 'I'm sorry, Brandon! I'm so sorry!'

Max saw his moment, and stepped forward. 'Excuse me, Mr. Safeword,' he said quietly, drawing everyone's attention. Into the dangerous silence, Max said, 'I've heard of you, of course. But I didn't know you had a brother. Brendan, is it? I've never heard of him. Is he someone important? You know, I think I'd have heard of him if he was someone important, don't you think?'

Brandon stared at Max for a long, tense moment; then his broad smile split his robust features. 'You must be the new boy! Welcome aboard!'

5.
homo vegetabilis

Sool Koobie tracked the tweed-clad professor from Culture Quo, staying always a half-dozen silent steps behind the man as he wandered the dark, ill-lit streets of the city's core. Don Palmister paused every few moments, his neck straining as he looked up at one dilapidated building after another. He mumbled under his breath and occasionally pulled out a small notepad and jotted down details, then resumed his peregrination.

This time, Sool Koobie knew, this one wouldn't get away from him. The last time had been a real mess. He'd thought his target to be a girl, and after piercing its belly and dragging the flopping body away from the rest of the small herd, he'd begun the task of dressing down the carcass in a dark alley. Although the victim was still alive, twitching and moaning, Sool immediately set his chert knife to its chest. Upon cutting away the select morsels that were the breasts, Sool found in his hands two blood-smeared bags of liquid. At that moment the victim screamed and rolled to its feet. Sool was a moment too late in pursuing, as the creature emerged onto the street and nearly ran into a passing car, which screeched to a halt, and the hunt was up for Sool Koobie.

Tonight, driven by hunger, Sool chose not to wait in ambush, but to stalk his quarry, and tonight, he'd make sure of things.

A wind was blowing, whining along the alleys and streets. Restaurants were closing up as the hour was late, and Don Palmister was alone, unmindful, and as far as Sool could discern, unarmed. The smell of various vegetables emanating from the man left an olfactory trail that made Sool's mouth water. He closed a step behind the man.

He'd made the proper propitiations, and the stars were kind in their glittering alignment overhead, the spirits at peace, the Mother casting down a benign eye on the natural process of things, to which Sool was intricately attuned. He'd danced the cycle of life and death, and a soothing calm had come over him, making him a part of all things, and each thing, and the thing to come.

As the quarry paused at the mouth of an alley and pulled out its notepad and pen, Sool Koobie leapt forward. The Neanderthal caught the professor entirely unawares, driving his spear into the man's back hard enough to plunge its stone tip out through the chest. The professor grunted softly, then sagged, his notepad and pen falling to the pavement. Sool paused over the body and crowed silently at the night sky; then he grabbed the body's ankles and quickly pulled it into the alley. A moment later he had the deadweight on one shoulder. Spear in hand, Sool Koobie jogged through the darkness. He would dress the kill far away – out beyond the city's edges, where grass and trees and abandoned buildings would provide him certain privacy.

In Sool Koobie's chest, his heart danced happily. He felt noble in his savagery, right down to the grime-rimmed curved nails on his wide, crooked toes.

6.
the late-night hate session

Minister of Art and Culture Paul Silverthump stood at the window of his office, looking down, with hands clasped behind him, at the city below. 'No,' he said, 'even lower than scum. Less than bacteria, more insidious than viruses, smellier than the crap stuck on my underwear after a minutes briefing. And what's worse, there's more and more of them, every day there's more. They should all be shot, crushed underfoot, ground into the grit and dust of their miserable hovels. I'm a believer in survival of the fittest, Andy, you know that. Me and my kind, we know what it's all about. I'm petitioning in my neighborhood for a high wall, Andy, the highest in the city. And private security guards. We'll keep them out, remove them from our sight, destroy them with our contempt and ministerial indifference. We're getting fewer, that's the problem, the imbalance is getting problematic, no doubt about it. We need to start systematically culling numbers: make a list, Andy. There's measures to continue: starvation, though that's slow; institutionally encouraged suicide through bureaucratic immobility – that's the other ministry's sphere of activity, of course, and let's face it, our SS boys and girls are doing a damned fine job, especially having added indirect support of substance abuse, malnutrition, bad education, and media-backed indifference. It's good, Andy, what they're doing is good work. We need to learn from them, we need to emulate their methods.' He paused. A pigeon slammed against the windowpane in front of him, but Paul didn't even flinch. 'Look at them down there – not that I can actually see them – who'd want to. The commonry. People. Suffering, miserable, deprived, poor, disadvantaged, disenfranchised, in-effectual people. The citizens – God, I hate them.'

He went on, but tonight Andy 'Kit' Breech's mind was on other things. He'd lost another non-staring contest with Kit earlier that evening, after Lucy had left and he'd changed the sheets. Kit's refusal to meet his gaze was all the proof Andy needed to confirm that something serious was going on, and that, added to what he'd discovered in the dresser drawer in his bed-room, was more than enough to leave Andy . . . scared. That's what I am. Damned scared. Someone rummaged through my box of condoms, someone leaving slime in his wake. Who could that be, I wonder? And it's a big box, five thousand condoms, each slick with slime, as if Kit had been . . . counting them. Why count them? What's he up to? What is it about my condoms? What do I do now? Where do I go from here? Take a memo. ASAP. My God, we're in trouble aren't we. Research the problem, pronto. I want contingency plans, I want scenarios, and I want them yesterday, dammit. Go to the library, go to the university, go to the fisheries branch, pet shops, diving enthusiasts, ministers, teachers, nuns – I don't care who, but find for me the answers I need. What's he thinking? What's he planning? What's he keep looking at out the balcony window? What's in that closet? How did he pick all those new locks? And why was he examining, one by one, five thousand condoms? I need to know these things, before it's too late, before I lose my mind. ASAP, hop to it, pronto . . .

'There's no hell more frightening than the world down there,' Paul Silverthump was saying. 'Normal people, my God, the sheer filth of their existence makes me want to throw up my veal cordon bleu, hah, that'll give those damn pigeons something to munch on. Have you instructed the exterminator, Andy?'

'Hmm? Oh, yes, of course, Paul. He says it's highly unlikely you are being individually pursued by the city's pigeons—'

'I don't care what the bastard says. I know what I know, Andy. They're after me. I can't step outside anymore. They kamikaze my windows, here and at home. In the car, in restaurants, in bars, in meetings. They chase me around, Andy. I want the city's pigeons dead, all of them, and I want it done now, this instant.'

'Of course, Paul. I'll make another call.'

'Malathion,' Paul said. 'We'll call it anticipatory spraying for mosquitoes. But I want pigeon-lethal concentrations—'

'Might prove human-lethal, Paul—'

'I don't give a shit. Let them all drop like flies. We're better off without all of them. Give us important figures gas masks or something, or open up those nuclear shelters down below – we can wait it out, no problem, and hey, only the fittest of the fittest will emerge from those shelters come the dawn. You and me, Andy, we'll be on top, and that's how it should be.'

'On top of what, sir?'

'Don't give me that shit, Andy. I know your soul. You sold it to me years ago. I know your contempt, that icy chunk of nadir you call a heart, pumping to the blood let by others, so shove the smarmy remarks, Andy. One snap of my fingers and you'll be pigeon feed – before they all kick off, of course.'

Andy smiled blandly at the minister. *Asshole, that's what you think. I've outlived every minister in this fucking office, and I'll outlive you and your minuscule career, Paul. Count on it. You stumble, like all your kind, but I slide. You've got your tricks, your evasions, your denials, your bald-faced braving it out with lawyers point, flank, and taking up the rear. If you're still clean, Paul, it's because I've kept you that way. And I've got the secret files to prove it, so don't fuck with me, Paul. Never fuck with me. Who the hell do you think trained all those pigeons?*

'Get outa here,' Paul growled, turning back to the window. 'Call that exterminator, set up the malathion program— '

'Could be difficult, Paul.'

'Why?'

'Well, why would the Ministry of Art and Culture issue a bug-spraying directive?'

'Find me an answer, Andy. That's your job. Now, stop wasting my fucking time.'

Andy kept his smile as he rose to his feet. 'I'm on it. Good night, Paul. Oh, by the way, the 'copter and limo and bodyguards have been arranged for the Awards Night.'

'Good,' Paul grunted. 'Make sure those guards are armed to the teeth, Andy. Someone might want to . . . touch me.'

Just the pigeons, Paul. 'See you tomorrow, then.' He headed out, leaving the minister alone with his rabid thoughts.

Not that he's exceptional in his beliefs. Just look at the bloody premier. But you're all making a mistake, fellas. That mob out there is getting all too hungry, all too pissed off with every fucking one of you. When they move, it'll be to take off your heads and stick 'em on spears. And that'll leave people like me, in the know, capable, sympathetic and righteous, victims of policy just like everyone else. We'll put things in order, and the beast's ugly head will subside once again into its comatose, vegetative state, and you and your cronies, Paul, will be fertilizer.

I could give Kit away. To the zoo or something. But I have to act quickly. Before he makes his move, whatever that is. ASAP. Pronto. Take a memo.

THREE

The Fruitful Church of Disobedience

1.
Thursday's Lounge

Seeking comfort, and more than a little concerned about his burgeoning appearance, Arthur Revell sought the companionship of his few friends, who would at this time of night be found in the establishment called Chesterton's, in the lounge next to the restaurant, known as Thursday's.

Arthur's friends numbered two. One was the owner of the place, Tobias Laugh, and the other was a successful painter of landscapes and wildlife, Elana Oxbow. He found them at a table near the kitchen entrance, at the very back of Thursday's. The other patrons in the lounge seemed to collectively recoil as Arthur walked past, leading him to scowl desultorily. It had been a miserable night already, and things just seemed to be getting worse and worse. He arrived at the table and, ignoring the stunned expressions on Toby's and Elana's faces, he pulled back the small chair and levered his massive frame into it. The chair creaked warningly as he settled in.

'Good Lord, Arthur,' Tobias said, 'what's happened?'

'I went on a date, with a lovely woman named Faye.

We'd just sat down to eat and she'd just asked me what I do for a living, to which I intended to reply that I'm a part-time professional specializing in part-time employment in various sectors in the service, maintenance, and other such industries, when I felt this indescribable pain.' He pointed to the two knobby horns that now jutted from above his browridges, one to either side of his forehead. 'Here, and here. And my teeth started hurting terribly, and the arms of the chair broke simultaneously, then the legs, and I could feel how much denser I'd suddenly become, and how much bigger. Poor Faye, she screamed, then fled. What could I do? What could I say? It was horrible, far worse than, say, finding a pimple an hour before the date, you know, the kind that gets redder and redder and then the white pustule rises like a volcano, and you know if you pop it, you'll have to squeeze all that stuff out, and then it'll bleed, and the red mark will get even bigger. So you put some kind of disguising cream on it, but it dries and cracks and you end up flaking into your soup, and the blood flows all over again, and you see how she's looking and looking at it and then, when she sees you watching, she tries to look away, to look everywhere but at the massive wound on your face, but she can't, not really, and that's the last time you ever go out with her.'

'Actually,' Elana said, eyeing him carefully, 'there's some spirits that look much like what you seem to be becoming – I know an old shaman—'

'No no.' Arthur shook his head. 'That won't be necessary. I phoned Dr. Payne – my gastrointestinologist – and he confirmed that there might be side effects to the medication I'm taking for my infection. He was kind

enough to send me a secondary treatment, by courier.'
Arthur reached into his shirt pocket and pulled out a
second pill bottle. 'I don't know what it is, but I do feel
better. The horns have stopped moving, anyway.'

'Moving?' Tobias asked, running a hand through his
wild white mane of hair. 'They were moving? How?'

'Well, waving about, I suppose. Reacting to, uh,
sounds, I think, like a dog's ears.'

'So,' Tobias said. 'Not horns at all, but antennae.
Let's see those pills.'

Arthur handed the bottle to his old friend.

'A hundred twenty-five milligrams,' Tobias read,
'malathion. Now, why does that word ring a bell? Elana?'

'Beats me. Do you mind if I touch them, Arthur?'

'No, I suppose not.'

The young woman reached up and probed the
projections. 'Can you feel this?'

'Oh, yes.'

'Well, they feel like horns to me. Wouldn't there be
some kind of tympanic membrane, Toby? Some kind of
obvious sensory apparatus?'

'You have a point there,' Tobias admitted. 'So you're
being treated for your ulcer?'

Again, Arthur shook his head. 'I do not possess an
ulcer, but an infection. It may be endemic, in that I am
physically responding to the country's economic ills,
making me susceptible to takeover bids.'

'Did your doctor suggest this?' Tobias asked.

'He expressed his concern. The insurance industry is
not doing well, after all. I've since given the situation
more thought. Clearly, I'm unwell. Now, as the news-
papers point out, the country is also unwell. I feel

poorly, and the poor are on the increase, even given the constant changing of the poverty level by the federal statisticians. My needs are not being met in innumerable contexts – for example, I'm still a virgin; I can't hold my liquor, as much as I might want to; I can't smoke cigarettes because it makes my cheeks swell, and I would surely love to indulge the habit; illicit drugs would interfere with my medication, not to mention my sense of reality. I'm not being socially served. Now, the coincidences continue. I'm getting hungrier, sicker, heavier, less inclined to physical motion, with an unquenchable taste for bad American television programs and infomercials. I'm also complacent, occasionally smug, with a growing coldness in my heart that is expressed in a lack of sympathy for my lesser fellows. If I had a dog, I believe I would feed it before I fed a homeless waif in an alleyway, then I'd kick the dog. Does this make sense? Without question, my friends, I believe I am a direct causal consequence of the pervasive collective misalignment of our nation's citizens with the natural exigencies of survival in the modern world. And if this is not sufficiently disturbing, I now have horns, weigh four hundred pounds without much increase in actual mass, and am four inches taller than I was this morning. The country needs saving, my friends, if only to purge me of my personal discomfort.'

'Dear me,' Elana said, genuine concern in her expression, 'I can't imagine you being coldhearted about anything, Arthur.'

'No, it's true,' he protested. 'I don't care anymore. I don't care about children, pets, disabled people, gays, lesbians, racial minorities, linguistically challenged people, juvenile delinquency, drugs, alcohol abuse, child abuse, spousal abuse, smokers, farters, nose-pickers, heart disease, radioactive waste, Native self-government, poor people, fat people, tainted blood, historical oppression, terrorism, the RCMP, the Jets, the Leafs, Hillary's fingerprints, insane cattle, endangered whales, the fur industry, baby seals, illiteracy, separatism, multiculturalism, technophiles, the Net, porcelain hedgehogs, cynicism, nihilism, and antiestablishmentarianism. In fact, I care about only one thing: money. I don't have any. Why not? That's what I care about, and I swear, once I've got it, I'm going to hold on to it, even if the whole world ends up in flames and ruin. Dammit.'

'So,' Tobias said, 'what makes you so different?'

Arthur stared at the old man. 'You mean . . .'

'Exactly,' Tobias said. 'You should run for office. Any office. The Big Office, in fact. You'll win.'

'But I would let everything dissolve into a chaotic quagmire through my cynical contempt and my affected indifference, and my insulated perceptions would ensure the social collapse of anyone remotely unlike me.'

'Right.'

'But that's inhuman, Tobias!'

The old man smiled. 'Bingo. And that, Arthur dear, is why you do not suffer from the country's ills. If you've come to reflect its ills, as it seems you have, then you must find an outlet – you must learn a means of reflecting back what is cast upon you. What else can you do?'

'I don't know. What's happening to me?'

'Self-discovery, I'd guess. Wait and see.'

'Is it safe?'

'Beats me. You trust this Dr. Payne?'

'I think so. He seems very busy, very much involved with work of paramount, and secretive, importance. In fact, he is constantly in communication with the entomology department at the hospital. It seems they require his assistance continually. I'm very impressed.'

'Entomology?' Elana asked.

'Yes. Containment Room B.'

'Will you be seeing him again?' she asked, frowning slightly.

'Well, not for some time,' Arthur said. 'I have three refills on both prescriptions, after all. Oh, and Faye told me he's been sent away, possibly for some time. Why do you ask?'

'Curious, that's all.'

'Malathion's a pesticide!' Tobias exclaimed, snatching the bottle from Arthur's hands. 'Stop taking this, Arthur! My God, you could've poisoned yourself! Killed yourself! Someone's made a terrible mistake!'

'But I need those,' Arthur pleaded, pointing at his horns. 'What if they get bigger?'

'Taking malathion's not going to change that, son,' Tobias said, looking shaken. 'Trust me, please.'

Arthur hesitated, then sighed. 'Of course I trust you, Tobias. You're a good friend. All right, you can keep the pills.'

'Arthur,' Elana said, 'have you seen John Gully around lately?'

'No, I don't think so. He's that dropped-out architect, isn't he?'

'Yes. I think he might be in trouble, him and his colony. If you see him, let him know someone's hunting him. Someone from the railroad.'

'Sure, Elana.'

'Cheer up, Arthur,' Tobias said, 'I'll buy you a big glass of milk.'

Arthur's expression assumed an uncharacteristic, nasty eagerness. 'Milk?' he snarled. 'The hell with milk, buster, give me a Jack Daniel's, doubled-up, no ice, no water!' After a moment his face cleared and he blinked bemusedly at his staring friends. 'Something wrong?' he asked quietly.

'Uhm,' Tobias said, 'no, Arthur, I don't think so.'

'Gimme a smoke, Elana,' Arthur growled, scratching the bristle on his chin. 'I ain't had a nail in hours!'

'My God,' Elana said to Tobias. 'He's changing.'

'You're right,' Tobias breathed. 'But into what?'

2.
the Sanger Sock

It was an hour past midnight. Wearing his combat fatigues, Joey 'Rip' Sanger shoulder-rolled across the tracks and slid down the gravel embankment into the high grasses in the ditch. He pulled down his IR goggles and scanned the countryside. Two of his beepers had chirped, less than ten minutes back, just down the spur's line. Ahead rose a leaning silo, a slightly glowing blotch through his goggles, the old wood still bleeding the day's heat. Summer came fast in the prairies – just two days ago it had snowed, and now everything was turning green under a blistering sun. Joey felt sweat trickle the length of his scar.

There was someone in the darkness up ahead. Maybe a runner, maybe a scout. Joey planned to take him down, apply some squeeze, and get a guide right back to the squatters' camp. He tightened the straps on his leather gloves, then hitched himself into a squat, paused a moment, then slipped forward.

The last thing he expected to stumble on, in the silo's inky shadows, was a scattering of split, bloody, flesh-streaked bones. His goggles showed them warmer than the ground they lay on, and then he found a blood-stained, ripped-up tweed jacket, carelessly half buried in gravel. Joey hesitated. This wasn't right. This was nasty, plain nasty. Still, he'd handled nasty before. If the damned squatters were cannibals, well, he'd seen worse. At least, he felt sure he had, somewhere.

A scuffling noise directly ahead alerted him to a nearby presence. Joey tensed himself, flexing his hands, getting ready for the Sanger Sock – he'd need it tonight, he was now certain. These squatters weren't pushovers, nosiree. They were mean, they were prairieboys down to their ugly, rock-hard, bloodthirsty core. Well, they were about to meet Joey 'Rip' Sanger from Scarborough.

A twig snapped behind him, and swearing, Joey whirled. Crouched in front of him was a naked, hairy man, his teeth bared and his eyes gleaming in the moonlight.

'A Luddite!' Joey hissed.

'Arlubye!' the man hissed back.

'Your time's up, bastard!'

'Yortimssup, basarr!'

'Come along peaceably, fella.'

'Guhmlahnbeesly, bela.'

Joey's eyes narrowed. 'You mocking my Ontario accent? Fine, have it that way. Ever heard of the Sanger Sock? You're about to make its acquaintance, y'poor sod.'

'Yablah,' the man said.

Joey jumped the man, his fists whistling a blinding flurry of blows.

The moon had almost set when Joey woke up, feeling

like death run over by Donald the Diesel Engine. There wasn't a single area of his body that didn't feel bruised, not a bone that didn't feel broken, not a hair left that wasn't crinkled and split at the ends. 'What happened?' he mumbled.

A clear, calm voice answered. 'Not sure, friend. Lucky we came on you when we did. Someone out there doesn't like you. Had you spread-eagled on the tracks. Lucky for you I keep a point, or we'd have rolled right over you. Jojum damn near stepped on you as it was.'

Blinking blearily, Joey tried to sit up, was surprised that he could, and looked around. He sighed. 'By God, it really is a 57 Wells, isn't it? Mint condition, too.' He saw the man who'd been speaking, disheveled but somehow clean-looking, thinning gray hair, a lean, strong frame, a face of solidly delineated angles and planes, and eyes that were sharp with intelligence. 'Who the hell are you?' Joey rasped.

The man smiled. 'The one you're looking for, Mr. Sanger. The name's John Gully. You're riding on *Gully's Block,* as the boys and girls like to call it. Ergonomically designed, a shantytown on wheels, fully self-sufficient, with a hydroponics car, a freeze-car stocked with meat purchased from local ranchers, and modestly luxurious accommodations to suit three hundred people. We stay out of everyone's way, we provide a safe house for the homeless of the city, we rehabilitate, teach trades, run our own justice system, use our own currency – gold, in fact.'

'How in hell you afford all that, bud?'

Gully smiled. 'I was an architect, once, from a

wealthy family. I inherited, invested, made bundles, then dropped out.'

'And that's it? You're some kind of eccentric patron of the poor? Geez, what a sorry story.'

The man shrugged. 'Not really. I just wanted out. Plain and simple, but the creative impulses remained. I needed a challenge. I found one.'

'Well—' Joey struggled to his feet, groaning softly before taking a deep breath. '—the challenge is over, Gully. I'm shutting you down.'

'I was afraid of that. And here I thought you, more than anyone else, would appreciate what I've done here.'

'Why in hell should I do that?'

'The history, the tradition. This city was built on the rails. No one cares anymore, and it's all going down the tubes. Faded glory. What a waste. We've gotten so scared of taking risks, we're just letting ourselves sink into mediocre oblivion. It's a damned shame, if you ask me. The people running your life, Mr. Sanger, they have no hearts, no sense of wonder, no ambition beyond self-serving greed; and they don't give a damn about you, so long as you do jobs for them. When it comes time for you to retire, they'll expect you to just drift away, find some hovel, cash your measly pension checks, vote conservative, and grumble about the youth of the day and live in terror of those who have not, but want. And they'll keep smiling and reassuring and feeding your paranoia until you're dropped six feet down and rotting in a pine box.'

'Not Joey "Rip" Sanger, they won't.'

John Gully laughed. 'You're a lifer, Mr. Sanger. A

product of inertia, collective malaise. Single-minded, stubborn, your own man – sure, all those things to comfort your sense of self-worth, but it's all an illusion because when it's all said and done, you toe the line just like the rest of them.'

'Heard about enough of your sermon, preacher. Lay on the steam and let's roll 'er in to the yards. I'm beat and my ears ache.'

'Sorry, can't do that, Mr. Sanger.'

With these words, three large men entered the engine room, carrying ropes. Joey groaned a second time. There wasn't enough left in him to resist. He glared at John Gully as the men tied him up. 'Plan to dump me off a trestle?'

'Trestle? As in trestle bridge?' John laughed. 'We're on the prairie, remember? There aren't any trestles. No, we'll just hold on to you till things blow over—'

'I won't blow over,' Joey said. 'You'll have to kill me.'

'Why bother saving you, then? Oh no, we're not murderers. We'll think of something, I'm sure. In the meantime, relax, Mr. Sanger. You've got some healing up to do. Who took you out, by the way?'

'A cannibal Luddite, I think. With a speech impediment.'

'Ahh, so you've met Sool Koobie, then.'

'Who?'

'A Neanderthal. It's a long story, but consider yourself lucky. He must've been well fed; either that or you eat meat three times a day—'

'Damn right I do,' Joey growled. 'I ain't no sussy.'

'Lucky you.'

Joey fell silent. At the moment, he felt anything but

lucky. His Sanger Sock had failed. For the first time in generations, it had failed. He was a broken man, and the feeling was new to him, and he didn't like it one bit.

3.
the table invites

The Habby Modeler's owner stood uncertainly behind the counter, surrounded by glass-fronted cases containing his military and science fiction model collection. He had one hand behind his back, and his T-shirt was a grayish white with the words SMALL IS BETTER emblazoned on it. The man peered at Max through thick glasses, craning his neck and shifting whenever Max edged down one of the rows and out of sight.

Sweat ran down Max's body, cool under the satin shirt he was wearing. He clutched a folded page of instructions in one damp hand. Habby. What an idiot. Happy, hobby, yeah, right. Cute as cow pies, fella. Shit, I'm running out of time. He checked his watch. He was due at the table at Culture Quo in ten minutes, and then, immediately following supper, they'd all trek off to the annual Awards Night at the Unified Cultural Workers Assembly Hall – otherwise known to city denizens as 'the Pyramid.' And then he'd receive his award as Most Promising Artist of the Year, and a check for ten grand.

Hissing in frustration under his breath, Max headed

toward the counter, and the sloppy, overweight man behind it. 'Technical question,' Max said, smiling.

'Only kind I can answer,' the man replied. 'How many King Tigers did Nazi Germany issue in 1944? I know. How close was the V3 rocket to full-scale production? I know. What size were Patton's army boots? I know. To what extent did Hegel's philosophy influence Adolf's private gardener? I—'

'Yeah, I know,' Max cut in. 'You know. But tell me this.' He unfolded the instructions and laid them out on the counter.

'Ooh,' the man said, 'Special Edition Klingon battle cruiser – you musta bought that years ago—'

'Yeah yeah, listen. Look here, the instructions says part 6B attaches to part 7A.'

'Yeah, so?'

'So, there is no 6B! There's a 6A, and a 7B, but no 6B! How the hell can I complete my sculpture without 6B!'

'Sculpture? That's a model.'

'Shut the fuck up. You're talking to an artist here, not some creepy weasel-faced chip-stuffed pimple factory.'

'Yeah, right,' the man drawled. 'Well, did you look in the box? Coulda come loose from the plastic trees.'

'Of course I looked. It's not there.'

'Huh. Well, sometimes the company screws up. Sometimes a part gets left out. That makes your kit a collector's item – something wrong?'

Max stared at the man blankly. 'Left out?'

'Yeah, sure. Happens all the time. You just have to send for the part. Or, hell, I'll swap you with one of the newer models – they look neater, anyway. Those guys' –

he pointed at the cardboard box – 'don't even know the cruiser's real name.'

'How can they leave a part out? What the hell am I going to do? I need a sculpture right now, in the next five minutes.' Max's gaze cast wildly around the store, fixed at last on the finished models behind the man.

Scowling, the man said, 'I don't sell my World War II stuff, and even if I did, it'd be damned expensive.'

'I can pay it. Give me that tank—'

'Like hell I will. That's a Swedish S-tank. Piece of garbage on the battlefield, but it's a collector's item.'

'I'll pay anything.'

'Not the S-tank.' The man still had one hand behind his back, and seemed to be working at something there.

'Well, what do you have that you'll sell?'

'Assembled? Well, I got two copies of the submarine from that old TV series in the Sixties. Remember *Voyage to the Bottom of the Sea*?'

'Imaginative title,' Max snapped. 'Let's see the damned thing.'

'Well, the one I'd sell has had some, uh, improvements on it. I did it when I was a kid, you see. Not even a serious collector yet, you understand—'

'Let's see it!'

The man reached with his free hand under the counter and pulled out a long plastic submarine, its nose dish-shaped. On its underside were four wheels. 'I stuck a motor in it,' the man explained. 'Nickel-cadmium batteries, probably still runs. Let's check—'

'I don't care if it runs, you asshole. How much?'

'With an attitude like yours, asshole, two hundred bucks, firm.'

Max pulled out his wallet and tossed down one of his many credit cards. 'Fine.'

'We don't take credit cards,' the man smirked. 'Cash. No check, either. Cash.'

'Scumbag, I'm a Nacht – recognize the name?'

'No.'

'The Nachts are in lingerie. Filthy rich.'

'Yeah, well, I'm outa that phase. I still want cash.'

'Fine!' Max pulled out a wad of bills. 'You just fucked up my supper, prick.' He counted out ten twenties, slapped them on the table, then had to wait while the man counted them again, all with one hand. 'Got a gun back there or something?' Max asked.

'I wish. Sometimes my anus closes right up. I gotta work it loose again, or everything backs up, if you know what I mean. You want me to wrap it?'

'Uh, no. A box will do.'

'Yeah but there's some highly breakable protuber- ances—'

'Do I give a shit? I paid for it. It's mine. I can do what the hell I want with it. Now, hand it over.'

The man had found a long flower box, but he now draped his arm protectively over it, his eyes wide, dribbles of sweat running down from his greasy hair. 'I made it,' he whined. 'You're not supposed to break it.'

'Just a joke, friend,' Max said, smiling. 'Honest. I'll take good care of it. Now, can I have it, please? I've got a dinner date with a table.'

'You're dating a table? Cool.' The man pushed the box toward Max, who snatched it up. 'Hey!' the man shouted as Max rushed to the door. 'I'm loosening up!'

Six minutes later Max reached the door of Culture

Quo. The restaurant was packed with pre-Awards patrons, and the air was humming with feigned excitement. Max pushed through the lineup, jabbing recalcitrant SOBs with the flower box until he stepped clear.

And there it was. The table. Where he'd dreamed of sitting, there in the company of greatness, or at the very least self-importance. And the empty chair – two of them, in fact – and Brandon Safeword gesticulating as he pontificated to his adoring audience consisting of his wife, Penny Foote-Safeword, and Lucy Mort. Max blinked uncertainly as he approached. Brandon's head looked too big, and Lucy's too small, as if someone had been messing with the camera lens through which Max observed – not that he was observing these details through a camera lens. Even so, what met his eyes seemed strangely skewed.

'Ahh, Maximillian!' Brandon called out. Many heads turned, the conversations at the other tables stilling for a brief moment as eyes fixed on Max, who arrived at the table and pulled out a chair and then sat down. 'Excellent timing, my boy,' Brandon said. 'We were just about to order.'

Penny thrust a menu into Max's hand. He set down the flower box, edged it with a foot under his own chair, then turned his attention to the menu.

Lucy's voice came out as a tiny squeak. 'I'll have the feral garden salad, wheat stir-fry with birch bark plain on the side, and a double lite alcohol. Thanks.'

Smacking her lips, Penny said, 'Were the scampi harvested in dolphin-safe nets? Excellent. I'll have that, and brown rice plain. No, no appetizer – I'd be stuffed! And a triple lite alcohol plain. Marvelous. Brandon, darling?'

Culture Quo
organic vegetarian dining

<u>appetizers</u>

barley soup

thirty-six-grain toast

feral garden salad

<u>main courses</u>

triticale quiche (sans eggs)

soya prime rib

scampi-shell salad

precious porridge

wheat stir-fry (with ginger)

bannock (made with canola oil)

<u>desserts</u>

oat cakes

soya-shell apple pie

yeast-free canola cookies

sugar-free ice water

(the fluffy slushy)

<u>beverages</u>

barley water

barley tea

wheat milk

soya milk

<u>on the side</u>

brown rice plain

soya rice plain

wild rice plain

birch bark plain

<u>alcoholic drinks</u>

lite draft

lite ale

lite red wine

lite white wine

lite citrus coolers

lite alcohol plain

'Oh no, Maximillian first, by all means.'

'Uh, thanks. I'll have the thirty-six-grain toast, the triticale quiche, and a lite ale, please.'

'Sounds perfect,' Brandon said to Max. 'Of course,' he added, leaning over to nudge Max with an iron-hard forearm, 'as emcee tonight, the last thing I'd need is all that roughage ringing the old bell below, eh? Hah hah! Ho ho! No, instead, I'll have the soya prime rib, with wild rice, and wheat milk to preserve my elocution. Wonderful, we're all set!'

'Where's Professor Palmister?' Max asked.

'Vanished,' Brandon intoned. 'A cause for great concern. Left not a trace of his whereabouts, and believe me, it's not like him to miss this of all nights. Nine out of the ten incipient award winners come from his class, after all.'

Max glanced at Lucy, who taught at the rival university. Her minuscule face was bent down toward the glass of mineral water in her hands.

'Next year, of course,' Brandon drawled, 'the balance will shift, right, Lucy?'

She nodded mutely, not looking up. The purse on her lap was inordinately large, long, bulky, and she reached down with one hand to stroke it a couple times, then reached back up to her glass.

The appetizers arrived. Max had hoped to add to the conversation somewhat, but the thirty-six-grain toast swelled into a glutinous, doughy ball in his mouth, and he was left chewing on his first bite until the main courses arrived. In the meantime, Brandon spoke. 'Ever been to the Pyramid, Max? Thought not. A wonderful work of art in itself, housing the city's finest publicly owned collection of fine art. Well, publicly owned is something of a misnomer, we'd all not hesitate to admit – at least in private, hah hah! The galleries are sealed against pollution, and that includes uninvited people across the board, and the wonder of it is, the Board of Directors ensure that few – very few indeed – are ever invited to peruse the collection. I, of course, have been many times. Truly remarkable. Brilliant work, all of it, packed chock-full with seminal meanings, dire significance, cultural value. There's even a copy of Penny's book, stored in an airtight, alarm-fitted cabinet, in a room all its own.'

The main courses arrived. Max managed to swallow down the mouthful of toast and, greatly relieved, permitted the waitress to remove the rest. 'Is the collection very large?' he asked. 'I've seen the building from the outside. It's huge.'

'There are seven works of art in the Pyramid,' Brandon said. 'Each a treasure in its own right. Most of the lottery funding went into constructing the edifice, naturally, and these days into the salaries of the two hundred staff members. A triumph of city planning, the envy of cities the world over.'

There followed five minutes of nonverbal utterances as everyone tucked into their suppers: crunching, slurping, gnawing, nibbling, chewing – mostly chewing, although the loudest sound assailing Max's ears was the twin cavernous whistles issuing from Brandon's enormous nostrils. His head appeared to have grown larger since Max first sat down, and each breath Brandon drew in seemed to create a momentary vacuum in the center of the table, followed by a hair-flicking gust. No one else seemed to notice, even though Lucy's head was pulled and pushed with alarming force, giving her trouble in matching her forkfuls of food with her mouth.

Desserts were then ordered, and when the plates were scraped clean, Brandon leaned back with a loud, atmospherically traumatizing sigh, and said, 'We'd best be off, ladies and gentleman. The Pyramid beckons, the Awards await our surprise and delight, and the day's light fades.'

'Do you think Don's all right?' Penny asked.

'Oh, I imagine so,' her husband replied as he and everyone else at the table stood. A moment later the patrons at all the other tables also stood. Max retrieved his flower box – he wasn't sure if he'd need to show an actual sample of his work, but he wasn't taking any chances.

'Well,' Penny said, 'he's awfully absentminded. But on Awards Night?'

'Perhaps just another case of acute constipation,' Brandon said.

'But it's been days!'

'Just like last time, if I recall. Shall we proceed?'

Max reached for his wallet, but Brandon waved a hand. 'Nonsense, we have dined on my account. After all, an artist must watch his coin, eh? Hah hah! Ho ho! By God, I'm feeling much better!'

4.
the dance of dances

Sool Koobie kneeled close to a wall of his cave, a bone tube in one hand, the fingertips of the other red with paint, his mouth full of spit and charcoal. The wall's red bricks were smooth with age, shiny with the greasy smears of Sool's shoulders in constant passage, and now crowded in painted images of the various spirits Sool had freed over the years – freed being Sool's unconscious euphemism for murdered in cold blood. Overhead, the cave's roof, consisting of woven detritus and misshapen pieces of corrugated aluminum, drummed and rustled beneath the night's light rain. The occasional rivulet dribbled down onto the smeared cobblestone floor, pooling close to the manhole cover, which led down into Sool's own private world of nether spirits and odd, bloodstained tubes of gauze that Sool threaded together to make his dancing cloak of death, which he now wore in homage to the god who was art, the gifts that were red ocher and charcoal paint, and the demonic angel who raced inside his head and gave painful birth to the images he now fashioned on the wall of his cave.

His was a world of magic, of gestures that were sacred, of dreams that were stories, and memories that were truth. In his propitiations before the hunt, and in the images he painted now the hunt was done, Sool had no sense of past or present, for each belonged to the central, tactile, physical truth that was the hunt itself.

Setting the tube to his lips, Sool leaned close to the wall and softly sprayed the wet charcoal, outlining the curving sweep of Don Palmister's back, then the heart-line – the perspective a perfect rendition of what had met his eyes moments before he'd driven the spear home. With the red ocher paint in his other hand, he daubed on the flesh, the hint of muscle beneath the corduroy hide, the color that was life and earth. In moments he was done. He spat out what was left of the charcoal, wiped the paint from his hand on his thigh and buttocks, adjusted the gauze-tube cloak, then cocked his head with a tense, febrile motion.

In the air, in the wet wind that drifted in from outside! A herd of vegetarians! A herd so large, so close! Sool Koobie's flesh quivered. A low whimper escaped his blackened lips. He spun into a flurry of gauze and beads and braids, the world in his perfect mind plunging into a dance of exaltation, communal propitiation, perfunctory mass extermination. The dance carried him into ecstasy, as he felt the spirits gathering, joining his flesh, surging through his veins and arteries.

And the sky blackened overhead, and thunder rumbled, and lightning flashed, and a Neanderthal turned his glittering, narrow, red-rimmed eyes upon the world outside, and thought of death.

5.
discoveries

Annie waited below with her three bodyguards and the limo, but Andy 'Kit' Breech gave little consideration to their likely impatience with this delay. He kneeled in the closet, the door open, the shoes flung out and lying on the living-room rug behind him, the secret trapdoor pried open, and the strange, mysterious electronic array spread out before him. Headphones, with an impossibly long headband between the speakers . . . Who the hell makes headphones for octopods!? A flat box, a round keyboard with strange symbols imprinted on each key, dials, switches, VU meters, frequency-finders. An aerial, wireless, made and sold by Radio Shack. A calculator, Texas Instruments, with trig functions and expanded memory, a diagram with penciled arc calculations, tensile strengths, velocity projections, angles, stress factors for some kind of mineral. Jottings, obscure notations, my God, what is all this?

'ASAP, give me a memo, please, help,' Andy babbled, pulling at his lower lip. He found a second diagram, illustrating – with a precise hand – no, tentacle – a condom. What? Stress calculations, elasticity factors, probability curves. He clambered out of the closet, realizing he was gibbering wordlessly but not caring, and crawled up to the aquarium. Kit wouldn't meet his eye. The octopus lounged under its rock, glutted with a half-pound of calamari, and slowly twirled one tentacle tip with another; still another tentacle tapped slowly in time on the gravel bottom, and still another held up its huge . . . head, or body, or whatever that blob's called. I used to know. I used to know everything about octopods. I used to ooze confidence when detailing my wonderful pet to each and every woman I brought up here – they'd see the incredible sensuality octopods exude, the strength of their sinuous limbs, the quiet awareness in their eyes, their startling explosiveness when they pounced – and they'd all damn near drag me into bed, wrapping themselves around me and grunting and gasping and begging – but now, but now I don't know anymore. I don't know anything. I feel weak, sucked clean, impotent. What can I do?

Then suddenly he knew exactly what he was to do. 'Kit,' he hissed darkly. 'When I get back, it's down the toilet with you. You brought it on yourself, Kit. You've left me no choice. You're pike-meat, Kit. Sorry, old friend, but this is what it's come to, after all these years.'

The intercom buzzed again, and Annie's tinny-squeezed voice called out, 'Andeee! Please, lovemuffin! We'll be late! And Stubble needs to pee! Why didn't you go with the minister? We weren't expecting this detour, Andeee. Hurry down, please!'

The minister. Ride with him? With those pigeons trying to nail him every minute? You must be insane. Oh no, no way. He scrambled to his feet and stabbed the intercom button. 'On my way, darling,' he said.

At the door he paused one last time to glare at Kit. The octopus had edged to the corner of the aquarium and was watching him, waiting for him to leave. It's all connected. I know it is. I just thought my underwear were stretching, but that wasn't it. My penis is shrinking, my testicles are withdrawing, the hair's all falling out. I think you've been poisoning my condoms, Kit. Is it jealousy? Are you, uh, gay? This can't go on – I didn't even notice the last time I had a hard-on – I can't keep making excuses, my answerphone's full, the bitches are getting nastier with every message they leave. I just hide in here, staring at you. I can't think. I can't do anything. You've got to be . . . removed, Kit. I never thought you'd be the one to betray me. The fatal kiss, the taste of your salty beak on my lips. E tu, Kitay?

Heartbroken but with a new resolution, Andy left the apartment.

6.
escape!

Jojum was the biggest bruiser Joey 'Rip' Sanger had ever seen. Of course, size was irrelevant, but it looked like the man could back it all up – he had fists that looked like stone mauls, and damn near the same color, too. And yet, there he stood, delicately, beautifully guiding the steam engine through the darkness, his touch a caress on the controls, his piggy eyes squinting into the darkness ahead.

Joey had been tied to a grab rail opposite the control station where Jojum sat. The knots were secure, the ropes unyielding. Gully and the other two scrubs had gone back to one of the other cars, leaving Jojum, just Jojum, but Joey knew it'd be enough. In any case, he was trussed up so tight, he could barely breathe.

Joey tried talking. 'Ain't no point in holdin' me, if ya think about it. Gully's got a problem, and it's me, and sooner or later he'll have to drop the black glove at my feet, and then the short straw will need picking. But I know Gully – I know people just like him. All heart and fairness to keep you sops in line, nodding your heads to whatever crap he delivers, but picking that straw won't be blind chance, Jojum. He'll have squirreled the whole thing, and it's my guess he's already picked you out to do the job. You're big, and dumb – as far as he's concerned. He's the brain and you're the meat, and the meat does what the brain directs. You'll end up with a murder rap, Jojum, and Gully will be clean grease sliding off into the sunset. You're young, boy, but I ain't. I seen enough in my day to know what I'm looking at – this here cozy world Gully's devised, well, he's the emperor, ain't he? King Shit of Turd Mountain, right? You're here to stroke his ego, all of you, and t'make him feel virtuous. So he's cleaned the homeless off the streets – that's exactly what the powers that be want – to not see you, so they don't have to think about you, so they don't have to do anything about you. If Gully's rich, it's cause he's being paid outa the premier's pocket, mark my words.'

Jojum slowly slid his flat gaze over at Joey. He blinked. 'You say something, bud? My hearing ain't too good. Say, that's two nice shiners you got there, bud.'

'Oh, bloody hell,' Joey swore.

There was a shout and all of a sudden Wild Bill Chan was clambering up Jojum to batter at the man's head, and the redcap was clambering in through the entranceway, knife in hand, and slicing at Joey's bonds.

'Hot damn!' Joey laughed.

Jojum and Chan were having a real set-to, grunting and grimacing and clobbering at each other, staggering back and forth, crashing into things, breaking things . . .

The ropes fell away and Joey leapt to his feet. 'Hey!' he yelled at the two fighting men. 'You two! Cut that out! Quit it, or you'll—'

Jojum slammed into the controls, snapping the handles at the far forward position. The train jolted, its wheels screaming, the dark scene outside quickly sliding past in a blur. Then Jojum, Chan clinging to him, caromed into the redcap, then Joey, and the fight got interesting for a while. Eventually Joey managed to pull himself away – he looked at the broken controls, then out the window. The redcap crawled to his side.

'Now we've gone and done it!' Joey swore. 'We got ourselves a runaway train, and we're all dead men!'

Jojum and Chan stopped fighting briefly to look over at Joey and the redcap – the boy's face was white with fear, since the train was already going too fast to jump off – then the two men resumed their battle royal. Joey thought about joining in again, but Chan and Jojum seemed perfectly matched, and looked to be having fun besides.

Joey sighed. 'Cheer up, redcap,' he said, patting his pocket. 'You're as close to earning your fiver as you've ever been.'

7.
revelation!

Arthur Revell stumbled down the dark, wet street, alter-
nately groaning and cursing. He'd swelled, burst
through his clothing, and was now able to glare
in through the dimly lit windows on the second floor of
the buildings he staggered past. Just for fun he punched
out a few, leaving a wake of ringing alarms. His horns
had grown long and they itched, as if eager for goring,
for rending flesh in a splash of fatal blood. 'Gimme a
Glenlivet!' he bellowed at the storm sky overhead, then
kicked a parked car across to the other side of the street.
He paused to stare at its crumpled remains, then
grinned. 'Cheap, smelly cigars,' he rasped. 'Days without bathing, picking my nose in public, farting in
restaurants, aargh!'

What's happening to me? What am I becoming?

He heard sirens approaching from behind. Arthur
spun around, spied the flashing lights. He picked up a
garbage bin – the kind that trucks hoisted up and tipped
into their backsides – and flung it at the patrol car.
There was a huge crash, then an explosion. 'Aaargh!'
Arthur crowed, shaking his fists. He threw his shoulder

against an old brownstone building, felt its foundations crack, heard all the crap inside rattle, shatter, and tinkle.

I am the ills of the nation! Awake with sour, deadly disposition. You all asked for it, every damn one of you, whoever you really are. Walls? I'll smash down your walls. Barricades? I'll crush them underfoot. Armored personnel carriers? One slash of my serrated tail and you'll be flying in ruin. Welfare cuts? I'll take what I need. Taxman at the door? I'll rend him limb from limb. Budget cuts in every social service left to us? I'll devour the banks – crunch crunch crunch – I'll incinerate the legislative assemblies, the house of parliament, the cronies on the Boards, the bloodless technocrats and vampire lawyers, the money-hoarders, the multi-national forestry companies, oil companies, insurance companies, chain restaurants, mall designers, pharma-ceutical companies, cut-price food stores, trucking companies, corrupt unions, reformers, liberals, con-servatives, separatists, unionists, lobbyists, bureaucrats, puritans, fanatic joggers, anti-smoking groups, anti-drug groups, bad television shows, the cynical, blood-hungry media. You've all made me ill. Terribly ill. I'm at the end of my rope, choking for want of com-passion, humanity, common sense, and the end – God, the end – to lies!

Arthur now towered over the core's turn-of-the-century buildings. He could see the dome of the legislature, he could see the peak of the Unified Cultural Workers Assembly Hall, and the skyscrapers housing the multinational companies and their tons and tons of useless paper and files and statistics and rules and pro-hibitions and secret codes – the reams of supposed authority, the chains of a dubious civilization, the bullshit breeding flics of misery and despair to a downtrodden, self-destructing species.

'My God,' he breathed. 'I know what I am. I know what I've become! It's all clear to me now, at last. I'm awake, at last awake, and the world will shake! The towers will topple! I am the monster you created, the one whose awakening you dreaded, sought to impede, tried to ignore – but it's too late! Aaargh! And aargh again! What will you do now that I'm awake, eh? Eh? *Eh? Eeehhh!* You see, I know what I am now! Finally! I'm an artist! *Aaarrghhh!!!*'

His sights set on the legislature buildings and the corporate castles, Arthur Revell began his rampage of destruction.

8.
liberation at last at last

In the way of octopods, Kit squeezed through the last keyhole and flopped out down onto the floor. He raised himself up on his eight legs and looked around. Silence, an apartment asleep in the absence of its owner. Outside the wind howled, thunder boomed, lightning flashed.

Kit slimed his way into the bedroom, moving from one cover to the next, darting and sploshing and oozing, and arrived at the dresser drawer. He opened it and extracted the large box of condoms. The box tucked under one arm, Kit returned to the living room.

The radio equipment had proved a perfect decoy. Andrew was confused. It was important that Andrew be confused, allowing Kit to complete his preparations. Squatting in the sunken living room, Kit opened the box and began ripping open the plastic envelopes of condoms, one after another, until he had on the rug in front of him 632 slippery, rubbery, multicolored tubes. Then he began tying one to the next, fashioning a rope of remarkable elasticity.

This completed, Kit carried the rope to the balcony door, which he unlocked and slid to one side. He slipped out onto the balcony, quickly knotted one end of the rope to the wrought-iron railing, and then the other end as well. He paused, turned to stare across the intervening distance to the balcony on the building opposite, and to the lovely pooch that sat there, watching him. Kit waved. The pooch's ears pricked up; its tail thumped once.

Kit returned to his task. He positioned himself in the center of the condom rope, then, using all his strength, and reaching for each carefully arranged piece of furniture, Kit pulled himself across the floor toward the closet door. The rope stretched tight around his soft body, but he contracted his muscles against it and kept on crawling, inching ever closer to the closet.

He finally reached it, wrapping the tip of each tentacle around the doorknob. The rope, now a slingshot, hummed taut across the length of the apartment. Kit slowly worked himself around until he was facing the open balcony door. He ran through the calculations once again in his mind, set his beak in a determined tight line, then let go.

The doorway flashed by in a blur; then he was out, flying through the air, the apartment and the balcony opposite him growing big alarmingly fast. He splayed out his eight tentacles, felt the elastic webbing between each limb fill with air, braking his murderous speed. He saw the pooch cock its head, its eyes widening as Kit raced straight for her. The dog ducked at the last moment and Kit splatted into the glass door behind it, then slid down to a crumpled heap on the balcony floor.

The pooch looked down at Kit. At the first sign of movement, her tail thumped once.

Kit shook himself, then podded himself upright. The dog licked him on the forehead and Kit sent two tentacles around the sweet quadruped in a brief but emotional hug; then he clambered swiftly onto the dog's back. He settled himself in, reached up, and slid aside the glass door.

'Is that you, Moopsy?' a quavering voice asked from inside.

Kit kicked Moopsy?' flanks and they entered. An old woman sat on the sofa, blinking bemusedly at the two of them. 'Have you found a date, then?' she asked. 'Oh, I'm so proud of you, Moopsy. Be sure to be home before dawn, dear, you know how I'll worry.'

Kit guided Moopsy to the door, freeing one tentacle to wave at the old woman before they left. Time had come, at last, to paint the town red.

9.
and they shall be rewarded

Max stood with Brandon, Lucy, and Penny at the foot of the steps to the Unified Cultural Workers Assembly Hall. 'That's a lot of steps,' he said, eyeing the climb.

'Six hundred and sixty-six, my soon-to-be-marginally-famous friend. Keeps out the riffraff, you see. The appreciation of art demands hard work, as you well know. Anything casually, easily received is crass commercialism, and let's not be naïve, such practitioners exist in this city, though of course we'll never acknowledge them. I can think of one off the top of my head, which is something in itself—'

Eyeing Brandon's expanding head, Max had to agree.

'—I believe her name is Elana Oxbow, her only positive feature being she is of a visible minority. Native, I believe. Despite that, her primary interest seems to be increasing her audience in size and appreciation. Can you imagine anything so . . . vulgar, but more than that, Maximillian, she's also plum dangerous, a threat to our subtle way of life.'

'I hate her,' Lucy squeaked from beside Brandon's knee. 'She should die, I think. That's what I think, and what I think is more important than you think, unless you think the way I think, making us think alike, and are you thinking what I'm thinking, that's what I want to know.'

'Indeed,' Brandon rumbled. 'We should be on our way.'

'Ooh,' Penny cried. 'Here comes Annie and Andy and Monk and Stubble and Nick. And a helicopter – that must be the minister, oh, what timing!'

Annie's limo rolled up and those inside climbed out. The thunder and lightning continued overhead, along with the occasional gust of wind, but it seemed the rain had passed, and the late spring air was turning sultry. Annie waved and, followed by her three bodyguards, approached. Andy hesitated by the limo, torn by some kind of indecision. Another limo approached, and the helicopter had landed, crushing a bag lady but otherwise uneventfully, and now waited, its props whirring.

Curious, Max watched. The limo stopped perilously close to the helicopter. The black vehicle looked battered, dented, with blots of feather stuck to it here and there. The door opened and the minister bolted, racing across the intervening space for the helicopter. The props made a strange budding noise and the night air was filled with gray feathers, and then the minister was inside, and Andy 'Kit' Breech was heading up to it at a more leisurely pace. He leaned into the cockpit and exchanged a few words with the minister, then turned and made his way toward the group.

Max swung his attention back to those who'd gathered around Brandon. Annie was speaking. '. . . and I really figured there'd be some kind of takeover bid at CAPSs, but Monk here intercepted two frustrated artists in the foyer. He castrated the man—' Her nose wrinkled momentarily. '—rather messily, in my opinion, and intellectually raped the other, who was female, it turned out.'

Max couldn't help himself. 'Intellectually raped, Annie?'

She nodded. 'At gunpoint, he forced her to knit a feminist quilt, right then and there, until she finally broke down and started foaming at the mouth. It was quite exciting, actually. Anyway, that's why we were late, that and picking up Andy – who's not well at all tonight, are you, Andy?'

Max looked over at the man, of whom he'd heard only hints of rumors, suggesting that here stood the real power behind . . . everything. An assistant deputy to the minister, or some such thing, a bureaucrat, a technocrat, a lifer in the game. The man looked like hell, and threw Annie an ill-disguised scowl when her words drew everyone's attention to him.

'I'm fine,' he growled. 'The minister will join us inside.'

'Excellent,' Brandon said.

They all turned to watch the helicopter rise from the street and skim up the steps to the Pyramid's landing platform on the roof.

'Shall we ascend, then?' Brandon asked the group, with a broad smile. 'Come on, climb aboard.'

Max stared as Lucy, her bulky, heavy handbag in tow, climbed onto Brandon's left thigh, wrapping her arms and legs around the tree-trunk-like bole of muscle and bone. Then Penny moved up and settled into Brandon's arms. Annie positioned herself piggyback behind his broad shoulders. Brandon grinned over at the remaining men. 'You'll all have to walk, I'm afraid, because I'm all man and certain things are just not done. I'm sure you can manage, hah hah! Ho ho! Tally ho!'

Brandon took the first steps two at a time, then three, then five, then ten, then twenty, leaping upward in powerful bounds, the hair on his massive head waving its licks in the wind of his swift, effortless passage.

Max glanced over at Andy, who was still scowling. 'I hear it's easier if you zigzag,' he said helpfully.

Andy curled his lip. 'Don't talk to me about zigzagging, you pup.'

In a flurry of motion Monk, Stubble, and Nick had their M16s out and laid down a spraying fire into a crowd of Boy Scouts who'd edged too close in their annual litter-collecting drive. Innocent voices screamed.

'Cut that out!' Andy bellowed.

The guns stuttered into silence, leaving a moaning pile of youthful bodies buried in black plastic and litter.

'I'm minded,' Andy hissed, 'to let the media hang you all on this one!'

The three helmeted men hung their heads.

'But,' Andy continued in a rasping tone, 'I'm in a generous mood tonight. Now, get out the climbing gear – Annie's feeling lost and fearful for her life without you at her back. Hop to it. As for you, Maxipad, get climbing – I'll be stuck to your tail like used toilet paper, count on it – because I'll tell you right now, I don't trust you.'

'Oh,' Max said. 'But I've brought one of my sculptures.' He lifted the flower box.

'You think I give a shit, boy? Now climb.'

They arrived at the glass and steel entranceway fifteen minutes later, Max drenched in sweat and seriously winded. Other guests had gathered around an oxygen tent set up just inside the doors, while paramedics worked desperately and, it seemed, unsuccessfully on another one to one side of the landing. As Max crouched at the last step, kneading out a stitch in his side, and Andy stood unruffled and barely pink-cheeked beside him, the three bodyguards arrived like an SAS team, on ropes, with grappling hooks, and in urban assault formation. They quickly took stock of the situation, checked their private frequency helmet transmitters, then headed inside to find Annie.

'Don't get near me inside,' Andy told Max. 'Don't even look in my direction. Got it?'

'Uh, yeah, right.'

'Fine. Now get out of my sight.'

Nodding, Max collected his flower box and staggered inside.

A few hundred of the city's select crowded the high-ceilinged hallway, recovering with glasses of white wine and nibblets provided by Culture Quo, which were brought to them individually by starving artists working part-time as waiters and waitresses. Off to the right was the entrance to the theater, where the awards would be handed out, but that was still an hour away. Max scanned the crowd until he saw Brandon's massive head – a brown hump like the shoulders of a bison rising above all the other guests – and the knot of familiars around him. Max headed over.

'Don't fret, Lucy dear, dear Lucy,' Brandon was

saying. 'I've ensured that the gaggle of critics are all seated in a single row, just as you requested. Right up at the front, as per your wishes, and thereby subject to your righteously baleful gaze throughout the proceedings.' It seemed Lucy would be sitting up at the front, on the stage platform, along with other important personages, including the minister, Andy, Penny, and Annie. Max had been provided a seat along one aisle toward the back, thus ensuring a long, momentous approach down to collect his award. 'Ahh, Maxmillian, my friend, I'm glad to see you survived the ordeal of the steps without much discomfort, such is youth, eh? Hah hah! Ho ho! Well, I must ready myself for the task at hand, so I will leave you for now, in the capable and expressive hands of my darling wife. Cheerio! The next time you see me will be as emcee, standing in the spotlight, my smile warm and my confidence emanating from every pore of my body, hah hah! Ho ho!'

He strode off, the crowd parting before him.

Max saw Annie receive a cellular phone. She listened, frowned, then gestured her three bodyguards closer. She gave them whispered, heated instructions, her face pale, and the men saluted, checked their gear, then headed off. Max followed them with his gaze as they found a door to a service elevator, Monk keying in a code. All three scrambled inside when the doors opened, and Max watched as the lights indicated their descent, down, down into the bowels of the structure.

Penny accidentally kneed Lucy into the lowest shelf of a passing service cart and ignored her dwindling yelps as she edged close to Max and murmured, 'Ready to perform for me tonight, darling?'

'Huh? Tonight? When? After, you mean?'

'I was thinking right up there onstage. Imagine the glory as, in front of a thousand politicians, administrators, professors, and obscure but powerful artists, critics, and media pundits, you were to install your art under my mnemonic mound – I'm almost certain that I was once Margaret Thatcher, you know—'

'But she isn't dead yet, Penny.'

'She isn't? Oh. Well, Joan of Arc, then.'

'Oh, well, she is dead, that's true. But, Penny – in public? I don't know if, uh, I can perform under that kind of—'

'Oh, don't be silly,' Penny said. 'I'm just kidding, besides. We'll polish the tip of the Pyramid after it's over, out under the stormy sky—'

'Sounds uncomfortable—'

She smiled. 'For you, maybe. Oops, what's Annie all heated up about?'

Max turned to see the chief administrator sharply gesticulating for them to join her. She had a set of earphones on, and looked to be in great excitement. 'We'd better see,' Max said.

They headed over.

'Someone's down below,' Annie hissed. 'An intruder. I sent the boys down to take care of him – oh, I knew there'd be a try, a takeover bid, something unsightly and crass. Come with me, we'll head to the security room and we can hear all the gory details – I've given the boys carte blanche!'

The security room housed a bank of television monitors and a com station. A technician sat at the station and nodded to Annie when they entered. He flicked a switch and removed his headphones as, through a vague buzz of speaker static, one of the body-guards' voices whispered, 'Nick? Where the hell are ya, buddy? Shit!'

A second voice broke in. 'It's Stubble, what's your position, Monk?'

'Coordinates 16G, level four. I sent Nick ahead – the tunnel's had its lights busted out. Now I can't reach him. You listening up there, Com? Check your cameras down corridor 32, switch to IR.'

The technician flicked more switches. 'Roger that, Monk. Going visual on my mark – you scoped?'

'No, dammit, there's a bug in the system – you're my eyes, friend.'

'Don't worry,' the technician said, 'I'll pull you through. Okay . . . mark!' He pushed a button, and a monitor to his left flickered. A heat blob was crouched over another one, the one on the floor swiftly cooling. The blob straightened, looked directly at the camera, then snapped out a hand. A black chunk of something flew up at the lens; then there was static.

Annie gasped. The technician now leaned forward in his chair. 'Monk, you reading me? Over?'

'Yeah, what's up?'

'Your boy's down. Intruder is heading your way. Heads up—'

'It's Stubble! Pull back, Monk, until I can support ya! Pull back!'

Monk said, 'I see something – no, just a shadow – no, what, wait – shit!' There was a burst of machine gun fire, then a scream, then the hiss of static.

Stubble spoke. 'Monk? Hey, bruiser, you hearing me?

Nailed the bastard, eh? Monk? Come in, Monk, over. Monk?'

The technician activated a second screen, sweat trickling down his brow. The image that came up was a floor plan of level four. A signatured heat blob was visible near the stairs, slowly edging toward Monk's last known position. Stubble, Max realized. Then he and the others saw another smudge of heat, moving swiftly on an intercept course. 'Stubble!' the technician screamed. 'He's coming straight for you!'

'Where? Shit! Where, dammit – I don't see a damn thing!'

Max stared as the two heat blobs merged.

Stubble was shrieking in terror. 'I don't see! Where, fuck, where – aaghhh!' Again a burst of machine gun fire, then nothing but static.

In the security room, Max and Penny and Annie and the technician watched in horrified silence as the blob made its way to the stairs, entered, and disappeared from the screen.

'Find him again!' Annie screamed.

But the technician shook his head. 'Budget restraints,' he said. 'We had the overall IR network set up for levels six to four, but then we ran out of money. He's taking out the cameras, too. We've lost him.'

'My God,' Penny whispered. 'And he's on his way, and there's not a thing we can do to stop him!'

From outside a bell gonged.

Annie cast Max a frightened glance, then straightened. 'The show must go on. There's only one of him. I'll be right at the front. The minister's guards are there, behind the curtain – you, too, Penny – we'll be safe.' She looked at Max with pity in her eyes. 'Sorry, Max.'

He shook his head, already resigned. 'At least I've been warned,' he said, 'and that's more than anyone else can say out there.'

'Good point,' Annie said. 'Keep your mouth shut, and you should be all right, just get ready to, uh, run, I guess.'

'Right.'

They quickly left the security room, leaving the technician furiously trying to track the intruder – with no chance of success.

Max found his seat, then sat and watched as Penny and Annie appeared on the stage and seated themselves behind the long table where they joined the minister, Andy, and the top of Lucy's head – which is all that was visible even from Max's vantage point. The assembly hall was packed, voices filling the air in a droning murmur.

A burst of applause greeted Brandon Safeword's approach to the podium. He inclined his prodigious head and smiled out at the guests. 'A wonderful evening, ladies and gentlemen,' he intoned, 'in which to celebrate the achievements of this city's talented, brilliant artists, all of whom saw their start as recipients of funding from Culture Assessment Promotional Support services – which we affectionately know as CAPSs. Not that such funding is a prerequisite to the receipt of tonight's awards – most certainly not, hah hah, ho ho! – rather—' He leaned forward on the podium. '—it is indicative of CAPSs's remarkable percipience at finding and supporting artists of exceptional ability, no matter which university they might have attended!

'Now,' he continued, smiling broadly, 'first a word or two about the panel of peers, who for the past eight months have struggled with the difficult task of choosing tonight's award winners. Each judge in his or her own right is an artist of renown and admiration. Since you all know them, I'll simply recount the List of Lists using only their first names. The position of chair, this year, hath been held with honor by dear Margie, who was a student who knew Donny and in union begat six grants and four major awards; whereupon Margie was gifted with a suitable post at the university, and came in time to know Chuck, Samuel, and Peter, and in the knowing thereof begat nineteen various awards and grants. In Chuck, knowing in time Elizabeth and Sally – though in each knowing an interval of time doth exist between the two, allowing for lawful propriety in the knowing thereof, was begat in twin succession twenty-two awards and grants; and in the gathering thereof, Chuck came to know Donny who begat funding for Samuel, who knew Sally and begat funding for Elizabeth, who knew Margie once more and begat funding for Peter, who then knew Donny and begat funding for Margie, who came in knowing to Lucy, and so knowingly doth Lucy begat Peter who, in begatting with knowing Elizabeth, begat Chuck, who remained at this time in the knowing with Samuel, Margie, and Donny, thus allowing in proper prescription the gathering of those in knowing, mainly these being the panel of peers who in all knowing begat the awards on this here night on behalf of nameless donors, a multitude of taxpayers, a slice of lottery funding, minus administrative fees and the knowing task of begatting, which in itself is known to be a costly thing; thus minus said trimmings these awards nevertheless being nearly a month's salary for said peers in their knowing universities and tenure and so worthy of sustaining an artist or two for a year maybe longer, we all begat in knowing the knowingly known, though some may not be known as yet by this night's end all shall be known at least in knowing circles of import and sacred truths, of which there are many and by swearing loyalty shall remain unwritten and so unopposable in the eyes of the public. Amen.'

'Amen!' the crowd murmured.

'And now,' Brandon continued, 'for your unrestrained enjoyment, Professor Lucy Mort shall read an excerpt from her most recent work, *Mommy Mommy Mommy*. Ladies and gentlemen, Professor Lucy Mort . . .'

The crowd roared. The crowd was on its feet – not in ovation, but in an effort to discern the tiny creature that scurried up to disappear behind the podium. Brandon quickly adjusted the gooseneck microphone until it, too, was out of sight. The crowd slowly sat back down, and silence fell.

A moment later a tiny voice cleared its throat, and the words followed.

> *I shun you and him and her and them*
> *for not giving me the golden pen*
> *I shun rivals for the almighty dosh*
> *and the critics who despise my success*
> *I shun for not giving me attention*
> *I shun, too, because it's fun!*

There followed a silent moment; then one of the critics at the front shouted out, 'What the hell has that got to do with mommies, Lucy dear?'

The crowd gasped.

Lucy jumped out from behind the podium, her head no bigger than an apple. She shrieked, 'I'm not finished! That's why! Wait!' She jumped back to the microphone, and the sound of her desperate breathing echoed through the hall, then,

I shun, too, because it's fun!
. . .
Isn't it, Mum?

Everyone cheered wildly, applauded frantically. Max stood with them, bashing his hands together and watching, along with everyone else, as Lucy climbed the tablecloth and stood up on the table in front of her chair. She reached down and hauled up her purse, which she unzipped, pulled out a tommy gun, and spun to the row of critics seated in front of her, and let them have it. The critics exploded in a messy expostulation of flesh, bone, blood, guts, and a few bits of brain, along with upholstery and clothing bits and pieces of shoes and notepads and rotten tomatoes previously stored in paper bags. Smoking cartridges spun wildly from the tommy gun as Lucy – visibly struggling under its weight and getting smaller by the second – continued pumping rounds into the amalgamated, sliced, diced, and ground-up critics, some of whom kept raising their hands to ask piercing questions revealing their sly, cynical erudition – but the gesture was wasted, and didn't in fact last much longer, as even the hands were pummeled into little bits. Then the gun was empty, and fell clattering onto the table in front of minuscule Lucy Mort.

At this moment the minister's six bodyguards were flung bodily through the curtain to flop and sprawl and roll and thump in blood-spewing messes onto the long table, knocking over every single pitcher of lemon water. And behind them appeared Sool Koobie, his sleek lithe body painted in frightening patterns, a hafted hand ax in one hand, his spear in the other, and wearing as his only item of clothing a long, billowy cloak of used tampons.

Annie, Penny, Andy, the minister, and Brandon shrieked in unison, then scattered as, with a weird, terrifying, ululating yell, Sool Koobie rushed the assembly.

Max made no effort to join the stampede for the doors. Instead he clambered over the heads and shoulders of the knotted mob and reached the thick heavy curtain against the wall, which he climbed with the zeal of an ape, still clutching his flower box. Fifteen feet above the surging, screaming, murderously panicked crowd, Max hung on for his life. He tried to shift the box under an arm but the lid opened and the submarine fell out, to land on the churning sea of coiffed heads below, where it slowly rocked and wobbled its way out through the exit. 'Shit!' Max hissed. 'Doesn't matter now, though, does it? Holy cow, look at that guy!'

Sool Koobie was slaying with wild abandon, cleaving vegetarians in twain right and left, driving the herd ever forward to the two narrow choke points of the hall's exits. Max scanned the overturned table on the stage, but saw no one. Meanwhile, the savage leapt everywhere, laying out red ruin wherever he landed and crooning eerily with every killing blow he delivered.

And yet the whole scene since Lucy's lead-filled refutation of the critics had lasted but a few seconds. All of a sudden Max found himself alone – the crowd had been driven out of the hall – and the screams continued as Sool pursued them. Max looked down, scanned the inert bodies below, seeing a few moaning and writhing in their death wounds, then falling still. Bodies, everywhere, bodies. He turned in his perch as he heard voices up at the front. There stood Brandon and Lucy, looking unscathed.

'There there, Lucy dear,' Brandon was saying.

'I'm out of bullets!' Lucy wailed. 'And I can't even hold up the gun anymore! Oh, Brandon, what am I going to do! There's commercial artists out there, all more successful than me! I have to kill them! I have to, Brandon!'

'Of course, dear, of course. But you're in luck – I have a penknife!'

'Give it to me!'

He handed it down to her.

'I'm off!' She leapt down from the stage and raced up the body-littered aisle.

'But where, dear?' Brandon called out. 'Where?'

'Chesterton's!' she squeaked. 'Thursday's Lounge! That's where I'll find them! They're dead! All of them, dead!'

Max watched her pass beneath him, then slowly

climbed down. That savage would likely be back, collecting trophies, finishing the last ones off. He had to get out of the Pyramid. But something made him pause at the exit and turn back to where Brandon still stood.

'Hey!' Max called, knowing the jig was up, the entire jig, and not giving a damn anymore. 'Hey, Brandon!'

The major macrocephalic man looked up. 'Maximillian! Well done!'

'I know all about your brother, Brandon!' Max yelled gleefully. 'He's a big star back East! Bigger than you'll ever be in this squat little piss-hole! Hah hah ho ho!'

Brandon froze, the veins bulged, the head swelled and swelled, and then, as he screamed his white rage, the head exploded, spraying Styrofoam chips everywhere. The body staggered, the hands groped, found the curtain, swept it aside; then the body ran away, disappearing from sight.

Max grinned, feeling better than he'd felt in years.

10.
from on high

Wild Bill Chan and Jojum had tied themselves up into an immovable knot that lay against the engine's back hatch, forcing John Gully to grunt with great effort as he pushed his way inside. He swiftly scanned the scene, his gaze coming to rest first on the broken controls, then on Joey.

Joey 'Rip' Sanger shrugged. 'An accident. Told you ya shoulda left me alone, or doused me right at the start. And now we're barreling along, outa control who knows where—'

'I do,' Gully said. 'We're heading into the city. We'll never make the turn before the station. There's gonna be one hell of a mess.'

Joey shrugged again. 'It was bound to happen, Gully. Screwing with the laws of nature, you've been, and now the piper's called you due.'

'The laws of nature?' Gully sat down on the floor, his back resting against the control sleeve. 'What on earth are you talking about, Mr. Sanger?'

'There'll always be poor,' Joey growled. 'Y'can hide 'em, y'can squirrel 'em away and get slipped the cool green by the powers that be, y'can pretend yer doin' good with this here housin' scheme a yours, but it's all pissing in the wind, Gully. Y'got the ones that have, and the ones that ain't, but want. Every now and then they have a set-to, at each other's throats – the ones that have defendin' territory, the ones that ain't trying t'carve out a piece for themselves. And maybe it turns right over, the faces switchin' right around, but you know what? Nothing changes. I figured you for a smarter buck than that, Gully, but you're just fooling 'em all, yourself included.'

Gully sighed. 'You missed the entire point, Mr. Sanger. Missed it by a mile. I'm not interested in getting my people to change places with those on high. My plans, which you have succinctly ruined this night, were far more profound, far more potentially devastating. I lead the Fruitful Church of Disobedience, Mr. Sanger—'

'Oh, hell, anarchists!'

Gully shrugged. 'People – all of us – got messed up in the Fifties, and we've been thinking and trying to get back to those days ever since. But it was a sham back then: the prosperity was singular, a blip in history's miserable line. It was false – the economy, even the society with all its icons shoved on us by television. Nuclear families Mom, Dad, the kids, and the dog? Oh, really. Look at the history of our species. Kids were meant to be raised communally. Aunts, uncles, grandparents, cousins. No single woman – or man – was ever considered to be wholly responsible. Tack on a nine-to-five job, then two of them, and you've got one royal fuckup that burned itself out within a single generation. Hence the Sixties, and now the Nineties, with that artificial construct all falling apart under immense, unreasonable pressures and unrealistic expectations. Single mums, single dads, screwed-up kids – it's all falling to pieces. And everyone walks around blaming each other, blaming the neighbors, the crackpots, the criminals, the strangers down the block. Tougher on crime, tougher on panhandlers, tougher and still tougher, keep breeding the paranoia, keep making isolated entities of us all, divide and conquer, divide and divide and divide, until we all feel powerless, dependent, until dignity disappears from the common tongue. Today's leaders – politicians and businessmen – have pulled off what kings and emperors and high priests only dreamed of in the back when. At least in the old days people knew when they were just meat, gristle, muscle, and bone and nothing else. Now, everyone still believes they count for something, even when they know that that something is one big lie. And so we keep trudging on, trying to make sense of things, trying to achieve the unachievable, sticking to the rules – most of us – and thinking that it all serves something important, but what it serves is the cronies on top and no one else.'

'Yeah yeah yeah,' Joey said. 'Big deal. So you want to tear it all down, start from scratch, but the guy who's missing the point is you. You got too much faith in human nature, Gully. You think we ain't naturally depraved, naturally vicious, naturally assholes – and that's your mistake, and it's a doozy.'

'Of course we're all those things!' Gully snapped. 'Doesn't mean we can't strive for something better!'

'In your dreams, Gully, and nowhere else.'

'Ohmigod,' the redcap whispered, his eyes widening on what he could see out the side window. 'We're coming to the bend, and that's not all – there's a monster out there, twenty stories tall at least, tearing up buildings, batting down helicopters and fighter jets!'

Gully leaned out the window, then stepped back, looking thoughtful.

Joey followed suit. 'Yup,' he said, 'that's one big bastard. Wonder who he is?'

'Arthur Revell,' Gully said. 'I know him only marginally, it's true, but I don't think I'm mistaken. He's . . . changed.'

'Let me guess, the horns are new.'

Gully glanced over at Joey, his expression becoming animated. 'There's your destroyer, Joey! He's discovered his inner self, who he is deep down inside, and now we're all going to pay!'

'Why, what is he?'

'An artist!'

'My God,' Joey breathed, experiencing terror for the first time since facing Sool Koobie. 'He's got to be stopped!'

'It's too late!' the redcap screamed, just as the racing train finally arrived at the bend. The 57 Wells engine seemed to leap from the rails, dragging the mass of cars with it, down the gentle slope giving the bend its rise, plowing up two huge waves of gravel, clinkers, dust, and sand – then, the engine reaching a street, the cow-catcher carved a swath through the concrete, then bucked upward – and the train of homeless victims was plummeting down the city's main street, flinging hapless cars to either side, barreling with unstoppable momentum straight for the legislative buildings a mere seven blocks distant.

Arthur Revell was suffering from an orgylike explosion of lifelong chemical deprivation – no alcohol slurring his veins and arteries, no nicotine hammering his heart, no tar clogging up his lungs, no cocaine from post-performance parties, no acid from wild-eyed friends, no hash, no grass, no hemp, no peyote, no Ecstasy, no speed, no mushrooms – he was in the hell of purified creativity, undulled by the oral/anal compulsive obsessions that strung out the spirit and forced on the body and mind a more reasonable pace – no longer the tortoise, but the hare; not a cicada but a moth speeding to the flame. Arthur saw before him his brief, apocalyptic glory, and answered it with a roar of soul-searing frustration.

His burning eyes fixed on the legislative dome, and beyond that, the Pyramid, Arthur took one gigantic step forward, his talons curling with desire. He opened his mouth, and a swarm of ladybugs poured forth in an eager, bloodythirsty cloud. He paused, confused, then – on a breath of cool wind came a scent that froze him in his tracks. 'Peaches!' he hissed. 'I smell peaches! Faye! Faye!' Arthur whirled about, found the faint scent once again, then surged forward on its delicate, wonderful trail.

Maxwell Nacht stepped into the hall beyond the theater and saw the remains of bloody chaos. The long tables on which sat the finest culinary profferings of Culture Quo had been shattered, strawlike foodstuffs scattered everywhere. More bodies lay about, motionless, horribly motionless. The waiters and waitresses all crouched against the far wall, their eyes dulled, their mouths hanging open.

One of them spoke. 'He – he didn't touch us. He came over and . . . sniffed us, then he left – he drove them on, on, ever onward!'

Max didn't spare them another glance. He went through the shattered entranceway and arrived at the landing. The wind gusted calmly across his sweat-beaded face. He looked below, down the 666 steps, and saw exactly what he expected to see. He also saw Penny off to one side, halfway down the steps – she looked up to him.

'My God!' she screamed. 'The city's entire art establishment is dead!'

The savage had driven them, like buffalo, Max realized, off the steps – and Max could see the horrible little man, down there among the piled bodies, cutting out tongues, collecting ears and other delectable trophies. And now Penny saw him as well.

'Ohmigod!' Max heard her say. 'She – she – she remembers! You! You down there! Oh, my noble one! You!'

The savage glanced up at all the screaming, and watched bemused as the scantily clad woman rushed toward him, down the steps, over the bodies, running straight for him, arms stretched out.

Sool Koobie bleated as Penny leapt on him, her legs spread wide.

Max stared as she writhed over the hapless creature.

'She remembers! Oh God, she remembers! I'm – I'm

– I'm . . . Croona! Queen of the Cavemen! I've come home! Home! Oh, take me take me take me take me!'

And Sool did, grabbing her thighs and boldly throwing her on her back, there atop the hundreds of dead politicians, professors, obscure but powerful artists, business leaders, he rogered Penny Foote-Safeword in the fashion of hunky, smelly, grunting primitive men the world over.

Max sighed, actually happy for them both, and wishing them well in whatever squalid hole the savage would no doubt drag Penny into. As for himself, well, enough of the loner jaunt, the gamble of youth – past at last for Maxwell Nacht of the Nacht Lingerie Empire. Time to go home to the millions, the swimming pools, the high society, the tennis lessons, and the maids in the bushes. He'd had his fun pretending to be the artist, he was tired of going hungry, tired of the cockroaches on the kitchen counter, tired of moldy bread and Kraft Dinner, and the endlessly arguing drunks on welfare next door. 'I'm going home,' he whispered. 'Home, my God.'

At precisely this moment, the 57 Wells tore through the legislature, destroying everything, absolutely everything, including the late-night session where politicians of various stripes had been arguing with no one in particular against any reduction in personal pay, benefits, and the double-dipping loopholes in their fat pension plans. The huge steam engine retired them all, permanently, but the train didn't stop and indeed was only marginally slowed in its passage through the historical edifice.

Max could only watch as the mechanical demon

plunged across the street and crashed into the 666 steps of the Pyramid, flinging bodies and concrete and dead Boy Scouts, and, as the cars behind the engine piled up and burst apart, hundreds of homeless people flew in all directions, thus providing a demographic slice of modern Western society.

Even before the dust cleared, someone flashed by close to Max and scurried down the steps – a figure that seemed able to disappear as it turned sideways, blinking into and out of existence as it descended toward the rubble below.

The minister. Paul Silverthump. Nice trick, that sideways disappearing act. Beauty. The man's a born politician. Look, not even a hair out of place. Gotta admire the bastard. Hell, he's the only one left, too. Which means he'll be taking the reins of power shortly, before the dust down there's even settled. And who says God isn't just?

Eight hundred and twenty-three feet overhead in the smoke-filled darkness, a wheeling pigeon outfitted with infrared goggles spotted its target. The bird banked, folded back its wings, and dived.

Few regarded pigeons with much respect, it knew, a lack that was about to be remedied in an act of singular, heroic self-sacrifice. The pigeon picked up even more speed, becoming nothing more than a blur of unstoppable intent, and it knew, in its last moments, that God was on its side, and failure was out of the question.

Max saw Paul Silverthump stop suddenly, entirely visible, and totter slightly on the steps. Something was sticking out of his head, fluttering darkly. Half a pigeon, in fact. The other half was embedded in the man's head, which even for a politician was likely fatal. And, true enough, Max watched the man topple limply onto the steps, then slowly slide down to join the disaster scene below.

Sorry for ever doubting you, God. Never again, I promise. My God, I'm going to join a monastery! That'll put the old man in a tizzy! One hell of a tizzy! Hee hee!

Arthur Revell arrived at the hospital, and saw her. The night shift, taking a smoke break outside the doors, dear Faye of the blushing bosom. His shadow swept over her and she looked up.

Arthur expected her to scream. It would have been an entirely natural response. Instead, she took one last, deep drag on her cigarette, flicked the butt to one side, and delicately held out her hand.

'I'm an artist!' Arthur boomed down at her.

'I know!' she said.

'I need – I need – I need—'

'I know! I know what you need, darling Arthur!' She pulled a metal flask from her hip, her pack of smokes from her pocket, and waved them both in the air over her head. 'I'm a nurse, remember!'

Arthur straightened for one last roar, a roar of intent, as dark a promise as it had ever been, but this time it was also a roar of sheer joy. 'I love life!' he bellowed. 'Aaargh!'

On a poorly lit, emptied street, Kit dismounted, hobbled Moopsy, then approached, in great curiosity, the tiny woman riding the motorized submarine steadily down the street's center. She held her penknife under one arm like a lance, and was muttering something about commercial artists and wildlife painters lucky enough to be born Native.

Kit felt a surge of inevitability deep inside his generally amorphous body, as if a thousand instincts had been triggered at the sight that met his eyes. He slimed forward on an intercept course.

The woman screamed as the submarine's splayed nose rammed into Kit, who tried a scream of his own and was pleased at its shrill, bestial madness. His tentacles lashed out, gripping the submarine and holding it fast. Lucy Mort stood up and hefted the penknife, her legs spraddled to keep balance on the pitching deck. 'Die, bastard from the deep!' she yelled.

Idly, Kit reached up, flipped the puny penknife from her hands, encircled the woman, and boldly lifted her into the air. Her arms thrashed, her hair tossed, her legs kicked, all with equal ineffectivity, and her last shriek was a tinny, hopeless cry. 'Help me! Help meeee!!' Kit studied her a moment longer, then ate her in a blinding flash.

He finished the scene by shrilling some more and bashing the submarine into pieces; then he returned to Moopsy, who'd watched the whole thing with tail wagging. Kit mounted up, and they rode westward to their date with destiny.

Max sat on a piece of rubble and observed the proceedings. The media had arrived, adding to the chaos of the scene at the foot of the Pyramid's steps. What was worse, they'd found the homeless – most of whom had survived the crash, which had proved unlucky for them, as the media crews, upon discovering real homeless people, had descended on them with a flurry of heart-bleeding angst.

The predictable end result was being played out below. A woman stood above the still form of Jojum, dead of a microphone shoved down his throat. A cameraman stood opposite her, a mounted spot bathing the reporter and the body in heavenly light. 'This is Sandy Grit, MFFB News, coming to you from the central scene of devastation, where an even greater tragedy has occurred. You see this man below me, a poor homeless man, victimized by – I have no choice but to acknowledge it – by a mindless, news-hungry media that views all humanity with a cold, cynical eye. I am ashamed to call myself part of this profession. My God, what have we become? All this just for ratings? For revenue? To shock and entice you with the depravity of modern civilization? Is that all we're here for? Well, let me tell you all right here and right now, MFFB isn't like the rest. We're not . . . animals, and we're not going to take it anymore! You'll see for yourself, my friends, soon enough, and that's a promise from Sandy Grit, coming to you live from the foot of the Pyramid.'

The light blinked out.

'Move it!' the next reporter snarled, being pushed savagely by the rest of the reporters in the long line. 'Mike! Get the camera rolling, dammit!' One of the lounging camera operators on the other side of Jojum's body straightened and shouldered his camera.

'This is Nick Steel, MKBM News Alive, coming to

you from the Pyramid. I'm ashamed, deeply ashamed. Good God, is this what the media has come to? Well, not us at MKBM News, not on your life, nor on his – this poor victim of my senseless, spiteful colleagues – colleagues, how that sad truth galls me—'

Max sighed. It was true, some things he was going to miss in the monastery, but, truth be told, television news wasn't one of them.

Miraculously flung half a block from the 57 Wells, Joey 'Rip' Sanger and John Gully strode quietly down the street. Each had faced death, had seen with wide-open eyes down its black, depthless maw, and each had emerged greatly changed, delivered, as it were, into a new, bright, promising world.

Joey well knew the redcap had survived, somewhere, and the mantle of the Sanger legend had fallen to the boy, and it didn't matter if he was ready for it or not, because that was the way of such things, to have it thrust upon you, leaving you no choice but to make do with what's landed in your lap. He'll do fine. So will Chan – just one more accident report to file, at least it straightened his back even if his head, striking dead-on that lamppost, was pushed right in until his eyes barely look over his collarbone. A survivable wound, for Wild Bill Chan. They'll do all right, they'll all do all right.

'Whatcha planning now, Gully?'

The philosopher shrugged. 'Leave the world-changing efforts to Art.'

'Art?'

'Arthur Revell. You see him anywhere?'

'Uh, no, I don't.'

'Exactly, he's been saved, twice, once by his own revelation, and once by someone else – whoever she might be. He's slipped back into the cracks, and you'll know in the years to come, as those cracks start spreading, that he's quietly doing his work, going about the task of intellectual disobedience, defying the rules of constraint, defying even the conventions of propriety, no matter what the context. As it all crumbles, my friend, you'll know where it started. Right here, right now.'

'Hot damn,' Joey sighed. 'What a night. And you, Gully?'

'Not sure. I think I'm done, for a while at least. You?'

'Same for me.'

They walked on in silence for a long time after that, and moments before they disappeared from view, their hands simultaneously linked – not in any sexual way, of course, but in a manly, proper way – and then they were gone.

Leaving at long last the end of the octopod's tale. Kit and Moopsy found Andrew clawing his way out of the mangled back door of the Pyramid. After a long chase, Kit lassoed his former master in a wheat field and trussed the gibbering man up and then unceremoniously dragged him toward a hilltop (really just a rise, but for prairie folk it was a hill, damn near a mountain) where waited a flying saucer. Its ramp was down, and two other octopods riding dogs patrolled the perimeter.

Kit rode Moopsy up the ramp, dragging a weeping Andy Breech in their wake, and then inside, into the blinding white light, where there waited an examination table and odd-shaped instruments with which to probe Andrew's shrunken genitals for all eternity.

After a moment the outriders also entered the shimmering craft. The ramp rose flush with the saucer's underbelly. The vessel lifted into the night sky and climbed blindingly fast into the heavens.

Annie Trollop had been crushed ignobly in the rush and subsequent tumble down the endless steps of the Pyramid. So badly mangled was she that no one knew her, no one at all. Brandon Safeword's body still haunts the alleys and streets of the city, seeking a head worthy of its astonishingly fit and trim body; and Penny Foote-Koobie lived her dreams out in the company of an increasingly exhausted but otherwise contented Neanderthal, who eventually gave up painting and became a stock analyst for four years before returning to his roots and a reunion with nature and the Mother and the cycles of life and death that, generally speaking, are packed with a lot of death.

Arthur Revell and Faye disappeared, but don't be fooled. They're out there. Doing art and thereby conspiring the ruination of modern civilization.

Hah hah! Ho ho!

FISHIN' WITH
GRANDMA MATCHIE

THIS IS WHERE
I WANT TO START

The Meaning of School and All That:

It's not my fault! It has to do with a lot of things. Special things, like Bigness. When I think of the world's Bigness I think of a ball of fishing line that's all tangled up and no matter how hard Dad tries he can't find where it starts or where it ends and the tackle box tips over then and he steps on a rubber worm that rolls and the next thing you know Dad's in the lake. It's like that.

So you follow the line this way and it loops into a knot and goes off that way. But you just got to keep following it, because Bigness leads to the Truth, and the Truth's important. If you don't know what I mean then I'll show you just like this:

Just like this:

In the Olden Days they used to have Jesters. Jesters talked about Plain Things as if those things were fat and skinny and tall and short. But sometimes the Jesters made those things too fat or too skinny or too tall or too short, and then they were bad and Not to be Tolerated, and then the king would stick them in a corner and make them wear a Dunce Cap.

Now, the corner is a funny place. You stare at the walls where they meet, and you begin to understand the importance of the Bigness of Things. And it all starts Making Sense. This is the place where children who are Not Yet Considered Adults go, when kings and teachers get all fretful about children with Overwrought Imaginations.

You see, when you're sitting there with your feet not even touching the floor, you stare at those walls where they meet and you know you can't fit between them because there's no crack. And that's when you suddenize that no matter how small you are, you're never small enough.

Which is just what the kings and teachers want you to suddenize.

LIFE starts with a Foolish Pleading of your case:

But it really happened. Just like I wrote it, three weeks during summer vacation, and summer vacation is the time for dreams. Just because school had started it shouldn't mean things that were true in the summer weren't true now. Isn't that right?

But the Bigness of Things tells you in No Uncertain Terms (that's what she says: 'in No Uncertain Terms'): No, Jock Junior, that is not right.

You'd think she'd know better.

Now, the first day of school and how it all came about:

My teacher was a nose and that's all she was, just a nose and some wispy hair around it. If she had eyes, they were hiding somewhere in the blackness of her giant nostrils. The nose gloomed over all of us, and snarted hotly, and we sweated a lot in that room.

The first thing you'd notice about that room is that it had four corners, all empty now because it's the first day of school. And the next thing you'd notice is that none of the corners have cracks, though of course you'd only see that if you were sitting in those corners, one after another. So you can trust me when I say there's no cracks in them, okay?

And by the window there's an aquarium with one fish in it. Sometimes I slip him notes, helping him plan his escape, but he never answers them, so I figure he's got a plan of his own. Thing is, I don't think he's very smart.

And I'll tell you a Secret. Something I've figured out. Look at the windows. See those cardboard faces pasted to them? There's a face for each one of us in the room, except Big Nose herself. Look at them. They have holes for eyes and holes for nostrils but drawn-in mouths. And that's my Secret. So don't tell anyone, especially Big Nose.

Of course I'm not old enough to see these things, nor to understand the Importance of Telling the Truth. I'm Not to be Tolerated, I'm Precocious. Only it wasn't me who said those things, which are Big things. And it wasn't me who knew how to spell them. But we're here to learn how to spell.

Tell the truth about what you did in the summer, Big

Nose told us sweating faces. And I made my eyes into slivery slits and thought about things, cool and calculating like. It may have been her understanding that there were no little jesters hiding among us, I think. She didn't say which summer, but we've already been taught to understand the need not to have to say Certain Things. But then I think: It may have been her plan to Ferret me out.

The Assignment that Ferreted me out:

I bet I know more than you do. I used to overturn big flat rocks, looking for the Devil. Satan Himself, Grandma Matchie always called him, and always with a shiver jippling all along her skinny shoulders. And her eyes spizzled, like she was showing me what Hades looked like, as if she'd been down there herself and armwrassled Satan Himself down to the ground (she did too, but that's another story). He was hiding, she told me, always hiding. So I overturned rocks, the big flat ones, but all I ever found were ants, carrying eggs back and forth, and getting on my shoes so I had to stimp and stamp and stromp.

I don't look under rocks anymore, and that's why I know more than you do.

And I'll tell you this too. I've seen him. I've seen Satan Himself. It was easy. All I had to do was follow that fishing line right to the end, and there he was! It was the third and last week in my summer vacation, but before I tell you about that, I have to tell you about the first and second weeks, because, you see, that's the only way to unravel fishing line.

And that's not the only reason. Sometimes the Bigness of Things is so big that you've just got to be prepared before you run into it. Which means you should take a look at smaller Bigness before you see the Biggest Bigness.

I'm doing this because Old Ladies say I'm nice, and since they got to be so old I figure they know the difference between nice and not-nice.

One last thing. Those Titles are Grandma Matchie's, one for each of the three weeks. She says Titles are important, and that's the way they've done things since Adam first broke the Egg. I'm not sure what that means, unless it's that all those Titles fell out when Adam broke the Egg. Personally, I don't think there's an Egg in existence that could hold all the world's Titles. Because if there was, who laid it and where does she live and what does she eat and does she ever visit Sudbury and if she did then why?

So, here's the first week, and Grandma Matchie's first Title. The rest of the stuff, and all those smaller headings, is mine and no one's Legally Responsible but me.

One thing worries me, though. What happens if all those people I talk about come after me?

NO REST FOR THE WICKED

Girls. My face is scrinching up already, but I'm forcing myself because it's Important to start here. I like pretending they're not there most of the time, even though they wear pants with zippers and I'm pretty sure they don't need zippers. They're funny like that and don't ask me why because I don't know why.

So I usually pretend they don't exist, and that makes them mad for some reason, and then there's this funny chase thing during recess, where you run after them until your chest hurts. And something Serious and Grim pushes the insides of your head all over the place, as if the chase was More Important than Anything Else on Earth.

It's sickening. And the girl you're chasing after looks Different from all the other girls. Stranger, uglier maybe, like she's always twitching her nose and pulling at her hair.

The fascination of ugliness:

But then you catch her. You force her into a red-bricked

corner behind the school, and suddenly she looks mad.
I can't figure that. She glares at you and she's breathing
hard and her cheeks are red and her eyes are wild in a
way that makes you think of stupid things, like
wrestling.

It's that corner stuff all over again. The Bigness of
Things that can make your face scranch up while you're
thinking of more stupid things, like mint-sucking piano
teachers and little violins wearing flowery dresses. I
know it's stupid!

And it gets worse and worse. You plant a grin on
your face like the ones you've seen in horror movies just
before the blonde woman throws up her hands and
screeks, and she stares at it, those eyes going big,
because you've grown fangs. It makes you even sicker
when you suddenize how dumb you look. But in spite
of all that, in spite of everything, you close in.

What do you do then? Maybe you punch her, maybe
she punches you. And you ask yourself in horror:
Whose arm is going to be sore? It's the most Awful
Decision of your life, that one.

Or, worst of all, nothing happens! And no matter
what, you feel luzzy for days afterwards. Ignoring her
giggling friends you follow her next recess, trying to
make her run away so you can splurt after her, so maybe
something'll happen this time. But it's awful, because
now she's ignoring you!

So I hate her and that's all there is to it. And my face
scrunches up when someone says her name, and that
Grim and Serious thing in me makes me want to barf.

The Secret of Wanting to Barf:

Oh, I know all about it now. I've studied the way those bumps on my sister's chest gromered all bigger underneath her shirt, until she had to tie them up so she could see where she was stepping, so there wouldn't always be dog-do on her runners.

Only girls and fat men have those things. And only girls tie them up, which is why fat men sag and slumple and I get out of their way so I don't get brolled on and skirbled flat.

I also know why girls exist. It all started that first week of summer vacation at Rat Portage Lake, when, feeling Grim and Serious, I threw a dead frog in Sis's hair and it came back to life. Up until then nothing I had ever thrown in her hair had come back to life. Not worms all liddlelimply gray, not minnows all bladed white, not even big black flies from the windowsill which are never really dead anyway! And the live things I threw in her hair all died instantly. It's true! The garter snake up and died! Went stuckled as a stick and stuck out its tongue and rolled up its eyes!

But the frog came back to life, all because Sis had grown those Infernal Bumps. I stood back in amazement and watched the poor thing struggle in the torngle of her long hair, while Sis blawed and screamed and clabbed at her pointy head. Then she managed to grab one of its kicking legs and she threw it high into the air. Limbs Splayed, it hung up there against the sky, then down it went hitting the lake with a batralp.

I'll never forget those Splayed Limbs in all my life. And now, when I chase a girl into a corner behind school, I know that those Splayed Limbs will be just another one of those stupid thoughts. The whole thing makes me sick.

And that's how it all started, as we stood by the dock with the tigerflies brazzling over our heads and the water purbling up on the little beach and the pine trees hisspering behind the cabin, the whole family every one of us waiting for Grandma Matchie to arrive.

Even normal families like mine got Secrets:

Grandma Matchie is that Secret. I'm not supposed to talk about her. I think it's because she embarrasses Dad alot, even though she's Mom's Mom. So I won't talk about the times she embarrassed Dad and I'll keep it to the Plain Facts nobody would argue about.

Grandma Matchie lives in a two-story wooden lodge that has been under water since 1899. That was the year the dam was opened. Fifty feet down, she says, all lit up so that the astronauts can see it whenever they pass overhead. She sleeps down there and comes up most mornings after breakfast, but sometimes earlier.

But it was already our second day at the cabin. And the sun was hot, making us all clampy while we tuddled around the cabin, or skiddled up on the Precambrian Rock skirmelling blueberries into our mouths and collecting deer antlers and putting them in trees and throwing pinecones at wasp nests and running away when all the wasps come stungling out. Our second day away from the city, away from Appalled Neighbors and Urban Miscreants who want to recycle everything in our house or at least bottles. Our second day at Rat Portage Lake, and Grandma Matchie hadn't come up yet.

So we stood there waiting, and waiting some more. Everyone figured she wasn't going to show. Mom and Dad kept arguing about it, and Sis sat down on a stump and tried to loosen the knots I'd tied in her hair earlier that morning.

Dad told her not to sleep in!

I kept my eyes peeled on the waves, because I knew better. I knew she was coming, just like she did every summer. And just like all the other summers everybody figured she wasn't going to show. Grown-ups have real short memories, if you ask me.

And sure enough there she was, her head bobbening to the surface in the middle of the bay. She gave a wave and we all waved back.

'See!' I said to Mom. 'I told you I saw lights down there last night! I knew she was home!'

'Well,' she sneffed, tightening her grip on the broom handle. 'Could've been lectric eels.'

Grandma Matchie swam towards us, her long skinny neck making a giant V through the water. Minnows leapt in little silver florshes in front of her, like she was chasing them, but I could've told them not to worry. Grandma Matchie didn't give a rizzling hoot for small fry.

'Ain't no lectric eels in Rat Portage Lake!' Dad gruzzled, scratching the thick black hair on his chest until the buttons on his shirt popped off. He turned to Mom with his big red-bearded face all scowllered up. 'Semper fey, woman! What've ya got for brains, anyway? Turnips?'

'That's a root crop,' Sis said. She was taking Agriculture in school and I hated everything she said, so I started looking around for something to throw at her. But then I remembered the frog and got scared.

'Lectric eels, Zeus!' Dad shook his shuggy head, making the fishing lures in his hat jample. He'd hung the biggest ones on the brim of the hat. For balance, he said. And so he had Red Devils in front of his eyes, and he looked out from the tiny holes where you tie the line. 'Lectric eels!'

Mom scowllered too, hefting the broom in her skinny hands. She looked down at her high heels again and tried feebly to pull them out from between the planks in the dock, but she was stuck fast, which made her scowller even more. It was just like every summer. 'Well, lamp rays, then.'

'Lamp rays!'

I left them binickering and ran down to the end of the dock to meet Grandma Matchie. Grinning, she clambered up on the weathered boards and began wringing the water from her bright red dress. She was taller even than Dad and skinnier even than Mom, and her gray hair sat on top of her head like a giant ball of torngled-up fishing line with only a little seaweed in it, and you could see she'd been lying on the rock all the bass like to hide under because her wrunkled skin was all tanned and anyway summer's when her Indian blood shows through, because Grandma Matchie's One Part Everything.

'How ya bin doin, Tyke?' Her hiking boots sloshed as, taking my hand, we walked up the dock. 'You ain't seen the Major lately, have ya?'

I looked across the bay at the Major's tiny island, but all I could see was his dock and his Blarny Boat and the flagpole with its Union Jack hanging there all lank and tired. 'I seen him out trobbling around, that's all. Yesterday. Whenever he comes near shore he just shakes his fist at us. I think he's mad at us or something.'

Tossing back her head Grandma Matchie laughed. 'He's mad, all right! Hah!'

Dad scowllered and said: 'We bin here since yesterday and you ain't been up once!'

'Aren't you ashamed?' Mom demanded, poking the air with her broom.

Making a rude noise at both of them Grandma Matchie turned and crucked an eyebrow at Sis. 'That hair sure looks funny, lass. In fashion nowadays, eh? Well, don't let the bees see you or you'll get stungled for sure!' And she laughed again.

Sis's face scrinched up and I could tell she was going to cry. And sure enough she let out a browl and raced away toward the cabin.

Mom scowllered even scowllier than Dad. 'Now look at what you done, Mother!'

Well, it didn't surprise me, that's for sure. Sis was older than me and I hated her. The way she made faces at dinner, and the way she started crying every time I kicked her under the table, and once she hit me when Mom wasn't looking, and nobody'd believe me, so I hated her, and that's why.

And she had purple hair too. It used to be brown, even when it wasn't dirty, but now it was purple. And she wore shiny shirts that made her chest look funny. Once, I saw her in the bathroom, miggling her hips so that her fat bum moved funnily. She was crazy, and if you don't believe me you just wait!

Grandma Matchie frowned. 'She bin cryin alot, Ester?'

Mom's face reddened for some Mysterious Reason, but she nodded anyway.

Dad caught my eye and winked. 'Woman talk, son. Don't you pay it no mind.' His eyes looked small as a gerbil's inside those holes in the Red Devils, but not just any old gerbil unless all gerbils are like the one that used to be in my classroom but got away when a Child with an Overwrought Imagination Assisted it to Escape. Eyes like that gerbil's, which were mostly suspicious even when I showed it the Plans. And all those flies snigged in Dad's hat made me think of when you accidentally drop a ten-pound jar of chocolate pudding on a rock and it breaks and there's a pile of ucky pudding just sitting there for hours before you tell anyone, and by then it's fly pudding and you can watch them sinking and disappearing until the sun goes down when there's none left and it's time for Sis to have a snack.

We were all getting ready to go up to the cabin when Grandma Matchie hissped 'Shhh!' and crouched, looking around. Everyone froze. Her eyes narrowed to slits and she sniffed the air. 'He's here, he is!' she hisspered. 'Somewhere!'

All at once we heard fladapping overhead and we all looked up.

'There he is!' Grandma Matchie screeked. 'Spyin!'

The Major hovered over us, wearing his usual navy blues and polished boots. You could see the fire gleamering in his eyes and he grinned crazzerly, his big red nose purlsing and his giant mustache bristlering. The two gulls holding him up screewled loudly and beat their wings madly, and feathers floated down all around us.

Water spraying from the eyelets of her hiking boots, Grandma Matchie splomped back and forth in a rage. 'Where's my duck gun!' She shook her fist skyward. 'I'll turn those gulls into paperweights! Hah!' Then she swirjerked around and tore off up the trail and prashed down the cabin door with both feet at once.

She disappeared inside. 'She's getting a gun!' Dad shouted at the Major, who shrieked. And the gulls shrieked too. Legs pumping the air, the Major tried to run home. The seagulls ducked their heads and drummed their wings, hurrying him toward his island. By the time Grandma Matchie arrived with her shotgun, the Major had shrunk to a speck. Looking miserable, she pumped a couple rounds after him anyway, then sniffed, her wrinkled lips pouping.

'Damn spyin! Did you see his beady eyes? Just aglowin!'

'How come?' I asked.

'He's fishin, that's what he's doin. An he's got it bad, sure enough if you ask me.'

'Got what bad?'

'The itch,' Grandma Matchie surplied.

I didn't know what on earth she was talking about, but I saw Dad grinning and Mom's face turning red. And for some reason I could feel my face starting to scranch, though it had no reason to that I could figure. It does that sometimes.

That night, in the cabin, Grandma Matchie cooked

us up a whole pot full of crayfish, but said they had to cool till morning before we could eat them. Then she sat herself down by the fireplace, streetching out her glongly legs and watching her boots steam.

Mom took over the kitchen and said no one was allowed to come in while she Baked Bread.

'Crazy woman!' Dad snargled, crushelling his beer can and throwing it into a corner, his eyes streaming in the smoke from the pipe in his mouth. Smoking a pipe's an important part of being a fisherman, he'd said between coughs. He had on his fishing hat with the thousand hundred fifty-two million lures snegged in it, and he stood in the center of the living room, wearing hip-waders and a fish basket clipped to his leg. Bing Crosby was on the tape deck and the sound of turckling water came from the bathroom where Dad had turned on the tap. 'Gotta have the sound of turckling water,' he'd said. 'It's a parta fishin. An important part.'

Whipping the air, Dad's fly rod swung back and forth, and fishing line torngled everything. It hung from the rafters of the A-frame like spiderwebs; it snarvelled the furniture and lay in twingled coils on the wooden floor. Sis was all wrapped up in it and hadn't moved in an hour. She just lay there, groaming every now and then.

I sat with Grandma Matchie, my feet growing hot as Hades in front of the mackling spunkering pafting fire.

'Crazy woman!' Dad repeated in a voice loud enough to be heard in the kitchen. Snapping open another beer can with his left hand he tugged the rod. 'Damn! Snaggered again! It's the worst parta fishin! If I lose another leader I'll scream!' He pulled and pulled and the moose head on the wall waggled and nodded.

The kitchen door swung open and a white-powdered figure stepped out and screaked: 'Didn't I tell you to do your fishin outside?' Clouds burst from her lips. 'Didn't I!?'

'I ain't goin out there!' Dad belbowed. 'There's dangerous beasts out there! A man could get himself killed!' He yanked savagely and the moose head jampled straight out from the wall all brown and blurthy like it was attacking him. Yimping, Dad ducked and the head sailed over and crashed down on a table. 'See!'

'Fishin's dangerous, Tyke.' Grandma Matchie nodded.

Dad straightened and glawered at Mom. 'Not only that! It's gothic fulla bugs and stuff!' He bared his teeth at her and snargled, 'Why don't you go out there if y'like it so much! Do your gothic bakin in the bush!'

'Look at your daughter!'

'Ahh, she's all right. Just sleepin, is all.'

'She's all tied up!'

'Bah!'

Crossing her arms, Mom whirled about. 'Well!' She slammed the door and flour gusted out around it.

Bing Crosby began dreaming of a white Christmas and I hissped, 'Shhh!' to Grandma Matchie and began wormening toward the kitchen, crawpelling from shadow to shadow like the Indians must have done, until I crouched up against the door. Reaching up, I grasped and turned the knob ever so slowly. I opened it a crack and peeked in.

It was white woman's territory for sure. In fact, the

whole kitchen was white, and loaves of bread were stacked everywhere, a million thousand seventy-two of them. And there was Mom, her fancy black dress all covered in flour and butter and dough, and there was more dough clinging to her fingers and arms and wrapped around her neck as she strubbled and pulled and pulled and strubbled, muttering and whimpering all the while.

Once Mom started she couldn't stop, and pretty soon the loaves of bread began showing up everywhere. Sloggy and swobllen on the beach, with groaming crows lying in piles all around them. Made into nests by squirrels, all hollowed out with flowery drapes in the windows. Hanging from tree branches with bees brazzling all around them trying to figure a way to get inside. And after a few days you could easily make bread igloos out of them. But this time she'd really gone overboard. Groaming softly, I closed the door and snucched back to Grandma Matchie's side.

'She done it again, huh?'

'Worse than ever!'

Grandma Matchie sighed, wrivilled her steaming boots. 'Ever drank crayfish wine, Tyke? I got vats of it down in the lodge. Canada's Finest, it says on the labels. Bottled it myself. Course, you're not old 'nough fur crayfish wine, anyway.'

'Soon?'

'Maybe. But I'll tell you somethin. You want hair on your chest like your Dad?' I thought about it and was about to answer but she went on, 'Well, drink some of Canada's Finest and I guarantee it, you'll never freeze in winter again.'

Frowning, I said, 'Maybe that's why the Major goes fishin and trobblin for you every day. He wants your crayfish wine.'

Grandma Matchie chackled. 'Not likely, though it does kinda get im a hankerin, 'times.'

'Every day he's out there! Rowin back and forth and trobblin bait past your windows!'

'Lubber don't know a thin about baitin,' she muthered distantly.

I looked up at her and I saw her eyes glowing like the coals in the fireplace. Before I knew it, my face scrinched up. 'Grandma Matchie! Snap out of it!'

Turning, she gave me a blank look. 'Snap out of what, Tyke?'

I sighed, feeling my face unscrinching. Whew! I'd almost lost her there! In the dull light I peeked out of the corner of my eye at Grandma Matchie's arm to confirm my belief. Yes, it looked too skinny to be punched. It'd break for sure. Right then and there I vowed to protect Grandma Matchie, no matter what.

Laugh if you want! You'll see I was right!

The next morning Sis was gone no one knew where. Mom sifted the piles of flour in the kitchen; Dad checked his fish basket; and I searched through all her clothes and stuff just in case anything interesting came up. But Grandma Matchie sniffered the air and then went straight over to the crayfish pot. Lifting the lid she peered inside and after a moment cried out, 'Aha! I knew it!' She slammed the lid down and whirvelled to us, her face grim. 'She's been kidnapped! And I know who!'

'The Major?' I asked.

Even more grimly she shook her head. 'He's small fry. Nope, this is bad, real bad. Cause it means he's back, an if he's back there'll be trouble for us all!' Suddenly she threw back her shoulders and roared a defiant laugh, then began barking orders: 'Ester! Get the canoe outa the boathouse! Jock, get me my spurs and saddle! Jock Junior! Pack us a lunch! An alla you – be quick 'bout it!' Hands on her hips, Grandma Matchie glowered at us until we all started scrambling.

Passing by the crayfish pot I paused to lift the lid and peek inside. They were all there, bright red and tasty-looking. 'But Grandma Matchie—'

'Aye, an look at em, Tyke. Look at em real good, now.'

And then I saw that each of them was missing a claw. 'Someone's stolen half the claws!'

'An you know what that means?' Grandma Matchie's face was grim and serious. 'It means he's back, and he was right here! An he stole Sis.' Fury smolgered in her eyes. 'He stole Sis!'

'Who?' Mom asked from the doorway, where the prow of the cedar-strip canoe had jammed in the frame and she was tugging frantically.

Grandma Matchie stared at Mom and said sandily, 'Ester, why are you bringin the canoe inta the cabin?'

'WHO?' Mom shracked, wrenching at the prow.

'One Armed Trapper, that's who.'

Mom shracked again, tearing at her hair.

The horror of He-Who-Stole-Sis:

The canoe had a big hole in it, but Grandma Matchie said, Never mind, that way we'll be able to see the lake bottom. That's important, she said. 'He'll leave tracks, he will. We gotta follow em, we do.'

After dravelling the canoe down to the little gravel beach beside the dock and loading it up with food and Grandma Matchie's silver spurs and range saddle, we all gathered at the dock.

'Don't you worry,' Grandma Matchie said to Mom. 'Me and Tyke'll bring er back. Rest easy now.'

Wringing her hands, Mom moaned, 'If only I wasn't halfway through my baking! You know how I hate to not finish things!'

'An I got all those flies to tie up,' Dad groamed. 'Can't let em get away, y'know.'

'Don't you worry neither of you. We'll hunt him down even if it takes us t'the deepest lake on Earth!' Grandma Matchie glowered. 'I gotta score t'settle with One Armed Trapper, I do.'

Then we were off, pushing out from the shore and drifting sideways. Sitting in the stern, I looked around and suddenized we had no paddles. But Grandma Matchie stood at the bow and spread her arms wide. Her red dress fanned out and filled with wind, and the canoe began slurping forward and soon was slickering through the water, the waves batralping against the canoe's sides.

I looked around. 'Grandma Matchie, I don't feel no wind.'

'Course not!' she surplied over her shoulder. 'It's cosmic wind, the kind y'can't feel, but it's always there.'

'Where's it come from?'

'The center of the universe, that's where.'

'Where's that?'

'In my lodge, where else?'

'Which room?'

'Never you mind.'

I scowlered. 'The kitchen?'

The back of her head shook, no.

'The den? The livin room? The dinin room?'

'Never you mind.'

'Your bedroom?'

I heard her chackle. 'You can't feel the wind yet, so don't you go talkin 'bout what y'don't know.' She shifted slightly and we rounded the edge of the bay. The Major's island went by off to our left and I could see him standing on his dock, shaking both fists at us, but Grandma Matchie just ignored him. What with his gnazzling garumphing and endless ormbling around and around his island's beach, and his Blarny Boat all borlupping with leaks, and all his meening away at night when he's drunk too much crayfish wine and sprouts purbling poems that drift moonily across the water, well, the Major's small fry.

Moving forward on my knees I looked down into the hole in the canoe. The water slid by as clear as glass and I could see down a million hundred fifty-one feet to the bottom.

'See his footprints, Tyke?'

Squimping, I concentrated real hard like she always told me to do, and then I saw them, crossing the mud bottom. 'Steady as she goes!' I shouted.

Boy, those sure were giant footprints.

The afternoon passed, as we followed the shoreline until we came to the river mouth, and then up the windering river we went, the forest going by on both sides in a blurthy blur. And below us the tracks of One Armed Trapper continued. When it got dark we kept going and Grandma Matchie, soaking up all that cosmic wind, started glowing in the darkness, and the footprints glowed too. The river narrowed and grew twimpy, with thick wild rice choking the channel and all the spiderwebs between the reedy stalks all shinnily and gothic in the moonlight.

I watched those footprints the whole night through and never even got tired. It was the cosmic wind, Grandma Matchie explained. 'No one ever gets tired with Cosmic Wind,' she said.

At dawn the river widened and currents swirvelled around us, making the water muddy. 'Winnipeg River!' Grandma Matchie shouted triumphantly. 'I know where he's gone to! He can't hide from me! Hah!' And the canoe raced through the churbling water. 'Eaglenest Lake, that's where! Hah!'

The river widened even more and I could see bays and inlets on both sides through the morning mist, which disappeared as the sun rose higher and higher. Staring down into the hole once again, I gasped. 'His tracks are gone! Grandma Matchie!'

The canoe stopped suddenly and she turned to me with a frown. 'Gone? Then that means he took a detour, don't it?' She held up her hands. 'Not a word, Tyke. Grandma Matchie has t'think.' And with that she closed her eyes and lowered her head.

Everything had gone quiet and I looked around. The river's current had stopped and the swirbles stayed in half-swirb, and the ebbies waited in half-eb, and over the trees flying birds were frozen in mid-flathap, and low over the water bazzling insects hung in mid-bazz. The world stopped when Grandma Matchie closed her eyes and thought. Suddenly I heard a tree crash deep in the woods a long way off and then Grandma Matchie's head snapped up.

'There's only one thing that could make One Armed Trapper take a detour.' Her face glowed pink and her eyes glimbered. 'Only one thing! I bin hopin for this!'

'What?'

She grinned. 'Get me my spurs, Tyke, I'm goin for a swim.'

The world started moving again but our canoe stayed where it was, the water purbling against the sides, as Grandma Matchie stepped to the center and bent down and picked up her saddle and leaned it up against the prow. Then she took the silver spurs and clipped them onto her boots. Jampling, she walked forward and sat down in the saddle. Then she leaned over the bow and yabbled, 'Gronomo!' and plunged into the water, vanishing beneath the brown swirbling currents.

I pulled a loaf of bread from the picnic basket in front of me, tied a rope to it, and heaved it over the side as an anchor. Then, peering down through the hole, I watched Grandma Matchie swarmle down and down until she disappeared in the muddy gloomb.

Minutes passed. A miscreant frog floated by in the water blinking snoozily and I thought about throwing things in Sis's hair. Never again, I vowed, would I throw a dead frog in her hair. No, I'd throw something bigger and better, like a giant dead tarantula. Sis hated spiders. I grinned as I imagined it coming back to life.

The water around me suddenly began to boil, steam rising up in wild sprouts. The canoe tossled and span crazily and I gripped the sides. And through the hole I saw Grandma Matchie coming up, crouched in her saddle with her bony knees up around her shoulders. The spurs glimmerined like fishing lures as she rose up into the sunlipped water. And then I saw what she was riding. The biggest snapping turtle I've seen. Bigger than Dad's Bronco, bigger even than the cabin, about as big as Dad's Bronco sitting on the cabin, but maybe even bigger. I gawped and stared as its beak opened wide and its long neck stretched upward as if it was going to swabble me and the canoe in one gulp. But then, with a kick from Grandma Matchie, it swirjerked to one side and broke the surface beside me.

'Ya-hoo! Jump aboard, Tyke! Afore you get capsized!'

The giant horny shell looked stlippery, all covered with slime and muddy seaweed, but I jumped anyway, landing beside Grandma Matchie who grabbed me before I could stlip and set me down in the saddle behind her.

'Yeahh!' she yelled, kicking her spurs until sparks flew from the turtle's shell. With a thrashle of its thick pebbly-skinned legs, the snapper surgled forward, clawing through the water so fast that steam burst out behind us. 'Tyke! Meet Leap Year! The biggest, meanest Grandma of em all!'

Eyes rolling, Leap Year nodded her huge head. Looking down, I could see that her shell was covered with carvings. Hearts and initials and arrows and stuff. B.D. LOVES O.A.T., G.L.H. AND O.A.T., O.A.T. LUVS L.L.

Thousands of carvings, thousands of initials loving O.A.T. and being loved by O.A.T.

'He's had it now!' Grandma Matchie screaked. 'We're all gonna get im! Hah! A thousand million ten fifty years I've waited fur this!' The water went by in a blurthy unplosion of foam and steam as Leap Year plommelled forward, smoke hissing from her upturned nose, fires spigging sparks from her enraged eyes, her lipstick-stained beak open and her tongue writhing like an inside-out backwards snake.

Then, with a nudge of her spurs, Grandma Matchie swung Leap Year shoreward, and I held on tight and let out a yabble as we hit land. Thunder shook the earth and Leap Year's front claws skraked gouges in the bedrock as we left the river. Then trees crashed down all around us and birds screaked and squirrels flew through the air until they caught hold of vines and swung away in shreeming flight.

Suddenly, the crashing stopped, and we perched on the edge of a cliff overlooking a lake. Leap Year snortered and stretched out her neck to turn and look at us.

Grandma Matchie nodded. 'He's down there, all right. I can feel it!'

The lake was round, and the trees and bushes grew in a tight ring all around its shore, making it look like a giant nest full of water. 'He lives down there?' I asked.

'Yep.'

'It looks like a big bird nest.'

'Course, it's called Eaglenest Lake, ain't it?'

'It musta been the biggest eagle in the whole world,' I said, and Grandma Matchie nodded again. I went on, 'It musta laid the biggest eggs too.'

'Yep.'

'Bigger even than Adam's Egg?'

Grandma Matchie rubbled her jaw. 'Don't think so, Tyke, but you never know.'

I squimped my eyes and studied the shore. 'I don't see him.'

'He lives right at the bottom. That's where he went down fifty years ago. Carried a cast-iron stove like the one we got in the cabin, a thousand hundred ninety-six miles through the bush, with his one arm. Winter, it was, and here he had his cabin. But crossin the lake the stove fell through the ice and he wen down with it. An there he be, tendin the fire in his stove forever more.'

'What fire?'

'The fire o' love, Tyke.'

Sure enough, scranch went my face. 'Yucchhh!'

Leap Year snortled again, her gaze belliful, grim and serious as she glarmored down at the lake. Behind us her tail thrashelled the torn-up forest, knockering down trees and overturning big flat rocks and stuff.

'An Sis is down there? What's he want her for?'

Grandma Matchie frowned. 'That's what I can't figure out an it's bin itchin me all over. He's up t'somethin, mark my words.'

And Leap Year nodded, shiftening nervously under us.

'Mebee he jus wants er, is all,' Grandma Matchie musilled. 'Mebee that's all there is, mebee.' Then she raised her fist. 'Like us all! Like us all!' she crackled. 'He'll steal em when he has to! Steal em and love em and leave em, that's what he does! He done that t'them all! Up and left em! Even his b'trothed!' Then her mouth snappered shut and she went white.

Grandma Matchie almost never goes white like that. So, remembering my vow to protect her, I said, 'Don't worry, we'll get Sis back. Don't you worry.'

Leap Year whimed and shibbered under us, her eyes lorling in her head.

Grandma Matchie drew a deep breath. 'No matter! The time's come an he's had it now!' Then she drove her spurs into Leap Year's hard shell. Suddenly we were in the air, sailing outward, then down toward the still blue water. And a head popped up below us, a bearded face with its mouth open in a silent scurm of terror, its eyes bugling out at us.

The crash when we hit threw me from the saddle, sent me tumbling, limbs splayed, through the air and hitting the water with a painful sralap. Down I went, the blue snirling in front of my eyes. With a thump my bum struck bottom and I looked around. A faint reddish glow warmed the water and I could see something like a baby sun burning in the distance. Jampling to my feet I ran toward it in slow motion. A terrible clanging sound filled my ears, like bells, but I couldn't see where it came from.

The glow grew brighter and the spot of fire grew bigger, and I saw that it was a stove, sitting on a bump of rock. Through its grille fire raggled, and blue smoke stained the water until my eyes stung. As I approached Grandma Matchie crampled up beside the stove and glarened about. Seeing me, she waved and I skuggled over.

'Where's Leap Year?' I asked.

'Dis'peared. I don't like this, Tyke. Not one bit.' She continued looking around from her perch on the bump of rock. 'One Armed Trapper's hidin somewhere round here, mark my words.'

'I saw him just before we hit the water, lookin scared to death!'

'Aye, an that's what's bothering me, Tyke. One Armed Trapper's never bin fright'ned of nothin in his whole life. Nosiree, he's up t'somethin, he is.' She shook her head, placing her hands on her hips and glowening about.

A faint scurm rode to us on the currents and we both turned in its direction. Far in the distance I saw Sis, being held by a small man wearing a tuxedo and the biggest shoes I've ever seen, as big as a sports car, though even flatter than the one Dad drove over in the Bronco in the parking lot.

'One Armed Trapper!' Grandma Matchie hissped, crouching. 'If I didn't know better, I'd scry he was baitin us. Only he wouldn't dare!' Then she scowlered grimly. 'Lessen he's got help!'

'Who?'

'Can't be sure. Could be Satan Himself!'

Sis screaked again and Grandma Matchie said, 'Well, Tyke, let's go get im! But keep yer eyes peeled, jus in case it's a trap!' Then she crampled down and we began running toward them, jampling from rock to rock and pushing our way through seaweed. Fish scattered in all directions when they saw the glow in Grandma Matchie's eyes and I didn't blame them. It was something Awful to Behold. As we got closer to where they were struggling, the clangening of bells grew louder and louder.

I could see One Armed Trapper's bushy face, and he was grinning, his teeth glowing white like pearls. Sis fought in the grip of his single arm but it was wrapped around her like a vice. When we were only a hundred feet away he gave us a little dance and tuddled off down a rocky trail.

'After im!' Grandma Matchie shouted and we broke into a sprintle. Rounding a corner we caught a last glimpse of One Armed Trapper as he plungered into a cave. The sound of bells filled my head until it felt like it was about to unplode, and things started getting dreamy like, as if I was being Hypnotized, like I saw in a movie once, when the blonde lady stopped screaking and skirking until all her clothes fell off.

We reached the cave mouth and Grandma Matchie took my hand and in we went. It was pitch black for the first dozen tuddles or so then we could make out a faint glow ahead of us and we skuggled toward it.

And before we knew it, we found ourselves standing in a chapel. There were pews carved out of solid rock, and a pulpit at the far end behind which stood a giant crayfish, old and gray-bearded. He held a Bible Delicately in his spincers.

And to one side stood Leap Year, all chained up and her head Bowed in Defeat. One Armed Trapper stood near her, smiling warmly. 'Ahh!' he squeaked in a high voice. 'The bride herself!' And he laughed and bowed.

We had paused at the edge of the long narrow aisle. I looked at Grandma Matchie and cried out. Her red dress had disappeared and now she wore a white wedding dress, and behind the veil her eyes were all dreamy and lost. Hypnotized!

'Betrothed!' exclaimed One Armed Trapper. 'Come to me at last! Oh joy! Joy!' And he did that little dance again and it made the old crayfish frown and push his spectacles back from his antennae.

Red fire was burning on Leap Year's shell and I could see new initials – bigger than all the rest – burning themselves into her back. She whailed Mournfully. The wedding bells rlang and rlang in the murky water and the red fire burnelled and burnelled, and Grandma Matchie began the slow march up the aisle as a hunchbacked carp with her gray hair in a bun started playing on an ancient organ.

'A trap!' I screaked, stumblering after Grandma Matchie. 'It was a trap!' But I couldn't break her out of the spell.

The old crayfish began reading the marriage vows and I whailed in Horror as Grandma Matchie and One Armed Trapper began repeating them. Lurchening forward, I stumblered over Sis, who was crouching against a pew, her eyes all crazy like.

'It's the fire o' love!' she hisspered. 'The Devil made it into a spell!'

'What do you mean!'

'It brings things back, dummy!'

The vision of the frog flashed in my mind. I stared up the aisle. Already, One Armed Trapper was rolling up his sleeve, getting ready to punch Grandma Matchie's arm. 'Wait here! Try and slow em down!'

And then I whirvilled and began to skuggle, out of the chapel, down the tunnel, out of the cave. And there, dim in the distance, burned that little red flame. The bells still rlang and I knew that when they stopped it would be too late, cosmic wind or no cosmic wind.

I skuggled and skuggled, almost flying through the water. My heart pounded until it was louder than even the bells. The smoke from the woodstove was getting thicker, and it was getting harder and harder to see.

I was almost at the bump of rock when a huge shadowy shape reared up in front of me and roarbelled. The sound hit me in a wave and I flew back, hippering the mud with a thump. All I could see through the smoke were two glowing slits, a hundred feet above me. They closed in, loombing right over my head.

The loudest voice I've ever heard thundered down on me. 'I WON'T TOLERATE THIS!'

Scramblering to my feet I almost slipped as a rock rolled out from under me. Lurchening forward I grabbed it, and suddenized it wasn't a rock at all. It was one of Mom's loaves. Grunting, I raised it over my head and screeked: 'Eat this!!' And then I threw it with all my strength right between its eyes.

'YEOWWWWWW!'

Those eyes reared backwards, scranching tight so that everything went dark all of a sudden. I jampled forward, passing between two huge pillars that must have been its legs. And there, right in front of me, was the bump of rock and the stove. I crampled madly.

Above and behind me I heard another roar, and currents swept over me, almost tearing my grip from the rock. But then I was on my feet and the stove wasn't more than five feet away, its flames licking eagerly at the grille. Springering forward I gave that stove the hardest kick I've ever given anything. The grille flew open as it torpled backwards, and the fire o' love shot out in all directions, pouring out sparks as the stove rolled across the rock and plumged over the far side. The glow of the flame went out and I hurried to the edge just in time to see the stove disappear in the deep mud bottom.

Sparks swarmelled off in all directions, and I knew the whole world was in a lot of trouble now that the fire o' love had been freed. My face scrinching, I looked around for Satan Himself but he had disappeared. And just then, far off in the distance, I heard a Horrible scrum of Frustration, then a Shout of Triumph. Thunder shook the rock and I fell to my knees.

We were saved!

'Nothin's over till I say so!'

Standing on the shore, Grandma Matchie shook her head and glarmered down into the croonbling waves of Eaglenest Lake. 'It's just no good,' she muthered. 'Ain't nobody beat me afore. Ain't nobody!'

The sun was going down and stars appeared overhead. I threw more wood on the small fire, then glommered at her. 'You shoulda punched him! That's all you had to do. Punch him afore he punches you!'

But Grandma Matchie shook her head. 'It's jus no good, Tyke.'

'Bah!'

Sis sneered at me so I sneered back, and that made me feel better. Glancing up, I asked Grandma Matchie, 'So, what're ya goin t'do, huh?'

Abruptly she squared her shoulders. 'I'm goin back down there, an that's all there is to it!'

'You can't!' I screeked, jampling to my feet.

'I gotta!' And with that she ran to where Leap Year lollered on a giant flat rock and climbed into the saddle. 'We gotta finish what we started!' Crackling, they plunged back into the water.

I kicked at the fire, and the sparks seemed to fly through the air forever, round and round. Sis stuck out her tongue at me but I ignored her, pacing back and forth and back and forth and dodging those crazy sparks.

'Ow!' Sis cried, and I turned around.

'What is it?'

She didn't say anything, but there was a strange gleemble in her eyes that I'd never seen there before and it made me frown.

'You and Grandma Matchie saved me, Jock Junior,' she said in this weird soft voice, standing up and walking toward me, smiling.

Suddenly I knew what had happened. 'Get back!' I screeked. 'Get away from me!' But I'd been cornered. The lake was behind me and there was no way on earth I was going in there. And Sis pounced like some Horrible Beast and trapped me in her arms and then she spotched my forehead with spit. With spit!

The Spotch of a Horrible Beast:

Oh sure! They call it kissing! Well, they can forget it as far as I'm concerned. Never again for Jock Junior!

It's just not fair. Everything gets so Grim and Serious, and things keep pushing the insides of my head around in helpless circles. I was pacing again but after a while I stopped and stared at the still, dimbled surface of the lake, and pretty soon it began to glow as if full of cosmic wind. It made me sick, and I bet you know what happened to my face too. That also makes me sick, and so does Sis. Everything makes me sick.

I hate recesses, and that's all there is to it. I used to think summer holidays were just one long recess, but it's not true. I won't let it! I'm gonna learn to tie flies like Dad, that's what I'm gonna do.

So I glarmed for a while at the glowing lake, then finally turned back to the fire and stokered it up with some of Mom's loaves. Sis was humming and I wondered how long it would take before that spark wore off. And the fire burned redly, and it made me want to barf.

That was the first week.

LUNKER, WHERE ARE
YOU BOUND?

Every word of it's true!

Just because I'm only nine years old and just because
I'm only four feet tall it doesn't mean I can't control my
imagination! I tell the truth and Big Nose twisters
my ear. I keep my eyes open and Big Nose sturffles my
mouth with cotton. Well, almost!

It's not fair!

I'd sure like to see Big Nose try and twister Grandma
Matchie's ear. Hah! She'd throw Big Nose in the lake
just to see what kind of lubber she was.

'The only kind,' Grandma Matchie'd conclude with a
sniff. Me too.

And it's that same ear – the one that's burning and
itching right now – that I keep pressed to the earth to
listen to all the whispering. Stories, a million stories!
And all of them true! They have to be, don't you see?
The earth wouldn't lie.

Big Nose forbids whispering:

It's a rule. No hisspering, no passing notes, no tellong-ing tales. It all has to do with respect, she says. You have to respect Certain Things, she says with fire and brim-stone. Things like Bigness, chalkboards and rulers, fire and brimstone. And of course Big Nose's Unwillingness to Tolerate any Precociousness.

And it doesn't end there, either. Just think about your last recess. Everybody's playing soccer. It's a mob of scrumming kids chasing a ball around in the snow. And you're leaning there, watching everything from the goal-post, getting numberled with the horror of it all. And they rabble all over the place, and their faces are set in gothic grimaces and nobody tolerates anything. After all, Big Nose is standing there at the edge of the field, and she has a big brass bell in her hand and I bet she's just waiting for someone to step out of line. Then, Whammo! And we're not talking wedding bells here, either.

Play within the lines, goalie gets the ball, penalty shot, all that stupid stuff. As if standing around between two goalposts is hard. As if keeping the ball out is hard. Dum. All you have to do is tie a string ankle-high from one post to the other and not a single ball will roll in. They can try and kick it high all they want. They couldn't get it between the posts if their lives depended on it.

Their lives depended on it:

That was my mistake. My big mistake. I should've known by looking at those pinchered faces as they chased the ball around. Grandma Matchie says it's an art to recognize a lynch mob when you see one, even in this day and age.

And worst of all, Big Nose was right up there, leading the pack, her bell waving about at the end of her arm as if her hand had turned to brass.

So there you are, Attila and her Huns are charging down on you all because the ball bounced back from the string while you were hanging from the crossbar. Just because something didn't look quite right about it. Just because their lives depended on that ball crossing that line or not crossing that line in a Manner Deemed Proper. In a manner you could Respect.

Nobody respects a string tied between two posts, I guess.

And I almost got away. Almost over the fence when Big Nose's hand – the flesh one, not the brass one – grabbled my ankle. They spizzled and snargled like wolves but kept their distance because Big Nose was there. You know, there's only one reason I can figure for why she didn't brain me: skulls find brass bells Intolerable.

So I got sent to jail, doing hard time, cleaning the chalk dust from the bushes and pulling the hairballs out from between the broom's straw. It was a strict school. Hairballs not allowed.

The mysterious world inside a broom:

You get to exploring, just sitting there on Big Nose's desk, putting all the hairballs into a careful pile and storing them away in her drawer beside the bruisbled apple she forgot to take home.

Gloria Feeb's apple, a present from Gloria Feeb's

house delivered by Gloria Feeb herself. I hate Gloria Feeb.

Pushing the apple far into the back of the drawer, I closed it and began picking out all the other things inside that broom. Pieces of crayon with chewbled ends – the purple ones were Margaret Pukeshank's for sure. She loved eating purple crayons and her teeth were always purple. Willy Dortmund liked the green ones but I found only the discarded paper wrapping from those. Willy was fat because he never let anything go to waste that couldn't be eaten first. Amy Greenfeet was a connoisseur – only yellow crayons were good enough for her, what with her pointy nose and plaid pencil case and all. Me, it didn't matter what color they were. I tried them all. Thing is, after a while they all get to tasting the same. Paper, of course, was another matter.

And then there were bits of eraser and chewing gum – though sometimes it was hard to tell them apart except for the smell. I think the real reason why the school has to buy new stuff every year is because we eat everything we can lay our hands on.

The best part about a broom is the straw itself. You'd think they'd glue it in, but if you shake the broom long enough and hard enough the straw fallers out and just keeps on fallering out, covering Big Nose's desk and all her notes and all over the floor. If I ate straw I could live for years on just one broom. This broom.

But when you think about it, they probably buy new brooms every year too. I'd have to ask Willy about that.

Well, the broom was clean, and all the chalk from the brushes was no longer on the brushes and I could make neat footprints all over the floor. All that was left was feeding the fish.

Fish always know when they're the only thing left:

You can tell by the way their mouths glape. They've got nothing left to say and even if they did they wouldn't tell you. They're like that.

I bet you think fish are dumb. Well, most of them are, I guess. Like the one in Big Nose's room. Just looking at it, I could see that its brain was wivening away. It'd been there too long, a prisoner under the shadow of Big Nose's big nose.

Even when I stuckled my head into the water and tried talking to it, it just swambled away and hid behind a rock. But after ten minutes or so it got used to me and came out for a closer look, glaping, glaping, glaping. I glaped back.

And I was just about to say something when I saw a blur come through the door. It screamed blurthily and grew really big really fast. 'Hide!' I yelled at the fish, who duckered into a plastic castle and peered out from one of the towers.

'Jlog Jlunlior!' I heard Big Nose yell. 'Glet—' Hands grabbed my shoulders. '—lout—' I struggled, but she began pulling my head from the water. '—thlis—' And then I was out, water spraying everywhere. '—MINUTE!'

'I wasn't doin nothin!'

'Jock Junior! Do you think I will tolerate this!'

Well, the answer to that was obvious. 'Probably not,' I said, lowering my head and watching the drops hitting the floor.

'Probably? PROBABLY!?'

'Jock Junior simply refuses to control his imagination':

That's not even true! I can control it just fine! It wasn't me who jampled to crazy conclusions, was it? Was it?

So there was Dad, and there was Mom, and there behind that big desk was the principal, who was all ears as Big Nose ran off at the mouth about all the things she Misunderstood.

'. . . And he had the gall to tell me he was talking with that goldfish!' Big Nose said in fruxasperation. 'I'm completely fruxasperated!' See! 'I mean, a goldfish!'

Turning to Dad I explained, 'That was my mistake. Goldfish can't talk. I should've known better—'

'I should think so!'

'Goldfish aren't like other fish. And of course you can't keep pike and muskie in aquariums cause they'd never stop complaining and it would disturble the class—'

Big Nose jumped to her feet. 'Aaaaghh!'

I've never seen her so red. Redder even than a boiled crayfish with its eyes bugging out in all directions. I started to get real worried when she clatched the sides of her head and began running in circles.

'You shouldn't get so mad,' I said as calm as I could. 'It just makes you intolerable.'

'Aaaggghh!'

The meaning of Aaaggghh:

Well, what could Dad and Mom say? They knew all about talking fish and they didn't even have imaginations! All they could do was sit there and help Big Nose drink down her medicine.

And the principal sat there frowning and gromering, drumbling his desk and cluhearing his throat and looking at his paperweight, which wasn't very big and a gull full of buckshot would've done the job much better. I vowed to give him one as a present for graduating me. Grandma Matchie would be proud of that!

'And that assignment!' Big Nose cried, her hands pressed against his cheeks. 'My Lord!'

My heart sank. Back to that again, eh? I knew right then I was finished. Turning to Dad I pleaded, 'Summer vacation at the lake. I wrote it just like it happened and—'

And. It's a funny word, isn't it? I mean, everything follows naturally, doesn't it? It shows up everywhere, and there's nothing you can do about it. See? The whole world turned into 'And' right then. And Dad's eyes bulgered, and Mom jippled out of her chair, her bum hitting the floor with a bathump. And Dad's cheeks bulgered, and Mom started repeating 'Oh my, oh my oh my—' And Dad's head bulgered and I started getting real worried.

And, finally, when I could take it no more, I leapt to my feet and screamed: 'It's all true!'

The point where you just can't take it no more and you scream: 'It's all true!'

It was the second week of summer vacation at Rat Portage Lake. Dad had given up the art of fishing and was putting together his new Jacuzzi in between bellowing at the ceiling and tearing at the instruction manual.

Mom finished sweepening up the forest trail out back and came in for a breather. 'My! But that was dirty!' she breathed, wipering invisible sweat from her brow and leaning on her broom.

'Gothic in heaven, woman! You know the roof needs fixin – but off you go without a damn thought for anyone else! What happens if it rains and water leaks down on your daughter's forehead? What happens then, eh? She's sleepin away and it's drip, drip, drip! Pretty soon she's droolin and chanterin communist slogans!' He glared up from the pile of cedar planks. 'What then, eh?'

'Oh, we'll put a bucket on her head long before that happens, dear,' Mom replied dreamily, since she'd already seen the tiny hairball trying to sneak into the kitchen. Her knuckles went white on the broom handle, and she began creepering forward.

Out on the porch Sis ruckled in the old ruckling chair, staring out at the lake with a scowl. 'I hate this,' she kept saying over and over again. 'I hate this. I hate everything about this and I hate you!' she hisspered at me.

The fire o' love had worn off, thank gothic.

Her hair was now blue, bright like the sky and if there were any clouds they were all inside her head. Every now and then she reached up, her fingers all turembling, and touched it, then she'd dart her hand back down and start ruckling like mad. Crazy. Just plain crazy.

Hearing footsteps on the roof I went outside and stood in the middle of the driveway and looked up. 'Hey, Grandma Matchie!'

She waved at me with the hammer, her mouth full of nails. Shingles sat in piles all around her like burnt pancakes and her yellow dress bilbowed brighter than the sun. I ran to the ladder and crawpelled up. The roof crucked and crackled as I walked across it to where she was working.

From the looks of it she'd finished patching the hole. Frowning, I asked, 'What're ya doin?'

Around the nails she whispered: 'Shhh! It's a disguise!'

Duckening down beside her I stared wildly about. 'Who are ya spyin on?'

'Take a gander, Tyke. The Major's island!' And with that she jerked her head ever so slitherly, her eyes squimbled to secret slits. 'He's up t'no good! I can feel it in m'bones!'

'Which bones?'

'Never you mind. There's trouble in the air, can't you feel it?'

On his island, the Major was humbering back and forth between his dock and his cabin, carrying stuff down, packing it into the H.M.S. *Hood*? his blarny boat. And every now and then he'd take out his long spyin glass and study us, and when he did that Grandma Matchie'd bend down and pretend to be hammering nails, and I'd look down too with a big frown of concentration on my face.

'He's preparin fur war, that's what he's doin,' Grandma Matchie muthered in a low voice, after checking the sky in case any gulls were trying to listen in. But the sky was empty.

'Against us?'

A shake of her head. 'Uh uh. Somethin else I can't scry. But come mornin you can bet your toad ranch he'll be gone. Right dis'peared inta thin air!'

We heard screams coming from below and I looked down to see Mom runnering out onto the dock, waving Dad's fishing rod over her head like she was trying to swat a horsefly out of midair.

'What's wrong?' I cried, jumping to my feet.

Grandma Matchie squimted. 'Damn girl! Sometimes I wonder how'n hell I . . .' Then she shook her head. 'She's bein chased by a wasp, is my bet.'

'Probably as big as the one Dad made last week,' I said.

'Probbly is the one Dad made last week! Still tied t'the line!' Grandma Matchie threw back her head and let out a wild laugh.

And she was right. You could see the fishing line glittering every now and then in the sunlight, as Mom frantically whippled the rod over her head, screeking and runnering round in circles at the end of the dock. Then, with a mighty swing, she flung the wasp down into the water, and there was a huge saplash and suddenly Mom was yelpering. A giant fish leapt out of the water and we could hear the drag winding as the fish raced out into the bay.

'Keep ridin im, Ester!' Grandma Matchie shouted, jumping to her feet and waving the hammer over her head. 'Keep on ridin im! Ya-hoo!'

It was a tug-o-war as the fish brolled the surface again and again, throwing spray everywhere. And Mom had her hand on the reel now and was pumpening madly, her legs spread wide and bent inward at the knees. Even from here I could see the terror in her wild eyes and if her high heels weren't stuck between the boards again she'd have been pulled right out into the water. But she pumped and she reeled, and the fish was dragged closer and closer, and suddenly it flew up and splanded right on the dock, flippening about between Mom's feet.

'Oh my! Oh my!' Mom plopped right out of her shoes and danced around, trying to avoid the slimy flippening fladapping fish. 'Oh my!'

Running forward along the roof, Grandma Matchie gave one mighty jump and landed clear on the dock beside Mom. 'You got im! You got im clean! Hah!' And with that she dived, grabbling the fish in a bear hug and they rambelled back and forth, struggling and torngling and grumting.

By the time I crawpelled down the ladder and raced around the corner of the cabin and down to the dock, Grandma Matchie had put the fish down for the count and was standing triumphantly above him, one boot on his gaspering head.

'Must be a hundred million ninety-nine pounds!' She shook her fist at him, and he mackled his eye and fladapped and squirmed feebly. 'We got dinner t'night! Hah!'

And sure enough Mom put the pot on the stove and stoked up the fire until the water boiled crazily, and then she added salt and a whole load of potatoes. Dad put the fish in the sink and filled it up with buckets from the lake to keep him fresh until the time was good and right. I sat on a stool beside him and watched him glape, glape, glape.

Everything was just about ready when we heard a browl from the porch and we all ran outside to see Sis standing beside the ruckling chair, a mirror in her hand. Her face was turning every color and so had her hair – yellow, red, mauve.

'Waaa!' Sis wayloned. 'Waaa!'

Behind me I heard a funny fladapping sound, then a wild laugh.

Whirling, I tore into the kitchen. 'Grandma Matchie!' I screamed. 'The fish is getting away!' And there he was, pushing at the window latch. One of his eyes winked at me and he laughed again.

Grandma Matchie flew toward him but it was too late, because just then he got the window open and plungered over the sill.

'Aaak!' Mom squawked from the porch. 'It's got my broom! Give me back my broom!'

We ran back out to the porch. A whufizzing sound came from over our heads and we ducked low. The fish had Mom's broom, all right, and he was flying on it all over the place, laughing hysterically.

He did one last loop then raced away into the west. Looking after him, Grandma Matchie put her hands on her hips and announced in a low voice: 'That, Tyke, was no ordernary fish.'

Numberly, I shook my head.

'I've known alotta fish in my day,' she muttered, 'but I ain't never known one like that!' And then she turned to me, shaking her head. 'You ever heard a fish laugh like that? I never heard a fish laugh like that.'

'Me neither,' I said. 'It sure was eerie.'

Next morning, just as Grandma Matchie had

predicted, the Major and the H.M.S. *Hood* were gone.

'Bad omens, Tyke. Bad omens.' Grandma Matchie paced up and down on the dock, while I sat with my feet in the water. 'Too many strange thins goin on round here.' Grimmerly, she stopped and faced me. 'Jus list em! First that fish, laughin like some demon. Then Sis, gettin a hangnail as if from outa the blue! An those potaters didn' taste like they shoulda at all. An, the most gothic damnin omen of all, Dad can't read those J'cuzzi 'structions – cause they're in French!' She began pacing again. 'Nosiree, I don't like this one bit!'

'Where d'you think the Major went?' I asked.

Suddenizedly Grandma Matchie slapped her forehead. 'O Course!' She whirled to me, her eyes burning merrily. 'Why didn' I think of it afore? Course! That's gotta be it!' She began stramping up the dock, then paused to straighten her dress and glare at me. 'Well, are ya comin, or what?'

I leapt to my feet. 'You bet! Where?'

'Where? I'll tell ya where! We're goin after the Major!'

'But what about the demon fish? And Mom's broom?'

'They all went to th'same place, or my name ain't Grandma Matchie! An we're goin after em!'

'Where?' I asked again.

A shiver jampled across Grandma Matchie's shoulders like there was a snake in her dress, and her eyes narrowed as she glared out over the water. 'We're goin t'the deepest lake on Earth! That's where we're goin!'

Well, it wasn't long after that that we packed all the essentials and readied ourselves for the trip. The deepest lake on Earth, I knew, was Westhawk Lake, over there in Manitoba. And it was made by a shooting star.

'Not just any old shootin star,' Grandma Matchie said mysteriously, but she wouldn't explain any further, only a burning kind of look would come into her right eye, then jump across to her left eye, then back again and back again and back again until I got dizzy just watching it.

By the time we were ready it was almost dark. 'Just right!' said Grandma Matchie as she stood at the end of the dock with her hands on her hips. 'An there ain't be no moon tonight, neither,' she said, nodding grimmerly.

'How're we gettin there?' I asked.

'You jus keep your eyes peeled on the lake, Tyke,' she growbled, 'an you'll see soon enough!' Bending down she checked her backpack and I heard clinking come from inside it.

'What you got in there?'

'Canada's Finest crayfish wine! That's what I got in there!'

By now it was night and the lake turned completely black, looking like a giant hole going down forever. I watched it like Grandma Matchie told me to do.

Then Mom and Dad and Sis came down from the cabin.

'Don't forget to bring back my broom!' Mom said, her hands all fluppering and her cheeks glowing red in the darkness. 'Oh my! Look at the dirt on this dock!'

Sis's hair glowed neon green but no one said anything about it so she wouldn't run off browling her eyes out. And there were funny little twigs sticking out of it now too. I thought back on it and was pretty sure it wasn't me who stuck them in there, so they must've grown naturally. Not that that made any sense, since Sis is so dumb she likes taking baths all the time, unless the water made those twigs grow better, I don't know.

'Don't you go brawlin bears this time, Grandma Matchie,' Dad warned. 'I don't wanta hear that my son has bin exposed to that!' He paused, frowned, and plungered his hand right into his beard and scritching sounds came out. 'You're s'posed t'be sensitive 'bout things with chil'ren, y'know. It's a turrible sight t'see a creature of the furest cryin and beggin like that.'

Grandma Matchie ignored him, thank gothic. 'Ready, Tyke?'

I nodded and with that she turned to face the lake.

'All right! Come outa there, you varmits! Afore I come down there after ya!'

And it wasn't long before the lake started glowing, and the water started burbbling and churmbling about. Then little streaks of light began flashing around the dock. Peering down I shouted: 'Those are lamp rays!' You could see their little helmets with those lights in them, flashing around as they swam in crazy circles and started fleaping out of the water. Then two big ones came up to the edge of the dock and poked their heads out.

'You two'll do jus fine!' Grandma Matchie said, then chackled, dancing a little jig.

It was then I noticed that she'd tied straps to her boots, with brass buckles. And all of a sudden Grandma Matchie jumped clear off the dock and landed right on those lamp rays. She bent down and strappered her feet to their backs, while they wraggled fumeously. 'Climber on my shoulders, Tyke! There's only one beast on Earth that knows the way t'Westhawk Lake – at least my Westhawk Lake – and that's a lamp ray!'

So I climbered over her backpack and onto her shoulders and she grabbed my legs and yelled: 'Here we go!'

Those lamp rays surgled forward and carveled deep grooves in the water, throaming white foam everywhere. The wind made my eyes tear and I leaned forward and stuck out my arms like you do in your Dad's Bronco when he's going a million thousand eighty-nine miles an hour and you got the windows rolled down.

'YA-HOO!' me and Grandma Matchie hollered both at the same time. And again: 'YA-HOOO!!' So it was just like the old-timers at the lake always grumped about – these days the whole lake was filled with bluddy Ya-hoos. Old-timers know everything, and they know what's true and what isn't, and the Bigness of Things doesn't scare them one bit.

Course, Grandma Matchie's the oldest-timer of all. 'I was here when this lake couldn even lick your boots! An the whole world was jus swamp!' she'd say. 'But them dinosaurs knew enough not t'mess with Grandma Matchie!' And she'd dance around like the Indians must've done when they tied string between all the trees and caused the extinction of the dinosaurs.

And boy did those lamp rays swim. Lakes whizzled by and when we came to the shore we just leapt high in the air and when we landed again it was in another lake. And then we crossed a big red line painted on the surface of the water and we were in Manitoba, which didn't look much different from Ontario except for all the buffalo swimming around. Course, they got out of our way! Hah!

And then, just as the sun was coming up in front of us, we stopped.

'This is Hunt Lake, Tyke,' Grandma Matchie said as she unstrappled her boots. 'An right over there on th'other side a those trees is Westhawk Lake. The deepest lake on Earth!'

'Are we gonna sneak up on it from here?'

'Yep. We gotta. There's demon fish spyin round all over th' place!' Off we jumped, hitting the water with huge spalashes and going straight down to the muddy bottom. Then we started tuddling, the water around us getting lighter and lighter and the bottom getting weedier and weedier as we crelpt toward shore. But all of a sudden a big black hole loombered in front of us and we planged into darkness.

'A secret cave!' I exclaimed.

Grandma Matchie paused to light a torch, since the lamp rays had gone home, and the fire made the water swirl with burbbles and the walls of the cave spackle as if they were full of gold.

We tuddled a long ways when Grandma Matchie stopped suddenly and crouched. 'There's somebuddy skulkin up ahead!' she hisspered, and we began edging forward.

We could see a light coming from around a corner further up the path, and Grandma Matchie put out her torch and ever so snuckily we came to the corner and peepered around it.

Grandma Matchie shouted and jumped forward and I followed, because there sat the Major, boiling tea over a fire right in the middle of a giant cavern. His eyes poppled out and he leapt off his camp stool.

'Gads! It's Grandma Matchie!'

'So there you are, eh? Jus as I figured – skulkin 'bout like the good-fur-nothin Major you are!' Grimmerly, she stalked toward him and he shrank back for a second then puffed up his chest and stood his ground. Grandma Matchie kept coming until their noses jambled together, the point of hers pludging into the red bulb of his. 'Good-fur-nothin Major!'

'Hah! And what 'bout you, hah? Spiteful ole witch!'

'Spiteful? Ain't I got reason t'be?'

'What ho? Reason? Whenever d'you need a bleedin reason?'

Uh oh, thinks I. 'Hey!' I shouted. Their heads turned at the same time and you could hear the Major's nose pop back out. Glaring at them with my hands on my hips, I said in my lowest, meanest voice: 'Tea's ready.'

And it was, and we all sat down round the fire and poured ourselves a cup. After a time Grandma Matchie sniggered, 'So, you're goin after er again, eh? Well, if you're one thing, Major, it's stubbern!' And she tilted her head back and shouted: 'Stubbern as a loaf of Ester's bread in a bear's belly! Hah!'

The Major glommered and his face got redder than the fire between them. 'Cripes! It's none o' yer bizness! None!'

'Oh, an ain't it, now? Ain't it? Well, somethin's saying t'me we're agoin after the same thin in the end. An jus like all th'other times you're agoin t'get in the way, afoulin thins up for alla us!'

Spluttering, the Major surgled to his feet. 'ME!' He began waving his fists around, making swirmbling currents so big even the fire pafted and wavered. 'I got ere first! I did! I did!'

'It don't matter one bit!' Grandma Matchie was on her feet now too, and the fire shrank between them. 'Yer daughter ain't got er broom stolen, did she? You ain't even got a daughter!'

'I do too! I do too!'

All of a sudden Grandma Matchie sat down, looking shocked. Then she got a hold of herself and glared at him. 'So he finally admits it at last, eh? Well, isn't this a pretty picture! A father, aren't ya? Afta all these years! Now you're a father!'

'An whenever di'you lemme be one, hah? Hah?'

I didn't know what in blazes they were talking about, so I stood up. 'Hey! Tell me some stories! Tell me some stories! You said we gotta wait till mornin, anyway! I wanta hear some stories!' And I put on my best little poor boy face and made my eyes real wide and pleading like.

Course it worked! It always does!

'The Major ain't gotta story in his hat worth picken!' Grandma Matchie sneerved.

'Hah! Is that right, is it? Is it? Well, I done thins that'll make yer stories look like they came from a Grade Fur Reader!'

'Iz that right?' Grandma Matchie leaned back and crossed her arms. 'Okay, Major,' she said in a low dangerous voice. 'Let's hear yer story! Come on, give it yer best! Hah!'

Pulling out a pipe, the Major settled himself in his stool and gave me a wink. And all at once his voice changed, getting all gravelly like Long John Silver's: 'Well, it wuz afore yer time, there, lad. Afore alla yer times—' Grandma Matchie snarted but the Major kept going. '—in th' Nort Sea, aye, an ya ain't seen waves as high o' those back then! An there I be, out fishin like a lad did in those days. An I was abaitin and ahookin an me boat wuz agettin lower'n lower wi' all the fish I wuz catchin. An in I throws the line, one last time, y'see, cause the waves wuz gettin a little big e'en fer the likes o' me – pullin down stars they were, makin em hiss and sputter in all kinds of steam!'

He was rocking back and forth on his stool and I could feel those waves making my stomach gasp like it was drowning.

'An then me line wen tight an started arunnin through me hands till smoke came out frum atwixt me fingers!' And he put his hand over his pipe and puffed crazily to show me what it must've looked like. 'Aye, I'd ahooked the biggest thin that lives in the sea. She's gotta thousand names, that sea snake, an ev'ry man, woman, and child o' the sea shakes when they 'ear em! Aye, so big she wen right round the whole world, akeepin all that water from aspillin out! So big she has t'bite er own tail so she knows where it is!' And he blew smoke rings that got bigger and bigger as they floated to the roof of the cave.

'No wonder the sea's astormin, thinks I,' the Major went on, leaning forward so his face glowed in the fire. 'I bin afishin er own backyard! Deprivin er a er own food! But I wuz a fisherman then jus like I am now! An

I started apullin on that line wi' all the strength in me young bones. An sure 'nough, up she comes, slow'n 'eavy, though still I cain't see er.

'Thirty-one days and thirty-two nights I'm adraggin up that line, eatin the fish in m'boat wi' one hand an apullin wi' t'other! Drinkin me own sweat when I got t' thirstin! An nineteen times 'roun the world she pulls me in that time, aye, an I seen sights the likes o' which no one's ev'ry seen afore!

'An so there I wuz, on th'thirty-third day and comin fer the twentieth time 'roun the world – an I finally sees er! Right there! Right there unner me boat!' And he points his pipe down and I look, but all I can see is the floor of the cave. 'Aye,' the Major chuckled. 'That's all I seen too! Er body's hard as rock an as fer across as the Kalahari Sea!'

'But the Kalahari's a desert in Africa!'

'Only after we apasst through it,' replied the Major, his eyes gleaming. 'She threw up so much water it plumb emptied the bowl! But where wuz I? Oh, aye, I seen er, an all at once I drop that line and dive inta the sea!'

I jumped to my feet. 'Did you get her?'

The Major nodded grimly. 'Aye, that I did.' He spread his arms wide. 'I grabbed er like this, apulled er cross me boat's thwarts. An she asquirmed and aslithered! But I held tight! An I heered er cryin and a'whimperin, an I realize't right then an there that I gotta let er go.' He bowed his head. 'I gotta let er go.' After a minute he looked up, and his eyes were full of tears. 'Y'know why, lad?'

I shook my head.

'I coulda took er, right then an there, but I realize't alla sudden that if I did, the seas'd empty an all th'water'd drain away! So I letter go and I cut me line, right then an there!'

'Bah!' Grandma Matchie scoffed. 'You call that a story? I coulda done better in my sleep!'

But the Major just leaned back and chuckled, relighting his pipe.

'An I ain't gotta go to no North Sea t'find my story, neither, cause it happened right here!' She leaned forward, her elbows on her bony gongly knees that peekered out from under her dress. 'Ten thousand years ago, it was, when the buff'lo filled the lakes from shore t'shinin shore! Buff'lo so big they left mountains behind em, if y'know what I mean, Tyke . . .'

I nodded, grinning snuckily.

'An if anyone ever asks you where the Rockies came from, you tell em 'bout the buff'lo an all the seaweed they et.'

I nodded again, thinking about how impressed Big Nose would be when I actually knew the right answer to one of her questions.

'Yessiree, Tyke, those were big buff'lo, an the Indians in these ere parts et their fill a them an made huts outa their skulls, an the buff'lo didn't mind one bit!

'But then one day the Indians look up and see alla the buff'lo are gone, an there's bones everywhere! Fillin the lakes so deep the bones at th'bottom turned right into stone, an if ever someone asks you where Tyndall stone comes from, you tell em 'bout the bones, Tyke, an they'll know you fer a wise man. An so, the Indians they start gettin worried, cause someone's et all the buff'lo, an this was way afore Buff'lo Bill's time, way afore Chris C'lumbus even!

'Not knowin what else t'do, them Indians turned t'me for help, like they always did back then. Only this time it was more serious than e'er afore. An not only were the buff'lo gone but so was the beaver and the bear and the deer and the mastodons – all gone!' Grandma Matchie paused to smirk at the Major, who was puffing madly on his pipe and studying the walls. 'Aye, so I start lookin fer signs, tracks, giant toothpicks with mammoth meat on em, an sure 'nough I pick up a mysterious trail, leadin north inta the backcountry. An I follows it fer days, till I come to this giant log cabin, tweeny stories tall, wi' bones piled up alla round it and smoke comin from the chimney.'

'Who lived there?' I demanded.

'I'm gettin t'that! Some thins you jus can't rush. So, up I go, right up t'that door and I starts poundin on it. "Whoever's in there better come out if'n know what's good fer ya!" I scream. Then I heared these footsteps crossin the floor in there, louder'n all the thunder rolled up in one! An the door opens up—' Grandma Matchie paused to sip delicately at her tea.

'And? And?'

She smackled her lips. 'An there he be, wi' me towerin over im! Wasn't no more'n five feet tall, but wearin the biggest boots I e'er seen!

' "Who in hell are you?" the little man screams. An I says, "I'm your doom, little man! Come on outa there, you puny runt!" Well, he goes all white, then red, an out he stomps, shakin his fists. "I was sleepin, damn you!" shrills the squirt, all indignant like. But I laugh in his face.'

'How brave!' the Major snickered.

Ignoring him, Grandma Matchie continued, 'This? thinks I, this is the one who et all those buff'lo?'

'An all those beaver and bear and deer and mastodons too?' I cried uncredulously.

Grandma Matchie nodded. 'Aye, them too? asks I. An I was gettin all ready t'give im the spankin of his life, when he jumps over to the biggest tree I e'er seen an pulls it up by the roots! An he starts swingin it like it was a twig! "Nobody wakes me up!" he roars, an if I didn't jump outa the way right then I wouldn't be ere telling this tale t'day! He hit the ground wi that tree so hard it split it right open from horizon to horizon! An if anyone e'er asks you where the Winnipeg River came from, now you know.'

Boy, no more D's in Geography for Jock Junior! Not after all this!

' "So! It's threats, is it?" screams I. "I arm-wrassled Satan Himself t'the ground an I can do the same wi you!" So we grab each other's wrists and sit down right there an the runt yells: "GO!" an the wrasslin started.' Grandma Matchie sipped more tea. 'Tree hundred years we sat there, locked t'gether, neither a us givin an inch! An grass grew up alla round us an snow covered us an birds nested on our heads. An that little man's cabin rotted away to nothin an all those bones turned to chalk dust and blew away—'

'An right into Big Nose's classroom!' I shouted.

'An right inta Big Nose's classroom, yep. An then trees growed up alla round us. An that little man couldn't budge me, an that was jus the way I wanted it—'

'Hah!' barked the Major.

'Jus the way I wanted it,' Grandma Matchie repeated. 'Cause by now all th'buff'lo had come back, an all th'beaver an bears an deer an mastodons too!'

'Of course!' I laughed. What a plan!

'But finally I start gettin turd a the whole thin, an wi the world back t'normal I figured it's time t'put the little man in his place. So I give it what I need to wrassle his arm t'the ground. Only he's bin sittin there so long, an strainin so long, that he's near turned t'stone! So – snap! His arm comes right off at the shoulder, an he didn't e'en twitch! But it awoked im up anyway, and up he stands, shaking his head.

'An he says: "I ain't never known anyone who coulda done that t'me! Not even—"' And Grandma Matchie sneered at the Major. '"—not even when I tied the sea snake's head to her tail!"'

'Liar!' screamed the Major, flying to his feet. 'That's not how One Armed Trapper lost his arm at all! Liar!'

Leapening to her own feet Grandma Matchie clenched her fists and shouted: 'I am not a liar! It was me who broke his arm off!'

'It was me! I did it long afore you!'

'You did not!'

'Yes I did!'

Well, it was obvious to me that this was never going to end, and I was exhausted, so I crawpelled off into a corner, and the shouting and boasting and accusing all jambled together as I fell asleep.

And next morning it was even worse. There were empty bottles of Canada's Finest all over the floor of the cave, brolling here and there in the lurzy currents. And Grandma Matchie and the Major weren't even talking to each other, and they wouldn't tell me nothing so I never found out who ended up with One Armed Trapper's arm.

The three of us packed up camp and started up the trail, going deeper and deeper into the cave. Pretty soon there were steps carved into the rock, going down. So down we went, nobody talking, nobody smiling. I just got sick of it and pushed ahead of them, holding the torch out in front of me.

The gold specks in the rock got bigger until they stuck out from the walls in nuggets, looking as soft as chewing gum. I remembered seeing some movie about these three guys in some desert who did nothing but try and kill each other over a whole pile of gold, and I remembered how one of them bit into one of the nuggets, so lots of people are fooled into thinking it's chewing gum. The only other thing I could remember from that movie was this fat guy saying: 'Badges, we don't need no steenking badges!'

Neither did we, and we didn't even care about all that gold. Gold? We don't need no steenking gold!

Finally I couldn't take it anymore and I whirled around. 'Will you two—?' And there I stopped, glaping. They were holding hands! And they didn't even pull them away when I saw it!

' "Will you two" – what?' Grandma Matchie asked, smiling.

I tried to say something but the words gaggled in my throat. And after a minute I turned back to the trail, all my delusions shattered. It was awful!

'Hold up there, Tyke,' Grandma Matchie warned.

'We're gettin close!'

Up ahead I could see reflected sunlight. Westhawk Lake! Thank gothic! I felt like I was going to die! And they didn't even look embarrassed! You'd think when someone got that old they'd know better.

Putting out the torch, we creepered to the edge of the opening. And there were stairs leading almost straight down, disappearing into the blackness. They looked like they went down forever – and even farther.

'Are we going down?' I asked, peepering over the edge.

'Yep, but first we gotta make sure there ain't no demon fish lurkin 'bout.' Grandma Matchie's eyes narrowed to slits and she glared around. 'I don't see none.'

'Me neither,' muttered the Major. 'It's a bad sign, if'n you ask me!'

'Aye . . .' Grandma Matchie made one last sweep with her eyes then straightened up and squared her shoulders. 'Let's go!'

She took the lead, then me, and then the Major. Down, down, and down some more, until the darkness turned the water into ink, and still we kept going down. The water went icy cold, then hot, then cold again. And little crayfish swambled around on the steps, wearing fur coats, so we had to watch our feet all the time. And then, slowly but surely, the water grew warmer, and a faint reddish glow seepened up from below, getting brighter and brighter.

'What's that?' I asked.

'Comes from the heart o' the Earth, lad,' the Major hisspered behind me. 'We're almost there!'

'Who lives down there?' I whispered back.

'Shhh!'

Now, I don't care how old or how small I am, I don't take 'shhh' for an answer to anything. 'Who's down there!' I cried, making echoes run off in all directions. The Major swore but Grandma Matchie glared at him.

'Tyke knows one thin, Major, and now you do too. "Shhh" don't count. Ever!' And with that she nodded at me. 'Problem now is, she'll know we're comin, and there ain't a thin we're gonna do 'bout it, neither!'

It wasn't long afterwards that glowing spots of light swam up towards us. Demon fish, riding the backs of lamp rays, only these weren't the normal kind of lamp rays at all. They were as long as snakes, glowing from the inside out, and their round mouths had a thousand million seven hundred twenty-one sharp teeth prangled up inside, stickering out everywhere. And the demon fish laughed at us, coming close then darpling away, hounding us all the way until we reached the floor of the lake. Then they raced off ahead of us and soon disappeared into the red gloom.

'She'll be waitin,' Grandma Matchie announced grimmerly.

'Who?'

Turning to me, she said, 'One Armed Trapper's mom, that's who. Lunker's her name, an she's the biggest pike you e'er seen!'

'She's more'n that!' the Major growbled. 'She's the heart o' the land! An a thousand years ago she ruled us all!'

'So she'd like t'think!' Grandma Matchie scowlered.

Glommering at her, the Major jutted out his chin.

'You talk now! But I didna heared you back then, did I.'

'She ain't ruled nobody who wasn't ready t'be ruled!' Grandma Matchie snapped. 'You ne'er saw me lickin er fins, didja?'

'I ain't ne'er once licked those fins!'

'Hah!'

And before they could continue we heard rumbling, growing bigger by the second. The Major reached into his pack and pulled out a tiny fishin' pole with a tinier hook and an even tinier worm hanging limply from it.

'So!' Grandma Matchie laughed. 'Y'think you're finally good 'nough, now, do ya?' And she laughed again. 'But I better tellya, Major, you weren't that good!' she added, smirkelling.

The Major's face went red and he began fiddling with his fishin' reel, muthering and grummerling.

Turning to stare off into the distance where all the rumbling and all the red light was coming from, Grandma Matchie frowned and said, 'But I got more important problems t'think 'bout. There's questions that gotta be answered, there is. And a course there's Ester's broom to get back!' She faced the Major again. 'You don't go doin nothin stupid afore I'm done, y'hear?'

'Bahhh!'

'Let's get goin!' And with that Grandma Matchie began stramping forward. The floor was flat and warm under my sneakers and seemed to stretch off forever in all directions. Pretty soon we started passing schools of demon fish with big-nosed teachers running about ringing giant brass bells, and we saw older demon fish walking pet lamp rays around on leashes, standing round fire hydrants and mailboxes whenever the lamp rays stopped for a sniff or two, or lifted a short stubby fin while looking off in some other direction.

But everyone stopped what they were doing to watch us pass, and they laughed and snickered and hisspered to each other, and the lamp rays barked madly and strained at their leashes. And after a while we came to a big door, barred like a cage, and the rumbling came from beyond it.

Grandma Matchie's frown deepened. 'This weren't here afore, nosiree. I don't like it one bit!'

Even the Major looked worried. 'I ain't bin down 'ere in a thousand years, so it must've bin built recently. Freshly painted too! A bad sign, aye!'

The rumbling stopped suddenly, but the silence was even worse. Grimmerly, Grandma Matchie pushed the doors open and in we walked. In front of us was a huge hall, with a domed ceiling that glittered every color I'd ever seen and then some. And there, at the end of the hall, sat Lunker on her throne – which was carved from a mountain – smiling evilly down on us. Raising a bejeweled fin, she beckoned.

'Come closer, dearies! Come closer!' And her voice crackled like the crackle when you crumple cellophane in the toilet. Just like that. 'I've been expecting you!'

Boy was she big. Almost as big as Satan Himself. Wearing a huge purple robe and a glittering crown made out of giant Red Devils. And she had a million thousand seventy-two sticks' worth of lipstick smeared round her mouth, and thick splatches of red on her gills, and false eyelashes made from pine boughs, and bright red hair wavering about like a burning volcano. And her teeth were longer even than the sleeves of Dad's woolen sweater after he's slipped on spilled chocolate pudding and fallen in the lake.

'You're lookin good, Lunker,' Grandma Matchie said, walking into the middle of the room. 'As pretty as a picture!'

Some picture, I was thinking to myself as I followed behind her and the Major.

'So you've finally come back to me, eh, Grandma Matchie?' Lunker chackled. 'You haven't been down here since I threw you out of my court two thousand years ago!'

Grandma Matchie chackled right back. 'An it's bin feelin pretty empty e'er since, I bet!'

Lunker fluthered her eyelashes and rolled her china-plate eyes at the ceiling. 'Yesss,' she drawled, stifling a yawn. 'I suppose jesters come in handy – even in this court. Too bad your tongue's too sharp for your own good, isn't it, Grandma Matchie?'

She snorted in reply then looked around critically. 'Well, it hasn't changed much from in here, I see.' Then she gazed shrewdly at Lunker. 'But that cage door's a new one, ain't it? Afeared a assassins, mebee?'

Lunker's eyes flashed, then dimmed as she let out a long sigh. 'Times change, Grandma Matchie.' Turning her head slightly she regarded the Major, who stood there with bent knees, holding his fishin' pole tightly with both hands in front of him. 'Why, Major! What we have there!'

'Where?' The Major's voice was high and cracking.

'Why, in your hands, of course.'

Looking down, the Major screamed as if he'd been

holding a snake and threw the rod down, staring at it in horror.

Lunker chackled. 'Still full of delusions of grandeur, I see. Oh well, and then there are some things that never change!'

The Major gasped and panted, still staring at the rod at his feet.

'And,' Lunker continued, 'it seems we have another guest!'

Uh oh, thinks I.

'Come forward, child! Let me see you more clearly! These eyes aren't what they once were, you know.'

So I did.

Lunker reached around with her fins and pulled her gown tighter about her, then leaned forward. 'And what's your name, child?'

'Jock Junior, and I'm not a child!'

Lunker's eyes widened and for a minute there I thought she was going to galobble me up in one bite. But with Grandma Matchie behind me I wasn't scared. Not scared at all!

'I'm so sorry! Jock Junior, you must forgive my failing eyesight! Of course I can see now that you're not a child! Yesss, you're something else, aren't you? Something more, maybe?'

'By my daughter,' Grandma Matchie said.

'A daughter! And a grandson! Oh my! I have been down here too long, haven't I?'

'Nobody's missin you, far as I can tell,' Grandma Matchie replied, her eyes blazening.

But Lunker just sighed again and half closed her eyes, and Grandma Matchie gave a little gasp, because you could tell she'd been expecting fire and brimstone.

'You've hit the proverbial nail on the head, there, Grandma Matchie,' Lunker said, and if you've ever seen a pike smile kindly then you're one up on me. Though she tried! She really did! 'And this brings us to the matter at hand, now, doesn't it?'

'You took somethin an I want it back!' Grandma Matchie said, stepping forward.

'Ohhh, yes! An item of laborious obsession, I believe?'

'A buhloody broom!' Grandma Matchie snarped.

'Of course. A broom. Well,' Lunker sighed, lifting a corner of her robe and pulling out Mom's broom. She eyed it critically. 'Oh, the awful things to be found in a broom!' she exclaimed, wrinkling her nose. 'Oh dear, Horatio, you'll never know what you missed!' Then she put it on her lap. 'It has served its purpose, I suppose. And since it's hardly the kind of trophy you'd mount on a wall, I suppose I can return it to its rightful owner.' And with that she beckoned and a demon fish appeared out of a small hole in one of the walls and scurried to her side. Lunker whispered a few words and handed the broom to the demon fish, who took it and disappeared. Facing us again, Lunker said: 'There! Now that that's done, we can get down to business!'

'What kinda buzness?' Grandma Matchie demanded suspiciously.

'I'm not likin the sounds o' this,' the Major muthered glumly, and I had to nod agreement.

'It's all really very simple, actually.' Lunker leaned back in her rock throne and made a small gesture with one of her fins. 'A minor inconvenience to take care of, and with your kindly assistance it'll be no great task.' And she reached down and grabbed the hems of her long robe. 'I simply need help in removing – these!' And with that she pulled up her robe.

We all gaspered, not because we'd never seen a pike's panties before (mind you, I don't think I ever had), even ones Royal Purple. No, we gaspered because there were giant black chains wrapped round Lunker, with their ends padlocked to the floor.

'Well, well!' Grandma Matchie exclaimed, her eyebrows raised. 'Now, whoever would've done such a thin!'

Lunker grimaced. 'Who else? My own son, of course.'

I stared at her. 'One Armed Trapper!?'

'Oh, then you've met him, have you, Jock Junior?'

'Met him! He come near to doin us in! For good!'

Sighing, Lunker let her robe fall down over the ghastly scene she'd shown us, and leaned back in her throne. 'It follows, naturally. With me out of the way, One Armed Trapper's ready to play! He's flexing the muscles on that lone arm of his, I should hazard to presume. Really very unfortunate, isn't it?'

'More'n that!' Grandma Matchie gritted, starting to pace. 'He'll be wreakin spite on us all afore long! Damn!'

'That explains why none o' us heared from you 'n ages!' the Major mused, rubbing his whiskered jaw. 'Not a story, not e'en a whisper!'

Lunker's eyes flashed for the briefest of moments, then she shrugged. 'And everyone's no doubt been lamenting on how silent their land is to their frail pleas. After all, you can't tell there's roots in the ground unless you see a shoot, or in this particular case, a tree. Such things pain me from time to time, but as you have seen, there's really very little I can do about it. Until, of course—' And Lunker paused to duck her head forward. '—I'm freed!'

'Aye, so you sent fer us by stealin Ester's broom – knowin we'd come after it! You always bin a sneakeny one, ain't ya?'

Lunker shrugged modestly, saying nothing though a spark flashed again in her eyes.

'An I bet One Armed Trapper's got the key to that lock!' I exclaimed.

'Very astute of you, Jock Junior! The problem, then, is: How will you get it from him? We can be certain that he's not likely to lay it at your feet with a shy smile and a bow!'

Grandma Matchie stopped pacing suddenly, looked up at all of us with a gleamy shivering in her eyes. 'It's quite simple, now that I done some thinkin on it. Easy pickins for the three a us!' And she let out a wild chackle that echoed through the chamber.

'Pray tell!' Lunker exclaimed breathlessly. 'Share with us your genius!'

Grinning, Grandma Matchie winked at me. 'We gotta present t'im an offer he can't refuse! An all it takes is the right kinda bait!' She whirled to the Major: 'You! You gotta do us jus one thin, an your part'll be done!'

The Major blanched, his eyes darting. 'What?' he asked weakly.

'Easy, lad, don't ferget you're the Major an none other!' And you could see him swell his chest out at that. 'So here's what you gotta do. Climb inta that blarny boat a yours an take out fast as y'can for th' North Sea—'

'What!?' The Major's chest collapsed and his knees started wobblering.

'That's right. The North Sea. An drop that fishin' line a yours inta the deep—'

'For the love o' Mike, why?'

Grandma Matchie's grin grew savage. 'You gotta undo what One Armed Trapper done, long ago! You gotta untie the sea snake's tail from er head!'

'But, won't all the water run away, then?' I cried.

'Nope. That ole she-devil was bitin her tail long afore One Armed Trapper played that turrible trick on er, Tyke! She ne'er did need any help holdin the oceans in, right, Major?'

'Eh?' The Major looked up, startled out of some pit of terror. 'Eh?'

'Never mind,' Grandma Matchie said, then turned to me. 'You'n me, Tyke, we gotta handle th'other thin, an it won't be as easy as what the Major's gotta do! But there's two a us, ain't there?' And she roared a laugh that sent waves through the water.

It was only a second before I threw back my own head and laughed almost as loud as she'd done. When there's important things to be done, you just got to be in the right frame of mind, Grandma Matchie always told me. And she's right. So we danced a little jig on our way out of the throne room, leaving the Major and Lunker behind.

And the journey took seven days and eight nights, riding the backs of lamp rays all the way, until finally we came to the sandy shore of Lake Winnipeg, and stood there watching the dawn turn that muddy water into sunlipped fiery gold.

Lake Winnipeg's as big as an ocean, I bet, because we couldn't even see the other side, even when I got up on Grandma Matchie's shoulders while she got up on mine and we added it all together to make us exactly twenty feet tall.

After breakfast Grandma Matchie picked up a piece of driftwood from the beach and pulled out her whittlin' knife and carved up a horn, which she then put to her lips and blew as hard as she could. And that moaning cry went out a thousand million two hundred nine fifty miles in all direction, going right round the Earth and coming back to us as loud as it was when it left.

Then we waited.

At high noon Grandma Matchie jumped up from the log she'd been sitting on and cried: 'Here they come, Tyke!'

Looking out over the lake I could see the dust cloud rising up on the horizon, and then a terrible rumble shivered up my legs and rappled my bones, and the lake got all chipchoppy and murky. It wasn't long after that when we could see them plain as day. All the buffalo in the world, crossing that lake in answer to Grandma Matchie's call. And these weren't regular buffalo, either. These were buffalo from ten thousand years ago – big as garbage trucks.

The next time you see a garbage truck in your back lane try and imagine it covered in shaggy brown hair, with big horns coming out of the cab. Go do that then come back, so that way I'll know you know what I mean when I say they were as big as hairy garbage trucks.

But the one leading the stampede was even bigger. Glue two garbage trucks together and glue a VW Bug on top and paint its headlamps to look like angry red eyes. Then go down to the river and find an old sofa that somebody threw away and pull out all the muddy filling and come back and paste it to the trucks and the Bug. Go do that then come back, okay?

When that stampede got close enough so that I could almost smell those buffalo, Grandma Matchie blew that horn again and they all came to a splashing stop right on the edge of the lake. And the big bull stomped forward, snorting fire from his nostrils and glavering murderously at Grandma Matchie.

'Whadya want?' the king buffalo demanded in a voice that sounded just like you'd figure a buffalo's voice would sound if that buffalo was as big as two garbage trucks glued together with a VW Bug for a head. He pawed the shallows and snorted some more.

'Well, well,' said Grandma Matchie, grinnering. 'No kind words for your old friend who's come to pay you a visit?'

The king buffalo just grunted.

Turning to me, Grandma Matchie said, 'Tyke, I'd like you to meet Bjugstad, the buff'lo of buff'los!'

'Hello,' I said respectfully.

'An this, Bjugstad, is Jock Junior. Grunt "hello," Bjugstad, afore I brain ya!'

Bjugstad grunted and fire blasted from his nostrils. 'Brain me, ay? I'd like t'see ya try!'

'You will,' Grandma Matchie promised, folding her

arms. 'Y'see, Bjugstad, this ain't jus a friennly visit for ole time's sakc. I've come t'bring you all back wi' me! One Armed Trapper's on the rampage again an he's got Lunker chained up in er throne room. And you gotta come wi' us, or else!'

'We'll see about that!' And Bjugstad bunched his shoulders and tore huge gouts of muck from the lake bottom as he plawed, plawed, plawed. And then he roared and flames poured out and turned all the water into steam for miles around.

Grandma Matchie roared back a challenge and hunched her shoulders and, ducking her head, charged. And then Bjugstad charged, and they were going straight for each other.

Everything you could think of and pile together happened when they collided. There was lightning, and thunderous shock waves, and fire, and steam, and mud, and falling trees, and tidal waves, and volcanoes, and birds scattering everywhere from swamps like you see in movies about Africa, and lots of other things you should think about before I go on.

When the smoke cleared there was Grandma Matchie, standing over Bjugstad with her hands on her hips. 'I tole you you was comin wi' us!'

Bjugstad didn't even have the strength to grunt. He just lobbled there, panthing with his white tongue hanging on the ground. All the other buffalo muthered and grumbled but couldn't do much else since most of them were dog-paddling like crazy. After a while Bjugstad was able to stand up, and then me and Grandma Matchie climbed up bchind his head and sat down on his hairy shoulders.

'Now it's your turn, Tyke,' Grandma Matchie said over her shoulder. 'I gotta be steerin Bjugstad wi' an iron hand so he don't try nothin. An you gotta keep your eyes peeled in case someone tries somethin.'

'Who?'

'Mebee One Armed Trapper, mebee someone else. I got an itchin there's more to this than what meets the eye. I gotta suspicious nature, Tyke, and right now I'm smellin more'n the fact that Bjugstad here don't know anythin 'bout takin baths.'

Putting her heels to Bjugstad's flanks, we jolted forward and were on our way. And all the buffalo followed, pushing up onto land even though you could tell by all the crashbanging and all the swearing that they didn't like solid ground one bit. Nosiree, give a buffalo a bridge and he'll jump right off it.

Fishing for buffalo's dangerous business, as Grandma Matchie told me last summer when we went trolling for them in Shoal Lake. You got to know what kind of weeds to snag on your hook too. Not any old weed will do, because buffalo will be the first to tell you they have sophisticated tastes.

Seven days and eight nights it took us to get back to Westhawk Lake, and we didn't see One Armed Trapper or anyone else the whole way, which had Grandma Matchie frowning something fierce.

Boy did those buffalo cheer when they plungered into that lake, and it wasn't long before you couldn't even see the water for all the buffalo heads. All the people who had cottages went down to their docks and shook their fists and tore their hair, but it didn't help one bit.

Bjugstad took us right out to the middle and then we

dived down, swimming and swimming until we finally reached the bottom, where all the demon fish and lamp rays scattered in panic. Hooves thumpening the rock, up we marched to Lunker's cage door, and with a tap from Bjugstad's head the doors flew open and once again we were face-to-face with Lunker.

'Is the Major back yet?' Grandma Matchie asked, all businesslike.

'No, I'm afraid not.' Lunker sighed, all depressed.

Grandma Matchie rubbed her jaw. 'One Armed Trapper been down here latcly?'

'Oh, yes!' Lunker's fins wriggled in sudden excitement. 'In fact, he's here now!'

Bjugstad groaned. 'Great, that's just great!' And you could hear his knees knocking. Just then we heard a scream from outside and the sound of running footsteps. Spinning around, wc saw the Major stumble into the room. 'I done it!' he cried. 'Hee hee! I done it!'

'Course you did,' Grandma Matchie snapped. 'You're the Major, ain't ya?'

The Major's navy blues were all in tatters, and his hair stuck out in all directions. And his nose blazed red too. 'You shoulda seen me!' he exclaimed, all breathless. 'That was the biggest knot I e'er did see! An it was days o' strugglin an—'

'Save it for another time!' Grandma Matchie griped, turning back to Lunker. 'Did you say what I thought you said? One Armed Trapper's here, now?'

'Oh yes. He is. Isn't that a wonderful coincidence?'

'I don't like the sounds o' that,' the Major muthered, all serious now.

'Me neither,' Grandma Matchie grumbled, eyeing Lunker like you would a wood tick.

'And now that we're all here—' Lunker smiled, her teeth grivdening together with pleasure. '—we can get down to business!' And with that a door opened behind her and in stepped One Armed Trapper, grinning from ear to ear, and even though he had the biggest ears I've ever seen, the grin was bigger.

'Hah?' the Major cried. 'We bin tricked!'

And it was true, because up stood Lunker then, and all those chains just fell away, and she was smiling even harder, and those fangs were grivdening so much that dust drifted away on the current in a white cloud.

'Now that I've got all the storytellers here, in one place, I can put an end to them once and for all! And I'll have all the stories myself! Or, rather, my story will be the only one anyone will ever hear in this land! My power will be complete! Ha ha ha ha ha ha!'

One Armed Trapper began advancing toward us, black chains dangling from his hand. 'Joy, oh joy!' he crooned. 'Now even the old tale about the sea snake is done with, and we can all forget about her too!' His eyes burned merrily. 'It was a childish prank of mine, in the days of my youth. Had I known better—'

'Had you known better,' Lunker snarled, 'you would have listened to me!' Then she smiled again. 'Of course, now all that's taken care of, thanks to Grandma Matchie's cunning little brain.' And she flaclapped her fins. 'Isn't it simply wonderful how all things come round in the end!'

All this time Grandma Matchie's eyes had been narrow like slits, and sparks flashered out of them every now and then. Bjugstad's bones rattled so bad I figured he would fall to pieces under us, so off I crawpelled and stood beside him.

The Major had fullen to his knees and was whimpering and bawbling his eyes out. Disgusted, I decided to ignore him.

'Only one story to tell!' Lunker laughed. 'And it's mine! All mine! And you'll hear it from border to border, shore to shore, shining sea to shining sea! You'll hear it even more than you do already! Oh, I'm so proud!'

'Grandma Matchie!' I cried. 'You can't let her get away with this!'

She leaned forward on Bjugstad's shoulders. 'I left this place once, Lunker,' she gritted, 'an you couldn't stop me then!'

'Oh, but then One Armed Trapper wasn't with me, was he? This time you won't get away, I'm afraid.' And she shook her head in sorrow, all her red hair flowing about like fire.

Grandma Matchie frowned. 'You gotta point, there, Lunker. But somethin's bin itchin me, so's I gotta ask. There's more'n jus you two involved 'ere, ain't there?'

Lunker fluthered her eyelashes, looking down. 'Well, I must admit that our mutual dragon acquaintance, Satan Himself, was very helpful in the formulation of our plans—'

'I knew it!' Grandma Matchie drove her fist into the palm of her hand. 'He's bin meddlin all along!' Then she shook her head, frowning again. 'Somethin's gripin him . . . wonder what?'

All this time I was thinking fast, real fast because time

was running out for all of us. And I studied Lunker, narrowing my eyes like the cowboys do when there's Indians about and they suddenly smell smoke coming from Old Lady Helpless's farm. And of course Old Lady Helpless has a daughter, Young Lady Useless, who faints at the sight of dirty toenails. Yesiree, I kept my eyes narrow and studied her face, those giant eyes all kind and evil at the same time, that giant nose with the big nostril slits, turning this way and that as if she smelled something bad. That flaming hair, so red it's just not natural. The way her fins gripped the ends of the robe, making sure it flowed just an inch above the dusty floor. The reddish tinge in her teeth from the lipstick. The splotches of rouge on her gills so thick they looked like the melted wax of a thousand crayons, and – wait a minute.

I had it! It was a gamble, but there was no choice. I had to try. I stared one last time at the biggest thing on Lunker's face, drew in a deep breath, then pointed down at the hem of her robe and said: 'Yuuccchhh!'

Lunker swung her head to me in a jerk. 'Pardon me?'

'I said: Yuuccchhh!' And I pointed down again.

'What is it?' Lunker tried to look down, but if you've ever seen a pike you'll know that pike just can't look down on themselves at all. And so she couldn't see anything.

'Can't you see them?' I exclaimed, a look of horror on my face. One Armed Trapper – I sawneaked out of the corner of my eye – had paused and was squinting like mad at Lunker's robe. 'They're all over the place!' I wrunkled my nose in disgust, then, looking up at

Lunker's face, I made my whole face scranch up. 'And in your hair too! Blagghhh!'

Lunker fluppered her fins futilely. 'What?' she screamed. 'Oh, what is it!?'

'Hairballs! Millions of hairballs! They're all over you! In your hair! On your robe! Your eyelashes, even!'

'Aaaaagh!'

Grandma Matchie and the Major and Bjugstad had been staring at me like I was crazy all this time, but then Grandma Matchie scryed what I was up to and shrieked: 'Billions of em!'

And the Major too: 'Yuucchhh!'

'Aaaaagggghhhhhh!' Lunker flailupped away with her fins and swam in wild circles. 'Help me! Oh help me!'

And that's when Grandma Matchie roared: 'Charge!' And One Armed Trapper's face showed one brief second of absolute horror before Bjugstad crashed into him, and then his flying body was blasting a hole right through the ceiling and heading for the moon.

Bjugstad bellowed and danced around. 'Revenge! At last!'

Only it wasn't over yet, because Lunker had by this time discovered the ruse, and now she glommered down on me and this time I was sure she was going to galobble me up.

Leaping off Bjugstad, Grandma Matchie stalked up to her. 'Game's over, Lunker!' she snarled. 'Now I'm gonna do somethin that I shoulda done two thousand years ago!'

And Lunker shrank back, whimpering. 'No, please! It was all a joke! Honest! Just a joke! Ohh, where's

One Armed Trapper? Where's Satan Himself? Ohhhh!'

'He'll know better than t'show up now!' Grandma Matchie said, though you could tell she was hoping he would, so she could take care of him too. 'Come on, Lunker, let me see em!' And she held out her hand.

Lunker tried to shrink back further but the throne blocked her retreat. Whimpering, she lifted her red wig from the top of her head – and there they were. Her ears!

And Grandma Matchie grabbed the nearest one and gave it such a twist that Lunker's yell was heard on Pluto, I bet.

And that was the end of Lunker and all her schemes.

Bjugstad was so happy that he carried us all the way home without even a garumble, and so there we stood on the dock, waving him good-bye.

And Mom had her broom and Dad had his Jacuzzi and a new VCR, and Sis's hair was pink with blue polka dots, which meant that things were back to normal.

Later on, me and Grandma Matchie went out to visit the Major on his island, and we sat around the fire roasting peanut butter marshmallows with olives in them, and told our stories just the way they happened. The whole truth, just like I'm telling it here! And then, when the fire was just a pile of coals, and everyone had gone all quiet and funny-looking as they stared at the embers, Grandma Matchie shook her head and said:

'I'm acursin m'self fer not seein the signs.' She looked up and her face glowed red and it wasn't just from the fire, either. 'There it was, all the signs a er schemin, right afore me! An I didn't see a thin! E'en when that one story kept showin up everywhere, till I was sick a hearin it! Still . . . I'm ashamed, jus plumb ashamed.' And she hung her head to prove it.

'Aye, me too,' muttered the Major. 'We shoulda both smelled the likes o' Lunker, hearin' that same story tole o'er and o'er again, from shinin sea t'shinin sea! Jus like Lunker said!'

Then Grandma Matchie cocked an eye at me and grinned. 'Tyke, canya figure out what story we're talkin 'bout?'

'I betcha can't!' the Major snickered, all superior like. 'It's right in fronta yer eyes, but I betch you can't!'

'I bet he can!' Grandma Matchie said. 'An I bet One Armed Trapper's arm on it!'

'An I bet One Armed Trapper's real arm!' the Major shouted. 'Yours is a fake! An if I win you gotta admit it once an fer all!'

'You're on!'

Then they both turned to me and waited, their eyes glowing brighter than the coals. I gave them a wide-eyed stare. 'You mean you'd give up One Armed Trapper's arm and the whole truth 'bout it? On some dumb bet!?' I jumped to my feet. 'Forget it! I want no parta it!' And I stomped off into the darkness.

After a moment Grandma Matchie's howl of laughter shook the stars. 'Atta boy, Tyke! Atta boy!' she called out behind me.

When people start betting stories on things, I want no part of it. I don't want there to be a loser, don't you see?

Sure, I knew the answer to that question, but that's not the point. Because the way I figure it, the next time I want to hear stories from Grandma Matchie and the Major, there'd be one less. And who knows, maybe some day there'd only be one, just like Lunker wanted all along. And it'd have more than one meaning too, if that ever happened.

Well, the answer's sitting there right in front of you, just like the Major said. And the next time you're sitting around a campfire, when someone starts telling you about the one that got away, you'll know where that story came from, and you'll be a wise man.

That was the second week.

THE DEVIL, WE SAY

It's a rule, I bet. And dealing with one just naturally leads to the other, and so on. Forever and ever. That's why I knew I was in trouble.

They were calling in one of the big boys, because when some little kid starts talking about Satan Himself then it's time to get worried. At least that's what the principal said, and if anyone should know, it's him. Besides, he had that look of failure about him. You know, the way I look whenever I bring home a report card.

Even jesters get report cards, and they're usually bad, so you learn to put on that face of failure so that everyone concerned can make appropriate faces to show how they're concerned. But people get concerned in different ways, so your face has to be a little bit different for each of them.

Take Big Nose, for example. She pretends it's her fault that I get lousy grades. So I make myself like a mirror, and we both look sadly at each other with exactly the same kind of failed poupy expression. 'I have tried!' she'd say with a shake of her head, trying to fit some kind of stern look into her failed face, and with a little burning flame of Indignation or something like it there in her eyes when she studies your face and you're trying hard to show how you've failed as much as her. It's a contest to see who's failed the most. 'What are we going to do with you!' Big Nose'd sigh. Oh ho! thinks I whenever this happens, now it's we, is it?

That's Big Nose, but with Mom it's different. For her, you have to put on a very special kind of expression, because Mom gets all dreamy-eyed and before you know it she's talking about when she was in school. And she's so understanding and everything that no matter what, my face scrunches up and I start crying. That's what's special about this kind of expression – I can't help it.

Of course, Dad's a whole other story, that's for sure. You see, you have to know Dad. He gets embarrassed by everything everyone else around him does. There's right ways to do things and then there's wrong ways to do things. Dad's way is the right way and everyone else's way is the wrong way. So the concern goes through two phases. First, Dad gets red in the face, showing me his embarrassment that his son has done it again. But that doesn't last long, because then he gets mad, and he says: 'It's that damn gothic school system! Now, if I was teachin . . .'

The point is, he's right as far as I'm concerned. Dad's a great teacher, and he knows the difference between doing things the wrong way and doing things his way. So pretty soon he's telling me how he'd run the school system, and I get all excited because he's brilliant when it comes to things like that.

Imagine watching old Westerns on a giant screen all morning, then going to restaurants for lunch, then watching more Westerns in the afternoon and other movies like *Tarzan and the Naked Lady,* or is it *Tarzan and the Leopard Lady*? Naked Leopard Lady? I can't remember exactly, but it's the one where Tarzan fights a guy in a lion suit, and then a stuffed crocodile, and then he gets taken prisoner by Lady Naked Leopard and she ties him to a stake and does terrible things to him until he screams out his Tarzan yell and all the birds in the swamps take to the air again, and this lion runs through the same section of bush over and over again, and all the animals stampede, and before you know it there's guys disguised as gorillas breaking down the walls and untying Tarzan just in time for him to get all moral about things.

Now that's education!

Showing concern in the right places is important:

And then there's the principal, and things start getting a little trickier. You see, his ears get redder and redder, and for him my lousy grades mean the whole world's coming down all around him. And when you start telling him about Satan Himself he looks like he's going to unplode.

And there's Big Nose crying and Mom and Dad trying to calm her down. So that leaves me one-on-one with the principal, and that's when I get mad.

'I don't look under rocks anymore!' I screamed at him. 'Cause I seen Satan Himself! And it's the truth!'

'Young man!' The principal surgled up behind his

giant desk and put his fists down on it – thumpthump!
'Young man! If there's one thing I won't tolerate in my
office, it's impertinence! Now, I'll hear no more of this
Devil stuff! Do you hear?'

Sneaking a look at those big ears, I figured that
there's no way he couldn't hear! Even if he had cotton
in his head! 'It's all true! And if you don't believe me,
you just wait! An I'll tell you what Satan Himself looks
like too! An you can't stop me!'

An he couldn't stop me!

It was the last week at Rat Portage Lake, and it was
awful! Two whole weeks had gone by and I'd hardly
done anything yet! And Grandma Matchie was going
on and on about how Satan Himself must be just steaming, since we'd foiled his sneaky plans.

'I can't figure it, Tyke,' she said. 'He's bin one step
ahead a us all along! Puttin Sis and Mom through hell
with his turrible schemin. An if there's one thing Satan
Himself is big on it's revenge! So what's he up to, that's
what I wanna know!'

Meanwhile, everyone was getting cranky since
vacation was almost over. So I moped around in the
cabin, watching all the normal boring things go on all
around me.

'Get outa the way!' Dad roared. 'I can't see a damn
thing!'

Sis ducked, scampered for the kitchen. Her giant ugly
feet swept through the tinder pile as she darted past the
big black woodstove, scappering scraps of wood in all
directions. She yelped, and I laughed.

'Gothic on a stick, girl!' Dad bellowed, like the whole world was coming down all around him. Twisting his head around, he hunted for Mom. She was sweepening dirt from the cabin doorway, as huge green flies, as big as birds, bazzled in and out through the gaping hole in the screen door. 'Ester! Sign up your daughter for ballet classes or somethin! Hell, I'll do it, come Fall.' Draining his beer, he let the can drop with a plop.

The Jacuzzi filled the living room. Dad sat in the middle of the fruthering water, which was full of floating beer cans. They bobbled and bumpled against the hairy islands of his knees.

Come to think of it, Dad was the hairiest man I'd ever seen. Hairier even than Grandma Matchie's upper lip, only everywhere like that. He had hair covering his legs, from the tops of his wide feet all the way up to his purple and pink striped shorts, and even more under them, I bet. And the hair was black, furry. When she kissed him Good Morning, Mom sometimes said: 'Get into that bathroom, Jock, and get that fur off your tongue!' So it was everywhere: hair growing out of his ears, hair growing in his nostrils, and yes, hair even growing in his mouth. His whole head was filled with hair.

The only place in the cabin big enough for the Jacuzzi was the living room. Water had splashed all the walls, and pooled in the fireplace where bits of tinfoil floated about. Grunting, Dad sat in the tub watching the new video screen and stabbing at the Remote and making the picture go backwards so he could replay his favorite scenes.

He had a thousand million twenty-nine thousand seventy cassettes, and all of them were Westerns. He'd squint like Clint Eastwood, and grimace like Lee Van

Cleef, and swell his chest like John Wayne. And the water burbled all around him and sank beer cans and made the hair part on his knees whenever he ducked them down then back up.

Sis hid in the kitchen. Her hair was orange and yellow now, and she cried all the time and it made me sick. And those bumps on her chest were getting bigger and bigger and I had nightmares about them filling up the whole cabin.

'Shoo! Shoo!' A broom whirvled in front of my face. I jumped back. 'Shoo, flies! Shoo!' I dodged another swing of the broom.

'Mom!'

'Jock Junior, you let all these flies in?' Like a big straw-haired head, the broom wanagged at me.

I shook my own head after it. 'Uh uh!'

'Don't you let any flies in, you hear!'

'I won't, Mom.'

'Jock Senior!' Holding her broom as if to swat a fly, Mom stormed up to the Jacuzzi. 'When are you going to get out of that damn thing? You've been in there since you built it!'

'Shut up! I'm not going anywhere! Now get outa the way so I can watch the picture!' He opened another beer can.

Ever since me and Grandma Matchie came back from Westhawk Lake, Dad's been in there, watching movies and eating bananas. He won't come out, and it's been three whole days. There must be a thousand million eighty-two beer cans floating around in there. And Mom's been on another sweepening craze since she got her broom back, sweepening everything: floors, walls, the ceiling, and the path out to the outhouse. Even the dock.

The whole world was getting desperate.

I stared at the giant screen that now hid the big window overlooking the lake. A man in a black suit sat in front of a saloon, ruckling in a chair while this dumb lady tried talking to him. But he just ruckled, pushing with his legs against a post, one leg, then the other, and the dumb lady didn't know what to do, and Dad drank his beer and grinned.

'Jock Junior!'

I looked at Mom.

'Go out and play, will you? Go find Grandma Matchie and make sure she's not getting into trouble. But don't you watch if she's wrassling a bear or something, you hear?'

As I passed by she swung the broom at me, but I jumped forwards and she missed. Only I forgot about the screen, and went through it again. I tore it even worse this time, and fell down on the porch.

'Damn you, Junior!' Dad's bellow made me jump up, and I leapt off the porch and fell again.

'Ballet lessons for alla em!'

Boy did I run.

I found Grandma Matchie down by the boathouse. She was dripping wet, which meant that she'd been down in her lodge, and she wore a long blue dress with white dots that went down to her flapping hiking boots. She winked at me when she saw me coming up the path. In her hands was an ax, and the door to the boathouse was all chopped up.

'What're you doing?' I asked.

Making a funny face she lifted the ax over her head. 'Can't find the key. Been so bloody long since I needed t'get in 'ere.' She swung the ax and the whole double door shook. 'Stand back, Tyke, or I'll be brainin ya.'

It took five minutes of chopping before that door fell open, and even then it fell open from the other side, where the hinges had rotted away. After pausing for a breather, Grandma Matchie heavered the ax out into the lake.

I watched it arc up and out, then make a big suplash about ten feet from the end of the dock. 'What'd you do that for?'

'Don't need it anymore. An what ya don't need y'throw away.' And with that she grasped my hand and led me into the darkness of the boathouse. 'Fifty years since I last come in 'ere,' she growled. 'Back then I wuz runnin yer cabin as a fishin lodge, an we had all them backhouses set up fur sleepin in, an we had millionaires comin up from New York New York bringin whole Jazz bands with em – boys who could play yer skids off. Yesiree, Tyke, those were the days!'

'How come you closed down the lodge?'

'Well, Tyke, there wuz a turrible acc'dent one day. We had one a them bands playin out back an the biggest blue heron you ever seen came right down an et them all up.'

'That musta bin some bird!' I shook my head.

'Not big 'nough, Tyke,' Grandma Matchie replied. 'Cause right then an e'en bigger eagle come down an snatch that heron right up, an they fought fur hours right up above the lodge. And then th'eagle gets his tal'ns roun the heron's neck and started squeezin. An the heron's beak opened wide an that eagle foun imself lookin right down its throat, an he saw that band, playin their brains out, an the eagle was so scairt by what he saw that right then and there he dropped the heron. Only the heron ne'er really did recover from that, and neither did the eagle, and that's why all the herons roun ere are blue, an that's why all the eagles got white hair on their heads.'

I'd always wondered about that.

'An that, Tyke, is why I shut er down. I was endangerin the wildlife, y'sce.'

I nodded, then looked around. 'Any rats in here?'

'Nope, they use the trail. Got no need fur comin in ere.' Pausing just inside the entrance, she turned to me. 'You know why they call this Rat Portage Lake, eh? Well, I seen them – jus once, mind you – giant rats, carryin bags on their heads and canoes, too. Comin down the trail, all in single file. Only seen it happen once, like I said, an that was a hundred years ago. They only come when they got good reason.'

Everything that had been black was now turning gray, and I could make out all the shelves on the thin sagging walls, and the old lanterns hanging from the roof. And sitting there in that black water was the neatest boat I'd ever seen. It was all wood, varnished and sleek, with brass things on it all glimmering and winking. I couldn't see a motor, so it must be hidden, I figured. It had a low windshield and a solid brass steering wheel.

'Does it still run?'

'Course it does!' Grandma Matchie chackled, striding forward with big steps and dragging me along behind. 'Ain't bin out in fifty years, jus sittin there, waitin.'

'Waitin for what?'

'You'll see!' She laughed, and laughed again. 'You'll see! Come on!'

Letting go of my hand she leapt across ten feet and landed behind the wheel. I jumped in after her and dropped down into the seat beside her. In front of us was the closed-up garage door, all boarded up and stuff. The motor roared to life and Grandma Matchie whammed that throttle forward.

The front lurched up and I was snapped back in my seat. Then – crash! Daylight exploded all over us and pieces of wood flew in all directions and we were flying out over the waves.

I shouted: 'Where are we going?'

One hand on the wheel, the other cranking the throttle, Grandma Matchie grinned. 'I've had it with the Major once an fur all! Him an his lyin! Him an his schemin!'

'But I thought you made up!' I cried.

'With that skulker!? Hah! I wuz jus takin a breather! An so wuz he! But now I'm gonna end it once an fur all!'

Staring through the windshield I could see the Major's island. We were flying right toward it. I could see the flagpole, with its Union Jack standing straight out at attention, a row of gulls holding it that way, fladapping madly. And then I saw the Major running down to the dock where the H.M.S. *Hood* lolled. Jumping aboard he cast off and surgled away from the dock, swinging about to face us.

'It's war he wants, war he gets!' Grandma Matchie shrieked, leaning forward. 'No more lyin, no more nothin!' Baring her teeth she yanked hard on the throttle and spun the wheel. We whirred by the Major, missing him by an inch. I saw his face, the wild whiskers, huge red nose flying by at a thousand million sixty twenty miles an hour.

'We've got im now!' Grandma Matchie laughed, turning us about. Directly ahead I saw the *Hood*, flundolering in the waves we'd left behind. Going at full speed, we raced for her. 'We'll ram em! That's what we'll do, laddie!'

Staring with wild eyes as we bore down on the *Hood*, I let out a yell just as we rammed her from the side. Everything shook until my insides rattled, and then we were through. Turning around, I saw the *Hood*, broken in half and sinking, but no Major.

'Got im!' Grandma Matchie howled.

'But where is he?'

For answer she jerked her thumb straight up and I looked and there he was, being carried back to his island in defeat by his gulls. He shook his fist at us, but you could see he was beaten.

'We got im! An never again will that blarny boat troll bait past my windows! Hah!'

Mom was sweeping the dock when we pulled up, and she started screaming at Grandma Matchie right away. 'Mother! Jock Junior's not wearin a lifejacket! Do you know how dangerous that is? Boatin without a life-jacket?'

Stepping up on the dock I stuck my tongue out at Sis, who was standing behind Mom. Her hair was now metallic silver, and the bumps on her chest had smaller bumps, making them look like bull's-eyes. I threw a dead minnow at her (minnows are safe) and she started crying when it got stuck in her hair. Rainbow trout minnow, Grandma Matchie said mysteriously when she finally dug it out from all those blue spikes and knots and things on Sis's head.

Mom tuggled my ear, but Grandma Matchie laughed so I grinned at her, which made Mom tuggle my ear again.

I don't mind things like that. After all, it's just show, so things look like they're supposed to. Discipline, Big Nose would call it, but what does she know?

Grandma Matchie wandered off, muthering about Satan Himself and his schemin, and me and Mom and Sis went back to the cabin. In the living room the Indians were killing all the bluecoats, but Arrow Flynn was grinning as he stood on a pile of bodies and blasted from both hips. Dad had a banana in each hand and made noises as he shot at the screen.

'Hey, Dad! Look at Sis now! Her hair looks like tinsel!' Pointing, I laughed.

'Gothic in panties, girl! Why not just stick yer head in a blender an get it over with!'

Her face turning red and scrunching up, Sis bolted for the kitchen, where she let out a bawl.

'Aaaaggghh!' Mom screamed, and I whirled. She had been sweeping round the woodstove and the broom had caught fire. 'Aaaaaggghh!' Screaming and running in circles, Mom waved the flaming brackling pafting broom above her head, trailing ashes and sparks all over the place.

'GET THAT DAMN THING OUTA HERE!' Dad bellowed.

But she ran right at him. Rearing back, Dad bleated as Mom swung that broom down into the ginurgling water. Hisspering sounds filled the air and clouds rolled up from the Jacuzzi.

'Ester! You damn near set my hair on fire! Are you nuts!?'

Mom started crying, standing in front of him. And Sis was bawling in the kitchen, and Arrow Flynn had bit the big one. I bolted for the door, escaped outside without anyone noticing.

Down the trail beyond the outhouse I caught a glimpse of blue dress, so I took off after it. Grandma Matchie was the only one who wasn't crazy around here, so I figured I'd stick with her.

Running down the trail, I didn't catch up with her until after we came out into a rocky clearing. At the far end was a pile of boulders as high as a house and as wide as a city block, stretching right across the clearing like a wall.

'Comin fishin, Tyke?' Grandma Matchie asked without even turning round to see who was coming up on her.

'Sure! What're we gonna catch?'

'Satan Himself, that's who.'

A deep-sea fishing rod in one hand and a bait box in the other, Grandma Matchie strode across the clearing, kicking rocks out of the way with her big boots. I followed as she climbed up the wall of boulders and stopped beside her at the top.

On the other side was a river of black water, flowing through a giant crack in the bedrock. The banks were steep and shadowy, and the water looked deep.

In a flat space between two boulders sat a rocking chair with a harness belt bolted to it. Grandma Matchie set down the rod and the bait box and stood at the edge, glaring down into the water. 'He's probbly plannin somethin, or my name's not Grandma Matchie!' She shook her head. 'Plannin somethin evil, no doubts 'bout it. If'n there's one thing he don't tol'rate it's the likes a you'n me messin up his schemin.'

'So what're we gonna do?'

'We're gonna get im afore he gets us, that's what we're gonna do!' And she grinned. 'We're gonna brin thins to a head, get it right out in the open! Satan Himself hates that! Hah!' And she settled herself down into the worn seat and buckled up. 'Hand me the rod, Tyke, an the bait too.'

I stared at the gloomeny water. 'How d'you know he's in there?'

'Where else would he be? An I've had nibbles 'ere afore, lemme tell you! But we'll get im this time – I've got an itch, an when Grandma Matchie's got an itch then sure enough Satan Himself's lurkin 'bout.'

'Where's it itch?'

'Never you mind. Now here, pull me out a worm, the fattest one in there, and don't break im now.'

Pulling up a handful of earth from the bait box I broke it up in my fingers, but there was only one worm and it was all skinny and oozing.

'That's perfect!' Grandma Matchie cried. Grabbing it from my hand she tied it in a knot around the biggest hook I'd ever seen. It was big as me, all shiny brass, with two barbs on the shank. Monofilament line was tied to the loop. 'Two pound test. Gotta be sportin, Tyke.' Adjusting the drag on the Abu reel she leaned forward and swung the hook out over the water and began letting out line. I watched the bait sink into the black river, flash once in the dark water, then vanish.

'D'you think he's hungry?'

Shaking her head, Grandma Matchie said, 'He's ne'er hungry fur long, Tyke. An he's probbly not hungry now, but it ne'er stopped im afore. He loves worms.' Her brow was all scrunched up and her eyes were burning slits. I felt sorry for Satan Himself.

You got to be patient when you're fishing, so I sat down on a rock to wait. Big flat bugs crawled up from the water and settled down on the warm stone all around me. Leaning close to one I stared into its bug eyes. 'What are these, Grandma Matchie?'

'Drag'nfly nymphs. They grow up in the water then come out an sprout wings when it's sunny. Drag'nflies are good, Tyke, cause they et skeeters an gnats, an gulls when they get the chance, which ain't often 'nough if you ask me.'

I watched as the bug's body dried up and then the back split open and after a minute the dragonfly's head came out and looked round. 'What happens in the water to make them grow up?' I asked.

'They get big, if that's what you mean.'

'But why do they get big?'

'Things in the water feeds em, that's why. But I'll tell ya somethin, Tyke, most a these ones 'ere won't be able t'fly, cause the water's bad. Their wings'll come out all shriveled up – I've seen it 'ere afore.'

And she was right. The dragonfly's wings were all

shriveled up, like crunched cellophane. 'Grandma Matchie! We gotta help him!'

'We can't, Tyke. Somethins are jus too big e'en fur me!'

'But a dragonfly's not big!'

'Nope, he ain't. But the well where all that water's comin from is bigger than Satan Himself!'

I frowned, leaned back on the rock. 'Grandma Matchie, how come Satan Himself lives here, in Rat Portage Lake?'

Grandma Matchie chuckled. 'Cause it wuz 'ere he wuz sittin when that shootin star came down, an it bounced right off his head and landed o'er in Man'toba! That's a bump he'll ne'er furget! Hah!'

'Where'd that shootin star come from?'

Grandma Matchie looked down at me, and her eyes spackled. 'Y'know what it's like when you sudd'nly get an idea an there's this lightbulb appearin right o'er yer head? E'er seen it?'

'Yep! Lotsa times!'

'Right. Well, that shootin star's jus a big lightbulb, know what I mean?'

I sat back up. 'You mean it was somebody's idea? Who?'

And she winked. 'Alla us, Tyke. Me'n Lunker an the Major an One Armed Trapper an Leap Year an a whole million other stor' tellers all o'er the wide world! You'n me, Tyke, that's who thought up that shootin star!'

'Then who is Satan Himself?' I demanded.

'Truth is, Tyke, he's somethin diff'rent fer everyone! He's jus a fancy name, is all.'

'But Grandma Matchie—'

'Got im!' she screamed, rearing back in the rocking chair and driving the hook home. The line hummed, then the drag shrilled, throwing out sparks as Grandma Matchie set the hook again and again. Driving the butt of the fishing pole into the belt socket she bared her teeth. 'I got im! I got im!'

She began pumpening, reeling up slack, pumpening and pumpening as she rocked in the old creaking chair. The river began churning, burbbling purbling and frothing. I could hear a roar and all the dragonfly nymphs scalampered for cover.

'Ere he comes! My God! I furgot the gaff! Tyke! Go get the gaff! Quick! Up in the cabin!' Satan Himself made a run, and the thin line whined and the drag whirnelled.

Leaping to my feet I scampered down the rocks, hit the flat clearing and tore across it. Screaming all the way, I flew down the trail. All the trees went by in a blur, but I could see every bump and root on the ground and I didn't stumble once. I never ran so fast in my life, and it was so easy I bet I didn't even touch the ground half the time.

Then I saw the cabin and then I was tearing up the porch, flying through the kitchen and into the living room. Everyone was screaming, Mom pulling Dad's arms as he stood in the Jacuzzi roaring at the video screen, where a thousand million twenty hundred nine Indians were riding down on us.

'Yeaagggh!' roared Dad.

'Jock Junior!' Mom shrieked over her shoulder. 'Come quick! Dad's got his foot caught in the drain! He's being sucked down!'

'Where's the gaff?'

'NO!' Dad screamed.

'Jock Junior! I won't let you use the gaff! This is your father! Help me! Oh my!'

'I'm being sucked down! Yeaaaggghhh!'

I jumped to Mom's side, grabbed one of Dad's arms and pulled. 'Sis! Get a rope!' I looked over my shoulder. She stood by the kitchen, her eyes wide and her hair green with leaves growing out of it. 'Look at her hair! It's green!'

Sis clenched her fists and brought them to her temples. 'I CAN'T HELP IT!' she bawled. 'IT'S NOT ME! It's just happening! I'm not DOING anything!' Acorns fell from her head and bounced on the wooden floor. 'Waaa!'

'Get a rope!'

Still crying, she stumbled away. Dad's whole leg from the knee down had disappeared into the drain, and the foaming water was up to his chest. Me and Mom pulled and pulled. The knotted end of a heavy rope hit me in the head and I grabbed it with one hand. 'Tie this round your waist, Dad!' I yelled, throwing it at him. 'Mom, you gotta hold on while I tie the other end to somethin!' Nodding, she gripped the rope while Dad looped it around himself and made a knot. I picked up the other end and looked around for something to tie it to. The closest thing was the big refrigerator, where Dad kept all his beer. Wrapping the rope three times I tied a knot and cinched it up until it was tight.

'Yeaaggghh!'

In the closet hung the gaff. Taking it down, I turned and looked around. Everything seemed under control, so I plowed through the door and leapt off the porch and raced down the trail. Then I skidded to a stop, because the trail was full of rats, plodding two abreast, with grain sacks on their backs and canoes too, the smallest aluminum canoes I'd ever seen. And they were singing in squeaky high voices some funny French song.

But I had no time to waste, so I edged to one side of the trail and ran past them. I heard their squeaks of surprise, then little cheers. Running and running, I came to a clearing and crossed it. I went up the rocks like a spider and reached Grandma Matchie's side.

She was still pumpening away, and the water boibled, full of bobbing beer cans and video cassettes. Not even breathing hard, she hisspered, 'I got im now, no doubts 'bout it, I got Satan Himself!' She cranked the reel and rocked back. 'Get down t'the edge an get that gaff ready, Tyke! He's gotta holda somcthin an he won't let go! Get that gaff ready!'

A huge hump rose from the water and a giant scaly head with a hook in its jaws reared up and glared at us. He was a dragon, with red and gold scales and flames for eyes, and he had giant crinkled-up wings and aluminum fangs, and giant ears that came to glowing red points. He was the biggest thing I'd ever seen and I screamed. Crouching at the edge, I liftcd the gaff in both hands.

'He's gotta holda somethin!' Grandma Matchie shrieked. 'Give im a poke, Tyke! Give im a poke!' She roared with laughter, pumpening and reeling and rocking.

Staring into the black water, I could see Satan's forearms clutching something pale and hairy and struggling.

Then I recognized it. 'Dad's foot! He's got Dad's foot!'

'So that's his game, eh! Give im a poke!'

Lifting the gaff skyward, I yelled and drove it home. 'That's the way, Tyke!'

I hit him in the belly and the gaff sank in halfway then popped out again.

'OOOOOF!'

Satan thrashed and hissed and let go of Dad's foot so he could clutch his belly. He gasped for a couple of seconds, then, wagging his head he raised his forearms and made fists and glared down at me. 'I WON'T TOLERATE THIS IMPERTINENCE!'

'Oh you won't, eh?' Grandma Matchie laughed, yanking on the fishing pole so that Satan's head snapped forward and he almost lost his balance and began falling forward, but then his fists came down – thumpthump!

'AAAGGGH!' he roared, chomping at the hook that was snagged in his lower jaw. 'IT'S JUST NOT FAIR!' he wailed, closing his eyes shut.

'Let this be a lesson t'ya, Satan!' Grandma Matchie was suddenly at my side, and in her hands she gripped the ax she had thrown in the lake earlier. 'Never mess wi the likes a Grandma an Jock Junior! If'n y'know what's good fer ya!' Grinning, she raised up the ax and with one slice cut the line. Satan Himself plunged backwards, throwing sheets of black water all over the place, and his wail turned into a gurgle as the river swallowed him.

'But we had him!' I shouted.

But Grandma Matchie just chackled. 'We sure did, Tyke, but I'm in it fur the sport, an that's all. Jus in it fur the sport. Come on, let's go have lunch.'

Walking across the clearing, I asked: 'I thought you threw that ax away?'

'I did, because I didn't need it then. But I needed it now, so 'ere it is. One thin you gotta remember, Tyke, an that's when you throw somethin away, make sure y'can get it back if'n ya need it.'

The trail was empty. 'Grandma Matchie! You shoulda seen all the rats! All over the place!'

'Course, this is Rat Portage Lake, ain't it?'

Understanding the importance of telling the truth:

Now they had some kind of doctor in the office too, and it was getting crowded. He was completely round, with his big wide tie all spotted with blueberry yogurt. And his face was round too, and so was his mustache and his glasses and his red-veined cheeks.

He puffed right up to the desk and started crowding its surface with all kinds of crazy things. 'Now,' he wheezed, 'if you'll just have a seat here, Jock Junior,' and he pulled a chair up to the edge of the desk, 'we can get started.'

I don't think the doctor was very smart, because he had me do all kinds of stupid things – puzzles and stuff that I suppose had him stumped so he wanted my help. And he had a watch that he kept looking at as if he forgot what time it was every few seconds or so. I felt sorry for him, so I finished all those puzzles as fast as I could.

'That's not possible!' the doctor exclaimed, looking up from his watch and goggling at the principal. 'That's just not possible!'

'Why?' I asked. 'What time is it? Maybe your watch is wrong.'

'No, no, it's not—' He frowned at me, and I put on that innocent dumb expression on my face, looking up at him and making my eyes as wide as possible. 'I mean,' he muttered, 'you don't understand—'

I smiled blankly, and he stopped, and his frown grew deeper the longer he stared at me. After a moment he started rummaging in his briefcase. 'I have a test here, Jock Junior. And I'd like you to try it. Don't worry if you can't answer most of the questions – they're designed for older people . . .' He found it and placed it on the desktop in front of me and gave me a brand-new pencil which I started chewing right away because that's what I do with all new pencils and pens and erasers and stuff.

'So, are you ready to start, Jock Junior?'

I examined the pencil critically, then said, 'Okay.'

'Right. Ready? Go!'

A couple minutes later I was finished. Those were the easiest questions I'd ever answered. And the geography section was a snap.

The doctor peered closely at the sheets when I gave them to him. He checked his watch again and then started reading. After a minute he looked up and gaped at me. 'But, but—' His round face was all sweaty so I found an old Kleenex in my pocket and gave it to him. Mopping his face, he stopped suddenly and stared down at the Kleenex.

'Sorry, there's some chewing gum in it,' I said. 'I forgot.'

'Who told you all the answers to these questions?' he asked, all fatherly now that he'd recovered. 'Because, I must tell you, they're all wrong.'

I made my eyes even wider. 'They are? But Grandma Matchie told me! She tells me everything!'

'Well, she's wrong, I'm afraid.'

'You mean the Rockies didn't come from buffalo droppings?' I demanded, a scrunch starting on my face.

'No, of course not!' the doctor said.

'Now, young man,' the principal said grimly. 'You know that Grandma Matchie doesn't really exist, don't you. I mean, there's no record of you ever having had a Grandma Matchie and—'

The doctor shook his head quickly, beetling his busy brows. Leaning toward me he gazed into my eyes. 'This invisible friend of yours, this "Grandma Matchie," she's—'

'She's not invisible!' I exclaimed. With a helpless, pleading look on my face I turned to Dad and Mom. 'Tell them! Tell them about Grandma Matchie!'

Mom looked at Dad and Dad looked at Mom. 'Well, uh,' Dad muttered. 'I don't . . . really . . . think we can, uh, say for sure . . . really . . . that is—'

'Liars!' I screamed.

'Now, son,' the doctor said, 'I'm sure you know the importance of telling the truth.' He cleared his throat and leaned back. 'Don't you?'

I bit my lip. 'I have,' I said weakly. 'I have told the truth!'

'Now, son, it's obvious that you're a very imaginative child, but—'

I scrunched my face until tears came out and I balled my fists. 'It's the truth!' I wailed, squeezing my eyes shut. 'You don't know what's the truth! You don't know!'

'Now, we are much older than you, you'll agree . . .'

Opening my eyes reluctantly, I nodded, staring down at the desk.

'And you'll agree also that we have a better idea of the truth than you do—'

'No!'

'Yes, we have, son. So you just tell your Grandma Matchie friend that she shouldn't go around telling you things that aren't true, because then she'd be lying, and—'

And that's just what I was waiting for. 'Tell her yourself!' I laughed, jumping to my feet. 'GRANDMA MATCHIE!' I screamed. 'IT'S TIME! JUST LIKE YOU SAID!'

'Jock Junior!' Mom was on her feet. 'You didn't!'

I let out a maniacal laugh like the ones I've heard in horror movies and ran to the window overlooking the playground.

'Gothic on a stick!'

'Oh my!'

After a moment the doctor smiled and said, 'Now. You see? There's no one—' Just then we heard a rumble, coming up from the floor, and everything began to shibble and shake. The pencil rolled off the desk and the doctor's briefcase tipped over, spewling tests and answers all over the place. He stepped all over them as he ran with everyone else to the window.

And coming across the playground, busting down the

wire fence, was Grandma Matchie, riding Bjugstad and holding a chain with its other end around Satan Himself's neck, who was being dragged along on his belly, and Lunker, thrashing about and roaring in the air like it was water, with One Armed Trapper sitting on her head. And there was the Major, rowing like mad across the grass in his broke-in-half H.M.S. *Hood*, and there was Leap Year, and a thousand million two buffalo and demon fish and glowing lamp rays and rats singing French songs and all of them.

We jumped back as Grandma Matchie – Bjugstad making one giant leap – came sailing up at us. With a huge crash they burst through the window and most of the wall, and everyone scattered. And there stood Bjugstad, legs wide, snorting and humphing and grunt-ing and shaking pieces of wall from his head (he had shrunk himself down so he could fit into the room); and Grandma Matchie jumped down from him and stood there with her fists on her hips. Glowering, her gaze fell on the doctor and the principal and Big Nose, all of them cowering in the far corner near the door.

'So, it's finally come, has it?' she growled, her eyes all afire.

I stepped up and said: 'They all want to be taught the importance of telling the truth, Grandma Matchie.'

'Oh, do they now? Well, Tyke, what should we show em first?'

I was feeling kindhearted, so I replied: 'How to be sportin.'

'Sportin, eh? Well, that's what we'll tell em, Tyke.'

By this time Bjugstad had calmed down and was

contentedly eating all the doctor's tests and answers. And from outside we could see (it was easy with all the wall gone) the whole playground filled with rats and buffalo and everyone else, playing soccer. They had strings tied everywhere, and the rats had barricaded their goal with canoes and bags and stuff, but the Major went round from behind and scored easily, sending the ball flying back out into the field. Shouts and roars of laughter filled the air.

The whole school must have been watching, I bet.

'We'll tell ya all 'bout sportin, now,' Grandma Matchie announced. 'An we'll tell it like this!' and she advanced on them, and they all tried to fit through the crack in the corner that wasn't there, and even if it was they were too big anyway. I could've told them all about that, but why bother?

'Doc. You live in a fishbowl and spend all day glapin, glapin, glapin!'

'That's not true!' he shouted, climbing to his feet.

'Course not!' Grandma Matchie snapped, then she grinned. 'But it could be, if'n I wuz t'say so.' And she turned to Big Nose. 'An you, you're jus a Big Nose breathin down all the kids' backs!'

'WHAT?' Big Nose jumped to her feet, grabbing her nose. 'But my nose is small!'

'Yep. An if y'wanna keep it that, use it less often an keep it away from where it ain't s'pposed t'be in the first place!' And she spun to face the principal. 'An you're the most impert'nent ear-flapper of em all!'

He leapt to his feet, his eyes blazing. 'I AM NOT!'

Grandma Matchie shook her head sadly. 'Fraid y'are.'

Then it was Mom's turn, and boy did she go white!

'Ester! Well! Have you anythin t'say fur yerself afore I pass judgment pon ya?'

'We, uh, I didn't think anyone would understand—'

Grandma Matchie raised her eyebrows. 'Oh? Mebee next time you'll let em decide fur emselves, eh?'

Wringing her hands, Mom nodded weakly and stared down at her feet.

'From now on,' Grandma Matchie pronounced, 'there'll be no brooms allowed in my cabin!'

'Oh my, oh my!'

But there was no room for argument – you could see that. And when Grandma Matchie glared at Dad, you could see he was wishing he was back in his Jacuzzi. 'So, I embarrass you, do I, Jock Senior?'

He went red.

'You'll have t'get used to bein embarrassed, then, won't ya? Cause we're all movin in with ya! Fur a whole month! Alla us!'

Cheering noises came from outside, and Dad gulped, but he didn't say one word of protest. He knew better.

And now, they all knew better.

Fishin' with Grandma Matchie:

Big jesters are just little jesters in disguise, that's all. I really don't mind being ferreted out every now and then, and that corner's not so scary once you suddenize that the last laugh is, as always, yours.

So the next time your Big Nose tells you to tell her what you did for summer vacation, you'll know what to do. The thing about Bigness is that when you're small it's easy to sneak around it, or under it. Pretend you're an ant carrying your favorite Adam's Egg under a big, flat rock. And when the time's right just break that Egg and eat it for breakfast.

You'll never be hungry again, I bet.